PENDANTS
OF FATE

PENDANTS OF FATE

A KNIGHT'S BEGINNING

JOEL HARE

MILL CITY PRESS

Mill City Press, Inc.
2301 Lucien Way #415
Maitland, FL 32751
407.339.4217
www.millcitypress.net

© 2018 by Joel Hare

Printed in the United States of America

ISBN-13: 9781545634127

To: DENISE

THE FIRST BOOK IN THE SERIES.

I HOPE YOU ENJOY THE ADVENTURES &

THE MANY MORE TO COME!

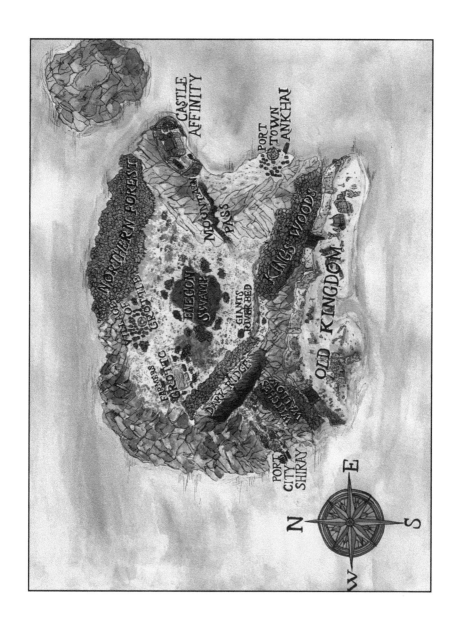

CASTLE AFFINITY

PORT TOWN ANKHAI

NORTHERN FOREST

MOUNTAIN PASS

KINGS WOODS

VILLAGE OF GROTILE

ENEGON SWAMP

GIANTS RIVER BED

OLD KINGDOM

FARMERS GROTILE

DARK RIDGE

VALLEY OF MOURNING

PORT CITY SHIRAY

N
E
S
W

CHAPTER 1

In the Eastern Kingdom on the edge of a cliff as far east as a man could travel by foot stood the Castle Affinity. Located at one of the highest peaks and towering over the vast ocean far below, Affinity, served as this land's capital with King Thesias as its ruler. Looking down from the highest perch, it seemed it would take a lifetime to reach the ocean if you were to fall. Looking west, one could barely see past the mountaintops barricading Affinity from the rest of the continent. Beyond was a vast plain in which many creatures dwelled, and a most humbling forest, which tamed the bravest knights to the north. On the western border of the Kingdom of Affinity, sharp mountains arose from the earth blocking most access to the sea. Across the sea was where great horrors and dangers are said to reside. This was where the Western Kingdom and Castle Towarden lay. The King that ruled over that land was said to be very powerful, as well as evil, although he had not been seen for some time.

In between these great and beautiful kingdoms is where our story begins. Set back from a rarely used crossing road bearing the signs of old age and forgotten paths stood a little wooden hut in the Farmers Grotto, belonging to the very happy family of Kadath, Evra and their newborn son, Arsivus. When Evra gave birth to Arsivus, she and Kadath knew he was a special child right from the start. He had very light blue eyes, brown hair, and was uncharacteristically silent during his young age. From birth, Arsivus was a quick learner. He started crawling very early and was walking and running much sooner than normal boys his age. Arsivus's craving for adventure and knowledge increased with seemingly unbound potential. He was ever so diligent to understand and to explore things, not fearing what lurked in the unknowns, or what dangers roamed about at night.

For Arsivus, growing up was a little lonely. His home and several others around him did not reside within the castle walls of Affinity. But their allegiance, was directly tied into the best interests of the Eastern Kingdom. They chose to supply Castle Affinity with herbs and supplies in exchange for sustenance. Their cottage was an oddly shaped hut made from wood; a stone fireplace was erected in the middle of the house to provide heat and light during the night. A shield and two black swords were placed above the ledge of the mantle, and a bowl of water was kept on top of the mantle with a pendant residing inside that reflected a beautiful blue aura throughout the entire room. When Evra would wear the pendant, its essence would glow brightly until it was placed back into the bowl. One small chamber of the hut was used for storage and another for sleeping. A wide-open room was used for cooking, eating, and sitting. They kept their stores and equipment in a dark and dusty cellar, and they had a big garden for their crops and produce outside. The garden loomed underneath the ominous presence of the forest that was to the north of them, which had been called the Northern Forest since anyone could remember. The Northern Forest was full of adventure and danger. Kadath told Arsivus about the Northern Forest quite often and the materials that could be acquired there, but he never spoke of how he knew these things.

A small stream ran right outside their house, so they didn't need to go far for water. Sometimes, if they were lucky, they were able to catch fish in the stream. They were a half-day journey from the nearest village of Grottel, which was east of them and on the path to the Castle Affinity. If they were towing their cart of goods, they were a several days journey from the castle, which was the capital of the Eastern Kingdom on the other side of the mountain. Although a light mount could make the journey in a day. Sometimes traders would come through, as they were near a crossing point that the kingdom's soldiers would often use on their way south towards the dark ridge to sail westward, and they would barter goods with the local residents. Common traders and merchants would usually pass through this area as well. Arsivus and his family seldom saw any representatives or royalty from Castle Affinity, and it was even less likely they would see knights from Castle Affinity, or Castle Towarden from across the sea. Although knights from Towarden were told to be fearsome and very dangerous, no one had seen any in quite some time, especially in the Eastern Kingdom.

Arsivus came to know the land very well; by age five he was learning to hunt by himself, even if it was small game. To him, the hunt was more important than the victory. On his land, he was able to catch rabbits, opossum, and squirrels. It wasn't enough to feed his family, but it helped him feel like he was contributing to his family's needs, and that was more than worth it to him. There was no real trouble for Arsivus to get into. There were only a couple small villages here and there, and he was usually busy most of the day helping with the farming, learning the ways of his father, and practicing with his father's hunting weapons. He could practice with the bow, work with his father in the field, use small knives for skinning animals, and run around doing whatever he wanted without fear of upsetting neighbors, as they were old and usually stayed to themselves.

Arsivus knew that there was an extremely large and important battle that took place back when his father was young. He knew his father took part in it, but Kadath never spoke openly about what happened or what part he played in it. In the valley where Arsivus lived, he could lay sight on the eastern and western mountains far off in the distance that permitted entrance into the Kingdom of Affinity in the east, and beyond the sea into Towarden in the west. The south remained a dried up fortress blocked off by the Giants Riverbed, Kings Woods and the Witches Wallow. Arsivus had heard tales spoken of witches and evil beings that lived there. There was an ancient war of magic in the south and it ruined many kingdoms over the centuries. There were only a few people remaining with the knowledge and courage to trespass beyond those obstacles to the kingdoms that once were.

Years passed with no excitement that involved Arsivus or his family. Arsivus spent his time pulling and planting crops, cultivating the land, and perfecting his hunting and tracking skills. Evra looked on with joy as she watched her son become a man in front of her eyes and was so thankful that he was a good boy. She loved her husband and son more than anything. She knew Kadath hadn't had a very good childhood and was pleased with how Kadath and Arsivus got along.

"The boy is strong, just like you!" Evra exclaimed.

"He has had his mother's strength in him from the beginning, one that is unwavering and fearless." Kadath replied. Evra blushed and gave a wink to her husband. Kadath wanted to make sure Arsivus had a better childhood than his own. He loved Arsivus very much and made sure to show him the affection and care that he deserved.

Kadath had established himself with the royal court for growing certain types of herbs that King Thesias desired. Kadath made an herb mixture that when diluted with water would heal wounds on soldiers that were injured. The herbs were placed on a soldier's injuries, and if they were held on top of an open wound, they would make the pain fade and the wound would heal itself. Upon removing the herb from the skin, they would find the wound had closed itself and the skin would appear as if the injury had never occurred. This had been shown and proven to the King on many occasions, although no one knew the true extent of the power of these healing herbs.

The possibility of growing limbs back had never presented itself while herbs were nearby for use, and no one was brave enough to try it on themselves. The most severe case had been when one of the King's White Guard had been run through with a blade on his thigh. He was immediately tended to and, with the help of the herbs, made a full recovery within mere minutes. Only Kadath and Evra knew how to grow these herbs, and the secret of how they made them had been kept safe for many years. This made Kadath and his family very important to Thesias and his court. The General of the King's army knew Kadath from a young age. He continually protected Kadath and his family from the King's need for power and his desire for Kadath's family's secret, as well as from poachers and ill-intentioned individuals.

Kadath worked the land every day to harvest the crops and to make sure the herbs would continue to grow. Evra would help with watering, but mostly took charge of caretaking of the house. Each year during the turning of the leaves, the herbs were harvested and brought to the King. Although Arsivus helped plow the fields and plant the herbs, he was told he wouldn't be taken to the castle until he was the right age. Arsivus watched his father work tirelessly in the fields, in the heat and the cold, and he noticed his father never took the sword from his belt, which struck Arsivus as quite odd. One hot and sunny afternoon, after finishing up harvesting for the day, Arsivus planted his shovelhead in the ground, leaned against it, and asked, "Why do you always wear that sword, father?"

"Because my son," Kadath replied, "in my life, I have always found it best to have it and not need it than need it and not have it."

Still confused and curious, Arsivus asked, "Isn't it toilsome to carry around, especially in this heat? You could put it down over there next to the fence and it would be just as useful as it is on your belt."

"Yes, but it makes you stronger wearing it and you can use it on anything you want," Kadath answered as he took out his sword and twirled it around. He continued, "You can use it for whatever pleases you." He swung it at the shovel that Arsivus was leaning on, knocking it and Arsivus down.

Arsivus got up and dusted himself off and gave his father a strange look. "I do believe that was uncalled for. Why did you do that?" Arsivus asked.

"You left yourself open for an attack, you see. You balanced all of your weight on the shovel, relying on it, and therefore giving me an opportunity to displace you of your footing with a very soft blow." Kadath replied.

"Ahh, I see. What other tricks do you know?' asked Arsivus.

"They are not tricks, my son. They are skills that knights have taught their own for centuries to use to best their opponent in combat." replied his father. "In time, I will teach you what I know. You may even find it useful later on as you grow older, and as long as you work hard in the field and listen to your mother, I will make sure you know how to defend yourself in battle, and how to master using this sword." Kadath showed him the sword and then put it back in its sheath. Arsivus gladly accepted his offer. From that time on, after the fields were tended to each day, Kadath taught Arsivus how to handle a sword properly, how to gain leverage in a fight, and how to distinguish certain elements that could prove useful in a battle. He also taught Arsivus about hunting larger animals (those that would put up a fight and those which were easy to hunt), how to cook his food so he wouldn't get sick, and how to survive on his own by building shelters, finding water, and mixing certain herbs that would help with illness.

A few years went by before Arsivus would be allowed to join his father on the expedition to deliver herbs to King Thesias at the castle. In the meantime, Arsivus kept himself busy working around the farm and increasing his knowledge about how to create herb mixtures, and how to hunt, track, and trap animals for food. He practiced his sword skills every day and grew stronger and smarter in the ways of combat. He also began practicing more with other weapons he was given and became very skilled with the bow and arrow. He was so very talented; he could hit a crow from the top of his house all the way by the edge of their farm. Evra saw his natural ability with weapons and knew that he possessed his father's ability and desire to become something great.

When Arsivus reached the age of eighteen, he was of a good build. He was strong and big and had some muscle on his bones. As he worked in the field on a windy morning, he spotted the leaves far off in the Northern Forest starting to turn an orangish color. He knew this meant his father would be leaving again, and this worried Arsivus because his father was getting older and wasn't as quick and strong as he used to be.

Kadath came up to Arsivus as he was cleaning his tools from his day's work and put his hand on his shoulder. "Arsivus, how are the crops looking?" asked Kadath.

"Very good this year. Everything looks great. Perhaps we should start to gather the herbs. I saw the leaves turning in the forest," stated Arsivus.

Kadath looked to the forest. "Good eye, son. I am having trouble seeing them from here, but your eyes are as sharp as a hawk. And yes, could you gather them all as quick as you can and I will go and prepare our, er, prepare the cart," he spoke with a smile. "Once you have finished with the herbs, come find me as quick as you can!" exclaimed Kadath. Arsivus, not wasting a moment, went to work pulling all the herbs that he could.

As he pulled the herbs, he thought to himself, "What did father mean our cart? Is he finally going to ask me to join him?" The thought filled Arsivus with energy and his work sped up, along with his anxiousness.

After several hours of laborious work, Arsivus finally finished loading the last of the herbs into the cart, and as he pulled the cover over, Kadath came up to him and rested his left hand on Arsivus's right shoulder. "Have you ever wondered what it is like to go on a journey through the mountains and lay eyes on the vast ocean beyond the Eastern Kingdom?" Kadath asked.

Arsivus replied, "Since the day I have learned of them, I have wanted to go." Inside the house Evra could hear the conversation between father and son and she smiled. She knew what would be asked next. Evra slowly moved over to the closet and pulled up a floorboard. She bent down and heaved up a wooden box that she placed next to the mantle.

Kadath laughed loudly and said, "Well, if it be your nature for excitement and adventure, then by all means, come and join me on our quest to Castle Affinity!" as he patted Arsivus's shoulders with approval. "Together," he continued, "we shall deliver this year's supply unto the Eastern King and have tales to tell your mother on our return." Arsivus jumped ecstatically with joy as he ran to get his bow and arrows and clothes for the trip. Evra, although happy that they were going together, as she knew it was Arsivus's dream to see the Eastern Kingdom, was saddened that she would be alone while they were away. Her eyes rested on the shining blue pendant on the mantle.

"Mother!" Arsivus yelled. "Mother, did you hear?" He came bursting through the door.

Evra, surprised at the outburst, said, "Yes, I have heard the good news." She folded her arms in a scolding manner and, joking with Arsivus, said, "Now you behave while you are gone, or there will be no more trips for you, and listen to your father as well."

"Of course! It will be an exciting adventure, and we will see knights and lords and a King!" exclaimed Arsivus. The creaking door interrupted the excitement as Kadath entered and walked toward the mantle to retrieve the wooden box.

He walked over to Arsivus with a half-smile on his face as Evra sat Arsivus down at the table.

Kadath placed the box in front of Arsivus and said, "Every adventurer needs proper equipment and has to look the part of an adventurer. While your bow and arrows will surely help," Kadath said, as he grabbed the bow and inspected it from top to bottom, "you need a reliable tool to protect you in all matters." Evra opened the chest, pulled out a black cloak, and walked behind Arsivus.

Evra said, "On the open road lay many dangers, not only on land, but within the weather. Best you have proper clothing to aid you." She wrapped the cloak around him and engaged the clasp under Arsivus's chin. The clasp had a symbol Arsivus had never seen before. It was a half circle with seven points. A hand clutched the top half of the circle and laurels encircled the entirety of it. The cloak was straight black on the outer side, but the inner side was pure white satin. Outlining the edges of the cloak from top to bottom were golden embraces.

The cloak was a little big for Arsivus, but Evra told him, "I made it overly long for you, so you may keep it as long as you like and grow into it. Perhaps one day you can give it to your children." That made Arsivus laugh as Kadath reached into the wooden box again and pulled out an item wrapped in cloth. He pulled the cloth away, revealing a beautiful sword with the words "Shadow of Life" etched onto the blade. It was magnificent. It radiated throughout the room, and Arsivus noticed the blue light from the pendant made the sword's blade seem stronger and brighter.

Kadath said, "This was given to me when I helped a displaced witch from the south regain her home and her people from the Northern Forest tribes long ago. It has served me well in the past and I believe it will aid you just fine. I have always intended to give it to my first-born son, and I know it will treat you well."

Arsivus was so overjoyed that he immediately put on the belt and sheathed the sword. Standing next to the table Arsivus now looked years older. He said, "I shall do both of you proud," and he ran outside to load the rest of his gear.

Rainclouds had started to form in the west, which was a usual occurrence as of late, when Kadath said, "We had better get on our way. We need not be caught in the open with such fine materials and equipment when this storm hits." He walked over to Evra, gave her a kiss, and said, "We will not be long." Evra had her own worries encased inside. She knew that thieves and rebels always lurked on the roads at night, especially at this time of the season. But she calmed her fears knowing that Kadath had a great deal of adventure in his past and had been trained by very formidable knights.

She hugged Arsivus after he threw the last of the equipment on the cart and said, "Be careful," to which he replied he would. And with that, the father and son mounted the cart drawn by two magnificent steeds as black as the night. Their eyes seemed accepting of the road ahead and their spirits seemed born anew when the reins came down upon their backs. The journey had begun through the ivory-covered mountains to the east, on their way to the Eastern Kingdom's crown jewel, Castle Affinity.

CHAPTER 2

They knew it would be days of riding to get to the castle with their cart full of goods, as they had grown an abundance of herbs for the King this year. Once the pair was well out of the range of their home, Kadath began to describe to Arsivus about the Eastern Kingdom's lineage and how Thesias had his council and knights, and the wars that they had fought in.

He told him about General Magnus, the elder brother of King Thesias. Magnus was the knight commander, and all of his fellow knights respected and adored him. Kadath described Magnus's skills with both blade and bow and told Arsivus of his own dealings with him.

Kadath said, "He is a very respectable commander; he values fairness and will always listen to reason." Kadath continued. "He does not judge a person by their status, or their skill; he looks into their hearts and sees their worth." As they rode a little farther, Kadath pressed on. "General Magnus being the elder brother initially was offered the throne, but he was dedicated solely to protecting his people and his lands. He believed that he could do better for his people as a knight, instead of a King, so his younger brother Thesias was made King in his stead when their father had passed. They were close in their younger years, and when Thesias became King, he immediately dubbed his brother the commander of knights and protector of his kingdom."

Thunder could be heard in the distance as Kadath continued, "Things started to change shortly after the war with the witches many years ago. Thesias became greedy, deceitful, and darker than before due to his power, wealth, and position, although Magnus maintained his oath to protect this land from all evil. They disagree on almost all aspects of this realm to this very day; Thesias for his own power, and Magnus for people like us."

As the raindrops begin to slowly fall, Arsivus replied, "He sounds like a very noble knight that I hope we meet."

Kadath responded, "Yes, he is, and he has a special set of armor that is only adorned to the knight commander that was given to him years ago. It is made of Origulaum, an extraordinary metal that is very rare and very strong. It is pure white and does not show scars, dents, or any other distasteful marks. It looks impervious to damage."

Arsivus replied, "Surely something must be able to damage it; otherwise, how was it made?"

Kadath replied, "Ah, keen observation, my son. It is susceptible to fire. Fire weakens the metal and makes it vulnerable to attack," Kadath continued. "There are even stories stating that the mighty Magnus fought a fire breather in his younger years during the war."

Arsivus's eyes lit up with interest. "What's a fire breather?" he quickly asked.

"Well," Kadath replied, "they are legends of a sort some say, and some say otherwise. The stories say they are two-legged beasts that can expel flame from their mouths, have claws sharper than a dragon's, and can run on all four faster than a horse." Kadath continued. "They have no mercy; anything in their way, they tend to destroy."

Arsivus asked, "Has no one seen any?"

Kadath replied with a laugh, "Not in a long, long while, if they even exist." Continuing along the road, the trees above them provided some shelter from the sky, but puddles began to form underneath the horses' hooves and the wheels of the cart. The rain seemed to be headed eastward with them, so Kadath bid the horses to engage in a trot with a flick of the reins.

"So, can no one else make the healing herbs like we can?" asked Arsivus.

"Well," replied Kadath, "it was a family secret that my father taught me, and with the help of your mother, we perfected it."

"You didn't answer my question," said Arsivus, as he tightened the cloak around his body to keep the warmth from fleeing. The cold air highlighted his breath as it left his body.

"No, we are the only ones that have that knowledge," Kadath explained. "But we must continue this later on as the rain is gaining the upper hand this night." They drove the cart to a secluded area on the edge of a small forest, and both of them dismounted the carriage to make camp for the night. The rain, now a constant drum beating upon the leaves and ground, forbade any movement as the night turned colder.

"Careful!" exclaimed Kadath as Arsivus swung his sword around the warm fire stoked with logs to keep the cold at bay. Arsivus tried to remember how his father had shown him before while they passed the time in their makeshift camp for the night. Kadath stoked the fire with a stick to battle the rain.

"You must remain the wielder of your sword," said Kadath with a caring but stern tone, "and not the bearer of your mistakes." Arsivus continued swinging his sword as Kadath grabbed some food from the cart.

"How long did it take you to master using this?" asked Arsivus as he patiently waited for his father to prepare the food for the night.

"It took as long as was needed," Kadath said with a smile. "Although, you never are the master of it, but more of a partner to it, I shall say."

"Partner," Arsivus repeated. "It's but a piece of metal. We should be the master of it, and it do our bidding."

"True!" Kadath replied. "But if you treat it well then it in turn shall do the same to you. But enough talk of swordplay for one night. Come and eat for we have a very long journey still ahead of us and it starts with first light." Arsivus grabbed the bread his mother had packed for them and reached for the bowl his father placed next to the fire that smelled of roasted cabbage. It was a whitish-looking soup that had the faintest look of garlic and carrots mixed in.

"It's not much, but it is enough to keep our strength up. Finish up, and I'll take first watch tonight," said Kadath. Arsivus spooned the last of the mysterious concoction that was given to him and laid down upon his blanket looking at the sky as the clouds slowly drifted off into the distance, carrying with it the storm.

"I wonder who else is looking at these very same stars tonight," thought Arsivus. As his eyes slowly closed, Arsivus felt the chill of the night envelope him and replace his thoughts with dreams of his warm and comfy bed, underneath warm quilts and close to a log fire.

The sounds of birds chirping in the distance, along with water being poured over a fire startled Arsivus from his deep slumber. A slight warmth embraced his face as he opened his eyes and saw his father packing up their cart.

"My apologies, father. I slept through the entire night." Arsivus lamented.

"No worries, son. You looked like you needed the rest," Kadath replied.

"Did you get any sleep?" Arsivus questioned quickly.

"I had enough to be ready for today," Kadath replied. "Come, load up the remaining items from camp. I have some bread here and more soup for you to eat." Kadath handed the food to Arsivus and said, "We shall be on our way as soon as you are finished." Arsivus ate as fast as he could so as to not hold up his father any longer.

"Sorry again, father" Arsivus shyly said as he got the horses ready to travel. "I will take first watch this night to repay you." Arsivus said as he grabbed a hold of the side of the cart and boosted himself up to the bench in front next to his father, who had already climbed up.

Kadath, pleased that his son had taken responsibility for his actions, said, "That will do!" as he brought the reins softly down across the steeds, forcing the cart to pick up speed and move along their way. Camping next to the smaller forests was ideal for their journey, as small game and water could be located in vast abundance if need be, and it was a road that Kadath was familiar with. Looking over at the Northern Forest so close to them made Arsivus shutter with worries over what strange animals or creatures were watching them.

"Is there no other path to use to reach the Eastern Kingdom?" asked Arsivus. "I mean, I'm not afraid," he said as he took out his sword and gave it a quick twirl with his wrist, which felt clumsy to him as he did it while he was sitting down. "I just wonder what is beyond that forest and what dangers may be out there waiting."

Kadath laughed. "Well, let me tell you about the beasts of the Northern Forest. Long ago, the beasts of the north were numerous indeed. Many walked upon two legs, some four, and even rarer were some upon six. They all flourished in the northern parts of the woods and rarely traveled south, but the lands above them and beyond were considered sacred." Kadath continued. "Some of the beasts looked wondrous and beautiful, and others were . . . others were not so much. They had a standing agreement with some of the lords of the land," Kadath said and continued on as he shifted his weight. "The agreement was that the beasts of the north would stay there and not harm any of the people of the Eastern Kingdom or its inhabitants, as long as no harm came to them. That was part of the initial agreement; the other part was that no one would trespass into the forest beyond the river running through it. The beasts of the north were civil, friendly, and helpful, but were also talented warriors and you did not want to cross them. Their truce held up for many years. When I was still yet in my early years, before I met your mother, I worked our farm with my father, and that was when I first met King Thesias and his White Guard. They were coming upon this very path on their way to explore the forest, even though it was forbidden."

"Why would they do this?" asked Arsivus.

"Because," said Kadath, "the King was young and foolish and greedy. He wanted more power, more land, more subjects, and he thought the beasts of the north would be excellent for that specific purpose. They were looking for the right place to enter the forest when they came upon our house. At first my father didn't know who they were, or what they wanted, but upon recognizing the banner, he informed me to set the dinner plates and fetch as much water as I could carry because we would be hosting royalty that night. Upon entering our home, King Thesias laid eyes upon our crops and found them peculiar. He inquired about them. My father was so pleased that Thesias was taking an interest that he told the King he was attempting to create a healing herb that could be dressed upon wounded soldiers and make their pain wither away."

"What did he say to that?" Arsivus asked.

"Well, Thesias was intrigued and asked for a demonstration. My father gladly pulled out our herbs, mixed it in the back room, and brought it to a knight of the White Guard who had a minor wound on his leg after a skirmish in the swamp. He laid the herb mixture upon the wound and within minutes the pain dispersed and the knight could fully rest upon his wounded leg. Thesias was so overjoyed that he said he wanted to employ my father to create these herbs and deliver them to his castle, and he would be rewarded handsomely. After Thesias and his White Guard left our cottage, they traveled north into the forest, and what happened there, only the Northern Beasts, Thesias, and his six White Guard know. When they returned, they had chests of gold, jewels, and silver, and it seemed a dark cloud followed them out. An ominous presence, an odor of regret or shame, if you will. As they passed through our land," Kadath said as he reached back and grabbed an apple from their basket, "their armor and weapons and horses were covered in blood. The King's White Guard were something else; when they were dining in our house, they didn't so much as say one word."

Arsivus looked curious but thought it best to let the story press on and inquire about the White Guard at a later time.

Kadath continued. "They sat and ate and watched with a perched eye of their surroundings. Very cautious they were, yes, very cautious. Word got around that Thesias and his men attacked a special holding that housed precious jewels and stones that the beasts had stored there and made off before any retaliation could be taken. By the time the beasts' force could be massed to help defend their storage, the King was already out of the forest and safely on his way back to the tall walls of his kingdom. No one could prove that it was the King and his White Guard that had begotten this disaster, so no counterstrike came from the forest. Instead, they tore up the truce and from then on have taken to have no outsiders crossing into their lands."

"Why didn't you tell the beasts what you saw?" Arsivus asked.

"Ha, if I had gone alone they would have made me but a memory, although it wasn't until Magnus came by on that very same path and inquired as to what happened that I would be able to speak my peace. I told him of our accounts and viewings, and Magnus asked if I would go with him to explain to the beasts what we had witnessed. Once in the forest, we were immediately surrounded and severely outnumbered. There was no chance but to request an audience with their counsel. We were bound and taken to their chief, Mujek. He was a magnificent looking creature. He had horns like a ram, but bulky shoulders that stood up to his jaw. His arms seemed as big as that tree over there. He wore a blue sash and his eyes had a thin line of yellow in them, that were otherwise black throughout. Once we were knelt in front of him, Magnus informed him of our actions, that we were there to make peace and help find the perpetrators who conducted the crime. Magnus was about the same age as I, but he had the tongue of a scholar. He informed Mujek that I had laid eyes to a party returning from the woods and I gave account of what I saw to Mujek. I had never been so frightened before," Kadath said as he shuddered remembering it.

"When I finished, Magnus looked over and gave me a nod of approval that warmed my heart. Mujek looked upon me and Magnus kneeling there. What he said still rings in my heart as of this day. He said, 'Go, friends of Mujek. I accept your offer of peace.' As we were silently leaving, Mujek said to us, 'Friends, find who did this and bring them unto justice.' And with that we were gone. Magnus had done everything he could to make it right, and he finally quelled the peace with Mujek. Magnus said he could not hand over his brother to them, as it would throw the kingdom into chaos. Instead, he offered his services to the beasts of the north and we went on many journeys together. From that day, only Magnus and I dared venture into the forest. From there, we went on many journeys past the forest and far to the north with the beasts by our side. But that is another story, son, and alas we have reached the town of Grottel. This place is small but has its dangers if you know where to look. Stay close to me and we shall be fine." Kadath said.

As they trotted into town from the west, the townsfolk gathered on balconies and in the streets hooting and hollering.

"Hello, Kadath. It's that time of year already, is it?" one asked.

"Showing your son the family business?" another hooted.

Kadath simply nodded and strolled on.

"They seem a friendly bunch," Arsivus said.

"Yes, they are simple farmers. They don't get many visitors, only those of trade and business." They wheeled up to the local tavern and dismounted the cart.

"Stay here!" Kadath said in a stern voice. Kadath went into the tavern as Arsivus looked around the town and down the road. It was a very bleak town; there were only ten buildings that could be seen from the main road and a big granary for storage right in the middle of town. The buildings were cedar in color and a little rundown due to usage and weather, and there were trees all around the buildings with a path driving through the middle of the village. There were houses all cooped up together behind the tavern. There was a goat path running through each of them where the people of the village lived and had gatherings. The sun was shining, but no one seemed to be out enjoying it, aside from when Arsivus and his father entered the town. Everyone now seemed to be going about their day, which seemed a shame to Arsivus. They were all either inside buildings or moving supplies into their local storage to prepare for the upcoming winter. He heard laughing from inside the tavern. As his eyes swept over the landscape again, he noticed two men on the edge of town leaning against an oak tree with bright green leaves that was divided into two as it made its way toward the sky. The two men were staring straight at Arsivus with a steely gaze. Shudders ran down his back and he gripped his sword handle tightly. "Those are freelancers," said Kadath. Startled, Arsivus turned around to see his father had returned. Kadath went on, "They are not to be feared, for they help protect the town, for a cost, of course."

"Ah, I see," said Arsivus "Why don't more people live out here with these resources and land?" Arsivus asked.

"Well, people like to feel protected. On the other side of the mountain, the ones that live in the kingdom, they are very well protected. Out here they have to fend for themselves," Kadath replied.

"It makes sense I suppose," said Arsivus. "If your business is finished father, let us be on our way then. There is a lot of road ahead of us, I would guess." With that, they continued onward toward the white-capped mountains highlighting the sky with their ominous peaks.

Night was drawing near after what seemed like hours upon the cart with his father. Kadath spoke only a few words for most of the day. Something about a bird on the road and a question to himself wondering what Evra was doing. Following a deep yawn that could have woken a mama bear from her winter slumber, Kadath said, "We should make camp here tonight." They both dismounted from their cart and began to unpack for the night. The night was very warm, so the flies were out in force. They were buzzing around so ferociously, it almost seemed as if they owned the path that Arsivus and Kadath were on. Swatting ferociously and trying to kill them all as fast as he could, Arsivus stumbled upon the wood he had laid down near the cart and his father laughed loudly.

"The more you swat and annoy them, the more they will bother you," Kadath said. Looking up from the ground, it appeared that the flies had only attacked Arsivus, as Kadath had none on him. Arsivus clenched his fists in anger and held them at his side as the flies slowly started to lose interest and move on to a more attractive target somewhere in the distance. Arsivus rose up and grabbed the last log lying next to him and laid it on the fire, while his father brought out more soup and bread for them to share.

"Tomorrow night we shall hunt for food. The game is good out this way and it is about time we had some meat instead of soup," said Kadath.

"Agreed," Arsivus said. As they sat down on makeshift benches, Arsivus pushed his soup around for a bit.

Kadath looked at him and asked, "Something bothering you, son?"

Biting his lower lip with a look of concern, Arsivus asked, "You said before that the White Guard were in your house. What were they like?"

Kadath looked down at the fire and without lifting his head again, answered, "They were cold."

Arsivus, not pleased with the answer, pushed a little further. "Who are they, where do they come from, and how did they become the King's personal guard?"

Kadath, still staring at the dancing flames, replied in a low voice, "What I know of them is limited. I do not know where they come from or how they became part of Thesias's court, but I do know they are dangerous. When they went into the Northern Forest, they were but in their teens. Even at that age, they were cunning warriors." Kadath took a sip of water and continued. "The captain of the White Guard is Atalee, a fierce warrior. He is said to have mastered the sword like no other. He is calculating and is said to have the ear of the King for any request he desires. His lieutenants are all equal in the eyes of their captain. There are two brothers who carry bows and are equally flawless with them; they are Korb and Malas. They are fierce and have the eyes of an eagle. They are very keen and agile and are seldom apart; if one is present it is best to expect that the other is unseen nearby. Tales are told that they are only seen when they choose to be." Arsivus shifted his weight with interest and begged Kadath for more information on these elite warriors.

"Another lieutenant is Helia," Kadath went on. "She can be identified by the two short swords she carries. The swords have handles that are as white as the clouds and blades as black as the night. Rumor has it she is nimble as a thief, and some even say she deals with witches in the south. She is also supposedly very beautiful from what I hear, although it has been years since I have last seen her." Arsivus's mind was imagining what they looked like in person and if they were as hostile, cold, and dangerous as his father said.

Kadath continued. "She is the calmest of the six but does not shy from a fight. Teslark is another warrior employed by Thesias; he has a belt wrapped around his shoulders that was equipped with more knives than I could count at the time. He carried two tomahawks sheathed on his waist belt that were as swift as they were deadly."

Kadath continued to look at the fire as he pressed on, "Finally, there is Korgal. He is the biggest, and also the strongest and slowest. He bears a hefty axe half the size of a man. He bears it with perfection and handles it like a knife. You can also identify him by the scars on his face, as he has seen many battles and walked away from them all, although not without his wounds. Upon creation of the White Guard, Thesias gave them each a token signifying their elevated status. Each one of them has a red jewel placed upon their breastplate in their armor. That jewel shows that they are special and above everyone else in the eyes of the King. Even more so than the General, which is sad to say."

Arsivus's appetite for knowledge had been satiated for now. He leaned back and said aloud, "I hope to meet them one day. Maybe they can help me become a knight like them."

"No," said Kadath, as he stood up and continued on. "These are not honorable knights. They do by harm and rule by fear. That is no way a knight should act toward another person."

Arsivus, realizing his father's sincerity and sternness, looked into the fire and said, "If they are not just, then someone should put a stop to them. But being a knight, aren't they to do what is commanded?" Arsivus asked.

Kadath put his bowl away, paused for a minute, sighed, and then spoke. "If they are just, then there may be hope for them, but not under Thesias's rule. While he rules them, they are as corrupt as he is."

Arsivus got up to place his bowl on the cart next to his father. "Why do we supply him with herbs if he is not for the good of the people?" he asked.

Kadath responded, "In my old age, it is a little tougher to get around like I used to when I was younger. You also came into our lives, so I had to choose to either live as an adventurer or create a stable home for my wife and son. Your mother and you were always my only choice. We continue to supply the soldiers and knights that are injured under Thesias's rule because they deserve a chance to live their lives. That is the way I can still make a difference for my child, my wife, and your future. You may understand this better someday, son."

Kadath lay down his blanket and lowered himself onto it as he said, "But enough for now. Tonight, you have first watch. Wake me when the fire dies and I shall resume."

With that Kadath closed his eyes and Arsivus pulled out his sword and said to himself, "One day I shall be a knight and show them what honorable truly is."

Kadath rolled over to face the empty blackness as a smile crossed his face. Arsivus leaned against a tree and looked into the sky seeking entertainment to help him pass the time. A cool wind started to blow from the north as the embers from the fire stained the ground red.

"Beasts of the Northern Forest, hmm," Arsivus said as he looked toward the north, "I would love to see them someday . . . someday soon."

CHAPTER 3

"Good morning, son." Arsivus awoke suddenly to his father's voice. Kadath was gathering up their supplies as he was leaning towards Arsivus on the ground. Arsivus stretched his arms toward the sky that was ominously riddled with dark clouds. "It's going to be a cold journey this day, for sure," Kadath said. "We'll have to move quickly to stay on pace. The path ahead sometimes floods when there is heavy rain." Arsivus immediately stood up to help his father pack up.

Kadath continued. "It looks like a storm is upon us. We will tighten up the cart and grab whatever warm clothes you need." Arsivus nodded his head in agreement. He pulled out his overcoat and tightened every string and rope he could find for the cart. Once he had finished, he hopped on top of the cart to start their journey again. He sat and waited patiently for his father. Once Kadath climbed up top, he grabbed the reins and handed them to Arsivus. "Your turn to guide today." Kadath said with a smile.

"But what if we get stuck in this weather and in the rain? You would do a much better job than I could, I do believe," Arsivus replied with an arching brow.

Kadath repositioned himself on the cart and put his hand on Arsivus's shoulder. He laughed and said, "No better time than now to gain some confidence." With that, Kadath unleashed a powerful whistle that energized the steeds and they took off in a gallop toward the east. Arsivus attempted to hold onto the reins while controlling his excitement at the speed and the power. He grasped the reins tightly and brought the strong-willed horses back to the beaten path.

"Now you want to be careful on this upcoming road. We are coming near the Enegon Swamp," Kadath stated. "It is very easy to become stuck if you aren't watching the land ahead of you!" Arsivus gripped the reins a little tighter and barreled down the path. In the distance, Arsivus could the see the mountains getting closer and the swamp his father had mentioned up ahead.

"Does anybody live in that swamp, Father?" Arsivus asked as he scratched his head as the first couple drops of rain hit his forehead.

"Lots of...things, really, but no people that I have heard of. I have never really hunted around the area. I usually just pass through as quickly as possible. No need to linger in a place that is better left alone to its creatures," replied Kadath.

"I would think that if someone was hunted by the kingdom, this would be a good place to hide," Arsivus spoke with certain eagerness.

"If someone was wanted by the King," Kadath said, "and the White Guard was after them, I suppose this would be a good place to remain hidden for a short while. If you can stand the bugs, the marsh, and the smell." Kadath put his hand to his chin and then tilted his head toward the forest.

"Do you think there are thieves and looters around this swamp as of right now?" asked Arsivus. He gulped silently, half in fear and half in excitement, as he has wanted to prove to his father that he was a warrior.

"I have heard tales that resemble criminals hiding out in the swamps, but I have never seen it myself," Kadath replied. "We have a long way to go yet, and I would hope that we do not meet any adolescent freeloaders on our trail."

"Very true," responded Arsivus. "Perhaps on the way back home, we can explore the swamp some more and see what we find!" he said with a smile.

Arsivus glanced behind him on the path they had traveled and noticed it getting very dark as they approached the dusty, narrow trail to the Enegon Swamp. The clouds seemed to be getting darker and the raindrops more frequent. Darkness had finally caught up to them and was angrily covering the sky. It seemed as if the light refused to venture any farther into the damp and dark swamp. A chill ran down Arsivus's back, one that was not unnoticed by his father. Kadath readjusted his sword, shifted his weight, and moved his feet wider apart to gain more stability.

"We must go quickly now!" Kadath said, as he looked around the horizon. "We must get farther into the swamp before the storm clouds open and trap us here." Arsivus cracked the reins down and the horses picked up speed, racing into the hallowed-looking marsh ahead of them.

"You must listen carefully to the woods now, son," Kadath said. "There are beasts out here that prefer solitude over anything. Best let them be." Arsivus looked down and stretched his legs out to mimic his father's.

"Can we make it all the way through the swamp today?" asked Arsivus.

"No, we cannot," replied Kadath. "Although we will make it as far as we can tonight. Tomorrow we shall be rid of this place and on our way into the mountain pass." The swamp was a crucial spot for the Kingdom of Affinity because of its location. A whole army would have trouble setting up and traveling through the land to trespass into the mountain pass if they chose the land avenue of attack. Otherwise they would have to come from the sea, which was heavily protected by Thesias and his navy. Narrow roads and dead ends would make for easy pickings of waylaid soldiers in a state of confusion. That slow-moving line of troops would make any approaching force easy to eliminate with well-positioned traps and ambushes. It was through there that Kadath and Arsivus had to go. As they progressed farther into the outlying trees that surrounded the swamp, Arsivus's uneasiness grew. He asked his father, "What is this place, and what is that smell?"

"This hideous place is a net for things long forgotten," Kadath replied. "If you get through here without seeing any beasts, you would be very fortunate indeed." As they pushed through the outer edge of the swamp, the clouds had turned against them, and the sky was the darkest that Arsivus had ever seen in his life. There were certain roads that were safe to travel, and certain ones that led to dead ends, pools of muck, and impassible obstructions that had claimed the lives of many unknowing travelers.

Kadath had traveled in these parts many times growing up before it was fully overrun by beasts, so he knew the correct way. But he had chosen to let Arsivus take the lead and see if he could find his way through with his navigation skills. Traveling a bit farther into the swamp, the path started to get narrow, too narrow for Arsivus's comfort. Arsivus peered down the dark paths in front of him. He saw a flock of unfamiliar-looking birds take flight directly above a three-way fork in the road. He realized he would soon have to decide their direction, knowing well enough that if he chose incorrectly, turning the cart around would take a bit of time. Arsivus slowed to a stop.

"You know how to track and scout, so bring us through the swamp and on our way," Kadath said as he looked towards the sky and continued, "but be hasty about your decision, as this weather will not wait for you to choose." Arsivus had no objections to moving forward but was more nervous than he let on. Looking at the paths that lay before them, he had three options: left, right, and center. He looked at the left one. It had less of an obstructed view but had a very narrow path on which to walk, so he knew he couldn't take that path with their cart of herbs. He looked at the center path and saw that it was very cumbersome with foliage but a wide path and less muck and water all around. He looked at the path on the right and it somehow looked darker than the other choices. But it looked as if it had been traveled very frequently by carts and man alike. He chose to go right and, with his father's consent, they followed the dark path.

Shortly after the fork in the road had passed, Kadath asked, "What was your reasoning that you chose right instead of middle?"

Arsivus replied, "The middle did look a lot better than our choices at first glance, but when I looked again it didn't bear any signs of travel, by any human I mean."

Kadath knew that Arsivus chose the correct path, but asked, "Well, what do you mean? It was clearly groomed and ready for travel by freight, cargo, and any other means of travel."

Arsivus replied, "This is true, but all I saw were animal tracks down there, non-shoed beasts with small strides, and I thought that would only mean that they wouldn't be friendly to our travel."

Kadath messed up Arsivus's wet hair and laughed. "Well done," he said. "You chose well." They continued on their way, fighting both the elements of weather and weariness that the swamp brought on. Birds deeper in the marsh started to fly high above the swamp in a seemingly threatened manner, as Arsivus and his father embraced the dark swamp and continued down the path together.

"We shall make camp soon, just a little bit farther, son." Kadath said as they pressed on.

CHAPTER 4

King Thesias stepped out onto the overlook at Castle Affinity, where he could view his kingdom far and wide. He looked at the sky and gazed at the dark clouds that were raging across the mountaintops on their way toward the sea. In the far distance hovering above the Northern Forest, Thesias spied lightning bolts roaring out of the clouds as they mercilessly struck the ground behind the mountain range. Thesias's older brother and commander of his army, General Magnus, came out onto the overlook from the castle as the King faced away from the door. King Thesias sensed his arrival without turning around and impatiently asked him, "Magnus, what is the status of your men in the north? Have they found my artifact?"

Magnus replied, "They should be returning shortly, brother. If all has gone well, they should be leaving the Northern Forest very soon."

Thesias replied back quickly and with a snapping tone, "How many times must I tell you. I am your King first and your brother when it suits me."

Magnus replied solemnly, "I understand, your majesty."

Thesias continued. "That is good. Come to me when your knights have returned and speak with me about their travels. I am curious as to what they have found," Thesias paused then spurted out in anger, "You may go now, commander!" Magnus turned away from the outlook in disdain, and his eyes fell upon two tax collectors sitting in the corner whispering to each other as they slyly gazed toward the armored General. Magnus gave a quick disdaining laugh in their direction and walked through the double doors leading out of the King's private chambers. As soon as he exited, the two tax collectors got up to close the door and then approached the King.

Upon reaching the perch, the taller tax collector said, "My lord, we have concluded the collections for this year. This year's revenue has far surpassed the previous thanks to the raised tolls you have implemented on the villages requiring our protection."

King Thesias replied, "Victar, you and your brother are from the Bordine clan, are you not?"

Victar replied, "Yes, out of the Western Fort. Vadeem and I have never been as grateful as when you appointed us as your personal envoys for the realm."

Vadeem chirped in, "As well as your hospitality for allowing us to reside in your palace. We praise your wisdom and are your loyal servants until the end."

Thesias replied, "This is a time that you can help me and, of course, none but us shall know of this request. Are we at terms?"

"Speak it and it shall be done," Victar replied.

Thesias continued. "There is a small outcropping in the west that is just south of the Northern Forest, a home that is occupied by a man named Kadath, his wife and boy as well." He continued. "You may know of them, as they produce a very valuable crop that I desire every year, but the secret to how they make it is unbeknownst to me. I would like to know every detail about it."

Vadeem replied, "Yes, we know of them. They paid their taxes on time."

His brother Victar continued. "Our father, Vergio, knows of them as well. He visited Kadath's wife once and asked for her hand. She refused and brought great shame upon our family name."

Victar replied, "They cannot be forgiven. We are wealthy and have land, something should—"

Thesias cut him off abruptly and shouted, "Enough of your spoiled squabbling. I care not what your family wants or thinks. I have called you here to perform a duty, and that is all."

Vadeem replied, "Of course, your majesty. We shall visit their home and inquire as to the process to produce this herb."

Thesias cut in immediately. "Of course, to be unseen, no one is to know of your task. Also, my irksome brother's knights are on their way back from a quest in the north. Let them not lay eyes on you, as I do not need Magnus's inquisition into my deeds."

After Victar and Vadeem agreed, Thesias gave them a bag full of coins to aid them on their journey and said, "One of my knights from the White Guard, Captain Atalee, will be joining you. He will be there to make sure this expedition will go forward with little trouble, and he is to be in charge. Listen to his every word and do not stray from it." The brothers agreed, bowed down to their King to show allegiance, and backed out of the room. Atalee was known to almost everyone as one of the most highly skilled knights, comparable even to General Magnus. But Atalee was given special status because he and his White Guard would sometimes commit actions that were less than honorable when sent on missions for the King, which Magnus would disagree with. The White Guard's missions were never spoken of. They were kept secret and no one ever knew what they were doing or dared ask.

Once outside of the King's chambers, Vadeem smirked as he gazed at the bag of coins. "Let us go prepare, Victar," he said.

"Perhaps we may speak freely to this woman who refused our father when we get there?" asked Victar.

Vadeem replied harshly, "Shhh. As long as Atalee does not hear of it, we just may, but do not get caught pushing our so-called squabbling in anyone's but our ears."

"Agreed," stated Victar.

Night was quickly approaching the castle as the trees swayed to the wind's will. Waves crashed harshly into the lower cliff's edge. Magnus descended down the spiraling staircase entrenched in white marble stone and stopped when he heard a girl singing in the courtyard outside of the castle tower. Magnus closed his eyes as he admired the maiden's voice, as she serenaded the surrounding area with angelic lyrics. As the General stood captivated by this voice, his second in command, Lieutenant Cardage, came up behind him and put his hand on the General's shoulder.

Cardage asked, "My liege, what did his majesty say?"

Breaking his fixation on the woman singing, Magnus looked up and smiled. "Ah Cardage, the King responded with dissent and impatience as usual, my friend. Although he is very well fixed on what our troops may have found in the north. I fear it may be something of great importance, as his majesty continually inquires as to what my men may have found. As I was leaving, there were two men in the corner, and I would like you to follow them wherever their journey takes them. They are from the west, I do believe, and if my memory serves me, their father is of the Bordine clan, although their particular names I do not know."

Magnus leaned closer to the stone etched window, gazing upon the ominous storm approaching. He rubbed his chin in a studious manner. "If that is true, and they are anything like him, we may have our hands full." Magnus said.

"But of course, sire!" responded Cardage. "Do you think their intentions be dishonest?"

Magnus replied, "I would not trust them, Cardage, and best not to let them see you either. Why don't you take Theros with you on this journey and remain hidden from their sight, if at all possible. You may need a tracker and hunter, and there are none better this side of the sea than him."

Cardage shuffled his cape atop his armor as he leaned near the window. "She is beautiful, isn't she, sire?" Cardage said with a half-smile, noting the lovely woman clad in white and surrounded by flowers in the gardens below, her brunette locks flowing in the wind.

"Are we hunting for anything particular on this mission, or just observing the dealings of those men?" inquired Cardage.

Magnus thought for a moment as his gaze was fixed on the woman in the courtyard. "Only observe. I am sure that this storm will bring other opportunities for glory. We need not be hasty; my brother is hiding something and I fear that it will come to light at the most inopportune moment."

"Very well, Magnus. Theros and I will depart shortly after them. They should be easy to track."

Just then, Captain Atalee approached the marble staircase on his way to the King's room. "Ah, General Magnus, are you enjoying the view?" Atalee snickered as he glanced at the woman singing.

"Atalee!" Magnus said with surprise. "Are there not logs that need be cut for the fire pits in the castle?"

Atalee gave a cold glance toward Magnus. "Why yes, there is. You make a good point," retorted Atalee as he continued on. "I suggest you have your knights continue their training and chop like a woodsman at a defenseless object. Make sure that my chamber is fully stocked, if you would please."

Atalee pushed his way past Cardage and Magnus, his armor clanging back and forth as he pounced up the spiraling steps.

"Sir," Cardage said aloud, "if it pleases you, I can reprimand him on charges of insubordination, or if it suits you I can challenge him to a duel."

Magnus replied, "That would not be wise. His skill is of the highest caliber." Magnus turned to continue down the stairs and muttered as he descended, "As well as him and his lot being privy to the King's personal attention and ear, I doubt any confrontation would end in our benefit, myself included."

CHAPTER 5

The rain clouds had passed and the sky was becoming clearer by the minute. They arrived at the usual spot that Kadath had used for camping in previous years and set up camp as the sun was almost vacant in the sky above them. Arsivus quickly hopped off the cart as his father unhinged the horses and tied them to a branch. Arsivus wanted to take some initiative and help out with dinner, so he went out to see if he could hunt anything fresh. After securing the horses Kadath looked up and saw Arsivus walking toward the woods. He smiled and went to collect some firewood for dinner.

Arsivus took his bow out with him as the moon was slowly ascending above the horizon in front of the storm. He walked at a slow and steady pace for several minutes until he found what appeared to be animal tracks through some brush. He decided to follow them away from camp and moved stealthily like a tracker would. He slowly crept through the fallen brush tracking his prey through a dark and dripping trail, which seemed to come alive with insects and flies. This forgotten trail seemed to lead into a dark area not meant for men, much less a boy. He pushed through the overhang with all his might as the thistles and branches tried to restrict him from discovering what lay beyond.

After what seemed like hours, he pushed through the final hanging limbs and arrived at an opening. Immediately he saw a full-grown rabbit sitting by the edge of what appeared to be a little pond full of weeds and leaves that were being corralled by the ripples of the water. He looked at the rabbit; it was facing away from him staring into the distance.

Arsivus thought about how he had practiced shooting targets with his bow back at home from the same distance. "Ahhh, back at home!" he thought. "I wonder what mother is doing right now." He gave a quick shake of his head to clear his mind and focus on the prey in front of him. He lined up the target and pulled his string back slowly, as the bow was old and he didn't want it to break. Arsivus pulled the bow back as far as he could until it made a creaking sound. He did not want to scare the prey so he allowed a little slack on the bow but felt his back arm shaking uncontrollably.

The rabbit, sensing it was not alone, raised its head in alarm. Arsivus held his breath and didn't move; his eyes were fixed on the furry creature that was unaware of its upcoming fate. He took aim and fired the arrow through the rabbit's chest, dropping it next to a small gathering of leaves floating on the shores of the pond.

He walked carefully through the brush as he didn't know the area at all and didn't want to disturb anything. As he pushed through the brush, he felt the cold chill of night come upon him and suddenly felt chills creep down his spine. Arsivus looked behind him but could see no trace of the fire from where his campsite was being set up. He took a deep breath and thought to himself, "It's only nighttime. You have hunted in strange places at night many times. Nothing to be afraid of here," and he pressed on.

He came up to where the rabbit was laying and found some unusual tracks that he had never seen before. It appeared that the rabbit had stopped at this place and was contemplating the unknown tracks before moving forward. He took a mental note of them, grabbed the rabbit, and turned around to head back to camp and his father. As he did so he heard a loud snort, similar to a horse but deeper in tone and shorter. He froze in place, his heartbeat thudding in his chest.

He tried to stay calm. He thought to himself, "A horse wouldn't be out here alone, especially in this thick brush," and with that thought his nerves began to rise. He felt a chill run through his back again. He felt as if he was being watched very carefully. He took another step away from the snort and heard a branch break to his left. Now frightened, Arsivus loaded another arrow into his bow and yelled as best he could in hopes his father would hear him "Who's there? Come out and do not be a coward!"

Nothing but silence followed, which increased his fear. He remained in place, legs frozen to the ground but eyes ever so alert. He was constantly scanning the darkness for any movement, his arms holding his drawn bow as it passed back and forth over the dark woods. After what seemed like hours, he lowered his bow and decided it must have been a wandering animal that was harmless and just as frightened of him.

He put his catch in his sack and slowly traced his steps as best he could back through the thicket, the branches and thistles cutting his arms. He finally came to the main trail and found his way back to camp. When he arrived, a boiling pot was cooking on the fire and the sweet aroma of cinnamon nectar filled the air.

"What did you catch out there?" asked Kadath.

"Just a rabbit. It could have been more if the sun had still been out, but this is all for tonight," replied Arsivus. Kadath took the rabbit from Arsivus and started to prepare it as he stuck it on a skewer after he skinned it.

Kadath could sense that Arsivus was nervous, so he said "Have a seat son, relax and dinner will soon be served." He cut some more onions and threw them in the stew and tried to ease his son's anxiety.

Arsivus sat down and looked up into the sky. His mind was racing and in deep thought at the same time. Kadath went over after a while and checked the rabbit and decided that it was ready to add to the stew. He took out his knife and started to carve the rabbit into pieces as he dropped the cooked meat into the pot. "Have you ever heard of the clans from across the sea?" Kadath asked, well knowing what his son's answer would be.

Arsivus looked up from gazing at the coals of the warm fire and thought for a minute. "I don't believe so. Who are they?"

Kadath finished putting the rest of the ingredients into the pot and gave it a quick stir with a thick oak spoon that had a cord tied to the handle.

"There are many stories that are told of them," Kadath said as he put the spoon down on a rock and continued. "Stories that say they retain the powers of the wizards from long ago, that they continued to fight each other over more power, more land, and more resources. The clans that are still existent today resemble only a fraction of the power of those that were present many ages ago. There was a group of warriors who banded together by some form of spells to give themselves immense abilities to combat the evil that was growing in the west."

Arsivus was very intrigued now, as he didn't even notice an ember land on the arm of his shirt. "What do you mean banded by some spell?" he inquired. Kadath picked up the spoon and scooped part of the contents into a bowl. He handed it to Arsivus.

"Well, they say that a force had to be created to counter the evil of the wizards in the west during their war. You see, the wizards wanted to rule all and be the lords of all the land. From what I can remember and what is known, there were wizards who refuted these claims and fought against those wanting absolute power. They fought against their own people to preserve peace and humanity as we know it today." Kadath reached behind him and threw another log on the fire to fuel the flames.

"Near the end of the war," Kadath continued on as he stoked the fire, "the wizards that rebelled were pushed back into their final stronghold. They were forced back into one of their castles and were quickly surrounded by hundreds, if not thousands, of troops and other wizards. They were outnumbered and lost all their other territories and smaller allies that were aiding them. Even though they were extremely powerful, they were on the verge of losing their war and revolution. When they initially started to fight back, they numbered in the low hundreds. But as the war waged on, they were dwindled down to only seven of them that remained tucked away inside their castle, and they were quickly running out of options." Arsivus's eyes were wide open as he slowly sipped from his spoon and waited for his father to continue.

"Shortly after them being surrounded, the siege of their fortress began. The numbers are vague, but it has been told that there were five hundred men that broke down the gates and gained entry into the castle. They wanted to end the war that night. There was nowhere that the seven could go. They were trapped. They went inside their largest keep down below the castle and braced for the final confrontation. There was one way in and one way out. This was where they were to make their last stand. The seven faced the doorway, with the leader in front of his throne. He had three wizards on each of his sides. The seven of them formed a half circle around the inside of their keep and started casting a powerful spell, one that would grant them the power they needed to protect themselves from the oncoming onslaught and give them a chance to end the war. At first, their intentions were pure." Kadath said as he paused to taste his dinner.

"What spell did they cast?" Arsivus asked.

Kadath took another spoonful and continued. "They casted a spell to summon a force to help end the war and put a stop to their pursuers."

"Well, that isn't so bad, I guess. Using magic for helping people is a good cause," Arsivus said. He looked down and saw there was a small hole in his sleeve from the ember. He took another bite and brushed his arm where the bitter damp air was coming through the hole.

Kadath took another bite and continued. "True, but the spell they cast had a very steep price." Arsivus looked puzzled as Kadath went on. "You see, the spell they cast was pure at first, but the feelings and hate that those wizards had inside of them twisted the outcome of the spell. It didn't summon a force to fight for them; it turned them into a fighting force together." Arsivus finished his first bowl and got up for a second helping. He quickly returned to his stump to listen.

Kadath continued, "When the spell was complete, the wizard's bodies were turned to stone and what was left . . . were seven beings with unseen power. Stories of their power are still spoken of to this day at the castle. They even have a tournament called the Seven Wizards Battle that you may be able to see one day."

Arsivus looked let down and confused as Kadath took another bite. "What happened to the seven wizards after they received their powers?" Arsivus asked as he sat impatiently waiting to hear the end of the story.

"Oh!" said Kadath. "The beings ascended back up to the castle throne room where the infiltrators were about to enter and waited for those that were waging war against them. They stood in the same half circle watching as the door to the throne room slowly opened. No one knows exactly how it happened, but reportedly, they let one wizard escape the Keep to tell the others of the horrors that they endured. She was able to tell her story, while the rest were slain. The rest of the wizards that were left outside scattered and fled because they were afraid and lost their faith. The reasoning behind them fleeing was that the small army of five hundred that went inside the keep were their best warriors, wizards and leaders. They didn't want to risk losing their lives to this new unseen power that seemingly decimated the best of their allies. I assume they lived quietly for a while, hiding in the shadows for fear of retribution. But the seven wizards hunted most of them down to ensure they never rose to challenge them again. After the battle and the retribution was dealt from the seven wizards, they were never seen again. There have been reports that they crossed the sea and are living here among us, but I don't believe it. After the battle, townspeople started calling them the Avocent. That was their clan name when they initiated the revolution."

Arsivus finished his second helping, put his bowl down, and looked at his father. "Has anyone ever been to see the Keep?" he asked as he placed his stump closer to the fire.

"Only one person that I know of has been there and back and that was King Argol," Kadath said as he picked a piece of an onion from his teeth.

"Argol? Isn't he the King of the Western Kingdom?" Arsivus asked.

Kadath stared deeply into the fire. "Yes, he is the only person that was able to go to the Keep. After he left there, the Keep was closed to all by a form of magic unknown to anyone. No one is sure what happened when he was there, but most agree that it was not good. But on to a more pressing note, let's clean up and find a comfy spot to rest for the night."

When they had finished putting the cooking tools away and gathering more wood for the fire, Arsivus looked around the darkness that seemed to be closing in on them. "Father, what kind of beasts roam this land we are in?"

"Many different kinds, son," Kadath replied. "You have your common woods animals, the deer, wolves, rabbits, as you well know, and then there are others you can never be too sure about. That's why it is always wise to be armed in case of an emergency. Why do you ask?"

Arsivus said, "When I was hunting, I came upon a print that was foreign to me. At first glance it appeared to be a hoof, but when I looked closer, it seemed to have three toes coming out of the front and at the back of the hoof there appeared to be something resembling a claw that dug into the ground."

Kadath stared into the fire and said, "It is probably just two prints on top of each other. There are many things out here we may never understand, but I think it's best if we put thoughts of strange creatures out of our heads for the night and let the stars blanket us with their light as we ready for rest."

His answer left Arsivus feeling a little worried. He sensed his father's unease in his response, which Arsivus wasn't used to. But trusting in his father, Arsivus brushed it aside and looked up at the stars while he wondered what his mother was doing at home at this time. He figured she was probably singing a song like she usually did when she was up at night and baking bread for their return home.

As they were laying there, Kadath spoke out loudly, "I'll take first watch tonight son." As Arsivus was about to drift off to sleep, he heard a faint noise that sounded like a horse's neigh coming from the same path he had hunted on. He brushed it off as the wind rustling through the trees and slowly drifted off to sleep.

CHAPTER 6

The leaves whipped through the open path as the detachment of knights from Affinity departed the Northern Forest. The sun was rising behind the mountains, shedding rays of light across the open and endless plains. Several of the knights were missing and even more were hurt from the scuffles endured while in the forest. They were galloping at a steady pace in formation with Mulik leading. There were twenty fully armed knights in front and thirty-one knights in the rear following behind a cart being pulled by two white steeds. On the cart, the driver cracked the whip for the horses to continue their pace. He sat atop a flat carriage that held a chest made of pure gold that was strapped down for safekeeping.

Once they were south enough and far clear of the forest paths and dangers, Mulik signaled for the party to halt so that he could give orders. "Hold up under these trees here," Mulik commanded. "We have no idea what evils have followed us from the forest, or what flies above us and scouts our path." Mulik disembarked his horse and walked over to the carriage. "You there, driver!" shouted Mulik. "You are to remain with these men behind you." He motioned to the knights behind the carriage. "Do not stray from them. They will escort you the rest of the way to the castle."

The driver responded, "But of course, sir."

One of the knights rode up toward Mulik's position. "Mulik, do you think it's wise that we split up? We are much more a force when we are together than apart," stated the knight.

"Janos, we need to send a party to the kingdom and let them know what has happened. We cannot tarry here for long. I shall lead a small group back as fast as we can. I need you to stay behind and lead the rest of them. Are you up for it?" asked Mulik.

"I will see it done. Which way will you take back?" asked Janos.

"I will take my group through the Enegon Swamp; we should make it home by midday if we maintain a gallop," replied Mulik. "Janos, I would recommend going south first and avoiding the swamp altogether. You will be too slow going through and open for an attack, especially with this caravan. Go around and I will send an envoy to meet you when I return home."

"Very well, Mulik. Safe journey to you and yours." Janos replied.

"And you as well," Mulik replied. "Knights, let's make haste!" Mulik shouted as he jogged back to his horse and climbed atop. As Mulik and his knights sped off into the distance, Mulik turned back to look at Janos and gave him a nod to wish him luck. Just then, he thought he glimpsed something in the woods, just at the edge of the trees, barely visible to his eyes. He was sure he saw something clad in black that had a strange forbidding glow to it as it swayed back and forth between the trees, and then it was gone. Mulik opened his mouth to say something, but no words formed. He thought he saw it again, but he could not make out anything or even assure himself that it was there.

Mulik shook his head to clear his thoughts and looked one last time. This time he saw nothing. "Ah, battle fatigue it must have been!" he exclaimed. He gave Janos another quick nod and sped off to meet with the twenty knights already on their way back home.

As he was galloping away he said aloud so his knights could hear him, "We shall be home this night. Ride with the wind at our backs and it shall be so."

The sun had started to rise in the east. It hovered just below the mountaintops but provided a small glimpse of light as it lay itself across the land. Janos turned in his saddle to face the remainder of the knights. In his head he pictured the nightmarish place they had just come from.

He looked at his companions and saw they were tired, worn, and beaten down. "Knights!" he proclaimed. "I know you are weary from battle, but we must press on. We will travel south, a good distance away from the swamp, so we can have a crow's eye view for those that pursue us. If all goes well, Mulik and a detachment from the castle will come to fortify our position just south of the swamp, near the mountain pass by the morning. Let us form up now and be on our way." The knights took position around the car-avan readying to ride out when they heard an ominous cry come from the Northern Forest behind them. All the knights turned their steeds toward the north and saw nothing except the trees swaying back and forth.

Janos wasted no time in commanding loudly, "Ride, we ride south now!" The knights turned back and started at full gallop while maintaining formation around the carriage. The band of knights and horses flew over the open plains like rapids gushing over rocks in a riverbed. Not wasting any time, Janos sprung to the front and led the company. He decided to maneuver more west than south because the sun was now peeking above the tops of the mountain. He hoped the sun would prove an ally, as it was shining directly at the Northern Forest from where that horrendous cry came. With any luck, the sun would highlight their potential pursuers, and give Janos and his knights a good target to shoot at with their bows.

They galloped until the sun was nearing the height of its ascent. After what seemed like hours of hard riding, Janos finally slowed to a trotting pace as he felt the wind howling through his armor. He looked back at the Northern Forest on the horizon, which was no longer a threat to them. He pulled aside and waited for the last knight to pass him as he peered toward the forest.

"Hmm, nothing followed us," he said to himself in a curious tone. He reached down and stroked the back of his steed's neck. "Very well done, my friend!" he said. As he turned around, he saw that the rest of the group had stopped near some trees to collect some shade. Janos rode up to join them and dismounted in proximity to the carriage.

"What was that in those woods, Janos?" asked one of his knights.

"I believe it was one of the nasty beasts whose treasure we took!" claimed the carriage driver. "Damned be the King for ordering us into that forest."

Shouts of "Aye!" came from the troops.

Another knight butted in "The beasts I saw, fought on all fours. Although some were fighting on two feet as well!"

Janos, feeling certain that sound came from something he had never seen before, said, "I believe it was something more evil than any of us have witnessed."

The carriage driver continued. "I am just glad we got out of there when we did while it remained in the forest."

Another knight came to join the conversation. "Why did we even go into the forest, Janos?"

Janos sighed deeply as he put his hand on the carriage and said, "What business do we have there, you ask? None that I can justify losing my men for. Although we should not disobey the King's orders, he must have his reasons and purpose to put us in danger. Rest assured I will inform Mulik of our journey home and ensure that General Magnus is aware as well. He will know what to do."

As he looked at the chest on the carriage, Janos shook his head in awe. "What is so important in that chest that noble King Thesias would want to risk the lives of my men?" he thought to himself. He attempted to take a sip from his water pouch but quickly found that it was empty, and there was none left in the reserve sack. He looked around and could see his men were visibly on their last legs.

He rose up with an encouraging tone. "Gents, we must get water and food into our bodies. I know of a farm a little way west of here that is friendly to our kingdom. I know not the owners, but they have helped knights out before. Let's be on our way." Janos climbed atop his steed and watched as the remainder of the knights followed suit. "We shall be there soon, my friends." Janos paused. "And then on our way home."

CHAPTER 7

Arsivus opened his eyes to see light pouring in through the treetops. He saw his father loading up some spare wood and the rest of the cooking tools. "How did you sleep?" Kadath asked.

Arsivus quickly replied, "Really good. I dreamed that I met with King Argol and discovered what happened in the wizards keep."

Kadath paused a second to gather his thoughts. "Perhaps I woke your adventurous side from the stories I have been telling you."

Arsivus sprung to his feet and said, "I'll go there someday; perhaps you and mother will join me?"

Kadath latched the last of the supplies in the cart, "Perhaps . . ." his answer faded at the sound of branches breaking behind them. Three men with their faces hidden by cloth and wielding weapons appeared from the depths of the swamp. From the looks of them, Kadath thought they had been living in the swamp for some time. The one in the middle had what looked like blood on his shirt and was carrying an axe. The one on the left was wide around the midsection and was bald.

As Kadath looked down, he saw that he carried two knives in his hands. The last man on the right wore all black and dragged a sack on the ground. In his other hand, he held a sword that had been witness to better days. Arsivus became aware of their presence and slowly walked to the cart to grab his bow. He rested an arrow atop of the string, ready to be nocked at any given moment. Kadath stepped beside him with his hand on the hilt of his sword still in the sheath. "Gentlemen, how may we help you?" Kadath asked with a stern and commanding voice.

"Ha ha ha, well, you see," said the man carrying the axe. "These here are our swamps. I am the leader of this outfit . . . I mean patrol, and I don't remember granting permission for merchants to use our paths." The wider man slowly started side stepping to the left of Arsivus and the man with the sword did the same thing toward Kadath's side.

Kadath, knowing what these men were, gripped the handle of his sword with more intent.

"Well, my apologies, but we are not merchants," claimed Kadath as he put his free hand on Arsivus's shoulder. "We are on official King's business delivering these goods to the King himself. And last I was informed, nobody owned these swamps." Kadath shifted his weight as he let his words sink in for a moment. Birds could be heard chirping high above and frogs were croaking somewhere near a pond.

Arsivus felt his heart beating faster as his eyes darted back and forth between the men.

Kadath broke the silence by saying, "Seeing as both of your claims prove to be false, it's probably best we all just be on our way then." Kadath shifted again, but this time managed to tap Arsivus's sword from behind, as it was sheathed on his belt. Arsivus put the arrow back in the carrier and rested his bow on the cart. He took a step away from his father and put his hand on his hilt just like his dad. The three men slowly started walking closer to where Arsivus and his father were standing.

Kadath, knowing what was going to happen next, took his free hand and motioned in the air to the thieves. "If your intentions are not good, I will offer this only once. Leave now and no harm shall come to you. If you do not regard my warning, there will be no quarter." Arsivus looked over at his father as he stood his ground mightily, his chest out, forearms tightened, and his massive hands gripping the handle of his sword. Arsivus had never seen his father like this. He was brave and menacing. Suddenly Arsivus was filled with courage and strength to be just the same as him.

The thieves laughed. "You are but one man, with a cart and a young boy. We are three experienced warriors. We will take all you carry and more," said the leader of the group.

The man in black jolted forward in the direction of Kadath with his sword drawn. Kadath drew his own sword and clashed metal with metal.

The wide man sprung toward Arsivus with his knives raised in the air ready to strike. He must have thought that Arsivus would be an easy target since he was younger. Arsivus pulled his sword from his sheath and it seemed as light as a feather in his hands. The fat man drew back his right arm to swipe at Arsivus and planted all of his weight on his left leg as he was getting ready to attack. Arsivus instinctively jumped forward and kicked the wide man's left knee out from under him. He fell hard to the ground, clutching his leg and writhing in pain.

Kadath continued to parry with the man in black as the leader went toward Arsivus. Kadath didn't want to leave Arsivus alone with him, so he ducked as a heavy fist glanced off his shoulder and leaned in with a hard slash to the man's left upper thigh. This knocked him down, giving Kadath enough time to jump in front of the leader of the group before he got to Arsivus.

Kadath was standing just as brave and strong as he was before the battle started. The leader had stopped in his tracks and he glanced over his men. Kadath looked back at Arsivus and then turned his attention to the leader. He was showing no signs of pain as he twirled his sword around in his wrist. The man in black got up and limped over to join the leader of the group. "My son has already bested one of your men without even swinging his sword!" Kadath boasted. "And your other man can barely walk, much less continue a battle," he continued. "This is your last chance. Leave now or never." The leader looked at his partner holding his cut leg and nodded toward him. The man in black nodded back. The leader looked at Kadath, then Arsivus, and then back at Kadath. Arsivus gripped his sword tighter and his father went into a defensive stance, expecting the worst to come.

"Never!" growled the leader of the group. The man in black yelled loudly as he limped forward to induce the battle. The leader raised his axe high and started to charge at Kadath when three arrows flew by Kadath's ear and landed in the man in black's chest, forcing him into the air. He landed several feet back from where he started. The leader paused and looked around, as did Kadath and Arsivus. Suddenly, the area was overcome with horses neighing from afar and men shouting loudly to proclaim their entrance into the battle. Kadath looked back and saw a large host of knights riding through the swamp on the same path they had come. Mulik was leading the pack of knights, and he charged up to the leader and dismounted very quickly and cleanly. Another knight joined Mulik as they drew their swords on the leader, while two other knights stood above the wide man with swords drawn upon him.

He was still clenching his knee, as tears strolled down his cheeks while he writhed in pain on the ground. Mulik looked back at Kadath and gave a nod of approval, and then turned to face the leader of the thieves. "Well, well, well, nice to see you again, Zather. Out plundering more goods?" Mulik asked. Zather lowered his head and kept it there.

"Ha, looks like you met your match finally. A man and his son bested the three of you. Perhaps it is time you find a profession that you are good at." Mulik said as he looked over at Kadath and Arsivus and continued. "Taking nothing away from this man and his son, of course. You two did a fine job."

Kadath put his sword back in his sheath and instructed Arsivus to do so as well. "My name is Kadath, and this is my son Arsivus. Thank you for assisting us. Although I do believe they wouldn't have been too much of a problem!" Kadath said as he smiled and gave a wink to Arsivus.

"Ha ha, I do believe you are right, Kadath. I am Sir Mulik, fourth lieutenant of General Magnus. Kadath . . . I have heard that name before. Where do you come from, if you please?"

Kadath motioned to Arsivus to go make ready the cart and said, "I served a while with General Magnus back in my day on ventures in the Northern Forest. We were good friends, and now I deliver the healing crops to the King for his army," Kadath explained.

"Ahhh, now I remember," said Mulik. "General Magnus still tells stories of your adventures. I see you have more herbs you are bringing to the castle. When you arrive there, find me and we shall have drinks and celebration with the court."

"That sounds very promising, I will ensure that we do!" Kadath replied.

Mulik walked over to his two knights standing next to the wide man. "You two, accompany Kadath and his son Arsivus to the kingdom. Go at their pace and we shall see you when you return."

"Kadath!" Mulik said. "I know you and your son can handle yourselves just fine, but I am leaving two of my knights with you to accompany you to the castle. There is no telling how many more thugs are out in these woods. As for us, we must be getting back as soon as possible. We must report to the General our current situation. I shall inform him of your arrival!" he said with a smile as he mounted his horse.

Mulik turned to face the path leading toward the mountaintops and said, "I shall see you soon. Safe journey, my friends." With that, Mulik directed his knights to load the two remaining thieves onto spare horses in the middle of the formation and rode off swiftly toward the kingdom.

Arsivus finished loading the cart and looked at his father. "Well, that was pretty interesting. I am sure we will not be telling mother about this when we return!" said Arsivus.

Kadath laughed out loud. "No, son," he said. "No, we will not."

CHAPTER 8

Birds were chirping over Kadath and Evra's cabin as the sun began to paint the roof with its warmth. Evra shuffled inside as she stacked some blankets in the corner of the storage room. She walked over to the door and opened it, filling the entryway with sunlight and heat.

"Another beautiful day!" Evra said to herself. While the heat was making its way into the cabin, Evra turned around and looked at the bowl on top of the mantle. She smiled deeply when she noticed the blue aura illuminating the room with its radiant color from the pendant. She grabbed a bucket and exited the cabin to walk toward the nearby stream. As she bent down to fill the bucket with fresh water, she saw in the distance three horses coming fast over the hills of the plains.

The dust trail flowing behind them resembled the mist that is left behind from waves crashing over the rocks of the shoreline. Evra rose to her feet, calmly walked back into the cabin, and put the bucket down. She looked around and fetched a sword that was leaning next to the mantle. As the riders drew near, she quickly leaned the sword against the chair and grabbed the pendant out of the bowl.

She ran into the storage room and put it in between the blankets to hide it from peering eyes. As she returned, she brought out some bread and some water for her uninvited guests. The sword remained resting against her chair. As she approached the open door, she heard the voices from the riders as they slowed down to a trot.

"Can I help you, sirs?" Evra shouted unnervingly.

"Ma'am, is this the house of Kadath that we have reached?" replied Atalee.

Evra shook her head in agreement and replied, "But he is not here at the moment. Is there something perhaps I can assist you with?"

Victar dismounted and started to walk toward the door. Evra immediately recognized him and his brother. "You are the children from Bordine, are you not?" asked Evra. "What business have you being here?"

Victar replied, "This is official business for the realm, woman. You will not insult us this day."

Vadeem laughed as he dismounted his horse and walked closer to Evra. "We require water and some food, woman." He marched his way into the house, followed by Victar.

Atalee dismounted his horse and walked up to Evra, "Ma'am, this is official realm business, and I am the only rep-resentative from the realm here. Please, give me a minute alone with them, if you would."

"If it pleases you, sir," Evra said, now visibly upset that the brothers were in her house. Atalee walked past Evra into the house and closed the door. From inside the house she heard a loud bang, a thump, and the sound of glass breaking. Evra ran inside and saw Victar laying on top of the table that was now upside down and Vadeem cowering in the corner holding his hand over a cut near the top of his head. "WHAT is going on in here?" yelled Evra excitedly.

"My apologies, ma'am. These two were just telling me how they wished to apologize to you for their behavior," Atalee replied. "Isn't that right, boys?"

Victar and Vadeem looked at each other, then directly at Evra. "We apologize," they said in unison.

"There, isn't that better? Ma'am, here is some coin for the table, the trouble, and the glass that was broken," said Atalee and handed her five coins.

"Thank you. Let's make sure it doesn't happen again, shall we?" said Evra who then flipped the table right side up. She walked to her pantry and brought out some more water and dusted off the bread. She took a seat with her back facing the door and noticed a slight blue aura radiating on the ceiling in the storage room.

Evra's heart skipped a beat. She did not want these intruders to see the pendant that she had just hidden from them. The scuffle they had must have knocked it loose from its hiding place and it was now on the floor. Victar, Vadeem, and Atalee gathered the chairs that had been thrown around and put them down at the table, then sat with Evra. Atalee started to speak. "Ma'am, if I may?"

Evra interrupted immediately. "My name is Evra!" she said.

67

"Oh," said Atalee in a surprised tone. He was a little taken back. "Evra, nice to meet you. I am Captain Atalee from the White Guard."

Evra looked at him closely and tilted her head. "I thought I had recognized your garb. I have heard many things about you, and most of them do not bring pleasant feelings to me," Evra said in a stern voice.

"Not all that we have done has been bad," Atalee responded. "And look at our friends here," he said as he pointed at Victar and Vadeem. "They know now not to say a word unless spoken to, out of respect for your home and you inviting us in."

Evra laughed. "You mean when all of you walked right in and started a fight?"

Atalee kept a straight face and looked over at Vadeem and Victar, then looked back at Evra and said, "You do make a good point." Evra stood up and walked into the storage room to grab some mugs of ale for her guests. But her motive was more to see how visible her pendant was.

As she was staring at it for what seemed like ages, Atalee spoke from the table. "Is there a problem, Evra?" He motioned over to Victar. "Victar, be a good lad and help the lady out!"

Victar rose from his seat and walked into the storage room. Immediately his eyes went to the ceiling. "That is fantastically wondrous!" he said out loud, which caught Vadeem's attention.

"What is that aura?" Victar asked, looking into Evra's eyes. Evra had to think quickly. She did not want this man to know about the pendant.

"It is merely a reflection off my mirror over by the blankets." And with that, Evra handed Victar a large cask of ale and guided him out of the storage room. As he was being shuffled out, she added, "Sometimes the light hits it just right where I have cleaned it, and it produces that aura." Victar, not being the wiser, accepted the answer as just and returned to the table with the cask and mugs with Evra right behind him.

"So, let's speak of this business for the realm, dear Captain. Why have you come here?" asked Evra politely. Victar went to speak but was quickly silenced by Atalee's sharp and angry stare.

Atalee returned his gaze to Evra. "Evra, our liege would like to know how you and your husband create the herbs that you do." Evra, a bit taken back, didn't quite know how to answer. She knew the secret of how she grew it, but she was not about to tell anyone that, especially these three that sat in front of her.

So, she lied. "It is all in how you prepare the crops, and how often it gets watered and tended to every day." She felt bad for lying, but even worse when she realized that although Victar and Vadeem could not tell that the truth was absent from her lips, Atalee did not change one muscle in his face and continued to stare at her.

"So . . ." Atalee said, "how often do you water it, tend to it, and how do you prepare the crops so they have healing properties?" His tone drew silence from Victar and Vadeem. "Are you sure there is nothing else you put in there, a ritual, a chant, magic?"

Evra, ever so keen to Atalee's tactics, now sought the offensive. "Are you accusing me of witchcraft?" she snapped. "That is all we do for the herbs, and if you don't like it, we will stop growing them. See how your army fares then!"

Victar and Vadeem were startled, and Atalee was caught off guard, "I didn't mean to offend," Atalee said. "But if it were that easy, why wouldn't anyone else be able to grow it?"

Evra leaned back in her chair. "I have no idea. I just know it works here, on this land, for some reason."

Atalee seemed satisfied for the moment. He stood up and motioned for Victar and Vadeem to join him. "Ma'am, I thank you for your time. You have been quite helpful." He paused as he looked around the cabin. His eyes stopped near the floor in the storage room.

Atalee smiled. "You shouldn't keep your precious gems on the floor, my dear. Thieves like these," as he motioned toward Victar and Vadeem, "make their living finding and taking things this way."

Evra maintained her calm and said, "My gems wouldn't be on the floor if your boys had shown some manners."

Atalee headed for the door but stopped and turned to face Evra. "Another good point!" he said. "Boys, come!" Victar and Vadeem stood up and followed him. Evra waited at the table for them to walk outside, and then she ran into the storage room to place the pendant back in the blankets for now. She straightened herself up and walked outside to say good-bye to the three men.

When she reached the doorframe, she saw that Victar, Vadeem and Atalee were mounted on their horses and were surrounded by Janos and his knights. Janos looked around and saw Evra in the doorway. "Ma'am, is everything all right?" he asked.

Evra looked sharply at Janos. "Yes, these men were just leaving as abruptly as they came."

Janos recognized Atalee on his horse and asked, "Sir, may I ask your business here this day?"

Atalee laughed. "Are you really going to try and interrogate me, the captain of the White Guard?"

Atalee turned his horse around, gave a sly nod to Evra, and looked back at Janos. "Move your plaything of knights out of our way. And make sure you get that cart back to the King as soon as possible. If it were me and my men, we would have been back days ago. But I understand Magnus runs things a little differently."

Janos moved his horse next to Atalee and said, "That's General Magnus, Captain."

Atalee stopped and looked at Janos with piercing eyes. "For how much longer I do wonder, if his knights weren't able to make it back to the castle with the King's treasure?"

Evra shouted from the door, "There will be no fighting here today, lords. You three," she said, pointing at Atalee and the two brothers, "Leave!" Then she motioned to Janos and his knights, "And all of you other knights, if it is water you want, I have some. I have bread and ale as well, and you are welcome to it."

Atalee pushed his way through the gathering of horses and headed off to the kingdom at a hurried pace, with Victar and Vadeem following. Janos watched Atalee as he rode away.

Janos dismounted and went over to Evra. "Thank you for offering us food and drink. We shall not take more than we need, and you will be compensated for it."

Evra replied as she headed into her cabin. "Hurry up now. I have more chores to do today than to feed the King's knights."

Janos smiled, looked to his knights, and said, "Freshen up, and feed and water the horses, for we shall not stay long."

He entered the cabin and looked around. "It seems there was a scuffle here, ma'am. Did they hurt you?" Janos asked with a concerned look.

"No, no they didn't," Evra said. Janos pulled out a chair and motioned his hand to it to ask permission to sit down. Evra nodded and Janos flicked his torn cape out from under him and took a seat.

"Why did those men come here?" Janos asked curiously.

Evra looked at Janos and could tell he was a genuine man. She put out some more water. "They wanted to know how we make our crops for the King and wouldn't leave here until I gave them a reasonable answer," she said. "I told them the truth, but they were convinced that I was involved in witchcraft, but . . ." she hesitated.

"But what?" Janos asked. Evra had a feeling that something bad would happen if Atalee were to return. Her thoughts were spinning as to why he grinned when he saw the pendant on the floor. She had never wanted Kadath to be home as bad as she did on this particular day. After a couple of moments passed in complete silence, an uproar stirred up outside. Janos immediately stood up and ran to the door. Evra tried looking past him, but his figure was taking up a good portion of the doorway. Janos, squinting his eyes for the source of the disruption, spotted it right behind the horses. "Brothers!" Janos yelled. "Ha, welcome! Have you been following us on our journey this whole time? You could have asked to join us if you had wanted. I'm sure we would have said maybe!"

Cardage patted his horse as he walked past it, with Theros right behind him. Theros pulled out three rabbits and four squirrels from behind his back that he shot with his bow.

"Anybody ready for dinner?" Theros asked with a smile.

Theros laughed out loud, as did some of the other knights. Janos stepped out of the cabin and said, "Still afraid to embrace hand to hand combat I see, even with harmless little pets as these!" This drew more laughter from the knights.

Theros smiled as he and Cardage embraced Janos.

Cardage walked into the cabin. Evra went and grabbed a couple more mugs for the new guests. "Shall I be expecting more knights this day, or is this it?" Evra asked the newcomers.

Cardage motioned to a chair to ask to sit, and Evra nodded once again.

The knights flipped their capes back and sat, and Cardage spoke first. "I must tell you that we were sent to follow and watch Captain Atalee and his two henchmen. We saw them approach your home and made haste to get here as quick as we could. Our mission was to not be seen by them. They were not to know that they were followed."

Evra looked at Cardage with a confused stare. "Why were you sent to follow them?" Evra asked with astonishment.

Cardage took a sip of the water and smiled. "This is good water, almost special in a way." Evra was curious as to where this was going.

Cardage continued. "Theros and I were sent to make sure no trouble or ill-advised actions took place by Atalee." He paused for a second and repositioned himself on the chair. "General Magnus, who knows Kadath very well, spoke of you on many occasions. You see, Janos and his men were with another detachment of knights led by one of our lieutenants, Mulik. They were to retrieve something from the Northern Forest for the King. Magnus, myself, and many others are curious as to why the King would dare such an adventure, especially knowing that he has done it in the past and brought disdain upon the land."

Evra asked, "Is the thing that the King wanted in that cart outside?"

Cardage went to speak but was cut off by Janos. "No, we found treasure, but it seems to be just normal gold and silver. Nothing that would justify sending men to die for."

Cardage put his hand on the table and nodded in agreement. "The item the King is searching for is a special pendant. It is something that has the ability to radiate light to pierce any darkness."

Evra adjusted her seat. "Why would he want a pendant?" she asked, trying to avoid any interest in the matter. "I am sure he has thousands of them in his mighty castle."

Cardage smiled. "Yes, he does, but this one is very special," he said. He looked around the room quickly and then focused back on Evra. "You see, there is a legend that was

74

told long ago. One told throughout the generations of the kingdom and passed on through heirs of royalty. There were five great beings that existed here centuries ago that lived among the people. Each of them represented a gift of sorts. These beings had special powers imbued within them, and they lived together to maintain balance and order. These beings were giants of men, and with their powers under one banner, they could conquer kingdoms in mere days if not less." Janos and Theros were staring intently at Cardage as he spoke, and Evra started to feel an uneasiness come over her.

Evra looked around the room quietly and then spoke up. "These powers . . . what could they do?" She wondered if there was any way her pendant was connected to this fable.

Cardage continued, "The powers were different between the beings. That is how the balance was maintained. You see, these beings had many abilities and talents. No one is certain as to what the full extent of their powers were, but it has been found that they were mighty indeed. We do not know where they came from, but from our royal scrolls in the castle, we have made some interesting discoveries. A particularly well-hidden scroll identified that one of the beings was able to heal the others, as well as itself with its power. The writings were very badly damaged, but this particular scroll that told us of the healing properties, was written with a radiant blue ink. There were riddles among the scrolls as well, but they were very vague as to where these powers might reside. From what we could decipher about the other beings, which wasn't much, did not give any other details as to the powers that they possessed. Although we think we have a small lead as to what we are looking for. One of the scrolls was written in the radiant blue ink, and the other four scrolls were written in a crimson red, burning yellow, blazing white and jasper green ink."

Evra thought to herself that this was impossible and couldn't be. Her pendant was blue, and was used in making the herbs, but there had to be more to this than he was telling her.

Cardage continued, "The story goes that the five beings grew bored of maintaining the balance with each other, which is when they decided to initiate a war. They wanted to see who the strongest being was. They fought for many nights, back and forth, and ravaged the land to an almost unrecognizable terrain. When they all finally realized what they had done to the land and forest and mountains, they swore never to take part in war against each other again. To ensure that this pact remained, they realized they must neutralize themselves to make it last. They combined their knowledge and desire to finally do some good and embodied their spirits and powers into five separate pendants that would radiate bright with their auras. I would only assume that their pendants radiate the same color as the ink that was written in the scrolls. Those pendants shine bright for all to see, and legend has it that their power can still be used if the person knows how to draw it out."

Cardage took another sip of his water and carefully looked into the glass as he set it upon the table. Evra was more worried now than ever. She feared that her pendant was the special one that Cardage spoke about, and if anyone knew that it was in her possession, her life and her family's lives would be in danger.

"So, this pendant," Evra said, "King Thesias thinks that the beasts of the Northern Forest have located it and are keeping it for themselves?" Cardage looked around the room and stopped on the storage room.

"Yes," he said while staring at the room. "Yes, King Thesias believes," Cardage paused and looked at Evra with a suspicious eye, "that one of the pendants resides there." Evra tried to look away but could not seem to break away from Cardage's stare.

"My lady," Cardage spoke quietly. "You are in very trusted company. We three are loyal to General Magnus and do not want these pendants to be found by King Thesias. In fact, we want them to remain hidden, but you must tell us the truth. Do you possess one of these pendants?" Evra stood up and gasped loudly. Cardage leaned back in the chair and swirled the remaining amount of water in his cup.

"Evra," Cardage asked, "is that what was helping you with your herbs that you supply the King with every year?"

Evra tried to fight the anxiety of being under interrogation, even though it seemed friendly so far. She thought back to when Kadath showed her the pendant, and what it could do, and warned her that others would want this special gift for their own. Her mind was frazzled. She could not contain her thoughts while these three men questioned her.

She kept frantically thinking, "Why did it have to happen on today of all days when Kadath was gone? How was she going to lie to the knights to hide the pendant that she was sure they knew she had?" Evra felt that her face was giving away her secret the longer she remained quiet.

Evra sat down calmly and scooted her chair in closer to the table and rested both of her hands in her lap. "How can you think that I would have such a token?" she asked.

Cardage leaned forward and spoke softly with a smile, enjoying the game. "There are scrolls in the castle from long, long ago, with riddles containing ideas and locations of where the pendants are. Not many know of them. Since Kadath is the only surviving member of his family, and his crest was seen on the scroll with the radiant blue ink, we thought it best to inquire of it here first and foremost." Cardage said as he leaned back in the chair, and Janos stood up and started to walk around the room.

"Well, I don't believe I have seen one of those around here, but if I do you will be the first to know," she said.

Janos suddenly shouted, "Sire, come look quick!" Cardage stood and went to meet Janos, who was peering into the storage room. Evra jumped out of her chair and rushed over to block the entry, but it was too late. Cardage, Janos, and Evra were now staring into the room that was radiating a pure blue aura in the back corner, as they stood to admire the glow.

Theros walked up behind the pack quietly and stopped at the door. "Well, looks like we found one of them, and the secret behind the herbs!" Evra was quiet. She didn't know what to do. There was no way she could best one of the knights, let alone three.

Cardage shook his head and let out a sigh of relief. "The stories are true!" he said happily. He turned and motioned to Theros to go outside and then turned to Evra.

"Evra, like I said before, we do not want this to fall into Thesias's hands. We want them to remain hidden from all who would abuse them. I need to ask you a favor."

Evra was a bit startled by this. "I will not give it to you!" she said with a stern voice. Cardage laughed, "Ha, ha, no, no, no, we did not come to collect this, only to locate it. The favor I ask is that you keep this hidden from all, in a better spot than your storage room. I am sure that Atalee is suspicious of it being here and will most likely return someday. I need you to put this in a spot that no one will look."

Evra felt relieved yet was still wary. She nodded her head in agreement. Theros came back holding a cage with a cover over it. He set it on the table. Inside Evra heard what sounded like a bird flapping its wings and jumping from perch to perch. Theros took the cover off and displayed a beautiful bird with fluorescent yellow wings, a red body, and a blue head with a black beak.

"No one but us three and General Magnus and his inner circle will know of this pendant, and we mean to keep it this way," Theros said. "This is a special messenger bird whose only purpose is to return to Castle Affinity. If ever you are in trouble or feel the pendant is as risk, release this bird from its cage. As soon as the bird returns, we will send as many troops as possible to come to your aid. I pray you never have need of it."

Cardage nodded his head. "We are not far, but if a situation were to arise, you must hide it at all costs. Do you understand?" he asked.

"Yes," Evra replied. "I have places I can go and places to hide as well."

"Good," said Cardage, as he looked at Theros and Janos. "We have lingered here long enough. Your troops should be rested," he said to Janos. "Let's return home with the treasure you have and speak nothing of the pendant until we meet with the General."

Janos agreed and looked at Evra. "My lady!" he said, as he bowed, then turned toward the door and yelled, "Let's go, gentlemen. We have a long ride yet and I do not want to be gone from home longer than I have to!" With that, the knights of Affinity mounted their horses and waited for Cardage and Theros to join them toward the mountains to the east.

Cardage looked at Theros. "Our mission is fulfilled, and we shall be on our way. But first," Cardage pulled out a bag of coin and placed it on the table next to the cage, "This is for the inconvenience and trouble for today. I do hope it wasn't all unpleasant," he said as he and Theros exited. They mounted their horses and turned toward the raised mountains in the east.

Evra came to the door and asked, "If you see my husband, Kadath, at the castle, please inform him of our meeting and tell him to hurry home!" Cardage looked back and nodded his head in agreement. With that, Cardage, Janos and Theros were off to the kingdom. Evra walked back inside and looked in the storage room. The emanating blue light was beautiful as it danced upon the walls.

Evra bent down, picked up the pendant again as it must have fallen, and put it in a small chest. "I don't mean to contain your essence, but for the time being we need to keep you safe," she said to the pendant as if hoping in the quiet and lonely room, a voice would come from it assuring her everything would be fine. Evra carried the chest outside to one of the fence poles and dug a hole for it to lay in for the time being.

As she filled in the hole with dirt, she brushed her hands to cleanse them of dust and looked at the sun shining elegantly above her. She closed her eyes and smiled as she thought of Kadath and Arsivus and hoped that the day they would come home would soon be upon her.

CHAPTER 9

Midday had passed and Arsivus and his father were now out of the swamp and leading down the trail at a steady pace with a knight on each side of them. "At this pace we should reach the mountain pass by nightfall," Kadath said.

One of the knights called Doran coughed quietly and looked at the cart. "When we get to the pass, we know of a spot to settle in for the night. From there we should be able to make it to the castle by this time tomorrow."

Arsivus bit down on an apple and chewed momentarily. He took another big bite and put the apple in a bin behind him. Doran curiously asked, "What are you doing?"

Arsivus replied, "I am saving some snacks for the horses." Kadath displayed a smile and Arsivus continued. "They like when I save them snacks, these two right here," and he pointed to the horses pulling the cart. "They are the most loyal horses I have ever had. They can always be counted upon when I need them."

Doran smiled and asked, "How old are you, boy?"

Arsivus proudly answered, "Eighteen!"

The knights looked at each other and the other knight said, "Old enough to be entered into training to be a knight."

Arsivus looked over at him and asked, "I thought you had to be born royal to become a knight?"

The knight shook his head. "No, not anymore. Ever since King Thesias opened the rite to anyone who deemed themselves worthy. It was probably the one good thing he has done in the last several years!" he exclaimed.

Arsivus felt his chest fill with pride and hope. He regained his demeanor and asked, "So what is the test to deem themselves worthy of becoming a knight?"

"It's the Seven Wizards Battle," Kadath said, not taking his eyes from the road. "You have to be invited to participate by General Magnus and earn his favor through different competitions. They only take one person every year to become a knight. It is the General's way of replenishing his forces that are lost on missions."

Arsivus looked at his father. "Father, you know General Magnus. Do you think he would grant me an invite if you were to ask?" he asked. The knights both laughed aloud.

"What's so funny?" Arsivus demanded. He could see that his father was smiling too. "What is it?" Arsivus asked in a more serious tone.

Kadath looked over at him. "I am sure your invite will be ready as soon as we arrive at the gate. Mulik will have already told General Magnus about us, and no doubt the General will want to speak to you and enter you into the contest. I had the will to ask him once we arrived, but my plan will have been foiled upon news from Mulik and our meeting."

Arsivus's heart was beating faster now with excitement. Images were racing through his mind. "Finally, a chance to prove my worth!" Arsivus thought to himself.

Kadath cracked the reins to go a little faster. Arsivus asked, "So what events are there to test myself in the Seven Wizards Battle?"

Doran responded, "No one knows. They will be chosen the day before the competition by General Magnus. They change every year to keep the competition fair."

Arsivus smiled, as he thought to himself, "I am sure I shouldn't have a problem with whatever the test is!" He leaned back on the cart and looked down the winding path they were on. He put his arms behind his head and started to imagine what it would be like to be a knight as he gazed into the clouds above him. Before he knew it, he was fast asleep on the cart as his father continued steering the horses down the dirt trail.

Arsivus was woken by a bump. He rubbed his eyes to chase away the sleep and looked around. The large mountains that were once far off in the distance seemed now only but a stone's throw away. He looked around and saw nothing but open plains and hills around him. He turned around and discovered that the knights were gone. Behind the cart, he could see that the Enegon Swamp was fading fast into the distance, and a thick cloud of dust rose from beneath the wheels. He turned back to his father and asked, "Where did the knights go?"

"They rode ahead to ensure the path was secure, and that the place we were to bed down for the night was prepared with wood," Kadath said. "They should be back in a little while." Arsivus continued to look around at the rolling hills around them, and they all seemed to flow in a symmetrical fashion toward the mountain. The sun had started to set and the mountainsides ahead of them were beginning to be covered by a sunlit cast.

There was a slight chill in the air. Arsivus grabbed his cloak and tightened it around his body. "How long was I asleep?" he asked.

Kadath looked over at him and said, "You were out for a little while. The sun is well on its way toward the horizon. You see there," Kadath pointed ahead toward the mountains and identified a path cut through the middle of it. "That is the mountain pass we will take tomorrow. We will make camp at the base of it tonight and rise early to arrive at the castle at midday."

Arsivus looked ahead and nodded his head in approval. "It looks like only a small group could fit through there at one time!" Arsivus said.

"Yes, many times that pass has saved the kingdom from enemies that wished to see the people of Affinity fall." Kadath replied.

Arsivus pulled another apple from his bag and took a solid bite. "So, who else will be put in the Seven Wizards Tournament?" Arsivus asked.

Kadath leaned back a little and raised his eyebrows as he thought of potential rivals for his son. "Well," Kadath began, "I am sure that the King's sons are of age and will attempt the tournament. Their names are Ruvio and Zenor. I have not had the chance to meet them yet, although I fear they haven't fallen far enough from their roots to be what we would call charitable. They will most likely be trained for the tournament, so that should be a little competition for you. Other than them, there may be all sorts of men from around the land. Perhaps someone from the Old Kingdom or the Western Kingdom will show up. Or even a beast from the Northern Forest. Now that would be a sight!"

Kadath chuckled to himself as he let out a yawn. Arsivus looked behind their cart quickly as Kadath went on, "Anyone could be invited, but only seven participate in this tournament, as that was how many wizards defended themselves in their Keep."

"Good to know," Arsivus said as he noticed a dust cloud rapidly rising in the distance in front of them. "Looks like our knights are returning to guide us the rest of the way," Arsivus said. Kadath squinted to get a better look at them. Arsivus was reaching back to put the other half of the apple back in his bag when he heard a loud crack.

Kadath had cracked the reins for the horses, sending them into a charged fury straight ahead. Arsivus dropped the apple from the sudden jolt of the cart rapidly picking up speed.

"Father," Arsivus said as he looked around in a mild panic. "What is the matter?"

Kadath did not break his gaze on the knights riding toward them. "Something is wrong, I can feel it." He gave the horses another whip. The distance between them and the knights was closing fast, and Arsivus could feel his heartbeat growing faster and faster. He put his hand on the blade of his sword, trying to remember the feel of it, wanting to become familiar with the weight and sharpness of the cold hard steel. Seconds seemed to pass like hours as they closed the gap between them.

Finally, the knights slowed to a pace, coming to a merge with the cart. "Gentlemen, we cannot stay at the base of the mountain tonight. We must return to the castle immediately," Doran said with a hint of alarm in his voice.

"What happened ahead?" Kadath asked intently. The knights dismounted and put on their chain mail, metal bracers, and shoulder guards. They quickly retrieved a drink of water from their reserves.

Kadath prompted them again. "What is the situation, sirs?" he said with a demanding tone.

Doran spoke again. "There are bodies at the base camp. Three of them, and we believe them to be a group of the General's knights, although we cannot be sure. They may be the ones that departed days ago. We cannot tell from the wounds inflicted upon them."

"They most certainly were!" the other knight pitched in worriedly. Kadath unhinged his sword and prompted Arsivus with a nod to do the same.

Doran secured the last remaining clasp on his armor with haste and looked at Kadath and Arsivus with intent. He said,

"I suggest if you want to come to the castle, that you batten down your cart before we reach the pass. It would be too vulnerable in the pass to defend with our party going slow."

"Aye, we will have to make swift travel through the pass if whoever did that to those men is still out there," said the other knight.

Arsivus had his sword ready and looked at the knights. "Who do you think it was that did that?" he asked.

Doran shook his head. "I don't know. Janos had thirty men and a cart as well, but they wouldn't have made it there yet. Mulik had eighteen knights, although this could have happened after they passed through. It may have been an ambush, but we best be prepared for anything."

"Agreed!" Arsivus said as he hopped in the back of the cart and started binding everything down that he could. After a couple of minutes had passed, they were ready. Both of the knights took their places on both sides of the cart. Doran was seated on Kadath's side, and the other knight stayed close to Arsivus on the opposite side. They began moving toward the impending mountain ahead of them as the sky filled with looming clouds.

Arsivus could feel the tension in the air grow thicker with each minute that passed. The closer they got to the pass, the more their speed increased.

The deafening silence was broken by Kadath as he leaned toward Arsivus. "Son, I want you on the bow in case someone charges at us. You will take them out before they get within reach. Can you do this?" Kadath asked, not taking his eyes off the pass. His eyes were scouring the edges and sharp risings of the mountain where looters and thieves could hide.

"Yes, sir," Arsivus responded calmly. For some reason, hearing Arsivus's confident voice made Kadath feel very comfortable. As they drew near the base camp, the party slowed back to a trot to fully observe the path ahead of them. They were cautious, as they did not want to run into a trap, or an ambush of men waiting their arrival. Even more perilous would be obstacles that could paralyze their cart.

"Eyes open," Doran said quietly.

"Mouths not," the other knight said.

As they crept along at a steady pace, the camp at which they were supposed to remain for the night came up on their right side. Arsivus looked over at it and saw the three bodies piled on top of each other. Their helmets and armor were aground and their bodies were burnt beyond recognition. One of them had what looked like an arrow with a glowing red tinge, sticking out of his back. It was the likes of which Arsivus had never seen. It was thick and looked as if it had metal thorns all the way down the shaft.

Arsivus threaded an arrow into his bow and pulled to ensure the tension was tight as his eyes blanketed the camp. He looked up and down but couldn't spot anything out of sorts.

"It is too quiet," Doran said softly. Nothing was moving and it seemed the wind was even hesitant to enter the pass. It slowly died down to barely a whisper the closer they came to the small opening. All that could be heard were the hooves of the trotting horses as they echoed through the tall mountainsides.

The wheels made of wood creaked as they rolled into the ominous pass. Arsivus's mind was consumed by thoughts of the bodies he had seen. He thought to himself, "Who in their right mind would attack a group of knights and live to tell the tale?" As they pressed on through the tall arches of the pass, the light continued to fade away as it was being held captive by the mountaintops. Kadath thought of a strategy and pulled out two long torches he had stored behind him in the cart. Once the sunlight was absent, they would have no other source to guide them through the seemingly unending pass.

"Kadath, best light those torches soon. We are almost out of light and I fear something is not far off in the distance and watching us," said the knight near Arsivus.

"Agreed," Doran quietly said. "As soon as those torches go up, mount them on the cart and we will move fast." Arsivus grabbed one of the torches and held it in his hand awaiting the call. They traveled a little farther down the narrow winding road when Kadath's whisper broke the silence.

"On my count, son." Time seemed to stand still and speed up at the same time. Arsivus's heart was racing at an incredible speed but you could not tell by looking at him. The natural silence around them was stifling. The hairs on the back of Arsivus's neck now stood up. His senses were tuned in to the environment around him, and he was slow to breathe in fear he would miss something.

Kadath's murmur echoed off the mountain walls. "On my mark, three, two . . . one." At that exact moment, the last of the sunlight retreated behind the horizon and darkness took its place.

"Now," Kadath whispered. Arsivus and Kadath both dipped the torches in oil and struck them with a sulfur spark. The explosion of light seemed surreal, and the flames highlighted the jagged crests of the mountain that seemed to trap them within its grasp.

Arsivus mounted both torches on the cart as the knight next to him quietly whispered, "Go." With that, they were off along the path. Kadath cracked down the whips on the horses in front of him while the knights galloped alongside. Arsivus quickly retrieved his bow and was looking toward both front and back for any danger. The torches obscured his vision from time to time and he could only see a few yards behind the cart. Beyond that was complete darkness.

The wheels continued to crackle beneath them as they spit out rocks along the path and the neighing of the horses resounded throughout the canyon. Time seemed to be slowly creeping by as the night got darker and darker. There was a faint breeze now coming from behind them and a vast coolness permeated the mountainous valley. Arsivus continued to scour their path ahead and behind, Finally, the cart whipped around a corner of the mountain pass and they started to climb into the rugged mountains.

The path was now straight and narrow and barely big enough for two carts to pass by each other. Minutes passed by with extreme hesitation. As they climbed higher, the cliffs began to disappear on the right side, giving view to the Kingdom of Affinity. After what seemed like hours, Arsivus was able to gaze towards the Eastern Kingdom unobstructed, and he saw the moon rising above the sea as it illuminated down across the land. In that instant, his thoughts and hopes were silent as he gazed upon the kingdom.

His fascination was brought to an end when Doran exclaimed, "We are nearing the high station path. From there it is downhill and rough. Be on your highest alert, gentlemen!" Arsivus focused back on the task at hand and gazed ahead and behind as he was taught. He suddenly thought he saw something cross into the opening of the cliffs some ways back, but the moving flame from the torches played tricks on his eyes. The moonlight was shining brightly now, enough to illuminate a bigger area in front and behind the cart.

As Arsivus looked back again, he saw there was a rider following behind them. Alarmed, Arsivus turned and braced his knee on the bench as he attempted a closer look. The moonlight suddenly dipped behind the large clouds in the sky and the area behind them was dark again. Arsivus, now holding his bow, stared impatiently into the darkness, waiting for the moonlight to come back so he could get another look at the shadowy figure.

Seconds seemed like hours as Arsivus dared not blink. He felt the cart turning again, so he stretched his upper body to keep as much of the area behind him in sight as possible. Just as the moon embraced the mountain pass, Arsivus saw the rider for a brief second in fast pursuit of them. He was now sure something was wrong and was about to tell his companions, but was cut off by Doran yelling, "The gate ahead has been destroyed!" Arsivus looked ahead of them and saw an enormous wooden gate with the door lying broken next to it. Beyond the gate, he only saw darkness where the mountain path crept back into the jagged cliffs. Arsivus took a rag from the cart and submerged it in the oil. He then took an arrow and wrapped the rag around the tip and waited patiently to cross back into the darkness.

"Someone is following us!" Arsivus exclaimed.

"Are they friend or foe?" Kadath asked as he continued to crack the reins, driving them faster into the mountain pass.

Arsivus positioned himself in a good stance by the lit torch, strung the bow back, and said, "We will find out soon!" As they raced through the busted gate, Arsivus hovered the arrow already laced in the bow over the torch and the rag burst into flame. He took aim and released the arrow into the dark side of the gate. The oil splattered on the wooden frame and spread the fire all around. He then took another rag, dipped it in the oil, and tied one end of the rag to a rope and the other end of the rope to the cart. He grabbed the soaked rag and touched it to the torch, and it erupted in flames.

Arsivus quickly threw it behind the cart on the ground, and it stretched itself out behind them a good distance away.

"What are you doing?" Doran asked as he continued to keep pace with the cart.

"Whatever is behind us will have to pass by the lit rag and show itself to us if they want to reach us. It will also help me to not shoot blindly behind us, and I might be able to get a good enough shot." Arsivus replied. He stood up and faced behind them as the cart raced through the mountain pass, swaying left and right as Kadath took the corners as fast as he could.

Arsivus drew his bow and aimed it slightly above the burning rag dragging behind them, "Whatever was back there was definitely gaining on us," he thought to himself. Kadath saw Arsivus standing there with his bow drawn back ready to fire. He looked back behind them and saw the rag on fire, but nothing else. He shouted loudly to make sure Arsivus heard him over the noise of the cart and horses. "What do you see?"

Without taking his eyes off the rag dragging behind them on the road, Arsivus shouted back, "I don't know, but there is going to be an arrow in it if it gets closer." Keeping his eyes peeled, Arsivus saw what seemed to be a shadow gaining on them. He blinked a couple of times to ensure his vision was correct.

The mysterious follower passed through the wooden gate, and as he did Arsivus saw that the pursuer was clad in black and rode on a steed as dark as the night. Arsivus got into position and waited until he could get an accurate shot. The black rider was now coming into view of the fire rope dangling behind the cart. Arsivus's heart was racing. Just a little closer and he could end this.

Just as Arsivus went to release his arrow, the right side of the cart hit a log lying on the side of the road. The arrow flew off into the air, lost into the dark night. Arsivus was knocked back onto the herbs but pushed himself up to a knee and threaded another arrow. He looked back at his target, and it appeared to not have gained any ground on them.

Arsivus thought to himself, "It probably doesn't want to be seen, or give me a target. It doesn't matter. This time I won't miss." He pulled back his arrow and took a deep breath. He exhaled as he released his grip. The arrow flew true and fast, right at shoulder height. He could see and almost feel the arrow strike its target in the chest. The rider fell back out of view, and Arsivus loaded another arrow and continued to look behind. He couldn't see anything else behind them, but noticed that the fire was hastily starting to climb the rope toward the cart. He reached over and cut the rope off, letting it fall behind them. He continued to watch but didn't see anything cross in front of it.

Once the burning rope was out of sight, Arsivus went back to his father and announced, "One arrow is in him. I see no more trace of him following us. He must be back there quite some ways, and I know I struck him good in the chest."

The knight nearest Arsivus said, "Good shot, son. The pass is almost at an end. We are free of it just up there." Arsivus looked forward and could see the stars shining brightly in the sky over the ocean.

"Almost there!" Arsivus thought to himself. He looked over at the knight, with his perfect posture and riding stance, and thought, "Someday that will be me." Arsivus took his bow in his hand and was about to put it back in his sack when he heard a high-pitched noise and then a thud. Arsivus looked up and saw the knight he was just admiring leaning forward in his saddle as his horse continued to race on. There was no movement from the knight, and he saw a small stream of blood dripping down the horse's side.

Kadath noticed this as well. "Faster! We must go faster!" Kadath yelled. "Arsivus, spread your arrows to all areas behind us; something still gives chase; shoot everything you have." Arsivus grabbed his arrows and stood up, and just as he was about to turn around to release his salvo, he saw the same strange glowing red arrow that he had seen upon entrance to the mountain pass sticking out of the knight at his side.

"No time," he thought to himself. He turned around, nocked his first arrow, and fired. He continued to fire into the night until he reached his last arrow. He waited in silence, as his eyes pierced through the darkness for any sign of movement. In the moonlight, he saw a black figure on the trail behind him with two arrows in its chest slowly come to a stop.

The dark figure appeared to be staring at Arsivus and his lot as they sped along the trail. The mysterious figure grabbed hold of the two arrows, pulled them out, and threw them against the jagged cliffs next to the path. As the figure turned away, Arsivus saw a strange blue light glowing from its chest. He watched as the figure moved off into the distance.

After a few moments, Doran said, "We are clear of the pass now. Let us make for Affinity as quickly as possible." Arsivus reached over and grabbed hold of the reins of the injured knight's horse. He leaned over and pulled the knight on top of the cart. Arsivus looked down at him and felt responsible for what had happened. The knight's eyes were barely open and there was blood dripping from his lips.

"I'm sorry," said Arsivus as he grabbed two herbs from the cart and placed them on the knight's wounds. "I thought I hit him. It was a perfect shot. There is . . ."

The knight reached his hand up toward Arsivus's mouth to silence him. "Shhh. If you are . . . to be a knight . . . show your confidence . . . even when it is broken," he said slowly, taking shallow breaths after every few words. "Never lose faith in what you are doing . . . or those that you are doing it for . . . remember this."

Arsivus grasped the knight's hand. "I will," he promised.

The mountain pass was finally behind them and they were now moving steadily along a dirt road that interweaved through rolling hills as it led up to the front gates of the castle. The moon was fully visible now and shone across the land. It painted the mountaintops behind them a bright white and highlighted the towers and buildings in the castle ahead. As they got closer to the castle gate, Arsivus was struck by the height of the castle walls surrounding Affinity.

"How is he doing?" Kadath asked. Arsivus, still holding the knight's hand, looked down and saw that he was breathing. "He is still with us, but he is resting now," he said. From the distance, a horn blared and Arsivus watched as the large steel doors of the castle were drawn open. The horn continued to sound as a rush of knights galloped their way out of the gate and toward Arsivus and his crew. Doran looked concerned and glanced over at Arsivus and Kadath.

Doran cracked the reins of his horse and moved at full gallop rushing toward the approaching knights. As he got closer, Doran saw that Mulik was leading the detachment and he immediately started to slow the horse to a trot. Mulik raised his hand to signal his knights to slow as well. They came upon each other and stopped at the top of a hill. Doran could not have been more pleased to see that his old friend had made it back safely.

"Doran, Janos hasn't made it back yet, but I am glad you have. We were just getting ready to head back into the mountain pass, for there is an evil that lurks within. We mistook it for a lone rider, but it killed three of my men without any effort at all. We sank arrow after arrow into it, yet it continued to attack. Whatever it was, it was not of this world." Mulik said. Doran looked back and saw that Kadath and Arsivus were drawing near them.

"We met this creature as well, and we saw your knights. Sadly, they were placed at the entrance to the pass. Young Arsivus said he struck the creature twice, but to no avail. Before we could get clear of the pass, we suffered an attack as well," Doran said to the men. They could see the injured knight lying in the cart beside Arsivus.

"Kadath, Arsivus, I am glad you both made it safely. We were just on our way to make the route safe, but I see you made it on your own. My apologies that you were set upon during your travels. General Magnus has already been informed of this beast and measures will be undertaken to rectify this situation," Mulik said.

"Thank you, Sir Mulik," Kadath spoke for the both of them.

"We shall not tarry any longer. Let us be on our way to the castle. You need to rest, for tomorrow will be a busy day, I am sure." Mulik said as Doran nodded in agreement. Mulik turned to his men and said, "Knights, continue through the pass to the other side and await Janos and his knights. Be prepared for battle. Best of luck to you." With that, the knights departed for the mountain pass and the horrors it held.

"Yes, let's be rid of this fateful night," Doran said as he turned his horse and joined Kadath and Arsivus. Together with Mulik, they rode toward the gate.

As they passed through the gate, Arsivus watched with awe as the doors that seemed bigger than the house he grew up in slowly swayed, granting entrance to the kingdom. The moonlight painted an enchanting picture of the town's buildings, roads, and magic that were hidden behind the large masonry border walls. Arsivus saw two men waiting with a cart by the entrance. They bid Kadath to stop.

Kadath obliged and Arsivus watched as they gently picked up the wounded knight and placed him on the cart. They covered him with a large royal cloak and lit two candles on the back of the cart as a symbol of a good journey for those injured in battle. They each grabbed a handle and slowly walked the cart down an alley, disappearing around a corner. Arsivus didn't know exactly what happened, but he had a pretty good idea as to why they did that, so he kept his mouth closed and just observed. As they continued through the corridors, Mulik slowed down and rode next to Kadath.

"This is where you will be staying while you are with us," he said as he pointed off to the right and highlighted a large structure perched on a hill. "General Magnus has taken care of your lodging, and all of your provisions are to be paid for by the crown. Relax tonight, for you are safe and well-guarded. Doran will stay here tonight if you need anything or have any questions or concerns. Do try and get some sleep, for tomorrow will arrive just as early as it always does," Mulik said. "Sleep well." And with that he rode off into the dark alleys ahead of him.

Kadath steered the cart up to the front of the building and dismounted, with Arsivus in tow. Doran dismounted and walked to the door to open it.

"Plenty of room for all of us. Let us put this night behind us," he said with a solemn tone.

"Agreed," Arsivus said as he walked in and plopped down on a bed near the fireplace. Kadath soon followed and closed the door behind them. He set his gear down next to the bed by the far wall. They sat on their beds, exhausted but unable to sleep, as thoughts from the day continued to race through their minds. No one spoke, as each was lost in his own thoughts. It was clear that sleep would not come easy this night.

CHAPTER 10

As daylight spread across the horizon, Arsivus rose to find he was the first one awake. He slipped on his boots to head outside. He had never seen the inside of Castle Affinity and was curious to explore it.

The old wooden door creaked as he opened it, rousing Doran who was quick to say, "General Magnus will have already examined our fellow knight this morning. So, don't wander too far, young master," Doran said. "We are to report to the General as soon as he sends for us. I am sure he has questions. No doubt he will be curious as to what you saw from our pursuer."

"No worries, sir," Arsivus replied. "I just want to use some energy up that has been bottled from last night. I will be back soon." With that, Arsivus closed the door and headed down the stairwell. His eyes were wide open and filled with excitement and cautiousness. He knew not what he would find; yet he wanted to find it all.

The sun was shining over most of the Eastern Kingdom. In the distance, Arsivus heard other tenants of the castle beginning their daily duties. Birds flew over his head and a couple of dogs barked at him as he passed, as they did not recognize his scent. He walked until he reached the main street that ran from the front gates to the stairs of the kingdom. Behind that gate was where the living quarters of King Thesias were located.

The streets were paved in a white stone and were bright as day. The buildings that lay across the busy street all had floral decorations hanging from their stoops that made them look inviting. Blue and red flowers hung from the armory shop and he could see a big man inside grinding away at what appeared to be a chest plate. Next to this shop and closer to the stairs to the citadel were more flowers and plants that decorated the shop fronts. Orange, green, and blue flowers highlighted the shop that dealt in fresh breads and oils.

On the other side of the armory shop, a man was serving cold ales to patrons. As he admired how many people were stopping to have a mid-morning drink, a beautiful young woman came up to Arsivus from behind. She ran her hand from one of his shoulders to the other and rested both of her hands on his arms as she came around to face him.

"My, my, my. Tsk, tsk," she said as she examined his stature. Arsivus was not sure what to do at this moment and replied with the only words that seemed to form in his head.

"Hello!" he said with confidence.

The woman smiled and withdrew her hands. "*You* must be new to the castle," she said.

Arsivus tilted his head. "Why yes, just as of last night actually. This place is wondrous, isn't it?" he said. The woman crossed her arms and leaned back to think for a moment. Arsivus gazed at her and realized how beautiful she really was. She wore a black sleeveless dress that extended just past her knees with a short-sleeved blouse underneath. Her arms were bronze-colored from the sun. She wore white shoes that contrasted against her tanned, toned legs. She had small hands and even smaller wrists, and her fingernails were painted white. A white hat with black accents shielded her golden blond hair from the sun. She had the brightest blue eyes Arsivus had ever seen and they shone with adventure.

"Where are you from, friend?" she asked.

"Just west of the mountains, near the Enegon Swamp," he replied. He loosened the cape around his neck as it suddenly felt too tight.

"West of the mountains?" she paused. "I have never even been fully through the mountain pass, but someday I would like to go," she responded as she smiled.

"Perhaps now that I know how to find this beautiful place, I can come back and take you," Arsivus said, surprising himself with his confidence. "Every woman should strive to achieve their desires, if that would suit you, that is?"

The woman blushed and gave another very captivating smile. "Well, it is nice to meet someone as well-mannered as you, and I will look forward to that trip!" she said as she extended her hand to him. "My name is Casily. What is yours?"

Arsivus gently took her hand and then placed his other hand over it. He looked into her eyes and said, "Arsivus. My name is Arsivus. Please remember it." He smiled as he let go of her hand and took a deep breath.

"So, what are you doing here, Arsivus?" she asked, patting down the midsection of her dress.

"My father and I are on a trip to make deliveries to the King," he said. "We were doing just fine and then ran into a little trouble last night in the mountain pass. Something came out of the darkness after us and we had to flee. We had two knights with us, and one of them was injured in the battle."

"Shhh, now!" the woman prompted. "You speak too plainly in the open. Someone may hear you." Arsivus was confused and started to ask why, but before he could, Kadath and Doran appeared and interrupted them mid-conversation.

"There you are, son!" Kadath exclaimed.

"I see you have already met one of our finer citizens here in Affinity!" Doran said slyly as he gestured to the woman and let out a quick laugh.

Arsivus, quick to defend her from that slight, responded quickly, "This woman has been nothing but pleasant to me, and if all people here are as caring as she seems to be, then this truly is a great land."

Casily smiled. "Why, thank you, Arsivus. Some people do lack the common manners around here," she said, as she gave Doran a glare.

Kadath, seeing that Arsivus was enjoying his time with Casily, decided to intervene. "Ma'am, would you be kind enough to show Arsivus around the town? Doran and I have to do some resupply runs for the trip home in a couple of days. Arsivus, meet us back at here at three. We have things to take care of, and General Magnus would like to meet you if he is free. Until then, enjoy the castle and all that Affinity has to offer, and do try and avoid any trouble." With that, Kadath and Doran headed off to tend to their business.

Arsivus looked back at Casily and she smiled warmly at him. "Shall we be off?" she asked with a playful tone.

"I thought you would never ask!" Arsivus responded, and they started down the street to experience the wonders of Affinity.

Thesias awoke with a smile. It was a bright and beautiful day, and he knew that General Magnus's troops would have arrived late the night before, which meant that his treasure would be presented to him today. He rose from his bed and walked to his balcony overlooking the ocean beneath him.

"What an age to be a King," he said aloud and laughed slightly. He took a deep breath and exhaled as a flock of bright blue birds soared across his view in perfect formation. He heard a knock at the door behind him.

"Come!" Thesias commanded from his balcony.

Victar and Vadeem entered. "Oh, it's you. What do you want?" Thesias asked as he walked across his chambers to another balcony overlooking the city.

Victar looked at Vadeem with a smile and they both started to walk toward Thesias. Victar said, "My liege, the day prior we—"

"STOP!" came a shout from across the chambers.

Taken by surprise, they all turned to the doorway where Captain Atalee stood. Atalee walked to the balcony and inserted himself between the King and the two brothers.

"You weren't going to ruin the surprise about our findings without me here, were you?" he said, scowling at the brothers.

"Well, of course not. We were going to fill him in on the general details of our visit while we awaited your arrival, sir," Vadeem said.

"I'm sure you were," Atalee responded with a sly laugh. "Your majesty, I have searched through the treasures that General Magnus's troops brought back with them from the Northern Forest." Atalee said. "The item you seek was not among them."

Thesias took a pear from a bowl on the perch of the balcony and bit into it. "I take it you have other news that is of a more impressive nature, Captain?" Thesias asked.

Atalee smiled as he looked at Victar and Vadeem. "Yes, why yes, we do. We traveled to the house of Kadath and Evra as you requested. Kadath and his boy were not there, but his wife Evra was. Also, our company here may need to learn some manners as they were less than charming to her inside of her own home; in fact, if I wasn't there, I fear something bad may have happened."

Thesias looked at the brothers in anger. "Did I not tell you that I care not for your spoiled squabbling? I will deal with you later. Carry on, Captain, as my day is starting to fill up."

Atalee continued. "I inquired as to the process of making their herbs. Evra was very adamant that all it required was proper care. She was defensive and protective of their craft of herb making. We were not there for long before we departed but..." Thesias dropped the pear from the balcony and watched it roll down the paved walkway to the gates.

"Captain, is there anything that is of good news?" he interrupted.

"Yes," Atalee replied. "Even though these two," motioning to the brothers, "needed to be set straight inside the house, if they had not been, I don't believe we would have located a precious gem that sounds like the ones you are looking for."

Thesias, now intrigued, looked at Victar and Vadeem with a smile. "Things are looking up for you two now!" Thesias said. "But how can you be sure?" he asked.

"The pendant fell out of wherever it had been hidden and shone a blue aura on the ceiling of the storage room. She was very quick to clear us out of that room, and legend says that the pendant of healing was blue, correct? It only makes sense that their herbs are being infused with the pendant's power and being sold to you." Atalee responded.

Thesias laughed out loud. "I thought as much, and now you say you saw this pendant of hers?" he asked the group.

"I didn't see a pendant," Vadeem responded.

"I saw the blue aura on the ceiling, but no pendant," said Victar.

"As I commanded them to leave, I saw into the room and observed the pendant lying on the floor, and it was cloaked in a bright blue aura," Atalee said.

Thesias clapped his hands in joy and said with a surge of excitement, "This is what I want; we cannot send any of the General's knights back to their house. That would be too risky and would draw too much attention and questions. Certainly, she must now know we are looking for something so she may try to hide it. Instead, Atalee, I want you to handle this. You cannot go yourself as she would recognize you, and you have to be at the upcoming tournament. Send one or two of your trusted men to take care of this matter. Do it quickly and bring me my treasure, Captain."

"Yes, sire," Atalee replied. "There was one other thing. As we were leaving, one of Magnus's knights, Sir Janos, and his detachment came upon us at Evra's house. No doubt that Magnus now knows we were there as well."

Thesias paused for a moment and took a deep breath. He paced back and forth contemplating this news. "Leave Magnus to me. Go about your duties as I have instructed. Have your knights leave within the next day, the sooner the better. Victar and Vadeem, leave now. I will call for you later to talk about your squabbles."

"Your majesty, there was one more thing," Atalee continued. "I am sure you will hear a report on it, but as I was checking the chests that were returned from the Northern Forest, Magnus's knights were talking about an attack that happened in the mountain pass."

Thesias, now a little perturbed, wondered aloud, "Who would conduct an attack against my kingdom? That is a very bold move indeed. Atalee, find out who did this when you have time, and we will take action. Until then, go about the tasks appointed to you."

All three of them bowed and bid the King farewell.

Thesias looked at his kingdom from his balcony. "The world is about to change!" he said to himself as he thought about the pendant. A smile began to spread across his face.

CHAPTER 11

Arsivus and Casily strolled down the alleyways casually enjoying the warmth of the sun. Casily stopped by a dressed-up little door that gave entrance to a little house.

"Can you stay here for a moment while I change into something more practical?" she asked.

"By all means," Arsivus said with a smile as Casily stepped inside briefly. "Is this your home?" Arsivus asked as he sat outside.

"Yes, this is where I live for the time being," Casily answered through the open window. "Although I am thinking about making a change in the near future for the better."

"It's good to have goals and dreams, although this seems like a very nice place," Arsivus said. He stood up and walked across the alley to look at some of the merchant's wares for sale. He browsed for a couple of minutes until Casily reemerged from her house dressed just like a commoner in the market.

She snuck up behind Arsivus and tapped him on the shoulder. "Ready to go?" she asked.

"Yes, lead the way," he replied. They strolled along with not a care in the world as the sun grew higher in the sky.

More people were out on the streets now and the market square was alive with shoppers. Casily turned to Arsivus. "You said that you were making deliveries to the King. Why would you want to help that man? He is naught but greed and lies."

Arsivus was a bit taken back but calmly replied, "Well, we supply him with the herbs that heal because that is how we make our living. The King said they are vital to the growth and success of this kingdom."

"Herbs that heal?" Casily said. "You and your father grow these herbs? How?" she asked.

"Well, perhaps I can tell you another time," Arsivus said, trying to avoid the question.

"Hmph! Very well then," Casily said disappointedly. "Well, your job seems very noble, to heal people. Is that what you would like to do? To follow in your father's footsteps?" she asked.

"No," replied Arsivus. "I would like to become a knight. Defending the innocent, protecting those that cannot protect themselves, and ensuring the safety and longevity of the kingdom."

"That is quite a charge; I think the kingdom needs more men like you, and less like the King." Casily said. Arsivus kicked a rock down the alley a little bit as they continued to walk by the doors that led to the chambers of the townsfolk.

"You seem very distrusting of the King. Is there a reason why?" Arsivus asked.

"No, it's . . . it's nothing," she replied shyly. Arsivus could sense the topic was bringing her discomfort so he didn't press any further.

"What would you like to do for a job?" Arsivus asked. Casily stopped in the street and looked down at the ground. She stared intently at a few pebbles on the road and then looked up at him. She stared into his eyes as they stood still in the center of the alley, people brushing by them as they went about their business. Casily finally spoke.

"I would protect my family and those I care about to the ends of the earth. That will be my job. By everything that is in me, I will see it done."

Arsivus saw a tear starting to take shape in her right eye. The moment seemed long lasting but passed as quick as a gust of wind.

"There is nothing more noble that I can think of than that!" Arsivus said reassuringly as the tear rolled down her cheek. She brushed it away and smiled at him.

"So, what do you do for entertainment in these parts?" Arsivus asked her trying to lighten the mood and cheer her up.

"You promised your father that you would stay out of trouble, so it looks like sneaking into the King's treasury is off limits," she said with a grin and continued on, "We could go to the overlook on the eastern side of the castle wall," she proposed.

"That sounds like an adventure. Let's do that," Arsivus said as he grabbed her hand and bid her to lead the way. She turned toward the shore and led the way through the multiple alleys to reach the overlook. Once they reached a set of stairs, Arsivus looked up and saw that they led up and around a corner. There were overgrown trees and shrubs along the stairs that looked much thicker the higher the stairs climbed. The top was not visible at all from the street. Standing at the bottom, he noticed the midday heat was starting to get more intense as the wind died down.

Casily walked over to a vendor and purchased a skin of water for them to share. She put it to her mouth to drink and Arsivus watched on as she tilted the skin of water. As she was drinking, a little blue and white bird landed on her shoulder.

Arsivus said, "It seems your little friend is thirsty as well. Care to give him a drink?" Casily carefully lowered the skin and poured a little water into the palm of her hand. She raised it to the little bird who was cautious at first, but then slowly dipped its beak into the pool of water. Casily and Arsivus laughed. She handed him the skin of water and he took a drink from it as well. As he lowered it, another bird swooped down and landed swiftly on the ground near Casily's feet. This one had a full red body with a small white stripe under its belly. Arsivus poured a small amount of water into the palm of his hand and bent down to offer it to the bird.

The bird was hesitant at first, but Arsivus extended his arm out toward the bird and made a chirping sound, "Knch, Knch, Knch." Arsivus repeated the same noise in hopes of gaining the bird's trust.

Casily could not stop laughing. She barely was able to say, "Oh! Is that the sound they make?" Arsivus looked up at her, smiled, and returned his eyes toward the bird. The small bird slowly hopped over to his hand and dipped his beak twice into the water.

Casily looked up at him and smiled. "It looks like we have made several new friends today!"

Arsivus nodded his head and smiled. After the birds had their fill, they flew away together toward the center of the town, no doubt looking for some food. Arsivus handed the water back to Casily, and she gave it back to the vendor and they began their walk up the stairs to the overlook.

There were several other people sitting on the stairs to the overlook talking and resting. They didn't appear to take notice of Casily and Arsivus as they ascended the staircase. One couple had their wineskins on the ground near their feet and the man was cutting into a loaf of bread while they sat on an outcropping next to the stairs looking at the sea.

After climbing stairs for what seemed like hours, they reached a part of the pathway where it thinned out, and Casily took the lead. The sound of the ocean crashing into the cliffs below echoed through the stairway as they continued to climb.

"That sound," Casily said. "It is so calming. I can never get enough of it." The cool breeze rushed over their bodies as it scaled the cliff's edge and dissipated halfway down the stairs. Finally reaching the top, Arsivus saw a little bench near the ledge that was constructed into the overlook for those to sit on and drink in the view. As they walked toward the edge, a cat strolled by their feet. It walked over to the nearest bench and crawled under to scratch its back, which prompted a snicker from Casily. As they approached the edge, Arsivus was completely amazed. The ocean stretched farther out than he had ever seen. The rocks below seemed impossibly small, but then he remembered that it was a long way down to the ocean.

The waves below were enormous and came crashing down upon the rocks with the strength of what sounded like a monstrous storm. The cliffs in the distance in all their beauty leaned up and out from where the waves were hitting, gigantic by comparison to the rocks below. Nothing was atop the cliffs but rocky jagged mountains filled with snow. From his viewpoint, they towered in the distance and seemed impassable. Aside from the snowy mountains, the rest of the land that could be observed cowered in the magnificent shadow of the overlook.

Arsivus, after gazing outward for some time, was finally able to say, "Where are we? It seems as if we are at the highest point in the Eastern Kingdom!"

Casily closed her eyes, took a huge breath, and let it out. "Almost! This is where I come to get away from it all. Not many people come up here for fear of falling. Or for fear that it's haunted with the past souls that flung themselves off in the name of love." Casily giggled. "The wind can be strong where we are at, this is true, and sometimes you hear the howling of the wind, which sounds like lamenting and sobbing from below. But I have never attributed it to spiritual beings. And if there are any here, they have conducted no wrong toward me."

Arsivus asked, "What is it that you get away from in particular, if you don't mind me asking?"

"There are many things really," she responded, as she continued to look out over the ocean. "There are horrors in this land, many of which people do not understand, or they do and choose to accept things the way they are. King Thesias is one of those horrors, ruling and judging from his tower what is good and bad. Whatever he desires he gets; your herbs are proof of that. Those he finds unusable or those that refuse to fall in line with his orders are abandoned and exiled to their own fate. I have known too many people that have dared stand up to him, and they are no longer looked upon as they should be. They are disgraced in the name of the King. I will not stand idly by and watch more people fall upon that same fate."

Arsivus motioned with his hand for them to sit on the bench. They took their seats and continued to gaze out toward the endless sea. "I am sorry you are so torn by what your King does," Arsivus said. "I have not had the chance to meet his grace yet, but I—"

Casily quickly cut him off. "He is not my King! I did not choose him and I will not protect him from those that wish him harm. He deserves every enemy he creates."

"I am to compete in the Seven Wizards Tournament, I do hope you do not look on me in this way if I were to win. I would have to protect his majesty in all matters," Arsivus responded, and let out a sigh as he looked at her. "From all people," he said quietly as he put his hand on top of hers.

Casily bowed her head in agreement and said, "I know you would be different, once you witness what *'his majesty'* is capable of, then you will understand. I hope you can be part of the change that this kingdom needs."

"I will do everything in my power to make this kingdom greater than it has ever been," he said solemnly. Arsivus slowly returned his hand to his lap as a gust of wind whipped over the ledge. After the breeze struck, a flock of birds flying in formation coasted up the cliff and toward the snow-capped mountains. Arsivus looked toward the mountains and suddenly his trip through the mountain pass surfaced in his mind. The black figure attacking them out of nowhere, the arrow, the men that were lost, all of this played out suddenly as he got lost in his thoughts and jolted back a little on the bench. Casily caught sight of the swift movement but said nothing.

Arsivus asked quietly, "You said there were other horrors in this land, what else do you know of?"

Casily kept her eyes on the sea and said, "There are reports I have heard that bad things are happening everywhere. In the Northern Forest, beasts are coming out of the forest and attacking travelers outside of their territory. That is very unusual of them, to be so actionable. Something is driving them out and no one knows what. I also have heard stories from knights returning to our lands, that there were ships that have shown up on the coast from the Western Kingdom. When they landed, there was no one found aboard. No food, no supplies, just an empty ship."

Arsivus thought for a minute and said, "Well, that is not too strange. Maybe they were attacked on the way over and were overcome?"

Casily shook her head. "I don't think that is it."

"Why is that?" Arsivus asked.

Casily turned to face him now. "There have been seven ships that have come across that I know of. From the reports, they were all the same, but they were all different."

Arsivus furrowed his eyebrows. "What do you mean?"

Casily looked down and then at Arsivus with a sorrowful face, "All of the ships were as black as night, but each one had different symbols throughout the ship. They all had a half circle engraved in white, which almost seemed burnt into the wood. Below each half circle was an image depicting something, it almost looked like a weapon. One of our knights traced the image and I was able to get a glimpse of it. It looked like an arrow, but not like any that I have seen. This one was different; it was drawn with a reddish glow, but had spikes coming out of it in complete disorder along the arrow."

Arsivus looked at her with shock. "Kind of like thorns on a rose bush?"

Casily, her voice rising with excitement, said, "Yes, exactly like that. Have you seen something like that before?"

"On our way here before the mountain pass, I saw it. One of the knights at the base of the mountain pass had one in him, and another knight riding with us was impaled with one as we were coming here," he responded.

"Do you think they are connected?" she asked.

Before Arsivus could answer, the kingdom bell rang with authority. She looked up at the bell and let out a sigh.

"You were saying that you were attacked in the mountain pass before. Were you able to see what attacked you?" she asked.

"I did not get a good glimpse at the time; it was far too dark." Arsivus said as he closed his eyes for a moment while the cool breeze continued to drift across the overlook.

"Wait, do you think whatever attacked us came from one of those ships?" he asked.

Casily shrugged, and the bells began to chime again. "We can talk about this later," she said. "I am afraid there is something that I must attend to. Would you care to meet me tomorrow?" she asked, looking at Arsivus and hoping he would say yes.

"Why, of course. Shall we meet tomorrow in the market at the same time?" he asked as the bell rang in the distance.

"I . . . I must be going. Tomorrow it is then. Take care, Arsivus!" Casily said as she ran down the stairs. He turned back around to face the sea and thought to himself, "Take care Casily. I can't wait!" He smiled as he stood up and made his way back to the inn to meet with his father.

CHAPTER 12

Arsivus reached the door of the inn and walked through the double doors while the sun was still overhead. He took a seat next to his father. Shortly after Doran came up beside them.

"How was the tour, lad? Did the woman fill you with novel ideas of patriotism and charity?" Doran asked with a snicker. Kadath took a piece of meat and brought it to his mouth while he awaited an answer.

"She was very delightful, proper, and passionate. She seems very nice, and I enjoyed her company. I promised her I would meet her again tomorrow around the same time, if that is all right, father?" asked Arsivus.

"That should not be a problem. We have a meeting scheduled tomorrow afternoon. Just be back in time for that and all should be well. What did you end up talking about? Did she show you the city?" Kadath asked.

"She did! We went several places. She showed me the market and the overlook, although she had to leave once the midday bells rang. She seemed interested in our travels through the mountain pass but left before we could finish our conversation."

Doran's interest was now peaked. "I wonder why she is so interested in your travels through the pass," Doran said with contempt in his voice.

Arsivus looked at Doran with an inquisitive look. "What is it, lad?" Doran said.

"You seem to know Casily. Who is she?" Arsivus responded.

"Well," said Doran with a sigh, "she is the daughter of a man who used to be a knight here. Her father stood up to the King and it did not end well for him or his detachment of knights that followed him. They were banished from the knighthood and she has been inflicted with a hot temper ever since."

Arsivus nodded. "I see why she was so passionate when talking about the King then," said Arsivus.

Doran continued. "I am surprised that she opened up to you right away. She rarely makes mention of this subject, much less with a stranger. She does odd jobs around the city. To tell the truth, I am unsure of what she really does, but she always has money and food. Makes me think something isn't right in what she does to procure those things." Doran said as he took a full drink of wine. Arsivus ate his meal and thought about his day so far.

"I would like to come back . . . more than once a year," Arsivus said.

Kadath looked at him and said, "Well, if you win the tournament then you will be staying here for quite some time, son."

"Even if I do not win the tournament, I would like to come visit her. I feel like I need to be by her for some reason," he said with a smile.

Doran laughed. "Perhaps you two went off and were drinking wine together! You are smitten, I do believe."

Kadath let out a chuckle as well and Arsivus joined in. "Perhaps I am!" he said as he finished his meal with a smile on his face.

The sun had come and gone, and night was fast approaching from the east.

"Go ensure the cart is secure with the new supplies, then bring some more wood in here please," Kadath said. Arsivus did as his father asked. Doran was reading a book, and Kadath was boiling water over the fire when Arsivus walked back in with an armful of logs. He set them down and placed two of them into the fire. Arsivus positioned the wood with a fire poker and slid another log underneath the blaze.

He pulled out the poker and it was glowing red on the tip. He started to think about the mountain pass and the thing that chased them, and the arrows that were shot at them.

"Has there been any word on who or what that was on the mountain pass?" Arsivus asked. Doran lowered his book and Kadath stopped checking the water. Doran moved the sword that was lying on his bed and placed it against the wall as he swung his legs up to lie down.

"No word yet, but no one has been talking if they do know anything." Doran replied.

Kadath joined in on the conversation. "Tomorrow we will ask around during our meeting if we have enough time. I am sure the wise men here will be able to give us some news, especially if General Magnus inquires of it," said Kadath. Arsivus leaned the poker next to the fireplace. He turned, walked to the door, and opened it. He gazed at the mountains in the distance wondering what was out there that he did not know. The conversation replayed in his mind of what Casily said about the seven ships that showed up.

"That has to be the same warrior that came across on the ship that was in the pass. It just has to be," Arsivus said to himself.

Kadath finally lay down on his bed and looked over at Arsivus, who was still in the doorway. "Son, let's get some rest. We have a very busy day tomorrow and we all need to be sharp for the meeting. Lock the door now." he said with authority. Arsivus slowly closed the door while looking at the stars above the mountaintops. He latched the bar on the door and wandered over to his bed. He set up his sword just like Doran had.

"Tomorrow will be a busy day for sure," Arsivus said to his father. To himself he thought, "I cannot wait to see Casily again. I wonder where she went today. I have so many questions to ask her, but most of all, I just want to spend time with her."

He brought the covers up to his chest and rolled to his side to face the door. "Until the morning then, gentlemen!"

Arsivus said, and with that, they went to sleep as the fire crackled.

The smell of fresh baked bread woke Arsivus from his sleep. He sat up and looked around, and saw his father was already up and getting ready. Kadath was shifting some of his gear around and it appeared he had already hauled some of it out to the cart. Doran was having a sip of wine with some leftover cheese and bread and saw Arsivus looking at him.

"Would you like some? It really fuels you up for the day!" Doran exclaimed. Arsivus laughed as he kindly waved his hand in rejection. Arsivus swung his legs over the side of his bed, stretched, and let out a big groan.

Kadath put some equipment down on the bed. "We have a couple more hours yet until we need to meet." he said. "Have some breakfast and feel free to explore the town again if you desire." Arsivus nodded, grabbed some cheese and bread from Doran's plate, and gave him a smile as he ran out the door. "Hey!" could be heard from inside as the door closed and Doran realized Arsivus took the biggest pieces from his plate.

Arsivus took in the morning sun as it began to crest above the walls of the castle. He took a bite of the bread and cheese and headed off to the market to meet Casily.

As he walked through the streets, he saw the business owners hurriedly trying to prepare their materials for the day's activities. Flowers were being set up in a decorative fashion, the churns from inside a blacksmith shop could be heard as they were heating up their forges, and the fresh smell of bread and vegetables filled the air. Arsivus wandered down the alley giving greetings to those that would take them, feeling as if he was already part of the city.

He finished his cheese and ripped up the remaining bread into little pieces for the birds to eat. He scattered it on the ground and wiped his hands. He saw an amulet shop on his left and decided to stop in and browse to kill some time until he could meet Casily. The amulets reminded him of his mother's amulet back at their house. A sudden feeling of angst rose up in him as he hoped she was doing okay and was not too worried about him and his father.

He continued to look around and spotted a necklace with a very pale blue gem in the shape of a diamond. He picked it up and found it was much heavier than he had expected. He held the gem in his hand and admired the fine piece of merchandise. He thought of Casily and immediately wanted to buy it for her.

His impulses took control, and he asked the shopkeeper how much it was. The shopkeeper took the pendant from him, held up a seeing glass to ascertain a better look, and then set it down again in his hand.

"Four pieces!" she exclaimed. Arsivus dug in his pouch, pulled out four pieces of silver, and handed them to the shopkeeper.

"Thank you, ma'am!" Arsivus said as he turned and headed down the alley.

The shopkeeper responded, "You are welcome!" As he was walking away, he heard her mumble something under her breath, but he couldn't make it out. He placed the amulet in his pouch to keep it safe until he saw her.

The sun was rising higher in the sky and Arsivus realized he should pick up his pace to reach the market before Casily did. His strides became more focused and he started to make good time. He stopped quickly to refill his flask of water in a fountain. When he arrived in the market, he realized that they had never discussed where exactly to meet.

He found a spot near the center of the market next to a bread stand that he thought would give him the best view. As he stood there scouting the crowd to find Casily, the market square started to fill up with people coming from all directions.

Arsivus thought it might help him to get up higher so he could easily be spotted and maybe could locate Casily faster. As he looked around for a stool to stand on, someone grabbed him from behind and began dragging him behind a shop in a gentle way. He turned and saw a woman standing behind him giggling with her head down.

He had no idea who she was or why she had grabbed him until she raised her head and he realized it was Casily. As he looked at her, his eyes widened. Her appearance had changed completely from when he saw her yesterday. She wore a black blouse with a diamond-shaped hole in the fabric around her navel that showed a white shirt underneath, black leather leggings, and a golden belt buckle wrapped around her waist. Her black boots reached up almost to her knees and had buckles on both sides for storage. She wore a blue overcoat that covered only her shoulders down to her wrists and fanned out from there down to her mid-waist.

Arsivus, who felt surprised and quite thrilled, was speechless.

"What? It's like you have never seen a woman before?" Casily said as she repositioned a dagger that was in her side belt.

"You look quite stunning, might I say?" Arsivus managed to spit out.

"Well, thank you, but we must be getting on now. We have things to do and see, don't we?" Casily asked as she started to lead the way.

"That scent," Arsivus said quietly. "Is that verick oil?" he asked.

"Yes, it is! Not many know of that oil. My father gave it to me long ago before he . . ." she hesitated.

"I'm sorry!" Arsivus exclaimed. "I had no idea that he had passed away."

Casily shook her head. "No, that's not what happened. He is alive, just not as he used to be," she said with sadness.

That confused Arsivus. He thought to himself, "What is she hiding and what happened to her father? Who was looking after her while he was gone and when would he find out?" The ringing of the church bells in the distance interrupted Arsivus's thoughts, signaling that it was almost midday.

As they left the market area, Casily seemed happier. She led the way down several alleys and pointed out significant parts of the city and places to keep away from that were always filled with danger. They passed by shop after shop, examining the goods that the merchants had for sale as they talked about their wants and dreams.

Casily led them down a street that looked darker than most of the ones they had been down. It seemed to go on for quite a while, and a small stream made its way down the middle. Arsivus looked around and noticed there were no shops on this street that he could see. He saw large columns built into the ground that continued on to the end of the street, which eventually intersected with the wall of the castle. He saw a small opening that peered out over the ocean below.

Arsivus looked carefully at the columns again. This time he could see that, at the base of each column, there was a cage that formed a circle no bigger than a man. Arsivus took a closer look at the cages and saw there were men and women inside each of the cages all the way along the street. Soft moans could be heard from some of them, and in a few of the cages, there were no sounds at all. Upon further inspection, Arsivus realized that the occupants of the silent cages had passed away not too long ago.

The cages were surrounded by dirt and the occupants inside were dirty as well. This became very evident the farther down the street Arsivus and Casily walked. Some of the occupants raised their heads to listen to the footsteps of Arsivus and Casily, and a few turned their gaze toward the visitors in an attempt to make eye contact.

Arsivus grabbed Casily's hand and said, "What has happened here?"

Casily turned to him. "I want you to see something. This place is called Fallen Row. You see, these people lying here were once knights that served under General Magnus. They were loyal to the General and served him faithfully. However, they were outwardly insubordinate to the King and thought his actions brought disgrace to the kingdom. They decided to voice their thoughts and fears. The King did not appreciate that at all. No matter the General's outcry or his defense of them, he could not stop their punishment. The King forced them to endure pain and tortures beyond imagination. Some were quelled by that alone. The King bid them never to leave Affinity but never serve the crown again. After the King outcast them, he made it a crime for anyone to help them or offer them assistance. So here they remain, living out their days eating scraps that they receive from supporters and sympathizers in and outside the castle, ultimately waiting for death to take them."

Arsivus shook his head in disbelief. Some of the knights were old and some looked younger than he did. "This is outrageous. These knights do not deserve this; no person should be treated like this!" Arsivus exclaimed, which caused more of the knights to look at who was defending them.

Casily turned her head to Arsivus and spoke just as loudly as he had. Her emotions had taken control and her feelings were evident. "These were knights of great worth and importance, and now they are just prisoners never to leave." Casily continued to stare at one particular caged man who still maintained a stout stature.

Arsivus noticed her resolve and asked, "Who is that man that you cannot break your eyes from?"

Casily lowered her head and whispered her answer in anger and sadness, "My father."

Arsivus pondered this for a moment. He reached out his arms and turned Casily to face him. "I promise I will become a knight before my time is done. When that happens, I will see these men and women freed."

Casily looked up at Arsivus and saw the truth and ferocity in his eyes. She slowly turned back toward the captives with the weight of sorrow sitting upon her shoulders. "You must understand that anyone who betrays the King ends up here, just as they are. I would not have you do this for me. The King is evil. He will not listen to you. He didn't even listen to his brother, and I wouldn't have you suffer for this."

"I will do it because it is right, and I believe someone would do it for me. I will bargain with the King if I win the tournament, and I believe he will listen to me," Arsivus said boldly.

Casily smiled. "You do have a fiery spirit inside you, which is something that we have lacked here for quite some time. Too many people will roll over so as to not create waves. Perhaps you can change this."

Arsivus reached up and wiped a tear from her face. He looked back at the cages and asked, "What does the General do about this?" Before an answer could be given, the church bell began to ring again to a count of twelve.

Casily looked to the sky and saw a flock of birds flying above them. "It is midday now. You will soon see what our

General does about this," she said as they could hear foot-steps coming up from behind him.

"Excuse me, young sir, but may we pass?" Arsivus turned around and saw a small group of what appeared to be knights, each with a sack over his shoulder and a leather water flask in his hands.

"Yes, why yes, sir, pardon me," Arsivus said, as he didn't know who they were or what they wanted. Arsivus continued. "Pardon me, sir."

But before he could say anymore, Casily stepped next to him, leaned in and said with a smile on her face, "General Magnus. That's General Magnus!"

Arsivus looked at her and back at him. "Excuse me, General Magnus. It's very nice to meet you, sir!" he said as he stood as tall as he could.

"No worries, my friends. Casily, it's very nice to see you again," said the General.

She replied, "And you as well, General. Right on time like usual."

The General gave a half smile. "These knights deserve it, and I see to it that they will never wait on anyone for food or drink."

The General looked at Arsivus and handed him the sack on his shoulder. "Would you be so kind as to divvy out portions to our brave knights, sir?" the General asked kindly.

"Of course!" Arsivus exclaimed.

"Knights, go ahead." And with that the knights fanned out and delivered bread, fruit, and vegetables to the caged knights. They carried on conversations with the prisoners as they doled out their food. A couple of the knights went to the cages that had deceased men and women in them. They opened the cages, very delicately took the remains out, and placed them in the same type of coverings and carts as Arsivus saw before when he first arrived at the castle.

Arsivus looked around to see who he could help, and all that was left was Casily's father. The General put his arm around Casily and walked with her toward her father's cage.

"Tell your friend to bring his items to your father," said Magnus.

"Arsivus, let's go," Casily said and she beckoned him over to her father's holdings. Arsivus walked over to the cage where the General and Casily were standing.

"It is very nice to meet you, sir. My name is Arsivus. May I have yours?" Arsivus asked as he handed over the water flask to her father. Her father accepted the flask and took a drink. He set it down to collect the food from the bag.

As he took a bite of the bread, he paused and looked at Arsivus, and then back at Casily, "Hello, daughter. It is good to see you again."

"Hello, father!" she replied.

"You brought a friend today. What is the occasion? Who is he?" Casily's father replied.

"This is Arsivus. He is here on business. He is competing in the Seven Wizards tournament to become a knight, and I think he has what it takes to do it," she said with a smile.

Her father took another bite of the bread and said, "A knight to be, eh? Well, in that case, my name is Romez. Any friend of my daughter is a friend of mine. It is nice to meet you."

General Magnus chirped in. "Sir Romez, to be correct."

Romez looked at the General. "Sire, you know we are not knights anymore. We are not worthy of that title. We brought shame upon the crown," Romez said sarcastically.

General Magnus continued. "You did what you believed the crown needed protection from, that is all. I never disowned you from my army or my table. Hence, you are still a knight under my command."

Romez laughed. "Still as stubborn as ever, eh?" He looked at the General. "I would be careful, Arsivus," he continued. "Once he has you in his command, he never lets you go!"

"As it should be!" Magnus said with a smile.

The General turned to Arsivus. "Arsivus, I thought your name sounded familiar. I saw it on the entrance list for the games. I know your father, Kadath. We have had many journeys together, both fortunate and the lesser. I am sure he taught you very well, for he is a knowledgeable man and has taught me many things. I will look for you in the competition."

Magnus looked down the alleyway as something caught his attention. Arsivus could see a slight scowl form on the General's face. Magnus returned his eyes to the knights in the alley.

"I'm sorry!" apologized the General. "Where was I? Oh yes, there are seven participants this year, as is custom, and you will have some tough competition. Although I am sure that we can talk about this at a later time and place. But we will definitely meet again before the tournament." After the food and water had been consumed, Arsivus realized that he was supposed to be at the market to meet his father and Doran by midday. Before he could say anything, the knights said their farewells for the afternoon and began preparing to leave.

"Arsivus, I believe you are supposed to be somewhere right now, correct?" Magnus asked.

"Yes, sir, I lost track of time. I was supposed to meet my father and Sir Doran at the market," replied Arsivus.

Magnus nodded his head. "Well, let us be on our way to your father then. Knights, return to the castle and continue making preparations for the contest. Casily, would you allow us the honor of accompanying you to the market?" Magnus asked.

Casily smiled at her father and waved goodbye. "Yes, I would very much like to join you." With that, Magnus, Arsivus, and Casily turned toward the market as the sun continued to peer at them from above the high walls of Castle Affinity.

CHAPTER 13

K adath and Doran waited patiently next to the smithy. Birds could be heard chirping in the near distance, and residents of the kingdom were strolling down the street admiring the goods and products that could be purchased.

"It is midday, Kadath. Hopefully your lad shows up before Magnus arrives," Doran said with contempt. Kadath leaned against a brick wall with his arms crossed in front of his chest. A glimmer of perspiration shone on his head from the heat of the day.

"He will be here, Doran, don't you worry. Arsivus knows the importance of this meeting," Kadath responded with an assuring tone. As they stood waiting, they discussed the day's events. Suddenly, a loud disturbance broke out several shops down from them. They both stopped talking and immediately proceeded to the shop from where the disturbance came. While they were walking, Kadath unhinged his sword to prepare for the worst.

As he grabbed his hilt to get ready, Doran said, "Careful, my friend. I sense you have not heard the latest proclamation from the King?"

Kadath looked at Doran with a puzzled expression. "What do you mean?" he asked.

Doran continued. "King Thesias has decreed that it be illegal for anyone but his White Guard to draw arms within the walls of Affinity. If it so happens, it is punishable by banishment."

Kadath released the hilt from his hand. "How did this come to be?" he asked solemnly.

Doran explained. "Ever since a group of knights rose up against Thesias, he has been afraid of what may come since the knights of General Magnus far outnumber those of the White Guard. He has banned all from doing so, except his precious Guard."

Kadath let out a sigh of contempt. "Well, we shall see what the matter is regardless, and settle it with our hands if need be." As they reached the shop, many of the towns-folk were surrounding something. As they moved closer they saw that in the middle of the crowd were two fully dressed knights, both furnished with armor, and each of the knights had a red jewel encrusted in the center of his chest plate.

"Those are the White Guard!" Doran exclaimed.

Kadath focused his eyes to determine if he could identify the guards. The one on the left was clenching the hilt of a knife strapped on a holster around his shoulders with his right hand. His other hand hung by his side holding a black and fierce-looking tomahawk. Kadath could easily see that this was Teslark, the warrior who was considered the master in hand-to-hand combat, as well as with his knives. Kadath had heard he had a temper from stories Magnus had told him when they were younger. The second knight bore a huge axe that rested on the ground. His arms were crossed and rested on his protruding chest. He was a huge warrior and looked like he had been in a few battles himself. Kadath knew immediately that this was Korgal.

Kadath looked at Doran and then at the open area where the knights were standing in a battle-ready stance. Right next to their feet, a man no older than Kadath was lying face down in the street with a stream of blood coming from his midsection. Upon seeing this, Doran and Kadath moved to the front of the group and confronted the White Guard.

"By name of the King, what has happened here?" Doran exclaimed. Teslark turned to face Doran with his hands still clenching his weapons.

"This man was caught stealing food for the disgraced knights upon Fallen Row. He was to deliver to them this afternoon, which is in direct violation of the laws created by King Thesias himself. We are just enforcing his commands. Is there a problem with that, Doran, o'mighty one?" Teslark said with a snicker.

Kadath spoke up before Doran had a chance. "What gives you the right to kill a man for an offense in which you claim he would have done? Should there not be a trial to ensure a law has been broken?" With that the crowd cheered and started talking loudly in support of Kadath.

Teslark, not liking the situation that was developing, tried to silence the crowd. "Those that break the law, or have plans to do so, are subject to immediate punishment befitting the crime." Teslark let out a small chuckle and continued on. "Unless you would like to prove otherwise?" He eyed Kadath and twirled his tomahawk around in his hand.

Doran stepped in front of Kadath. "Is this what the White Guard has become, a bully to the citizens of Affinity? How low must you be to attack an unarmed man? How capable are you against one your equal, I wonder?" Doran said as he unsheathed his sword and held it in plain sight of Teslark.

At this moment, Korgal looked at Kadath and Doran and took a deep breath as he hoisted his axe high into the air and let out a spirited roar. Teslark grabbed one of his knives in his right hand and looked at both Kadath and Doran. "Are you sure you want to do this here, lads?" Teslark asked. "You know it is against the law for you to brandish your weapon in the kingdom," he concluded with a smile.

Kadath also unleashed his sword from his side, as they both prepared for whatever may come. "He does not stand alone!" Kadath said with dominance, as he made ready for battle.

"Enough of this!" a man commanded from between two of the shops in the alleyway. The men stepped down from their battle stance and turned to see who had spoken. The crowd began to part as a man made his way through.

"General Magnus!" Doran exclaimed. "Sir, we were on our way to meet you when we heard this disturbance in the market. We came to examine it and found these two standing above this unarmed man who lies before us."

Teslark remarked slyly to Doran, "Hmph, never could fight your own battles, eh?" General Magnus, seeing Teslark and Korgal standing there with a lifeless body on the ground, took action immediately.

"Knights, you will sheathe your weapons now!" exclaimed the General.

"You two," as he pointed to the White Guard, "report to the castle immediately, and send for the gravedigger while on your way."

Teslark replied, "Our job is not to—" but Magnus cut him off.

"You will do this now or find a much bigger problem on your hands!" as he grabbed hold of his sword.

"As you wish," said Teslark as he tapped Korgal on the chest, and they made their way toward the castle.

Magnus turned to Doran and said, "Doran, you know it is against the law to draw your weapon within the castle. I will speak to the King on your behalf, but I cannot make any promises."

"I understand, sir. No need to be worried for me," said Doran.

"I wouldn't expect anything less, Sir Doran." Magnus replied. It took a while for Kadath to realize, but behind the General was Casily with her right arm upon Arsivus's shoulder, and Arsivus had his hand on his sword as well.

"Arsivus!" Kadath shouted. Arsivus looked over and saw his father with his weapon drawn. Arsivus nodded to acknowledge his father, and Casily gently removed her grip from him. Kadath smiled at the sight of it. He knew Arsivus would be just fine in the big city with this girl by his side, and there appeared to be a connection between them. General Magnus looked over at Arsivus and Casily and then back at Kadath and Doran.

"Kadath, my friend!" the General proclaimed. "It has been too long since our last meeting. I have already become acquainted with your son, and if I dare say so, he is the spitting image of you at that age."

Kadath put his sword back in his sheath. "General Magnus!" he exclaimed as he walked over to him and put out his arm for a warrior's shake. "It is nice to see you in good health, and my how the years have been good to you!"

The General extended his arm. "How many times must I persist? Call me Magnus."

Kadath said, "Very well, Magnus. I believe we have some important things to discuss?" he said as he looked to Arsivus, who was standing next to the body on the ground, examining it closely with Casily.

Magnus also turned around and could see the frustration in Arsivus's face as he contemplated why this had to happen. "Why yes, yes I believe we do, my friend," he replied. The group came together and began to walk toward a tavern down the alley away from all of the excitement.

Kadath and the group walked with Magnus into a nearby pub called the Blue Night Tavern and found a table that could accompany them all. Magnus and Kadath immediately engaged in conversation, while Doran walked to the bar. Casily and Arsivus were still visibly upset over what had happened in the market, and they struggled to hide it.

"Arsivus! Arsivus!" Arsivus looked up to see his father and Magnus looking at him.

"Apologies!" replied Arsivus.

"No worries, son," Kadath said.

"Your father has entered you into the competition, which you have been made aware of." Magnus said. "It begins tomorrow morning. Make sure you are ready and well rested. The tournament will only be one day, so you will need to do your very best to come out on top. Casily will be able to go over specifics with you as she has seen these tournaments before. I cannot give you any information on it because I reside as judge over the competition. However, I do wish you the best of luck. Your father and I have some more to talk about. Why don't you two take a stroll around the city?"

Arsivus nodded and he and Casily stood up. "Of course, sir," he said. "We will be back in a little while."

"Very good," Magnus replied. As Arsivus and Casily were about to leave, Magnus shouted out with a smile, "Do try and steer clear of trouble!" With that, Arsivus and Casily walked out of the Blue Night Tavern. Magnus ordered a drink from a patron and called Doran back over to the table to join them.

"Kadath, it is good to see you. This kingdom is long overdue of men like you and your boy," Magnus said.

Kadath smiled and nodded his head. "It is good to be back here. Arsivus hasn't stopped talking of coming here for quite some time now. I know if he wins the tournament he will be in good hands here."

"There is no doubt of it," Magnus replied. "Although there is something I must inform you about. A while back, I sent a company of my knights into the Northern Forest to acquire a treasure on the King's orders. The men went as directed and returned but found themselves short of supplies on the return trip home. They were briefed upon departure of areas still friendly to the kingdom, and more specifically, of houses nearby that would be able to provide assistance. Long story short, your house was one of which I spoke and made recommendation to. By the time they arrived at your home, Captain Atalee of the White Guard was leaving with two men from the Bordine clan, I do believe."

Kadath was now visibly upset, as he knew who the two men were, and said their names out loud with an unsettling tone. "Victar and Vadeem, they are as crooked and evil as their father. I see the King is employing thieves now. What came of the visit? Was Evra hurt?" Kadath asked with fear in his voice.

Magnus shook his head. "No, your wife is just as tough as you are. She held her own and told them to leave. I had two of my men, Cardage and Theros, follow the brothers wherever they went. By the time they arrived at your house, Sir Janos and the company of men had arrived prior to them and assisted in removing Atalee and the brothers. Evra was visibly upset. Although after some talking, she confided in my men. Atalee was looking for the secret of your herbs and how they work." Kadath, visibly anxious, straightened up in his chair as the wind howled through the open cracks in the tavern.

"What happened next?" Kadath asked.

Magnus leaned in as Doran made a quick look around the room to locate any peering eyes and ears. "We are trying to protect certain things and have them remain out of the King's hands. He is searching for some powerful pendants of which he will use to start the fall of the Western Kingdom. These pendants are of immense power, and it is best if he never finds any of them, for he would conduct the remainder of his reign as a fool. My mission is to stop him from acquiring any of them. My men went to the Northern Forest to look for these pendants under the King's orders and to secure them by all means available. I am sure you are aware of the legend?" asked Magnus.

Kadath nodded. "Yes, I know of the legend. Were there any pendants in the treasure they brought back from the north?" asked Kadath.

Magnus smiled. "No," he said, "not a one!" Kadath lightened up a little bit. "As I said, we want to prevent the acquisition of these from the King, so if one were found, we would not take it here. I would go to war to prevent any of them from falling into the hands of Thesias or his precious White Guard," Magnus said.

Kadath nodded in acceptance as Magnus continued on, "Evra did talk alone with three of my knights that were there, Sir Cardage, Theros, and Janos after . . ." Magnus paused and took another look around the room to ensure that no one was listening. "After everything happened, they saw something in your house!"

"Is that so?" Kadath replied.

Magnus continued with a reassuring tone. "It is still there. She was instructed to make it disappear for worry that others may come look for it. We could not leave anyone there to sit and watch as it would draw the wrong attention." Kadath bit his lower lip as he stared at Doran and then back at Magnus in frustration. His brow was bent as he thought about what Magnus had told him.

After a brief moment, Kadath spoke up, "I must return home as soon as possible then, also, I think it would be best if we did not tell my son. His mind should be focused on the tournament!"

Magnus looked around the room and then back at him. "All of the King's trusted agents are within the castle and are constantly being watched by my men. If any of them leave, I have issued orders for my men to follow after them."

Magnus took a sip from his drink and continued. "She is safe right now. My men also left her with a bird from Goj. It can get here within hours and then we can return there within a day. If that bird were to show up, I will send all that I have to her aid."

Kadath, still a little uneasy about the entire situation, felt better that Magnus had thought of her and the protection he was willing to offer.

Magnus leaned back. "She also says to hurry home soon. So, after the tournament, I will send a detachment of knights to escort an old friend, although I do suspect Arsivus may be staying here!" he said with a smile. Magnus continued. "If your boy makes it, I will even accompany you on the trip home and congratulate Evra myself on a good and just upbringing!"

Kadath smiled. "That does sound good indeed; I shall hold you to that." With that settled, they enjoyed the rest of their drinks, and talked and laughed about old times as the sun began its journey to the far and distant sky.

CHAPTER 14

A shopkeeper slammed his rug against the post of his shop as Arsivus and Casily strolled by.

"Every day is the same here," Casily said, breaking the silence. "Merchants are out selling goods and gifts for more than they are worth. People are going hungry in the streets, and the same bartering goes on up and down the alleys just to get through the day. On and on it goes, all the while King Thesias sits perched up in his castle overlooking those that either fear him or don't have the strength to act. Sometimes I wish I could be clear of this place and live a simple life, but there is too much vested here for me!"

"What do you mean?" Arsivus asked.

Casily stared at the ground as she walked. "I would like to leave, but I would never abandon my father here alone. Not while I have the ability to help him escape."

Arsivus slowed his pace and grabbed Casily's hand as he turned her around. "What do you mean escape?" he asked.

Casily smiled a little, and then tried to maintain a serious appearance. "I think about it all the time. Running down to the alley, being able to free all of the prisoners from their torturous life and then leaving here for good. Although, I am positive that I would need the assistance of friends and more to accomplish this. But without a major distraction, I would never be able to get away with it. It would have to be big, something that would draw the King's gaze away from Fallen Row." She looked into his eyes and smiled. Arsivus returned the smile, but an uneasy feeling came over him.

"Let's go!" she said as she winked at him. She withdrew her arm from his and continued down the stone path.

"Wait! Wait up!" Arsivus said as he took a couple quick steps to keep up.

"Your tournament is in a little less than a day. We should get you ready as best we can," Casily said.

"I don't know the details of the events or what to even expect when it starts," replied Arsivus.

"Well then, we shall have to teach you, shan't we?" Casily said as she grabbed a piece of bread out of her satchel and broke it in two pieces. As she did, her eyes caught his and remained fixated on them. Arsivus could not help but be drawn into her beautiful steely gaze.

"She is impossibly beautiful!" Arsivus thought to himself as he felt his face begin to express his innermost desires.

"One day we will change the very fate of this kingdom!" Casily said as she grabbed his hand. "There are big plans and obstacles ahead of us, ones that would crush a normal person by their lonesome." She took the bigger piece of the bread and gently placed it in his hand. She closed his fist around it while she looked into his eyes. "But together!" she said as she gazed at him. "Side by side, we will conquer them all!"

Several moments passed without them speaking. Arsivus felt certain there was no other place for him to be but where he was. Casily slowly let Arsivus's hand go and looked down shyly for a moment. Arsivus grabbed her hand again with his and gently pulled out the pendant from his satchel with his other hand. She looked down into his hands and smiled.

"What have you there, in your hand?" she asked with curiosity. Arsivus turned her hand palm up and lay the pendant in it.

"I saw this in the market. It is far lacking in the beauty you hold, but it is a token of—" but before he could finish the sentence, she giggled and cut him off.

"It is lovely. I shall wear it always!" she said with a smile as she looked at him. Her eyes moved from his eyes to his lips and back. She turned around and held her hair up so he could put it on her. Arsivus unclasped the hook, reached around her and re-clasped the hook. She turned around and looked down at the pendant resting on her chest.

"It's beautiful! Thank you so much!" she said with a smile.

Arsivus returned an adoring smile and said, "You are more than welcome."

"Now, let's get you ready for this contest!" said Casily, as she led them down a side street. A sudden gust of wind caught her hair and brushed it back toward Arsivus.

"Wow!" Arsivus thought to himself. "Her hair smells so wonderful! My heart is racing! Maybe this is what love feels like, or am I just imagining it in my head?" He shook his head to snap out of his reverie and looked ahead. He saw Casily examining the goods at the stores in the street as she moved from one to the next. "No," Arsivus said aloud. "I wasn't imagining it at all!" and he ran to catch up to her.

Casily turned as Arsivus approached. "There you are!" she said with a smile. "For the tournament, there will be some sort of archery test as always, so we will buy some small items to practice with. I will throw them in the air and you have to be able to hit them." Arsivus reached down and picked up the smallest item that was on the table next to them, which was no bigger than his closed fist.

"This should suffice, I do believe," he said as he handed it to her to put in her satchel and handed money to the merchant.

"Are you sure?" Casily asked curiously.

"Yes, that should be plenty big," he said confidently.

"Well then, it seems you are pretty versed with the bow, so let's move on to the next task, shall we? Another event will be based on combat abilities," Casily said.

Arsivus nodded his head. "That shouldn't be a problem," he said. "I have trained . . ." His voice began to fade as he saw two men about his age accompanied by the same two guards, Korgal and Teslark, they saw earlier. Casily noticed his behavior and turned around to see what had interrupted him. She saw the four men walking toward them. She took a step back toward Arsivus so her shoulder was touching his chest and grabbed his hand.

Arsivus sensed something was not right and realized that whatever was about to happen was making Casily very afraid! Arsivus stepped out in front of her while maintaining his hand in hers as the four men came up to them.

"Out of the way, peasant. Our business is not with you," the man with short brown hair shouted at Arsivus. Arsivus looked around and saw the merchants and townsfolk quickly packing up their belongings to leave.

Casily squeezed his hand harder as the area began to empty. The sun vanished behind the clouds and the shade began to overtake the immediate area they were in, almost foretelling of a dark outcome. Arsivus gave a reassuring grip back to Casily as he addressed the young men.

"Who are you to conduct yourself in such an elevated manner?" Arsivus asked.

The smaller one snickered and responded, "Why, we are your royal princes, my friend. You should pay us your respect and do as your told."

Casily leaned closer to Arsivus and whispered in his ear, "That is Zenor with the brown hair and the other is Ruvio, King Thesias's sons. They are as arrogant as they come." Arsivus looked at them both. Zenor had wider shoulders than Ruvio, although Ruvio was taller with blond hair down to his jawline.

"No secrets now, my dear," Ruvio said to Casily. "We have business with you and you alone. No need for any trouble here today."

Arsivus stood firm and looked Ruvio in the eyes. "Her business is my business. What do you require of her?" he replied. Korgal shifted his weight and let out a sigh as he was getting bored with this already.

"Well, since you must know, she was seen feeding the prisoners in Fallen Row, so upon this information, she is to be tried for breaking the law," Ruvio said.

Arsivus laughed and said, "And by chance, who made this discovery? Because if it were accurate they would have seen—"

Casily interrupted while she nudged Arsivus in the back and stepped in front of him. "It is true, I was there seeing my father, and I was there alone."

She turned back around toward Arsivus and spoke softly while still holding his hand. "I will be fine. You must compete in the tournament and win it, for us. I will find my way out. Please inform Magnus of this when you see him."

She put her hand over the pendant he just gave her as she backed away from him. "I will see you soon, trust me!" she said as she let go of his hand.

"Is there something else you would like to tell us, peasant?" Zenor asked, referring to Arsivus with a smile.

"His name is Arsivus, a name you shan't be forgetting anytime soon!" Casily retorted.

"It matters not. Our time is precious and we can't be wasting it dealing with a lover's goodbye. Let's go, Casily," Zenor said. With that the four men and Casily headed toward the castle keep as Arsivus watched, feeling helpless.

Magnus took a bite of his drumstick and sipped the last of his ale just as the bar attendant came and grabbed his plate.

He leaned back, stretched his arms out in front of him, and let out a chuckle.

"I say, we did have some good adventures back in the day, didn't we?" Magnus said as Kadath nodded his head and they all laughed. Magnus stood up, which prompted Kadath and Doran to follow suit.

"Gentlemen!" Magnus said as he nodded his head in preparation to leave. He placed a couple of coins on the table. "This one is on me!" he said as he reached to put his money satchel back under his belt when a loud yell came from the entrance into the bar.

"General!" All the patrons looked to the door and saw Arsivus hunched over and breathless.

Kadath quickly sprinted over to him. "Son, what is the matter? Where have you come from?"

Magnus quickly found himself next to the pair as he looked outside and back at Arsivus. "Where is Casily?" he asked sternly. Arsivus stood up and looked them both in the eyes as sweat dripped down his brow.

"Teslark and Korgal, they came upon us in the market and took Casily. I would have stopped them but Casily forbade it and went willingly with them and two other men that were with them."

"Who were the other men with them? Did you get a name?" Magnus asked. Now Doran joined them while the other patrons returned to their mugs and conversations.

"Casily said they were the King's sons. The first was Zenor, and the other was . . ."

"Ruvio," Doran said. "They are nasty little beings, always meddling in affairs that do not concern them. If I had the mind, I would like to see if their swordplay is as profound as their attitudes."

"They said she was to be put on trial for feeding the prisoners of Fallen Row." Arsivus told them. "I tried to reason with them only to have Casily silence me and tell me to come inform you."

Magnus looked at Kadath and back at Arsivus. "You did well. Fighting them, I am afraid, would have ended badly for you. Leave this matter to me, and I will do what I can. Doran, I would like you to stay with Kadath and Arsivus until the competition is over. I have a bad feeling that something more is at play than what we are aware of. Anything you see that is of uncertainty or concern, bring it to my attention as soon as you can. Arsivus, continue to train and prepare for the competition. Kadath, if there is anything you need, inform Doran and he will take care of it. Zenor and Ruvio are also in the competition and are very capable fighters. Be careful. If you see them again, do not engage them. I will speak with you soon." With that, Magnus departed, leaving the three to contemplate the recent events.

Kadath looked over at Doran and back at Arsivus. He put his hand on Arsivus's shoulder and said, "I wouldn't trust anyone to be able to do anything better. Casily means a lot to General Magnus, and he knows how much she means to you. I would not worry too much. Instead, let us worry about your training."

"Indeed, let us do that!" Doran exclaimed.

Arsivus looked at both of them and solemnly agreed. "Where shall we start?" Arsivus asked with determination and continued on, "If I am to compete against the likes of those two then I want to be at my best." Kadath smiled an encouraging smile, as did Doran. Doran walked over and opened the door. He could see Magnus walking the main path. The castle keep was high above, looming over the entire city. He could see the big golden archway hovering above the steel gates that allowed entrance to the royal partition of the city. That was where all of the knights, all of the elders, and all of the nobles lived, including the King and his White Guard.

"Did the lady ever get a moment to speak with you about the tournament and the events?" Doran asked while watching his General march toward the oppressor that sat high above them.

"Not all of them. She got through archery, and that's when they came for her," Arsivus replied. Doran looked back at Arsivus but kept the door open.

"Well, we will have to go practice them all, won't we now?" Doran posed to him. With that, he tilted his head in a manner to make Kadath and Arsivus follow him out the door and to whatever Doran had planned for them. Arsivus held the door as his father passed by. He took one last look around the room before he exited the tavern. As he did, he saw a man leaving at the opposite end of the bar. Arsivus peered toward the man but all he could see was a black cloak that had a blue cape over the shoulder. On his shoulder, he carried an enormous sword that he held steady as he walked away. Arsivus's curiosity was peaked, but now was not the time. He exited the same door his father did and saw both of them sitting upon their horses, holding the reins for Arsivus's horse.

"Where are we going?" Arsivus asked the mounted warriors.

"To show you what you will need to accomplish to win this tournament. Hurry along now, we have much to learn and are hard pressed for time!" Doran exclaimed. Kadath let out a reassuring smile while he dropped Arsivus's reins to hang freely in the air. They dug their heels into the horses and departed toward the gates of the city. Arsivus grabbed hold of the reins and quickly looked around the outside of the tavern trying to find the man with the black cloak he saw inside, but to no avail. He then looked up to the perch of the kingdom where King Thesias sat throughout his days.

A feeling of rage began to set inside him as he thought about Casily. "Where is she? Is she all right? When will I see her again?" Thoughts raced through his head. He tried to shake them loose, but they kept surfacing like an itch that could not be scratched. He relented and hoisted himself up and dug his heels into his steed to catch up with his father and Doran.

He willed himself to concentrate. "If I could not do anything to save her in the alley, then I will train as hard as I can to win this tournament. Perhaps then, I may be able to help her somehow," he thought. In the distance, he could see his father and Doran galloping along. Going a little bit faster he finally caught up to them and saw the gates opening. A fresh breeze blew through the opening. For the first time in a long while, as the breeze brushed by his face, he felt a sense of tranquility and a sense that everything was going to be just fine . . . somehow.

CHAPTER 15

The sun was beginning to set in the cloudy sky. Night would soon be upon the kingdom. A knock resounded throughout the decorated walls of the chambers. A voice bellowed from deep inside the room, "Enter!" The wind whipped past the door while it slowly opened. Walking inside, Magnus saw a fire roaring in the center of the room. The tapestries on the walls swayed back and forth and the drapes floated above the ground from the wind. Magnus looked toward the balcony facing the city and then to the balcony facing the sea and saw King Thesias perched on the railing admiring the ocean and its majestic strength. Thesias turned his head and saw Magnus standing there with a serious expression on his face.

Thesias sighed loud enough to make it known that he was agitated. "Argh, what is it this time? Can't you see I'm busy? Is there nothing better you can be using your time for? Like instructing your knights on how to do a King's bidding!" he said with disdain.

Magnus shifted his weight and gripped the handle of his sword with contempt. "I have yet to speak with you about the conduct of which your men and lackeys showed at a very loyal and close acquaintance's home. But that will come later, as well as a discussion of the treasures that you were so eager to attack the beasts in the Northern Forest for. But for right now, my bidding is that I wish to speak with you about a young woman who your men took captive."

Thesias whipped around to face Magnus with a face as stern as the iron forges and just as red. "Who are you to question my intentions, General?" he said as he paced over to the other balcony overlooking the courtyard below him.

Magnus took a couple of steps toward him maintaining his posture and kept his hand on his hilt. He tried hard to keep his anger from rising. "I am the protector of this city," Magnus said with a commanding tone. "I defend our walls from all enemies on the outside as well as inside. When someone needs questioning, it is by my command and from knights that I have trained to do so. Your sons cannot conduct official business based off their name alone, much less your White Guard accompanying them as they do. I want the woman they took to be released immediately, and for your sons to be held on a tighter leash from now on. Finally, I want you to leave the policing and protecting of this kingdom to real knights," Magnus finished, his rage completely obvious.

After a few seconds, Magnus heard a scuffle on the marble floor behind him. He turned to see Captain Atalee in the doorway leaning against one of the parchments. Magnus made eye contact directly with him, and Atalee smirked as he returned the stare.

Thesias responded, "General, I ordered my sons to detain that woman specifically because she was seen giving aid to the wretched souls residing in Fallen Row. Everyone knows my decree; they are traitors to the country and are banished to suffer for their crimes. Giving aid is strictly forbidden, and she has defied my law and, therefore, must pay the price."

Atalee chimed in. "Some say others have been seen taking part in the sympathetic gestures for those in Fallen Row, General. There is even some talk of knights in your command visiting on a daily basis. How bad would it look upon the great General Magnus if this were to be true?" Atalee scoffed with a smile as he stood straight up and made his way toward the King.

"Prisoners must also eat, *brother*!" Magnus shouted back toward Thesias. "I will see her free by the morning as she was there on my command."

Atalee laughed aloud and said, "So you think you can break the King's commands because he is your younger brother? I see your loyalty to your King comes second to your selfish nature. Perhaps that is why —"

But before he could finish his sentence, Thesias shouted, "Enough!" as he knocked over a golden vase seated near him.

Thesias faced Magnus and said, "You purposefully committed an act I deemed traitorous. Not only this, but you admit to it freely. This will be the last time we have this conversation, *brother*! How can I trust my General to do right by me and my kingdom if he blatantly disobeys me?" Magnus looked at Thesias with a disheartened stare, and then noticed Atalee smiling as he adjusted his armor. Thesias shifted his attention back to the courtyard. He touched the ivory banister running along the sides as he chose his next few words carefully.

"Normally I would have you thrown you into Fallen Row with your friends. But I am feeling merciful in light of recent news of long lost-treasures." Thesias smiled and returned his gaze back to Magnus. "You will preside over the tournament as originally planned, after which I shall decide what to do with you. Until then, Captain Atalee will be privy to any decisions you make and will give guidance where it is due."

Magnus gaffed and gritted his teeth. "As you command, your highness!" Magnus said. "What of the treasure you sought in the north that you may have started a war over? And what of my acquaintances that were treated harshly in your fine Captain's name?" as Magnus motioned toward Atalee.

Thesias's face remained stone cold as he murmured, "The treasure was of utmost importance, and we found what we were seeking. As for how your friend was treated at the hand of my Captain and his cohorts, that is being handled in due time." Thesias turned and headed back to look over the sea. "That is all, General Magnus. Go about your duties and protect something!"

As Magnus turned to walk through the door, he heard Atalee whisper, "She is very beautiful, General. It would be a shame if anything happened to her while her husband is here and she is all alone." Magnus immediately grasped his sword with his right hand and brought it from his sheath. In one sweeping motion he spun around and brought the sword swiftly through the air and down toward Atalee. Atalee, taken by surprise, barely managed to get his sword out in time to bring it high enough to parry the heavy blow off to the side, and both blades crashed into the marble floor.

"Enough! Magnus, stop this child's play immediately!" Thesias commanded from the back of the room. With that, Magnus looked deeply into the eyes of Atalee, who was rattled from the strike that he delivered.

"We are not finished, you and I!" Magnus said as he sheathed his sword and turned to exit the room. His strides quickened to be free of the wretchedness that had become his brother and his place of ruling. He knew he must get to Kadath soon and pass the warning that was blatantly directed toward him. As Magnus walked down the white marble steps, he stopped at the little nook overlooking the courtyard, hoping to see the woman singing as he did before but she was not there.

He let out a sigh and continued down the staircase thinking, "What did Atalee mean? Was it a veiled threat or did he say it just to get under his skin?" Magnus knew he was going to be watched; he understood this and frankly would do the same in this situation so knew he should expect it for himself. Freeing Casily would take a great deal of effort not to draw any further attention on himself, so he knew he must wait for now. But first things first, he must warn his old friend of the plight that was so thinly veiled by

Captain Atalee. Kadath must know, and he must hear of it immediately.

Once Magnus reached his room, he sent for Mulik. Mulik was downstairs in the courtyard and arrived immediately upon being summoned.

"General, I was told you wanted to see me?" Mulik said with purpose.

"Yes, my friend!" Magnus replied immediately. "I need you to send a small detachment of knights to my close acquaintance's house. These need to be formidable knights that can carry themselves among the best. I do not want to draw attention to this, so here is an order to have the gates opened tonight. Send at most three knights to this location and let them know that danger is coming. I will send more when the opportunity presents itself to me, but it will not be until the morning. Your men need to depart immediately."

"Yes sir," Mulik responded. "Request permission to join them on this task?"

Magnus shook his head. "No, I need you here for the tournament. If anything happens, you will be on the first detachment to leave, understood?"

Mulik nodded in agreement. He took the order to open the gates and before he turned to leave, asked, "General, which house are they to go to?"

Magnus, not turning his head from overlooking the city, responded solemnly, "Back to Kadath and Evra's house. They are to remain there until further direction is given."

Mulik gave a nod of approval. As he walked out of Magnus's room, he said, "Understood, my men will depart immediately." With that, Mulik left to give the orders to his men. As Magnus lingered overlooking the horizon, he heard a familiar voice.

"My oh my, he seemed to be in quite a rush. Wherever is he going at this time, and what was he carrying?" Without having to turn around, Magnus already knew who was in his chambers, and standing in between him and his sword that was resting upon his bed.

"Well, Captain, if you came to strike the cowardly blow, here I am. Unarmed and upon the world's edge with naught but rocks to catch me below," Magnus said to Atalee.

The captain took small strides to join Magnus on the balcony overlooking the kingdom's borders. "It truly is magnificent, how so much can be out there for grabs, yet it remains untouched. And here we are on the doorstep, seemingly able to witness its beauty from afar." Atalee said gently as he rested his hands dressed in gauntlets upon the railing.

Magnus, not breaking his gaze, asked again, "What is your business here?"

Atalee continued. "While we have not always seen eye to eye, I have come across some rather disturbing information. This particular information would not be pleasant for either one of us, as it involves the King's children."

Magnus turned his head slightly so he could see Atalee out of the corner of his eye. "What information do you have, and who is the source?" Magnus asked with strength in his tone.

Atalee returned the half stare to Magnus and spoke softly, "I have suspicion to believe that the King desires his sons to join my ranks in the White Guard. Although my source will remain unbeknownst to you at this time, this may be a serious threat. There needs to be something in place in case this does happen. I think we can agree that having those children in positions of power would prove very unfortunate for me and my Guard, as well as you and your knights. I think it is best if that is not allowed to happen."

Magnus nodded his head and said, "For once, Captain, I think we can fully agree on this. I take it you have a plan to ensure that this doesn't happen?"

Atalee laughed and responded, "We could kill them!"

Magnus joined in the laughter, but only for a moment. "No, if this is true, neither of us should have any linking to this. Let us have a drink, and we can solve this problem together, what say you?"

Atalee nodded his head in approval. He took his left gauntlet, brought it down by his waist, raised his right one, and patted Magnus on the shoulder. He said, "You pour, I drink, we talk!"

Magnus let out a quick laugh and they turned and walked back into Magnus's chambers.

Casily opened her eyes and saw a rusty gate door that was wet from the water dripping down from the ceiling above. She squinted her eyes to get a better picture of her surroundings and saw a bucket near the rusted door. She slowly got up off her makeshift bed and started to walk around a little bit.

"How did I arrive here?" she thought to herself as she stretched her arms and legs. Her arms ached painfully, which brought forth a memory. "I was dragged down here by Zenor and Teslark. They threw me in the last cell. As they shut the door I grabbed Teslark through the bars and he looked back with a solemn, almost sorrowful gaze. Before he could react, Zenor hit my upper arms with a rod incredibly hard and I fell to the floor. The last thing I remember is seeing Teslark hostilely grab Zenor by his collar and hold him against the brick column next to the door, and everything after is blank."

As she moved to the door, she looked to the right and it was silent. There were only a couple of torches that were burning in the distance. She looked to her upper left and saw an opening at the very end of the corridor. It allowed fresh air to enter and exit, but it denied any hope of escape, as it was too small to fit into if given the chance. In addition, it would not be any good to use as she could hear waves crashing below, so she determined that she was on the outer perimeter of the castle.

That information lowered her optimism that this particular day would have any type of good outcome. She looked down into the bucket and saw a loaf of bread that was rotten and had bugs crawling on it. There was a whole carrot, which also appeared rotted. She gracefully slid the bucket away with her foot as she grabbed hold of the bars.

"Hello? Is there anyone there? I would like to put a request in for a meal, if I may?" She laughed to herself silently.

"And what would the lady like to order?" A man's voice came from down the corridor.

Casily was stunned at the response and tried to peer down the corridor. "To be honest, if you would just open this door and walk away, that would be good enough for me. We could just skip the whole meal entirely," she said.

"I can open the door when I am told to. Until then I am afraid that I must tell you that I am unable," the voice replied.

"May I at least have the name of the only other person being jailed with me?" Casily replied quickly to try to gain sympathy from the captor who shared her empty prison. A chair could be heard scraping against the cold and damp stone floor. She heard clanking as the mysterious man clad in armor approached. She could tell he must be bigger than most, due to the echoing of the metal clashing against the stone floor. Immediately she recognized the red jewel in the armor as it moved slowly toward her.

"The King's elite!" she thought to herself. "That's just great." Her eyes settled on the great big axe that was in the jailor's hands. She closed her eyes in disappointment, and when she opened them back up, she was face-to-face with a smiling Korgal. His smile unintentionally sank her spirit to the far-thest depths that darkness could reach.

"Hello, my lady!" he said as he put his giant left hand on the iron door bars.

"Korgal, so nice to see you again!" she said sarcastically. Korgal tilted his head to the right and let out a sigh. Casily con-tinued. "So, what could you have done to be marooned in a place like this guarding a defenseless woman? Aren't you one of the high and mighty knights, and not some lowly jailor?"

He looked toward the opening in the wall and took a deep breath. "The young masters commanded your detainment. They said something about you being on Fallen Row and feeding those men," Korgal stated with purpose.

Casily shrunk back in her cell a little bit, as Korgal went on. "You know that is a punishable crime, do you not? Why then would you do this, in broad daylight?" Korgal asked sternly.

Casily came back to the door with fury and anger in her voice. "You want to know why I did it? Because that is no way to treat any person, especially a knight who loved his kingdom and would give his life in an instant to protect anyone that lived within it. For me to be jailed for showing mercy is utter ridiculousness. Do you not agree?" She finished as she realized that she was now squeezing the life out of the iron bars that obstructed her freedom.

Korgal's face remained the same, although he was now looking into her eyes and could see the passion that she harbored. "When and if you are released, knowing what you do about the laws and the severity of them, would you continue to feed those knights?" Korgal asked with curiosity.

Casily released her grip of the door. "You know I would," she said solemnly with purpose. Korgal brought his hand down to his waist as he leaned his axe against the column of bricks outlining her cell.

"The King's sons are ruthless and unrestrained; they do what they please, and there are no repercussions. They wanted to make an example of you but were too afraid to do it alone. They did not know the man who was with you and, for that reason, commanded Teslark and I to accompany them on the task of arresting you." Korgal looked down the hall toward the doorway and back at Casily. "I told them they were fools and not to waste my time. I am not here to be an errand boy for two spoiled brats. For that reason, even though they made me accompany them to retrieve you, I was banished to sit here until they decide to come and fetch you. I very much dislike taking orders from lesser folk."

Casily asked in a pleasant and polite tone, "What do you mean?"

Korgal continued. "Teslark is being punished since he refuted the order as well. He is being made to clean out the horse stalls, which is beneath us great knights, but we cannot disobey the King's sons."

Casily felt a little regret for him. "You understand that although I see their abuse of power with you and Teslark, I do not feel bad for either of you since I am down here because of them as well," said Casily with a softened voice.

"I understand this, and nor was I seeking pity. I just want you to know we are loyal to the cause and the cause alone." As Korgal finished his sentence, he grabbed the door with both of his monstrous hands. He bent his knees a little and arched his back, and with one mighty thrust backward, he broke the door off the rusted and wet hinges and let it fall to the floor. Casily stepped back, stunned. "What are you doing?" she asked nervously.

Korgal made a gesture to invite her out of the cell. "You are free to go, my lady. I have already sent word to Teslark to be ready while you were sleeping. Do you know the layout of where you currently are?" Korgal asked.

Casily hesitantly took a step toward the opening and mustered the courage to speak. "Not really, but once I can get topside, I will be able to find my way. What about you? Aren't Zenor and Ruvio expecting me? Won't they try to hurt you knowing that I escaped?"

Korgal grabbed hold of his mighty axe and hoisted it to rest on his shoulder. "I would like to see them try!" he said with a smirk.

Casily smiled back and stepped out of the cell. She felt as free as the wind and the urge to be just as swift. "His name is Arsivus!" Casily said. "He is . . ." she hesitated for a second, "important to me, and I think he is destined for great things!"

Korgal tilted his head. "Why do you tell me this?" he asked.

"Because he is a good man, and I just thought you should know," she said as she turned to walk down the corridor.

Korgal laughed as he walked next to her. "Well then, I shall be on the lookout for him in the future, if it pleases you!" he replied.

Casily reached the end of the corridor and paused. "Thank you for helping me. I shall remember what happened here!" she said cautiously.

He grabbed the door and opened it. "I cannot go any farther. From here you must go alone. Teslark is waiting at the stables. He will help you as well."

Casily finally felt hope breathe back into her body. "You are very kind," she said quietly.

Korgal rested his hand on her shoulder. "Be safe, my lady!" he said as she exited the doorway and pounced up the stairs on her way to the fresh cool air and freedom that now was before her.

CHAPTER 16

The sun was well set into the sky as the day drew to an end. A thud echoed over the horizon. Arsivus hit the ground with his ironclad fist while he lay upon the hard and dry dirt.

"Ha, you must learn to keep your feet hitched while you attack on your weak side, Arsivus. Your opponents will surely know this!" Doran shouted as he rode around his fallen foe.

"Again!" Arsivus shouted as he raised himself to his feet and grabbed the strap of his horse.

"Remember son, maintaining your balance and speed takes as much strength as swinging your sword. Most warriors think their strike will give them a victory, but in fact, anticipating it and countering is the key to success," Kadath said.

Arsivus threaded his foot into the stirrup and swung his leg over his horse. He looked around the enclosed stable yard they were training in and saw nothing but old fences surrounding them to keep the animals locked in. The pastures that were neighboring them ran over the seemingly never-ending hills that hid underneath the mountains.

"Keep my feet hitched and dig down. All right, let's go again!" Arsivus said as he swung his horse around to face Doran. Doran pulled on his reins to align his horse with Arsivus and readied his sword again. They darted toward each other as clouds of dust rose from the ground in a steady trail behind them.

Kadath moved from side to side as he watched from the fence post, trying to see through the veil of dirt that now filled the sky. Doran looked up from the ground and saw Arsivus spinning his horse around as Doran's riderless horse galloped toward the gate.

"Doran, my friend, where have you gone?" Kadath said with a laugh. Doran unbuckled his armor strap while he lay on the ground.

Arsivus rode over to him and leaned over. "I believe your feet came unhitched at some point this last time!"

Doran let out a deep chuckle as Arsivus jumped down to the ground and extended a hand to help him up.

After Doran had finished dusting himself off, he walked over to the railing and set his armor and sword down. "Now that we have finished for today on riding combat, it is time we see your proficiency with axe throwing in case it is an event. It is very simple and very effective if you understand the basics of it," Doran said with a smile. Doran just finished speaking when Arsivus picked up a hand axe resting nearby and flung it toward a water bucket, impaling itself with ease into the deep, dark cedar lining.

"Mercy be!" exclaimed Doran, as he looked back at Kadath. He turned back toward Arsivus and said, "Well, that is how axe throwing is done, my lad," and gave Arsivus a slap on the back.

"All right kiddo, now starts the real fun," Doran stated with enthusiasm. He grabbed his armor and slid it back on. While he did his, Arsivus saw his father also donning his armor and strapping his sword back onto his waist as Doran did the same.

"Well, arm up, boy. This is where you will earn your keep!" Doran yelled as he fumbled with the leather straps to secure the sheath. Arsivus grabbed the armor sitting by the railing that was for the challengers of the Seven Wizards tournament to wear while in competition. The armor looked as if it had just been retrieved from a battle and the previous tenant had not survived the wounds. There were a great many dents and cuts throughout the bold and tarnished chest plate, couplings were loose and strewn about the neckline, and what appeared to be dried blood coated the creases of the folds.

Arsivus found it was a perfect fit, but the stench that remained on the inside of the hot steel made his eyes water.

"What is this horrendous stench?" Arsivus asked in a worrisome tone.

Kadath could smell it as well. "Doran, is there anything that can be done to acquire some decent gear for my boy?" Kadath asked.

Doran was about to slide his helmet on but answered calmly, "It has already been taken care of. Now, let us begin the dueling sessions!" The three of them stood in the open field with a wind that was starting to come out of the east. It was strong enough to pick up leaves and clippings off the ground hundreds of yards away and deposit them throughout the dueling area. The dust rose everywhere except for where the three men stood.

"This last portion of the trials involves dueling. The person with the highest points will be our champion," Doran exclaimed with his regal voice.

Kadath leaned in toward Arsivus and spoke to him. "They choose the names the day of to see who competes within each battle. It is best to prepare for all of them, for you never know what fate may deal you!"

Arsivus nodded in agreement and unsheathed his sword with his right hand. "Well then, are we ready, or did you need more time to rest?" Arsivus asked his two elders as he charged into combat resembling a lion seeking its prey.

The hours passed quickly as the sun began to fade into its nightly slumber. Doran slowly lowered his guard and went to remove his helmet.

Arsivus, still trying to perfect his blocking and attacks, took notice and slowed his movements. "Are we done for the day?" Arsivus asked hopefully.

Kadath lowered his sword and removed his helmet as well, and said, "I think that is enough for today. We do not want you exhausted once the tournament starts tomorrow." Arsivus agreed and fetched a pail of water for them to share. When he returned, he handed it to his father first to drink. While he did this, he gazed across the ridges of Affinity admiring how majestic it appeared. He suddenly noticed a figure standing in the shade of an archery tower. He looked around to see what this mysterious individual who had been watching him may be looking for. Perhaps it was just a soldier who grew tired of guard duty, or a fan of the tournament looking for entertainment value. Arsivus watched as the mysterious individual took two steps out into the light and turned away as to almost show himself before he vanished. Arsivus knew at that moment who it was — the blue cape, the black cloak and the enormous sword over his shoulder — it was the same man he had seen at the tavern many hours before.

"Who is that man?" Arsivus asked Kadath and Doran. They looked where Arsivus pointed and Doran recognized him in an instant. "That man is not from this land. He comes from the Western Kingdom. I do not know his name, but his reputation precedes him everywhere he goes. You can always pick him out because of that large sword he carries over his shoulder like a bag of flour," Doran said. "He is a great warrior but had troubles with the laws of his land, so he came east to live peacefully. Although, this is the first time that he will be competing in the games. I wonder what brought him here."

"So, he is in the tournament?" Arsivus asked. "Who else is going to be battling for the knighthood?"

Doran looked at Kadath and then at Arsivus. "The names that I have heard from the General were; you, Zenor, Ruvio, one of Ruvio's friends Huply, that man with a sword, a common burglar (they always throw one in for a redemption vote), and last, a squire who has come of age. You shall make up the seven, and from there, one shall be named champion!" Doran said again in a regal tone. "But enough of this chatter. Let's get some food into your belly, and some wine into your gullet, for tomorrow starts the festival of competition." With that, the three of them packed up their equipment, and loaded it onto their horses, and returned back to their quarters.

A quick breath escaped Teslark's mouth as he lifted the shovel of manure into the air and threw it into the ever-growing putrid smelling pile.

"Ugh, what type of work is this for a knight of the White Guard?" Teslark said to himself as he returned his shovel to the discarded pile of waste.

"I swear by the gods, if I ever get those two spoiled brats alone, they will learn what it means to possess actual power!" Teslark left the shovel buried in the mound and stepped outside of the stalls to pull out his tobacco pipe and light some of the local weed the villagers called "Starlight." As he put a match to the barrel opening, a horse neighed in the distance as it dug down on the dry and coarse oats that were strewn about on the ground. A foul wind filled the air as the tide in the ocean below changed direction, and with it, the breeze.

"Blessed be!" Teslark exclaimed aloud as he whipped around to lay blame upon the mighty steeds. "It's all of them cursed oats you've been eating that stink the place to beyond our sky. Maybe if you —" Teslark stopped suddenly, as he peered past the assembly of horses near the stalls and spied Casily leaning against one of the saddles hanging on the door. Teslark walked to the exit and peered outside but saw no one paying any attention to what was happening within. Teslark returned to his position and took a long drag from his pipe. He looked down the stable aisle and nodded at Casily. With a quick head jerk, he motioned for her to join him in the stall to his right where he had been shoveling. As Teslark entered the stall, he turned to find Casily right behind him.

"It is not often that you see a White Guard not wearing his armor, although it is clear to see why in this case," Casily said.

Teslark laughed aloud. "Well, well, well, the infamous Casily. How nice of you to join me here. I'll have you know, this is all because of you. Well, partly you, more because of those two spoiled brats who need to be taught a very serious lesson, and very soon!" he said. Casily leaned up against the open stall door as Teslark reached out to straighten the shovel in the pile of refuse. As he spun around, he kicked the shovel over and excrement landed all over the wall. Casily, stunned, stood up straight and let out a quick smirk but, was hesitant and worried about what was going to happen next.

Teslark leaned back against the opposite wall and looked her in the eyes. He took another puff out of his pipe and said, "Those two boys have something out for you. We had reports of other people that were feeding the prisoners, much higher-ranking individuals. But those boys were dispatched just for you. Why is that?" Teslark asked with a serious tone.

Casily looked confused. "I . . . I don't know. There were others there with me, but I do not know why someone would just want me!"

Teslark felt she was being honest. "Hmph!" he exclaimed and went on. "I believe you, and I also believe there is more to this that you may not be privy to. Therefore, I will fill in what I can. Thesias despises your father and those that followed him. He knows that Magnus was there, as well as a few outsiders, but he wanted to make a point to your father. He wanted your father to understand that he is powerless, as are you, and there is no protection within this kingdom that can match the King's desires. He sought you, because your father would have heard by now. Perhaps that would give the King the leverage he needs to control the masses, as well as gain information on the treasure he seeks."

Casily looked bewildered as Teslark went on. "Those boys, they are as crooked as crows. It was their idea to throw you in the prison cell, as well as their idea to instill these punishments upon Korgal and I. They did this because we bluntly disobeyed their orders, and King Thesias directly commanded us to accompany them to retrieve you. Captain Atalee may not be fully privy to our punishment, but he will be soon. The King left us at the mercy of his two spoiled potatoes to be their playthings. That is unforgivable for us."

Casily was now starting to understand the situation as Teslark spoke again. "We told the King's sons to go take a bath with each other. My best guess is that our statements were frowned upon highly!" Teslark said with a smile. "Anyways," he continued, "here we are."

Casily finally spoke. "Korgal spoke of you being able to assist me, but my question is why?"

Teslark answered almost immediately. "If yours was a grave error, then our cause to collect you would have been just. Your actions in our eyes did not justify the punishment that was sought; therefore, we see to do as we must to uphold the peace in the name of honor. When we are pushed, we will retaliate, but when others are pushed, we protect."

Casily smiled a little bit, finally understanding more than she previously had. Teslark motioned for them to exit the stall and gather out by the horses with a simple nod of his head. As they walked out, they heard a loud dragging sound coming from the end of the stables. Teslark peered his ears and listened. He looked at his armor hanging upon one of the hooks near where he was working. Then his eyes drifted down to where his belt full of knives hung. He slowly walked over and rested in front of them as the heavy dragging sound came closer.

Casily, now worried, dashed into a stall and waited.

"I could smell you from the alley across the street!" a familiar voice rang out.

Casily, a bit surprised, heard Teslark respond, "With that big axe cutting into the street, I am surprised you haven't woken the underworld, you big oaf!" With that, laughter filled the stables as Casily saw it was Korgal who had arrived. She came out to see Korgal standing with Teslark.

"Hello, my lady," Korgal said with his charm.

Casily responded, "Hello, my big friend."

Teslark walked further into the stable and returned with a horse in hand. "I thought you were supposed to stay in the prison and wait for those two little yams to see their reaction?" he asked Korgal.

Korgal leaned his axe upon the stall that Casily had been hiding in, tightened his oversized gauntlets around his massive wrists, and responded to Teslark. "I got bored, figured they would never show. It was very lonely down there as well, and I wanted to make sure you didn't mess everything up without me."

Casily smiled brightly and said, "Well, I appreciate your concern, and it is good to know that there are two of the White Guard that I can trust. Now, how do we all get out of this predicament?"

Teslark started strapping a saddle on the horse he brought over for Casily. As he was doing so, he started talking. "This horse has witnessed many battles, some fruitful, and some not. His name is Vex, and he will treat you right if you do the same."

Korgal chimed in. "You are to ride this horse and meet your Arsivus. You will do good to stay with him until after the tournament if he is to still compete."

Teslark butted in. "Who is Arsivus? Was he the one you were with when we —?"

"Yes, that was him," Casily interrupted. "And he is still going to compete!" She looked at Korgal.

Teslark nodded his head in approval. "That is a well-built man. He will do good in the tournament. What joy that would bring me to see him embarrass those two little cabbages in front of the whole kingdom. It would save me the inevitable punishment of doing it myself."

Korgal laughed and said, "Yes, that would be grand indeed. I already gave the girl my word that we would look out for him." Casily smiled as she mounted the horse. Teslark retrieved his armor and put it back on. He strapped his weapons back to their original place as Korgal heaved up his heavy axe from the stable floor.

When Teslark finished strapping his knives back down, he said to Casily with a serious tone, "Beware the two young turnips. From what I could gather, they are planning the combat to be lethal. I hear there is a young squire that is to compete and he will be selected for that competition. If you can bring word to your Arsivus and see that he intervenes if need be, you would have my thanks!" Teslark said with sincerity.

Korgal injected softly, "That young squire is his sister's only son," as he motioned toward Teslark.

"It will be one of the first things I mention to him," Casily said. "He will handle it, I know he will!"

As Casily steered Vex around to face the exit, she said appreciatively, "I will not forget this gesture, believe me. I will pay it back in full when I am able!" With a nod from both Teslark and Korgal, she was off through the exit of the stable, and would soon be in Arsivus's comforting arms. Teslark and Korgal looked at each other and smiled. They turned their attention toward the exit as they were fully armed and ready to go.

"Where to now, friend?" Korgal asked quietly.

Teslark responded, "Well, let's go tell those two little radishes that she escaped. That should be fun!" They both laughed while they walked toward the Royal Chambers of Affinity.

King Thesias paced back and forth on his balcony between his master's chambers and the grand stairway leading down to the massive double doors that opened into the Royal Grand Hall. The large ivory doors swung open with force as the sun beat down upon the marble floor. Thesias looked down the staircase and saw Atalee standing there with a smile on his face.

"My liege!" Atalee exclaimed as he took a couple steps up the stairs. "The riders have been dispatched. They should be there by tomorrow midday, or later if they are slow, but I have given strict instructions as to what to do."

Thesias responded excitedly, "Good, good, and these men are capable of the task given? Are you confident that they will not fail you, Captain?"

Atalee shook his head. "Yes, these men have undertaken tasks such as this before and are well versed in the art. They are not part of my White Guard, nor are they part of your idiot brother's legion, they are . . ." Atalee hesitated for a quick second. "Specialists, if you will." Thesias nodded as Atalee continued. "They will ensure no blame can come back to the crown, or ourselves. Two days from now, you shall have one of the treasures that you seek, and no one will be the wiser."

Thesias smiled and clapped his hands together. "Captain, you have done well. As you are well aware, my sons are fighting in tomorrow's tournament. Upon their successful completion of the tournament, I would like them both to join your White Guard. I have changed the decree that no longer will there be one champion. This year there shall be three — my two sons and one of their accomplices. That is who I would like to win. I am counting on you to make it happen. Do what you must, you understand. Don't you?"

Atalee hesitated for a second. He thought, "My sources were correct. There is no way those little brats are White Guard material. They wouldn't even survive normal combat against any of my knights, even if both of them could fight at the same time. I cannot let this happen."

"Captain!" Thesias yelled. "Is there a problem?"

Atalee responded quickly, but slyly, "No, your majesty. We would be honored to have them join our ranks. I will see that they have the easiest competition and ensure that anyone in their position would be able to win!"

"Very well!" Thesias exclaimed. "You are excused." He said as he turned around and walked into his bedchambers for the night. Atalee turned around and descended the stairs and closed the heavy doors behind him with ease. He overlooked the Grand Hall before him, vast and empty. Candlelight's were fading out one by one and the cool wind from the ocean was filling the room.

"What do you want to do, Captain?" a voice spoke softly out of the darkness. Atalee, not phased at all by the mysterious voice, began to walk through the Grand Hall with a quick pace, his steps echoing off the marble encasements. He walked up to one of the remaining lit candles near the exit and stared fiercely into it.

Another voice broke the silence, but on the opposite side of the hall. "Captain, what are your orders?" Atalee put his fingers up to the flickering golden flame and held them steady above it.

Atalee let out a sigh. "Now, we must wait. That is what we will do. We must be patient," he said as he closed his fingers around the flame and extinguished it completely. "Be patient, but be ready," he said as he walked through the Grand Hall exit and made his way to his chamber for the night.

"So, we wait then!" one voice echoed through the room, only to be met with a simple response from the other side.

"We wait!"

"Almost there," Casily thought to herself as she rode through the alleys trying to remain unnoticed. She rode swiftly, but with purpose as the night began to creep over the city. She gripped the reins a little bit tighter than normal, not knowing what to expect around each corner.

"Nobody that rides back here has anything but bad intentions," she thought while she peered into every nook and crevasse she passed. The wind began to howl through the alleyways like one thousand steel arrows being fired at once. Vex was getting a little on edge as he was trying to navigate the stone causeway amid the darkness and breeze. Casily felt an odd chill come about her as she strode through the alley and started to get nervous.

A very damp feeling ran up her spine and stayed upon her neck like a chill she just couldn't shake. She remembered that she had no weapons, had no means of contacting anyone, and was alone at this very moment in a dark and somewhat frightening place.

She encouraged Vex to pick up the pace. "The sooner I can get to Arsivus, the better off I will feel!" she said aloud. With that, she increased to a steady gallop through the dark and twisted alley, faintly remembering what part of Affinity that she was in, as it all seemed completely different in the dark. As she went faster, the wind seemed to pick up speed as well as become louder. Everything seemed to be moving around her at high speed. Through one of the gaps in the alleys, she swore she saw riders that were matching her speed and going in the same direction.

"That can't be!" she said aloud. "No one should be riding these streets at night, especially at our pace unless they are hiding something." Casily slowed Vex down as best as she could and turned down one of the alleys that would connect her with the riders on the next street over. Once she came to the end of the alley, she looked left and could see the two riders had slowed as well. Casily, now understanding that she was almost to the main gate, which meant that Arsivus was also just as near, started toward the main gate where the two cloaked riders were heading.

The riders did not seem to notice Casily turn toward them and continued their gallop towards the main gate. Casily maintained a good distance behind them as to not be noticed, but to keep them within sight. From the corner of her eye, she could spot Arsivus's temporary residence and his horse outside. Casily slowed to a light trot to make it up the big hill leading to Arsivus. Once there, she dismounted and peered into the distance toward the main gate. She quieted her heart and stroked Vex to calm down as well and listened with an ear of patience.

"Open the main gate! Open the main gate now!" She heard the gatekeeper yell as she saw that the two cloaked riders were not breaking speed and were barreling down on the gate to exit the city. Casily continued to listen and heard two gate guards arguing about strict orders being issued to have it open at a certain time to allow two messengers from Captain Atalee to depart.

All she could hear were the guards rambling on about already having to open the gates once tonight on request from General Magnus, and that they were not sure if these individuals were allowed to depart, but King Thesias demanded it, so it had to happen. The rest of the conversation was muddled as they returned to their shack as the gate was closing. Casily could not focus on this right now. She needed to speak to Arsivus at once, so she turned around and faced Arsivus's hut in front of her. She knocked every so lightly and waited, but to no avail. No one could hear her.

"I do not have time for this right now!" she thought to herself and opened the door without hesitation.

"Who is there?" shouted Doran, as Arsivus turned the dial up on the oil lantern in the room to shed light throughout.

"Casily!" Arsivus shouted as he jumped off his cot and ran to her with a multitude of questions. "Are you all right? Did they hurt you? How did you escape? Were you followed?"

Casily smiled and sank into his arms. "I am fine, thank you for your concern!" she said happily. By this time, Kadath and Doran were up and standing behind the two as they embraced.

"What happened, madam?" Kadath promptly asked. So Casily told them everything that had happened since her departure from Arsivus, as well as everything that Korgal and Teslark did for her. She even mentioned the two cloaked riders that departed the castle gates only moments before.

When she had finished, Arsivus was enraged. "Tomorrow, at the tournament, I will —"

But Doran interrupted him before he could finish. "You will do as you have trained, and that is all. Casily will be with us the entire time, and we will be in General Magnus's company, so she will be in a much safer place than you, I am afraid!"

Kadath, Doran, and Casily found humor in this, while Arsivus was still thinking of all the punishment he would like to give to the King's sons.

Casily then said, "Teslark also mentioned something about his relative coming of age as a squire and being able to compete. And that he heard that his nephew was to be in the duels with the King's sons and their friend. And they are planning very horrible things for him."

Doran jumped in immediately. "If those little rats think they can dictate how the tournament shall run, then they have another thing coming. I will speak to Magnus prior to the start of tomorrow's events and remedy the situation at once."

"Korgal and Teslark, they assisted you in your endeavor to escape, did they?" Kadath asked Casily. "That is interesting. I will have to remember your words exactly!"

Arsivus looked at his father, and then back at Casily, and saw the worried look on Casily's face. "Father, I believe her. I believe what she said is true and of pure intentions."

"Very well, son. We shall see." Kadath laid back down on his bed and faced the wall, still within arm's reach of his sword that was leaning against his headboard.

Doran patted Casily on the back and gave a nod of approval as he remade his bed and sat down on it. "You are more than welcome to stay, my lady. There is a cot next to Arsivus with fresh linens upon it. Sleep well, and tomorrow will be a new day."

"Thank you," Casily said just loud enough for Arsivus to hear and continued on as he helped her make the bed. "Your father doesn't trust me,"

Arsivus laid down at the same time Casily did, and he looked into her eyes, "He does trust you. He has always been that way. He is wary of situations like these, especially since we don't see them too often on our farm."

Casily smiled. "Well, thank you for trusting me. I will repay you for your kindness!" And with that, she leaned over and gave him a soft kiss on his lips, as she gently ran her fingers over his ears and down to his shoulders.

"You need to get some sleep champion, for tomorrow is going to be a very busy day!" Then she turned over and faced away from him and quietly hummed herself to sleep. Arsivus lay still as his heart felt like it would beat out of his chest. He craved more but stifled his desires for the moment.

"After the tournament!" he thought to himself, "Then I will inquire more about that kiss. After the tournament." With that last thought, Arsivus quietly and quickly nodded off into the world of dreams that were filled with nothing but her.

CHAPTER 17

D awn broke upon the horizon as the morning birds began to fly across the sky. The cold brisk air was slowly erased by the warm embrace of the sun. The humidity brought a musky aroma that was heavy in the air. The day-lilies began to crest and the flowers bloomed as the sun began to shine upon the anxiety-ridden kingdom — the Seven Wizards tournament had arrived. Magnus placed his left hand on the wash basin and looked out over the distance from the balcony in his room. The view was not as regal as that of King Thesias, but Magnus's quarters offered him a peninsula balcony that stretched out from his main chamber and overlooked the mountains, the ocean, and the mountain pass with views virtually unobstructed. It was here that General Magnus would spend some of his time in free thought, or even just examining his homeland in peace.

"Today," General Magnus thought to himself, "shall be a monumental day, one that will shape our history forever. I just hope that it is in the right direction." He straightened his black ceremonial attire, which encompassed a gold theme throughout, while gazing into a mirror. He shifted his cloak emblem so that it sat level and looked proper. His sword hung heavily from his belt, and his black cloak laced with gold trim fluttered in the wind, as a banner would do on a ship caught in a mild sea storm.

From outside his room, Magnus heard a loud knocking accompanied by some voices. He took one last glance upon himself in the mirror as he walked over to the double oak doors that sealed his room tightly from the outside. As he opened the doors, he saw Doran, accompanied by Theros, Janos, and Cardage close behind him.

"My friends!" Magnus said with a happy tone. "What brings you up here on a morning such as this? Shouldn't we be concentrated on the events of today?"

Doran wasted no time and immediately walked into Magnus's room.

"General, we may have a problem!" Cardage said aloud as they entered his quarters. Doran went to the balcony and gave a quick look around the area to ensure they were truly alone. By this time, Magnus had closed his double doors, and all of the knights had joined Doran on the peninsula over-looking the kingdom. Theros and Janos walked over to the balcony that looked over the ocean and leaned on the railing that protected them from the steep fall down below. They turned their attention to Cardage and Doran.

The sun started to crest in the sky and the light began to dance down the stone and marble structure. Once it hit Magnus, it was truly a spectacular sight. Their leader, standing in his armor, was daunting and strong in front of his men.

"General, permission to speak freely?" Doran said while looking at his companions standing in front of their leader.

"Of course," Magnus replied.

"Your brother is attempting to dictate certain aspects of the games. We have it on good faith that your nephews are plotting to kill a young squire during the games. They are conspiring to have the duels be unfair, and they are apparently set on attempting to kill their challenger, a young squire, in front of everyone," Doran said.

Magnus looked unsurprised as he soaked in the information. Theros was the first to speak. "Sir, you seem to not be phased by this information."

Magnus took his time and formulated his words carefully. "I have heard my brother intends to make both of his offspring a part of the White Guard upon completion of the tournament. It seems that he has already determined the winner for this year's competition."

Janos replied with a snarky comment almost instantly. "Like they have the stones to even match the capabilities of anyone in the White Guard. I wonder what Atalee thinks of that?"

Magnus, not breaking his concentration or poise, responded with care. "Captain Atalee is the man who informed me of this. He is not happy with the decision either." This drew the complete attention of the four knights.

"Sir, why would he give you that information?" Theros asked.

Magnus gave a quick but stern reply, "Even though we have our many differences, I think we both agree that those kids are not good for this kingdom in any way."

"Sir, there is another matter," Doran said. "Last night, Casily said that after she was set free and assisted by Teslark and Korgal, she came upon two riders cloaked in black departing the kingdom after dark. No orders were run through us to have the gates opened, but your brother issued orders for them to open the gates and to tell no one."

Magnus replied, "I was aware of a threat made against our friend Kadath, the herb supplier. He is like a brother to me. Atalee had spoken of an ill-gotten fate toward his wife, so I ordered Mulik to dispatch three of his best knights to depart immediately last night. They were to report to Kadath's home to ensure nothing bad happens until we can get there. These other individuals must have been sent after Mulik's men departed. That is troubling news indeed. If the reports I have heard in the past are true, they are assassins from the Western Kingdom that are sell-swords to the crown. No one has seen them, but it was rumored that the White Guard uses them for tasks that need to be unassociated with the crown or his group. They are very dangerous men," Magnus said. "You said Teslark and Korgal assisted Casily in her escape. That is very interesting," he said with a half-smile.

"What shall we do, sir?" Janos asked as he stretched out his back as if preparing to go to battle.

Magnus gestured toward his door and they all started toward it together. "We shall go about the day as if nothing was amiss. I need to meet with Kadath immediately and inform him of the recent events. He may want to depart as soon as possible. Doran, bring him to me at the coliseum, as well as Casily. Janos and Theros, round up twenty of your best knights and be prepared at the main gates ready for battle. Prepare to ride light and fast, for if we depart westward to Kadath's home, I want no reason to stop. Cardage, before the tournament, find out what you can about the events, who is in which one and any potential conflicts that may arise. We play our parts with intent, and after the tournament, all who can will ride west. There may be danger outside of the castle, but I fear that there may be a greater danger within for today's competition. Does everyone understand?" Magnus asked.

In unison, the knights in his presence answered proudly and with strength, "Yes sir!" and departed as Magnus closed the door behind them.

"This indeed will be a monumental day," Magnus claimed as he gazed upon the sunlight breaching his chamber with a solemn look upon his face.

An hour had passed and Arsivus awoke to find Casily lying beside him still, although her eyes were wide open and looking into his. She smiled at him and he returned it with confidence. The salty smell of bacon was in the air as Kadath was cooking a hearty breakfast for his son and guest. Doran had long since been gone this morning, and the sun has started to extend its grasp upon the land. Casily stretched out her arms and playfully hit Arsivus in the shoulder.

She said to him, "Today is going to be a big day. I hope you got some decent sleep last night!" Arsivus had actually wondered how he fell asleep since he felt like he could do nothing but think of her the entire night.

All he could say was, "I am well rested now, and I feel I am as ready for the tournament as I will ever be."

"That is good to hear," Kadath said as he pulled the bacon from the pot stove in the corner. He placed a fresh baguette down on the table and put bacon on everyone's plate, serving Arsivus the most since he would need the most energy. Fresh red berries from the market and cold milk from the local farmer completed the meal. As Arsivus and Casily took their seats at the table, Kadath continued to eye Casily suspiciously as she picked at her food. Arsivus noticed and immediately brought up the events of the day in an attempt to distract his father.

"Father," Arsivus said with purpose. "Will Casily be with you when the tournament starts?"

Kadath looked at his son. "Yes, she shall be in the company of me, General Magnus, and Sir Doran for the entirety of the day. I assure you, there shall be no safer place than within our company!" he replied. Arsivus, somewhat relieved by the news, calmed himself down and looked toward Casily. She gave him a hearty smile. He continued to eat his meal but could not fight the feeling that something was amiss with Casily this morning. Her mannerisms had changed. She seemed more reserved, more careful, and more calculating than how he had known her to be in the past couple of days.

Arsivus looked again at his female friend, and as their eyes met, he returned the smile to assure her that he trusted her fully, as well as cared for her very much. Kadath looked over and recognized the look. It was the same stare that he and Evra continually gave each other.

Not to be drawn into a place of endearment, Kadath broke the silence with a laugh and said, "Well, son, today is the day. Finish up your meal, for we have much to cover in a short amount of time before the activities start. Casily, make yourself ready, for we must depart within the hour to make it to the coliseum in time to prepare." Casily glanced at Kadath and nodded her head in agreement.

She took one last bite of bacon and said to Kadath, "Thank you for the generous meal. I agree, we should be departing very quickly. The other contestants will be arriving shortly and it would be nice to speak with them prior to the contest and learn what we can from them."

As Casily finished her sentence, Arsivus pushed his empty plate away and said, "I am ready. Let us go and learn of these other contenders. I am most anxious to meet the man from the Western Kingdom. I do have some questions for him."

Kadath let out a quick smile, yet Casily seemed more worried now that Arsivus brought up the strange man. A horse could be heard galloping toward the home and stopping right outside. Within seconds Doran busted through the door.

"Hello, friend!" Kadath said. "There is breakfast if you would like. We are getting ready to depart for the coliseum as we speak, so you had better hurry if you wish to join us."

Doran, not willing to waste any more time, cut in. "Friends, we must hurry indeed. Casily and Kadath, you are to come with me immediately to General Magnus. Arsivus, you as well, but we need to leave now. Gather all of your things. We must go."

Arsivus was a little confused and worried. He started putting his gear together and could not help but ask, "Sir Doran, what is the matter? Why are we being rushed into the coliseum?"

Doran not wanting to speak out of turn simply said, "The General has very important information for all of you. We must not delay any longer."

Kadath said, "Son, no more questions. If General Magnus needs us, he has a very good reason as to why he sent Sir Doran to get us. We must go." Arsivus finished gathering his clothes and gear and walked outside of the lodge with the rest of his crew. By the time they mounted their horses, the sun was already starting to climb high in the sky. The heat was starting to penetrate the land and most of the city was awake and on their way to the games to get good seating. As they hurriedly made their way toward the coliseum, the pathways were starting to get clogged with the townsfolk.

As they got closer to the coliseum, more people started to notice Doran and Casily. Their eyes quickly turned to Arsivus as he was of the right age to compete, and they immediately started drifting toward him to learn his name and where he was from. This slowed the process significantly as more people were drawn toward them. They reached a standstill and not even Doran could keep them moving.

The crowd that formed around them was quite extensive, and everyone seemed to be speaking at once, which brought more confusion. Arsivus was attempting to be polite, but it was starting to get very hot out with all of their gear and they needed to start moving soon. In the distance, Arsivus could see the coliseum in all of its glory, standing tall and ominous overlooking parts of the city. As he peered farther, he could see a man slowly walking through the corridor.

Upon his back, he saw a giant sword draped across a blue cape. "The Western champion," he thought to himself. As he tried to move forward, he was met with more and more people and stiffer resistance.

Out of nowhere, a bellowing voice could be heard, "Make an opening, let them pass!" Casily smiled as she immediately recognized it. Everyone in the surrounding vicinity stopped what they were doing and looked around.

From a couple shops ahead, a giant could be seen walking toward the four as they were trying to get to the coliseum. "Korgal, so very nice to see you again!" Casily exclaimed as he drew near the group. Teslark appeared from behind him. Doran, still a little hesitant from their previous engagement, remained steadfast. Kadath gave a reassuring nod to the rest of the group to follow. As the crowd started to part, Korgal and Teslark responded with a smile. Once Arsivus and his group reached the two White Guard, they slowed down for an instant.

"You have my thanks," Kadath said to each of them and was met with a nod from both of the elite fighters.

"Thank you, Korgal, and fear not, Teslark, I have passed word of your nephew. Arsivus will see it done," Casily said as she turned her gaze to Arsivus. Arsivus looked at Teslark and nodded in agreement. This brought a half smile to Teslark's face as he motioned with his head for the group to continue on toward the coliseum.

As the group proceeded several strides past the White Guard, Teslark shouted out to Arsivus, "Nothing but your best, kid." Arsivus heard him loud and clear and understood what he meant. Teslark was telling him to give it his all and do what he must to win, and to protect his nephew. Without turning back, Arsivus raised his right hand to signify he understood. This brought not only a smile to Arsivus, but also to the rest of his group, even Doran, as they continued to move forward.

"Let's go. We are of limited time and need to be in position," Janos shouted from behind his troops as they were massing near the stables just out of view of the main gate. The armory was stocked full of equipment to supply Magnus and his knights their swords and armor, although Janos and Theros had far greater equipment than the common knight. Janos was outfitted with a beautiful broadsword sharpened and taken down to be swung with one hand, while his other hand grasped the shield designated for General Magnus's most trusted knights. Its crest, which was centered on the face of the shield, was a picture of a sword shining bright, and in the background, a castle on fire.

Their armor maintained its brilliance under the intense rays of the sun. The clasps glowed with strength, and the chain mail covered all of the vital parts while allowing for greater movement. Each one of Magnus's Lieutenants had the same armor and also had blue capes that flew behind them, that complemented the darkish white armor surrounding their bodies. The Lieutenant's horses were black Friesian breeds and the fastest in the land. Even the White Guard were not privy to steeds such as these. As the knights started coming in, Theros and Janos could be seen nearest their beautiful horses and ready for battle. Most of them coming in were familiar faces from the raid in the Northern Forest, but there were a couple of new knights that were present. Theros left Janos's side and went around to inspect everyone's gear to ensure that they were traveling light and ready for anything.

"Sir, what exactly are our orders for this mission? You haven't told us anything yet." one knight asked as she was packing her saddle.

Another knight chimed in almost instantly. "I heard we are to ride west again, toward the Forest." While they were all clamoring about, Theros started to fill them in on the details of their mission while the knights sat in disbelief.

Theros said, "There has been credible information that one of the allies to our kingdom will be under attack. Actually, attack is the wrong word," Theros said as he tightened one of the straps on his men's horse. "The word I was avoiding was assassinated. She is an innocent woman and defenseless, from what I hear. It is the General's wish that we depart upon his command to prevent that from happening." With his final inspection, he turned back to the men and looked them over vigorously.

Janos shifted his weight and could see the questions forming in their men's minds. Before they had a chance to ask, Janos answered it for them. "The assassins that were sent were two, neither from our ranks nor the White Guard. We have had reports of individuals from the Western Kingdom, very nasty men that have infiltrated our city walls and are providing less than honorable services to our King. Mulik sent three men from his banner last night to provide protection. We are their backup. What Mulik's men do not know, is the caliber of the enemy that is coming their way. Once the General and his friend Kadath are with us, we shall depart immediately. So be on your guard. It will be a hard and fast ride."

The knights remained silent. A few nodded their heads in acceptance of their task. Janos went back to grooming his steed. Theros approached him from behind.

"Not sure we needed to tell them everything about the assassins that left last night," Theros said as he rested his arm upon his saddle.

Janos let out a sly laugh and continued to brush his horse down. "It is a mistake to wait. We should be departing right now. Too much can happen in this small amount of time, and we are already behind."

Theros quickly acknowledged the statement but refuted it, saying, "I know exactly what you mean, but it is the General's orders that we stay. We cannot break his command. He must have a reason as to why we must wait for him."

Janos, not liking the answer, abruptly responded, "I know. I just hope we don't go north after we reach the house. I would much rather stay out of the Northern Forest again . . . for the rest of my life if possible. It was beautiful, but whatever resided within the perimeter of those trees certainly did not appreciate our presence in the least bit."

Theros smiled as he nodded his head in agreement. "You are right. It certainly was marvelous that way. So much land, so much potential. One day when my duties are served to the King, I may retire in that area. It would be fit for a knight indeed."

The morning bells were ringing throughout the kingdom as a warm breeze moved through the alleyways and seeped through the large castle gates. A loud clang could be heard from across the way, behind the group of knights waiting to depart on their General's command.

As they all turned about to face the clamor, they saw that a young girl was running through the alleys knocking over pots and plates as she went. A distinctive cry could be heard from her as she continued to run briskly through the corridors.

Theros looked to Janos, and Janos quickly nodded his head and whistled for his bannermen. "Gents, let's take a look, shall we?" Janos said with optimism. With that command, four knights departed their steeds and followed Janos into the alley after the girl. What started as an initial trot quickly changed. The little girl continued to swerve in and out of pedestrians and poorly made kiosks standing in the alleys. Luckily for the knights, they were clad in their lightest gear, which greatly improved their mobility. This allowed them to stay within visual range of the girl as she sprinted through the market and down alleyways.

They continued the chase as one of the knights from the back shouted out to Janos, "Sir, I am glad you decided not to wait to start our mission but shouldn't we at least have brought our horses to go that far west. I mean, I am okay with running there, but I am not sure about Parcy here making it all the way." He motioned to the knight several steps behind him who was having a tough time catching his breath.

Janos, not breaking stride or focus, quickly retorted, "Well, if you can't make it to the west on foot, what good are you to me?" which encouraged all the men to give a quick chuckle as they continued on. Janos knew his kingdom well and started to get a tingly feeling in his spine as he started to realize where they were heading. After a little bit, he held up his right hand to bring his troops to a slow stop as they were nearing the alleys close to Fallen Row. Once they were at the entrance to Fallen Row, they approached slowly and cautiously.

At the very end of the cages, they could see some commotion happening, but none of the prisoners along the way were aware of the events. As they got nearer, they could see that there were two groups of people forming around what looked like one of the cages. On the left side, there appeared to be three individuals all wearing black cloaks, and on the right, there were another three individuals dressed the same. They were all facing the cage, but Janos could not tell if they were men or women because they all had the same build. Janos now had a very suspicious feeling come over him.

"Parcy, stay here and keep watch of the exit," Janos commanded. Parcy stopped and found a wall to lean upon and fixed himself into a more comfortable position.

"Himus, Darius, and Ioma, come with me," Janos said as he motioned to the other three knights. "Look alive, and no joking here," he said to Darius, as he was the one that was making fun of Parcy. As they formed up into a wall of four, they started to walk carefully down the alleyway with the cages in clear view of them. The prisoners inside were motionless and did not look up. The knights gave their best effort to not show their remorse for them as they passed by on their way to the two groups down the path. Janos looked at the crowd and saw the little girl loitering around the right side of the cage.

She was wearing a bright red hood, white shoes, and a black dress, as black as the others that were there with her. Her blonde hair flowed back like a windstorm was forming right in front of her. Janos motioned toward his men to take notice and then gave them instructions via hand gesture to split into two groups in case there was danger.

Janos and Darius went to the right, and Himus and Ioma went to the left. All but Janos had their hands on the hilt of their swords as they slowly approached the groups from behind. From this viewpoint, Janos could see the group on the left had two men and one woman all staring intently at the cage, which was covered with a cloak.

From Ioma's viewpoint, he could see that there was one man and two women on Janos's side along with the little girl who now had centered herself on the cage between the two groups of individuals and was facing in the knight's direction with her head down. Her hair was still flowing wildly, although Janos came to realize that it was extremely cold and there was no wind coming down the alley. Janos looked back at his men and brought his gaze down to their weapons and nodded slowly. Ioma and Himus gripped the hilt of their swords and slowly started to draw their weapons as Darius quickly followed suit. Parcy was still leaning against the wall enjoying his breather and listening to the birds and market dealings that were being shouted through the air.

He was surprised that he could even hear it for how far away they were. But then he noticed a chill come over him as he sat there. He looked into the sky and saw the sun rising fast into the early afternoon and squinted his eyes in confusion. He pushed himself away from the wall. "That was odd," he said as he turned his attention to his comrades down the alley. He saw Janos from a distance slowly starting to draw his blade and giving himself distance between himself and the girl. Parcy immediately drew his sword and started walking quickly toward the group when he noticed the prisoners in the cages were all looking directly at him.

Their eyes glowed a fiery blue and it felt as if they were burning a hole directly into his body. As Parcy took a couple more steps toward Janos and the group, the prisoners started breathing quickly and in unison.

"Hgh, hgh, hgh, hgh, hgh, hgh, hgh," Their loud grunts could be heard echoing down Fallen Row. Parcy looked toward Janos as Janos and his men looked back at him, for they could hear it now too. Parcy quickly began to trot toward his comrades. As he neared them, the gaze from the prisoners followed him, as did the chanting. As Parcy came to a stop in between the two groups of knights, the chanting stopped, but the gaze remained and looked more menacing than ever.

The position in the alleyway from where they just came, appeared dark and ominous, and nothing like it should be with the sun rising in the sky on a beautiful warm day.

Parcy turned to Janos with a look of concern. "What do we do, boss?" Parcy asked as the other knights looked around cautiously. Janos looked over his men. They are well-built men, tall, strong, great fighters, and had seen many battles together, but he could tell they were nervous. They have never seen anything like this before, nor had he. Janos summoned his courage, tightened his grip on his sword, and turned back to the little girl who started all this in the alleyway. He assumed his position in the middle of the knights.

Being the one in command, Janos issued the first words toward the group and the little girl. "Little girl, what is the matter? Why have you run all this way with tears clouding your eyes?" There was silence. Not even a breeze could be heard. The sounds from the market had ceased completely and the warmth of the sun was now gone. All that could be felt was a constant chill in the bones and the feeling of danger. The little girl was motionless. The knights remained steadfast, not moving but ever ready, and continued to wait.

Janos tried again. "Little girl, what is your name? What business have you here?" A low growl could be heard from the girl. Slowly she raised her arms above her head.

Janos, a bit taken back, continued to press. "Little girl, where have you come from?" The little girl slowly tilted her head up toward the sky with her eyes closed. Before anyone could say anything or question her any more, she turned her back to them with her head still tilted skyward. Himus licked his lips and appeared ready to attack at any moment, his hand clenching his sword with all of his strength. Normal tactics for them would be to sort out their enemies, "But what about the little girl? Was she a threat? Was she a combatant?" These thoughts were rummaging through each of the knight's minds.

The little girl slowly lowered her head down, her eyes still closed. She lowered her arms and turned to face the knights, as did the two groups of black-robed people now behind her. The five knights spread out to give themselves room as they were expecting the worse. They faced the seven individuals. Janos stayed strong in the middle and continued to look at the girl.

"Little girl, answer me. Who are you, and what are you doing here?" The little girl opened her eyes suddenly and stared directly through Janos with solid black eyes void of any light.

Darius gasped aloud, "Ugh!"

Silence was all that could be heard until the girl opened her mouth. "We were the ones before, and we will be the ones after. Our return is imminent," she said in a very low tone.

Janos, appearing unfazed, asked, "What is it you seek, little girl?"

She looked directly up into his eyes and said with a slow deep voice, "Power, destruction, death." With that, a gust of wind came up and thick black smoke exploded in front of all of them. When the smoke cleared, there was no trace left of the seven that had just been there.

"Witchcraft!" Ioma said.

"What did she mean, sir? Where did they go?" Himus asked. Darius was not in the mood for any jokes now as he was debating whether he was losing his mind. Parcy looked back and saw that the prisoners in their cages had returned to normal, although none of them were speaking. Janos looked at the cage that the seven had been huddled around. It was still covered with a black cloak. Janos took his sword and put the tip into the cloth on top of the cage and slowly drug it off. There was nothing inside, except for one piece of parchment paper. There was smoke coming from it as it lay upon the floor of the cage.

Janos quickly opened the cage, grabbed the paper, and pulled it up for all to see. It appeared to be a map of a continent. On the map, the smoke continued to rise up as an X was magically being burned into the map.

"What is that? What does that mean?" Ioma asked quietly. Janos had studied the maps of the world in his younger years and he knew what this map displayed.

Janos replied, "Gentlemen, this is the Western Kingdom. That X is where the Great Hall of the Seven were before they ended the war!"

Parcy jumped in. "We must report this at once!"

Janos nodded in agreement, "Yes, we must. It is odd that on the day of the Seven Wizards tournament we might have just seen them ourselves, or at least a version of them. Something is happening and this cannot be ignored. Someone needs to go west and investigate. We will consort with General Magnus and Cardage and let them know, but until then, we keep this to ourselves, understood?"

His men all agreed as they sheathed their swords and turned back down Fallen Row to return to the gate. None of the prisoners were speaking or even looking at the knights. Janos was unsure of what they saw and experienced, but he did not want to bring it up again. The walk back was silent. No one said a word, for the words never formed on their tongues that could make a sensible statement.

CHAPTER 18

C ardage stood in the middle of the coliseum training
arena where all of the events of the tournament would
take place. His gaze was fixated on a slow-moving cloud that
was seemingly being drawn into the rising sun but had no
escape. The people of Affinity were starting to slowly filter
in. Armorers and smithies were preparing their workshops
for the tournament, as vendors were setting up their stands.
The fresh smell of herbs and bread drifted through the air.

The constant chatter of people haggling prices echoed
loudly off the coliseum walls and fell upon Cardage's ears.
His eyes were wandering through the crowds of people, not
looking for anyone, but at the same time seeing everyone.
His observations stopped when he spied King Thesias's sons
walking through the doorways into the coliseum.

Zenor and Ruvio were uncreative in their attempts to
stifle their laughter while they looked upon the noblemen
and women in their finest garments, whose value appeared
well worn and outdated, much unlike what the two young
princes were wearing. As the princes continued down the

path, the townsfolk appeared discouraged and even embarrassed about their attire, for no other reason than the way the two spoiled children acted toward them, believing themselves to be better than everyone else. They stopped at a bread stand and took a loaf off the front stand while the baker was pulling another out of the brick oven. Zenor grabbed the loaf and broke it in half and gave one half to Ruvio.

The baker saw this and immediately protested. "By what means and rights have you to steal from my shop?" the baker yelled for all to hear. This caught the attention of the metal workers nearby, as well as a single guard, who paid no attention and averted his eyes back toward the sand beneath him. Ruvio took a bite of the bread and chewed contently for a couple of seconds while Zenor broke his half into smaller pieces and took a bite out of one. Zenor immediately spit his chewed-up piece out at the baker and threw his bread on the table. His toss knocked over a couple more loaves that had just come out of the oven and were resting on the table to cool.

Zenor said in a loud tone matching the one in which the baker had addressed them, "Do you know who we are, my little peasant? We rule this kingdom. Who are you to bring judgment upon us? What have you to say for yourself?"

The baker still angry and yet taken back, managed to mutter, "Royalty or not, that is still stealing and you will answer for it." Ruvio took an unimaginably large bite from his loaf and stared directly at the baker as he chewed it.

Zenor continued. "Well, well, well, stealing. That is quite an accusation. Have you any proof of this? A false statement like that, especially against your rulers! That could prove to be very costly."

The baker pointed toward Ruvio. "My proof is right there, in his hand!" Now the metal workers stopped their preparation and were slowly starting to gather closer to the baker's stand. Ruvio stopped chewing. His mouth was full of chewed-up bread and he looked back at Zenor and gave a quirky smile. Ruvio opened his mouth and let the bread fall out slowly and as disgustingly as he could. Once his mouth was empty, he raised the bread and dropped it on the sand floor and began to slowly walk away. Zenor continued to smile.

He turned back and said in a spoiled tone, "What proof have you?" as they continued toward the entrance to the inner rooms of the arena and disappeared around a corner. As they disappeared, the baker shook his head in anger and two of the metal workers came up and offered their apologies for the princes.

Cardage began to walk over to the baker and see if he was okay when someone called out to him. The voice came from the main gate that led into the underground area of the arena where the fighters would rest between their matches.

"Sir, sir, may I have a moment? It is of utmost importance. You need to see this." Cardage turned around and saw the games coordinator running toward him with scrolls in his hands.

"Sir Cardage, a moment please!" he said as he finally reached Cardage's side.

"Hello, good sir, how may I be of assistance?" Cardage asked as the coordinator adjusted his tunic.

"My name is Yura. I am planning the events for the tournament. This will be my — "

Before he could finish his sentence, Cardage cut him off. "Yes, Yura, I remember you from the last tournament. I was hoping you could help me with a couple of tasks."

Yura nodded his head in agreement and said, "Sir, I would love to, but I have an urgent need of your counsel at this moment. I will be more than happy assist you with your tasks, but I must ask for your assistance in the meantime. Shall we be off then?" Yura asked with impatience as he turned to leave.

Cardage nodded and followed Yura back under the big metal gate to go underneath the coliseum. Cardage had not been down here in a long time and had forgotten how long the corridor was. He looked up at the ceiling, at least thirty feet above the floor, and admired the way it was rounded and arched all of the way around the coliseum. They began passing the statues carved from ivory that rested every hundred feet from each other on the outer edge of the ring that enclosed the arena. As they walked, Cardage noticed that one of the mighty statues was lying on its side. Where the statue normally rested, there was a partially broken wall and behind the wall was an iron lever attached to the cage. Through the wall, they could see iron bars running vertically to the ceiling.

A musky, damp smell seemed to be coming from the broken wall. As they stood looking at the hole, Cardage picked up a hammer that was nearby and gave a heavy swing with it against the wall. The impact echoed through the corridor and more of the wall came crumbling down, which revealed more of the iron lever. Behind the wall was a thick iron gate that was now revealed. Through the gate, they could see stairs spiraling downward, but they fell into darkness and they couldn't see anything after a certain point. Yura walked toward the gate and pulled out a very extensive ring of large metal keys and began to sort through them.

Cardage didn't understand. He looked around and saw they were alone. He looked back at Yura. "How come I have never known of this hidden door before?" Cardage asked sternly.

Yura continued to flip through the keys until he found a very unique small and thick key that looked unlike any key Cardage had ever seen. "That was the reason for the urgency, sir. This wall was just recently uncovered, it looks like one of the legs finally gave away which caused it to fall. And now we are hearing very concerning sounds from down below. None of the guards here will enter. That is why we need you to go take a look," Yura said.

Cardage was a bit taken back. He looked slyly at Yura and at the key in his hand, and then at the iron gate. "If this door was recently discovered, how did you come by that key then?" Cardage asked.

Yura gave his immediate answer. "When I came into this position several years ago, I ensured that I knew every key on this chain and its home. Throughout this entire city, I have never come across anything that looked like a match for this one. I just assumed that it was some type of weight or fancy gift made for the key holder. I never would have believed it had an actual use for something."

Cardage found solace in his answer but responded quickly as he unsheathed his sword from his hip. "This is a journey that we are going to take together, my friend. You shall hold the torch behind me, and we will descend together." Yura turned the lock to the left and several clicks and latches could be heard coming undone. The door swung and creaked forward into the stairwell as it opened. Yura gave one look at Cardage as Cardage started his descent down. Yura ran to the opposite side of the corridor and grabbed a lit torch off the wall and returned to the hidden door to join Cardage. They headed down a very large and twisted staircase that had smooth walls and stone footings that were sturdy and old. As Yura caught up to Cardage, the torch started to reveal claw marks carved into the stone wall on the way down.

Yura, his voice shaking but within close proximity to Cardage, managed to ask, "What beast could have done such a thing? This is solid stone. It would be impossible for any animal to make these marks!"

Cardage paused and looked for a moment, but then pressed on. "We won't find any answers up here, now will we?" he said as he continued down the staircase. Upon getting close to the bottom, a very frigid chill began to creep up the old and trampled stairway and a faint light could be observed from below. After only a few minutes, the chill had penetrated every part of Cardage's body. Cardage kept his calm and wits about him and finally reached the bottom. He felt the wind flowing freely even though they were underground. It provided a cool atmosphere as their eyes began to adjust to their surroundings.

Cardage turned to Yura and said, "Leave the torch lit, but keep it in the stairwell so whoever or whatever is down here does not see it." Yura, against his own desires, followed his order and ran up about ten stairs and left the torch on the ground. He came back down and joined Cardage on the bottom as their eyes adjusted fully to the chamber. Across from them, there was a massive table with at least twenty chairs surrounding it. There was fresh water flowing through the corner of the room into a reservoir and then disappearing below the surface. Off the main chamber, it appeared that there were doorways leading into different rooms.

On the far side, two torches could be seen lit and hanging in the wall offering an end to the room they were standing in. Nobody appeared, so Cardage took a few more steps into the room. They saw that the rooms off the main chambers were sleeping quarters that contained evenly spaced beds in each. There was a stairway between the torches at the end of the corridor that led up.

"What is this place?" Yura asked with wonder. Cardage, still running ideas through his head, could only think that they must be a long way down, which meant either they were down at the surface and that was ocean water coming in through the corner, or they were partially under the mountain and it was a water runoff from underneath the mountain.

Cardage looked around and said, "This was created a long time ago, you can tell by the design. Rooms and chambers are not built like this anymore. What is over there?" he asked quickly. Yura turned around and they both looked at a grand iron door with reinforced braces that dug deep into the ground below the door, as well as above it. There were six bars in the middle of the door that were evenly spaced about two inches apart in a span of a foot that ran from the ceiling to the floor. Cardage and Yura walked slowly up to the door and saw that there was a keyhole in it that looked exactly like the one that led them down there.

"Open it!" Cardage commanded as Yura fumbled to retrieve the key. As he was searching for it, Cardage took a closer look through the bars.

"Stop. Don't move!" Cardage said as he peered closer through the spacing. "I do not believe my eyes, but I know this to be true," Cardage said as he leaned back from the door.

"What? What is it?" Yura asked as he looked through the door himself. On the other side was a wide walkway that narrowed into a bridge that extended deep into a great chasm. After the path narrowed, it ran into a central platform that was attached to a ceremonial bridge with another platform at the very end. The ceiling was incredibly high, which made it impossible to determine its height, and it was rounded like a bowl that dropped down into the walls and continued to descend straight down into blackness. There was light shining in the middle of the room from what appeared to be a hole in the ceiling.

The sun shined into the room and lightened it up, but only to the main floor that they were on. What resided beneath was covered in blackness and mystery. At the end of the narrow stone bridge was a circular platform that was suspended by what appeared to be a thick stone column that extended from the chasm's ground level. Upon the platform were three gigantic totems carved in the images of past kings.

One was at the far end of the platform and the other two were on the sides, forming a perfect triangle. Their positions were that of men bracing themselves against something pulling away from them. Their arms were extended outward, and in each of their hands were thick iron chains that were attached to something imprisoned in chains between the three of them. The light from above continued to spread over the figure sitting down. The creature was enormous, but the iron chains ensured it stayed put and only allowed for a little movement. Even from that distance, it could be seen that the creature was breathing slowly and heavily.

It sat upon the floor facing the same iron door that Cardage and Yura were looking through. Its face was level, staring at them both as they peered into the dark and ominous chamber. The creature's face was that of a bull with extended horns that curled down and rose up sharply. Its massive shoulders rode up to its neckline and were rigid with muscle and battle scars. The arms were built for destroying whatever got in their way and were protected by arm bracers that were made from thick metal. At the end of each arm were five claws grown from deep within the hand that showed lethality and strength.

The torso was built from muscle and bulk, and around its waist was an iron belt made into circles and odd shapes. There was a sackcloth of red strewn from the belt and a skull on the very front of it. The red cloth was flowing behind it as it was seated, but the large metal bracers could be seen wrapped around its legs that were encased with muscle. Looking at the face, all that could be seen were complete white eyes staring back at them.

Cardage pulled Yura back and looked him in the eyes. "Open it," he said again as Yura shook his head no. "Open it now," Cardage said as he gripped his sword tightly.

Yura put the key in the hole and said only this, "You're a fool!" He turned the key and the lock mechanisms and the door started to creak open just as the one in the stairwell had done. With the opening of the door, the creature stood up immediately and settled into a battle stance. Cardage paused for a moment and just admired what was before him. The creature was just about double his size in height and massive in its own right. He could see the breathing had picked up as the creature's muscles were flexing with hate and power at the same time. Cardage did not know what he had gotten himself into, but he knew that this creature was not here of its own doing. Although that did not give him any more comfort in the fact that he was down here alone with this massive beast. Time seemed to stand still as Cardage admired the beast, while the beast maintained its battle stance without moving an inch. "Such power, such steadiness, beautiful," Cardage thought to himself. When the silence began to get too much, Cardage was the first to break words, as Yura stayed at the door. The distance between them and the beast was great, so Cardage took several steps closer and announced loudly, "I was unaware of us having a guest, my apologies. My name is Cardage. I am second in command here for General Magnus, protector of the realm," Cardage said with a tone of apology and with as much comfort as he could spare regarding the circumstances. He stopped proceeding and waited for a response. Nothing. No movement, no words, no actions whatsoever from the beast.

Cardage took several more steps until he was where the path narrowed leading up to the large creature and asked, "What is your name? How did you come by these restraints and how long have you been here?" he asked of the beast. The only movement that could be seen from the beast was its chest rising and lowering with every breath it took. Cardage continued to walk closer to the beast. He was now crossing over the narrow path, and as he walked, he looked down and saw darkness staring back at him. He felt a cool draft coming from the center platform where the beast was and heard trickling water falling in the back of the chasm as he got closer. Cardage could see a large reservoir by one of the statues that was collecting water from the opening in the ceiling. Clearly this was meant to be a torturous prison room for very bad individuals.

The only feasible way of escape was along the bridge that was ahead of Cardage, over the narrow path he had just crossed and through the large iron gates, which seemed almost impossible to destroy, even for the beast. As Cardage came upon the bridge, the beast began a low growl that would stop the hearts of lesser men. Cardage stopped in his tracks and slowly put his hands up. As he did that, he realized that his sword was still drawn. Immediately regretting this, he hurriedly put the sword back in its sheath and then removed his weapons altogether and placed them on the bridge. He lay down the sword and a couple of knives and then removed his armor and placed it atop the weapons.

With this done, he turned and faced the gigantic beast and said, "My apologies, I did not mean to offend you or make you think my intentions were impure. I have never been down here and I did not know it even existed. Do you have a name?" Cardage asked as politely as he could as he moved a couple steps closer.

The beast seemed to understand and relaxed his stance a little. Cardage looked to his left and right and saw that he was just outside of the reach of the creature.

"I mean you no harm or ill will. I would like to talk with you," Cardage said as he took four more steps closer, putting him well within range of the beast. Cardage's heart had never beaten as fast as it was beating right now. His legs began to tremble a bit and he did everything he could to stop them.

"Who are you?" Cardage asked again. Before he could think of another question, the beast rushed forward and stopped within inches of Cardage. The beast towered over him by several feet and just stood there. Cardage could see the slack in the chains lying behind the beast, and he realized that it could have killed him if it had wanted to, but it didn't.

"Who are you?" Cardage managed to ask again, only this time his voice was a little shakier.

"You are brave. I could have killed you. You know this?" the beast said in a deep and terrifying voice.

"Yes, of course I do," Cardage responded, "But I mean you no harm.

"My name is Midemos. I am an Eglician from the Western Kingdom. By your look, you have never seen one of my kind before?" Midemos said with a challenging voice.

Cardage shook his head. "You are absolutely correct. You would be my first. How did one such as you become captive?"

Midemos let out a quick grunt. "Eglicians are strong, but betrayal is very strong as well. Sometimes stronger than Eglician. I journeyed to this land with a companion several years ago. He and I had intentions to come to the Eastern Kingdom for some time. He had a great desire to explore all of the land, and I was on a spiritual journey. Upon arriving on the western shores of this kingdom, we were led into a trap.

We fought well, but in the end the cowards used sleeping agents to render us defenseless. When I awoke, I was being sold to a man who wore a crown and my friend was gone. My guide received the payment of gold and they draped a cloth over my cage as I was shipped away. I was chained down and they continued to use their sleeping agents on me so I could not break free. I fought them at every chance I had. The last time was down those steps over there, and I killed two of their men. But here I ultimately reside, chained up. My life has been flowing by as I watch the sun and moon do the same above me."

Cardage looked at the iron chains and saw that they were the same type of lock that was on the iron door they unlocked. "What did they want of you? Surely not to parade you around as a trophy or the King would have already done so. What is it that he desired?" Cardage asked.

Midemos took a step back and sat back down. "The man with the crown wanted to know if my kind had any strange powers or magical trinkets!" he said.

Cardage immediately perked up and responded, "So he has been looking all over for those then. It seems for quite some time as well." Cardage thought for a second. "What did you tell him?"

"I didn't answer," Midemos said. "You are the first person I have spoken to since I've been here. There was nothing more your King could do to me. No one dared get close enough."

Cardage smiled and continued. "Good. Our King cannot be trusted. I am second in command to General Magnus, the King's brother. There has been a deep rift between the two for several years now." Cardage proceeded to tell Midemos of everything, the raids in the Northern Forest, the pendants, the King, and the tournament.

Midemos rose after their conversation. He gave a quick stretch and said, "Your King promised my freedom if I were to intervene in this tournament. I was told that if I were to be called up, I was to ensure the King's sons were victorious in the tournament. Then, and only then would I have my freedom."

Cardage shook his head. "I shall free you before that, my friend. You will not remain hostage while I still have breath."

Midemos pulled his hands back and said, "I do not want you to suffer for setting me free. Find a way to have me summoned during the contest and give me a weapon, preferably my hunting staff, which I can feel is still in the chamber where your friend continues to lurk. It is impossible to miss. It is almost as tall as I and is made of thick black oak with massive blades on each end. Have that ready for me, and I will make my own escape."

Cardage agreed, but gave warning with his response, "I will do what I can, but I must also say, there are four individuals in the tournament who are not under direction of King's decree. They are innocent, if you can and are able, you must spare them. Our General would be very grateful if you did and would give you what you ask in return."

Midemos nodded his head in acceptance. "I will do what I can to see that they remain unharmed," Midemos responded. Cardage smiled as Midemos relaxed a bit more.

Cardage looked back and saw Yura continuing to stare through the doorway at him and Midemos. He turned back to Midemos again and said, "My friend, the tournament shall start today. With that, I am to be topside near the General. I shall inform him of this conversation, as well as these chambers, and together we will devise a plan to ensure your appearance."

Cardage went to grab his gear that was lying upon the bridge when an idea struck him. "Midemos, hold on one second." With that, Cardage yelled for Yura. "Yura, come here. I am in need of your assistance." Yura, still hiding behind the doorway, peeked his head out and leaned out of the doorway.

"Yura, come here!" Cardage commanded. With that, Yura started his slow walk toward the platform where Cardage and Midemos were. Ages seemed to pass before Yura reached them, and when he finally did, Cardage asked only one request. "My friend, I need the key that opened these gates. This shall not be counted upon as your loss. For I know the key master to the city has certain duties to uphold. I shall take blame for losing this key."

Yura was hesitant but asked anyway. "What do you mean for losing this key? What do you intend to do?"

Cardage held out his hand for Yura to place the key within it and said only this, "We are doing what is right, as well as what is required. Midemos will hold the key to his fate!"

At this point Midemos, interrupted and said, "My friend, Cardage, I will not accept this key as of yet. If your plan for me to appear comes to fruition, then deliver me the key. Until that moment, you shall hold it, as I trust you, and you will determine the best time for my escape."

Cardage looked at Midemos with questionable eyes, but ultimately agreed that this was the best option. Cardage looked at Yura, and then at Midemos and said, "You shall be free by the end of this day, on my life I swear it. It shall be the most opportune time for you to leave this land and return home. I will see to it myself!" Cardage said as he put the key within his cloak.

Cardage turned to Yura and stated, "The events of today did not happen. You were never down here and you never witnessed any of what you have just seen or heard. Do you understand?"

Yura nodded his head and said, "I will not repeat the events of today until my dying breath. You have my word."

With that, Cardage looked back toward Midemos and said, "I must be off. We will close everything back up, but be ready, for you shall be called upon yet today. Be safe and await our word."

Midemos nodded his bulky head in agreement as Cardage picked up the remainder of his gear and put it back on. "Let's go," Cardage said to Yura as they both turned toward the large iron gate that sealed the chamber. Upon reaching the doorway, Cardage commanded Yura to go and retrieve Midemos's fighting staff. Yura followed the commands and ran over to the wall that the weapon was mounted upon and attempted to lift it off the mantel. He picked one end up and the weight surprised him as it quickly fell to the floor. Yura went to the other side and picked it up and set it down on the floor as well.

Cardage looked over and gave an inquisitive look toward Yura.

Yura, sensing that he was being watched, immediately looked up at Cardage and said, "I have this. Let's go. I believe we both have things we should be doing." With that, Yura picked up the large staff and hoisted it upon his shoulders. It was extremely heavy and Yura bore all of the weight with discomfort and pain. As Cardage closed the large iron door and prepared to lock it in place like they found it, he looked at Midemos one more time and Midemos returned his gaze. Cardage raised his right hand to signal a goodbye, and Midemos simply nodded his head in return. With that, Cardage put the key in the hole, closed the iron gate, and sealed the locks into place in front of them. He pulled the key out and he and Yura began their journey back up the winding spiral stairwell into the main coliseum floor.

Cardage gave Yura back the key, and said, "As the master of events, you should have it and set him free. It will be less conspicuous that way."

"Understood, my lord. I will do just that." Yura said as he took the key and put it back into his pocket as Cardage made his way to find Magnus and report their findings.

CHAPTER 19

A rsivus and his crew reached the coliseum entrance and were immediately met by event specialists who took their horses and led them away as the group formed around Doran.

"Where are we to meet General Magnus?" Casily asked as they looked around.

"His balcony is where we will find him, and it is up on the third level. We should make haste while we can," Doran said.

As they started to walk away, someone yelled, "Doran, am I glad to see you!" Doran and the group turned to see Cardage and Yura coming out of the iron gate from below the coliseum grounds. Yura was out of breath from carrying Midemos's staff and Cardage had a look of intent on his face.

Doran smiled. "Sir, we are all here. We were just about to go meet up with the General," he said as the group started to walk and meet them in the middle of the coliseum floor.

"That is good. Yura and I were going to speak with him as well, and we were on our way as we saw you. We have some very interesting news to share with him."

Cardage paused as he looked at Doran's group. "My apologies. Where are my manners? I am Cardage, second in command of General Magnus's knights, and this is Yura, he works at the coliseum."

Doran let that sink in for a moment then spoke for his group. "This is Kadath, a longtime friend of the General." Kadath nodded toward Cardage. "This is his son, Arsivus, who is in the tournament and," he paused for a second and looked at Arsivus, "their close friend Casily," which brought a smile to both Arsivus and Casily.

Cardage nodded his head and said, "Nice to meet you all. Kadath and Doran, we should be going at once. The General will be waiting for our news. Arsivus and Casily, if you wouldn't mind joining us with the General, I would appreciate that."

Cardage turned to Yura. "Go and make preparations. We must be ready, and remember, tell no one."

Yura nodded his head in agreement. "Understood, sir!" he said, and with that he walked back toward the underground corridors through the sturdy iron gate.

Cardage turned back to the group and said, "Friends, the day continues to move on. Shall we depart?" as he motioned with his hand toward a very well-lit corridor that led to the upper levels of the coliseum. With that, the group entered the corridor. Kadath was the first through, followed by Doran and Casily, and then Arsivus with Cardage behind him. As they were passing through, Arsivus noticed the doorway had a gate that shut and sealed to prevent the combatants from exiting once the competition had begun.

Cardage walked a little faster and caught up with Arsivus. "So, you are one of the competitors. I am anxious to see you fight. The General already seems very impressed with you, I hear. Have you been in competition before?" Cardage asked.

"Only what my father has taught me, as well as an actual fight in the Enegon Swamp on the way here," Arsivus responded.

Cardage nodded his head and said, "Yes, Sir Mulik informed me of that engagement. He said he was very impressed with your skills. It was just you and your father, and you took on three full-grown bandits. I have come across them before; they are not opponents to take lightly. They fight with dishonesty and shame. If nothing else, they are still quite deadly if left unchecked. No honor in the way they fight, but you appear to have quite a skill in taking care of yourself. That shall serve you well in both this competition and in life."

Arsivus, a little shy that their exploits had reached the castle, didn't know what to say. He finally said, "Thank you. I hope I have what it takes to compete and win."

Cardage smiled and said, "So do I. I had those same nerves when I went through, but once the gates are closed and it is just you and them, your instincts will kick in." Somehow this comforted Arsivus, although it left him anxious to actually start the competition.

They reached the bottom of the stairs, and Arsivus looked up and asked, "What should I expect when those gates close?" as he gestured to the gate they just walked through.

Cardage grinned. "You shall soon find out. When we reach the General, I am sure he will have some helpful words for you. Instructions will come from him and him only; the rest of us are only spectators at this point."

Arsivus smiled. He had a feeling Cardage would respond like that. "Good!" he said, and he began climbing the stairs to the third floor.

A loud knocking resounded through the chambers. It continued at a steady pace.

"Argh, what now?" Thesias said aloud as he came back into the room from his balcony. "Come in already. What business have you?" he barked as the door creaked open. "Ah, Captain, what brings you here? Shouldn't you be prepping for the tournament to ensure our victory?" Thesias questioned.

Atalee closed the door slowly as he peered outside to ensure no one was listening or observing their dealings. He turned around and saw Thesias grabbing an apple off a platter and rubbing it back and forth in his hands to get the dust off. The sweet smell of jasmine and fresh bread was in the air from the market below.

The King was half dressed in a gold cloak, white button-down silk shirt, and black trousers with the royal emblem embroidered on each leg. His hair was disheveled, but he wore his crown anyway. Atalee, on the other hand, was dressed in slim-fitting armor reminiscent of his battle armor. It looked almost the same but smaller, more tactical and lethal for close quarters. He bore his sword upon his hip as usual, but his armor was made of a chainmail-like substance that allowed airflow and free movement of the body.

"Sir, the competition will begin soon. Shall I summon your chambermaids to assist you with your gear?" Atalee asked calmly.

"I do not need assistance getting myself dressed, Captain. You will do good to remember that. I am not old and feeble yet," Thesias responded hastily.

"Understood, my lord," Atalee said. Thesias gave a quick glance toward Atalee before heading back out to his balcony. He watched the ships entering the city docks, as he spoke to Atalee behind him. "Today will be an exceptional day. We shall see a most prominent fight, shall we not?"

Atalee felt a little uncomfortable, but quickly created a lie. "Everything is set in place. It shall be a monumental day indeed," he said. Thesias smiled as he took a bite of his apple.

"I never thought the day would come when my boys would be welcomed by the White Guard and become part of their esteemed legacy!" Thesias said. This made Atalee feel extremely uncomfortable since Atalee informed Magnus about the King's request. "I would like them put directly under your command at the soonest available time, Captain. They are to be your immediate underlings. They will fall second in line to you and then the rest of your White Guard will be beneath them, am I understood?" Thesias demanded as he stared at Atalee while chewing a bite of his apple obnoxiously.

Atalee nodded and said, "It has been taken care of, my lord. As long as they win the tournament like we have planned, it shall happen." This brought a level of doubt into Thesias's mind.

"What do you mean, *as long as*?" Thesias demanded.

Atalee responded, "Sire, it is set up for them to win. All they have to do is take it. I can only do so much for them. They have to earn the rest. Rest assured, they are well on their way to knighthood as long as they keep their wits about them," he said with a hard tone.

Thesias did not like that answer. He spun around and once again gazed over his kingdom.

"Captain, they had better win, for your sake. I shall hold you completely responsible if they fail to succeed in this tournament." Thesias said with contempt.

Atalee, not knowing how to respond or what to say to appease his King, simply responded, "My liege."

Thesias, not to be one to not have the last word, softly muttered into the wind, "If you fail me, Captain, I have another way to ensure their success. Needless to say, it is a beast of a plan to guarantee their victory today."

With that, Atalee nodded his head in agreement and turned to take his leave. Thesias laughed out loud as Atalee closed the door.

"Today shall be a glorious day for the house of Thesias, it very much indeed will be." Thesias let the apple drop out of his hand onto the hard terrace. It rolled toward the edge with the wind pushing it. Thesias looked again over the seas and spied all of the ships coming in for the tournament. He recognized some of the lords from their banners and colors. The Highmark from the Western Kingdom stood out with its royal blue mast and golden stripe splitting it in two, the Vasterly from the western coast of his kingdom with its electric red mast that could be seen for miles, the Luriels from the eastern seaboard, and many others. As he scanned the crowded seaport, one ship in particular caught his attention. It was resting upon the shoreline, just out of view from the harbor and docks where his guards patrolled. From his viewpoint, Thesias could see that the ship was as dark as night and appeared to have no movement on board.

"Hmm, it is strange that a ship as burned as that should still be afloat, is it not, Captain?" he asked as he turned back and saw no one. "Ahh, that's right, he left," Thesias said to himself. He returned his gaze to the harbor and the ship, but it was nowhere to be seen. "Hmm, that is odd indeed," he said to himself as he took a step closer and kicked the apple off the balcony and watched as it hit the rocks on the way down the cliff. His thoughts quickly turned back to the tournament at hand. "I must make myself ready." He returned to his room and rang for his chambermaids to assist him with his armor and apparel.

When they arrived, he immediately yelled, "Tell no one you helped me, is that understood?" The chambermaids nodded in unison and began dressing the King to make him look presentable on this day. "It shall be a good day indeed!" Thesias said with a smile as his clothes dropped to the floor and the maids draped his ceremonial gown across his shoulders.

Magnus was standing at the back wall of the master of events room looking over the event board for the tournament. He was deep in thought, his arms crossed in front of him.

"This cannot be right," he said to himself as he studied the event listings and shook his head in disbelief. The door creaked open and Doran, Casily, Kadath, Cardage, and Arsivus entered.

"Doran, Cardage, I am glad you made it on time. And hello again, friends!" Magnus said as he looked at Kadath, Casily, and Arsivus. "Thank you for bringing them directly, Doran. Were there any problems?"

Doran leaned against the wall. "No, my lord. A little mobbing on the way in, but that was taken care of thanks to Korgal and Teslark. After that, we ran into Cardage in the arena. The crowd was starting to get rather large, even this early before the tournament. It should be a great turnout to watch our future champion," Doran said as he smiled at Arsivus.

"That is good to hear, Doran." Magnus looked to Cardage and asked politely, "What did you learn, Cardage?"

Cardage took a bite of bread and quickly washed it down with some ale. He set his glass down on a stone ledge and gazed into the open arena, noticing every ledge, rock, and grain of sand on the floor.

"Sir, the first thing I learned is that the King's sons are reckless, arrogant, and unworthy to even be considered for becoming knights. They lack all of the moral fibers that most of us take for granted. They cannot be allowed to win this tournament. Although I fear that there are motives at large that will most certainly assist in them achieving their goals." The group now turned to face Cardage as he continued to stare out at the arena.

"Behind those gates," Cardage said as he nodded in direction of the large iron gates, "there is a large corridor that is outlined by statues of old. I discovered one of the statues concealed a very old and large cavern behind it, which was hidden in plain sight, albeit secured with a very odd key." By this time, the entire group was intently listening.

"It is not the fact that there was a hidden chamber underneath our noses this entire time, it is the contents of what was hidden within the cavern that has worried me."

Magnus shifted and asked, "What did you find down there?"

Cardage turned to face the group that had huddled around him. "Yura and I found a prisoner, the likes of which I have never seen. His name is Midemos, and he is a very large, full-grown Eglician." Everyone gasped.

"An Eglician!" Doran exclaimed. I have never in my life witnessed one. I only believed them to be in the legends of old."

Everyone began to speak at once until Magnus silenced them. "Cardage, go on," he said. "What did you learn from this Midemos?"

"He said he was captured a long time ago. He and his companion were coming east. He was on a spiritual journey and was captured once he landed on the western shores. A trap was sprung on them, and apparently his companion had disappeared. But Midemos was transferred here through a variety of tactics, mostly sleeping agents. He was interrogated many times over the past couple of years about magical trinkets Thesias was looking for."

Magnus looked at Kadath and Arsivus and, seeing no telltale signs from them, looked back at Cardage and asked, "What did Midemos tell him?"

"Nothing. He has not spoken to anyone. I am the first person he spoke to. I told him about our King and what he has been doing over the past couple of years, and he did not seem too pleased."

"We should do better to keep our interests our own, Cardage," Magnus said. "We do not know Midemos's intentions as of yet. Better that he doesn't know everything about us, agreed?"

Cardage nodded his head in agreement. "My apologies, sir. I got carried away like a child getting a gift. I shall do better next time."

Magnus nodded his head and asked, "Anything else that he told you?"

"Yes, it appears that your brother offered him his freedom if he were to interfere in the tournament to aide his sons in winning. He told me that he was to be raised up and to hinder everyone's chance of winning aside from Zenor and Ruvio. I offered to free him from his captivity, but he neglected. He said that the blame would fall on me, and he did not want that. I told him I would speak with you and we would not let him be used like this. That we would give him his freedom." Cardage replied.

Magnus turned and drank from a mug of ale then gently set it down. He turned to the board of events and stared at it with intent. Nodding, he pointed at it and said, "It will be the three-on-one competition at the very end. It appears the traditional events are no longer part of the competition. This year, the events that are taking place will be archery and dueling competitions, and variations as to how those are conducted. There will be one-on-one, two-on-one and three-on-one. I would venture to claim that Midemos will be the deciding factor in the three-on-one as it is already determined that Zenor, Ruvio and Huply will be fighting against Wallace, a squire, it appears."

Casily cut in. "That is Teslark's nephew, the one he told me about, General. They plan to do him great harm to satisfy their sick desires."

Magnus gave a quick nod. "Three-on-one, surely they will be victorious, unless someone were to intervene. Arsivus, I do not know of the last two competitors, but it has been decreed by the King that this tournament can be fatal. I do not want any deaths while the competition is underway. Can I count on you to ensure that does not happen?"

Kadath rested his hand on Arsivus's shoulder as Arsivus went to speak. "Yes, sir. I shall do everything I can to see it through."

Magnus responded, "That is good. It may be tough, but we need to ensure that—"

Before Magnus could finish his sentence, the door burst open and Janos appeared. "General, we may have a problem," Janos said as he immediately grabbed a pint of ale and took a sip. He looked around the room and said, "Hello, everyone, glad you could make it!" He took another large drink from the ale, and then turned back to Magnus. "Sir, I believe we have some witchcraft in the kingdom today."

Magnus, a bit taken back, simply said, "Continue."

Janos took another sip and began to tell his story, while the others listened on.

As he finished, Doran shook his head in disbelief and recapped everything they had just heard. "So, you chased this girl into Fallen Row, and when you got there, all of the prisoners were in a stasis mode with glowing eyes. There were seven individuals surrounding a cage, and they spoke to you and then disappeared, leaving all but a piece of map that was burning a location into itself?" With that Doran slowly took the pint of ale away from Janos, which prompted Arsivus and Janos both to laugh.

"Where was the location on the map?" Arsivus asked as Janos handed him the piece of parchment.

Arsivus looked at it and said, "This is —"

Janos interrupted. "The Great Hall in the Western Kingdom," Janos said, finishing Arsivus's sentence. He went on. "Whatever those spirits are, or were, are linked to something there. Someone needs to investigate this and soon."

Magnus nodded in agreement and said, "After the tournament, we will send a detachment to investigate as soon as we are able."

This brought delight to most everyone in the room, but the moment was soon interrupted by the chiming of bells.

"What is that?" Arsivus asked.

"Those are the tournament bells that signify the tournament will start soon. You had best be on your way to prepare," Magnus said. Everyone turned to Arsivus as he took a deep breath.

"Where do I go?" he asked as he looked around the room.

"I can show you. Come with me," Janos said and he opened the door to lead him out.

"Here is your map back, sir," Arsivus said as he handed the map back to Janos. Janos looked at Magnus, and Magnus gave a quick nod. Janos took the map, and with that the two left the room. As they did, everyone wished him luck. As the door was about to close, Arsivus glanced back and saw Casily holding her hands close to her chest above the pendant he gave her as she stared longingly at him. She gave a nod to which he reciprocated as the door closed with a quiet thud. Janos and Arsivus started down the stairs, and Janos led him through a bunch of corridors that eventually led into the inner chambers of the coliseum, which contained an armory, resting quarters, and a place to be treated with medicine if things went wrong. On the far side, a large barrel of water slowly dripped into a giant wooden structure that housed different kinds of plants. As they got closer, Arsivus immediately recognized them as the herbs Arsivus and his father had recently brought to the kingdom.

"Those are healing herbs," Janos said. "Although I am sure you are familiar with them," he added with a smile.

Arsivus returned the smile. "I am just glad they are being put to good use. Tell me, Sir Janos, will all of the fighters be down here before the tournament begins?" Arsivus asked.

"Yes, everyone shall be down here and Yura will be giving instructions as to what is to be expected. There will also be guards down here to ensure that there are no unnecessary quarrels before the competition starts. We don't need anyone being disqualified prior to the festivities," he said with a smile, although both of them knew that he was referring to the King's sons. Janos and Arsivus walked over to the armory and observed the choices that lay before them. Multitudes of swords and shields were leaning against a large steel rack built into the wall. The heat was immense from the kiln on the other side of the room. It made its way toward the entrance room, dousing everything with its sweltering warmth.

"They are all made from the same metal, each to be exact copies of one another to ensure the competition remains fair!" Janos exclaimed. "The other shelves are off limits for the competition. And over here," he went on, pointing to the other side of the room, "are the suits of armor that you can wear, complete with gauntlets, helmets, chest and leg plates if you so wish. The General wanted everyone to be equal in this competition. Of course, you can choose not to wear it, but it is here if you decide to."

Arsivus nodded in approval and asked, "What of the bows? Are they wood frame, or made from steel?"

Janos put his hand on Arsivus's back and walked him out of the room into the large foyer. He pointed toward the distant wall next to the herbs and said, "Those are the bows that will be used. Crafted from the finest wood, they are replicas of what the knights currently use in combat. Best to get whoever is victorious to train with them as soon as possible."

Arsivus went to the wall and picked one up to get a feel for it. He held it in his hand and pulled back the drawstring. "Good weight, good resistance, it feels strong," Arsivus said as he twirled it in his hand and noticed the arrows next to the wall. He pulled one from the quiver and nocked it, pulling the string back and slowly releasing the tension while still holding the arrow. "The arrows are nice and straight, also a good weight to these. I like it. This should do very well." As Arsivus put both the arrow and bow back into their places, he asked, "Will there be a practice round for this event?"

Before Janos could answer, a loud voice echoed across the stone walls of the chamber. "Ha ha, did you hear that brother? He asked if he could practice before shooting. He must be really scared of the bow. I can't wait to see him with a sword!" Zenor exclaimed, mocking Arsivus.

"I thought this event was for knights, not farm boys who are afraid to hurt themselves in combat. It will be interesting watching you compete, if that is what you will call it." Ruvio said as he joined Zenor in laughter. Arsivus held his tongue, while Janos gritted his teeth with disgust.

"Say, boy," Ruvio continued. "You do know how to fire a bow, don't you? I bet the safest place to stand would be right in front of you. I'm willing to bet that you couldn't even hit the ground if you aimed for it!"

Zenor laughed and said, "You best stay out of our way, unless you want to get hurt, really bad!" He patted Ruvio on the back and they made their way into the armory to look at the weapons. As they did, a wider man came in who looked to be around the same age as Zenor and Ruvio.

Janos leaned over and said to Arsivus, "That is Huply, one of the King's sons' acquaintances. He is no quality fighter, but he fights dirty. When combined with those two melons, he can be quite formidable."

Arsivus took note. "So, those are the three that are planning on going after the squire? I shall keep that in mind," Arsivus said to Janos.

Shortly after, a woman was hauled into the room wrapped in chains to keep her from escaping. She wore a long-sleeved red leather top with buttons down the right side that secured it in place, black leather pants with straps and holds sewn in to secure weapons and tools, and black boots with silver buttons. Her thick brown hair was worn loose and she wore a silver necklace around her neck.

Janos continued, "Ah, here comes Raeolyn. She is a criminal and has earned the chance at her freedom. She doesn't speak much to anyone, but from what I have seen she is a very fierce fighter. She wields a sword better than most men that I know. She will be one to watch if you find yourself on the other side of her blade. There has been talk of her being a freelancer, or a sell-sword, but the tattoo on her face shows that she served in the Western Kingdom."

Arsivus asked how he could tell she served in the Western Kingdom. Janos pointed to the tattoo and said, "That is their sign of betrayal. That symbol under her eye means that she must have crossed someone very important to earn that. They don't do that practice anymore for the amount of cruelty and pain it causes."

As the guards pushed her toward a bench, her eyes met Arsivus's and they stared at each other. He could not break contact and felt as if he were frozen and she was in control. She smiled as she passed him. It seemed very genuine and almost loving. Arsivus felt her smile meant something more but he did not know how to describe it, or the proper way to react, so he gave her a polite nod. She broke eye contact with him, but he continued to watch her as she made her way to the bench.

"She is an attractive woman, no doubt about it!" Janos said quietly.

"She is very beautiful!" Arsivus said out loud, although he meant to keep the thought to himself. Raeolyn looked at Arsivus again and winked.

Flustered, Arsivus shook his head and Janos laughed. "Welcome to the city, boy!" he said, and patted Arsivus on the back. They looked up to see a man enter the room. Arsivus recognized him instantly and his face filled with wonder. The man had a large sword strapped across his back, a flowing blue cape, and all-black attire. Arsivus couldn't believe his eyes.

"That is the champion from the west. His name is Dricaryo and he is a force to be reckoned with," Janos said. "Although he will not be able to use his sword during the competition, his skills from the stories are far above most men in this kingdom."

Dricaryo was a little bit smaller than Korgal, but well built, and his arms looked solid, yet limber. Every step he took was with purpose, and his stoic appearance was intimidating and inspiring at the same time. He walked straight through the room into the resting quarters, laid his sword on the bed, and sat down next to it. Everyone in the room took notice of him.

Within minutes, the squire came in. He was by far the smallest person in the room, even compared to Raeolyn. He looked around, spotted a bench in the corner, and immediately walked toward it. He seemed very uncomfortable and a little scared. He looked around at everyone in the room and appeared to be about to speak but then quickly thought better of it and looked down at the floor. Arsivus saw this and then looked toward the armory where Zenor and Ruvio were standing with Huply. They had suddenly become very quiet and were whispering back and forth to each other.

Arsivus looked at Janos and then back at the squire then got up and walked over to greet him. "My name is Arsivus, a friend of your uncle. And your name is?" he said as he extended his hand.

"Hello, so glad to meet you. My name is Wallace. I am not really sure what to do down here but it looks like everyone else feels the same," Wallace said with a grin.

Arsivus returned the smile and informed him of what would happen with the events of the day but made sure not to mention the plot against him. "A man called Yura will be down soon to relay the instructions of the tournament. Until then, I believe we are to wait. Have you been preparing for this?" Arsivus asked to get a gauge on his abilities.

Wallace replied, "Somewhat. I have only just become a squire, but I have been around weapons my whole life."

"But have you used them, boy?" Ruvio interrupted, as Zenor and Huply held back their laughter.

"Not as much as I would like, but I believe this will be a good learning experience for me," Wallace replied back in a hopeful tone.

"This most assuredly will be a good learning experience if that is what you are hoping to acquire, lad!" Zenor said.

"And what about you?" Huply asked as he pointed at Arsivus. "What is it you are going to show us today? How to farm your herbs?" he and Zenor and Ruvio laughed.

Ruvio then yelled, "What does a farm boy like him even hope to accomplish in a tournament of fighters?" Arsivus knew they were trying to get a reaction out of him.

Janos had heard enough and went to speak, but Arsivus beat him to it. "It is simple. Nothing but my best," he said as he remembered Teslark's words to him upon their entry into the coliseum. Thinking of that, and of what Casily told him about Ruvio and Zenor planning to kill Wallace, filled him with a strength he had not known before.

Arsivus thought, "They are planning to attack someone for fun. They have to be brought to justice!" And with that thought, Arsivus spoke so the whole room could hear. "We shall all soon be parted with your imprudent chatter. Maybe you are better suited for the crowds as opposed to holding a sword."

With that Zenor pushed past Ruvio to charge at Arsivus but was stopped in his tracks by a command that thundered throughout the room, "Your majesty arrives!" With that, all the attention went to the doorway where Yura stood. He stepped aside and King Thesias appeared.

Everyone went to their knee as the King walked toward the middle of the room. "Rise," Thesias said and everyone obeyed. "I have come to wish you all well in this tournament, and to tell you that upon this special occasion, I have decided to alter the rules a little bit. This year, there are to be three champions crowned. Master Yura will speak of the events and how they will be graded, but rest assured everyone will be given fair chance to be crowned a champion at the end of this tournament. Give it everything you have, as if your very life depended upon it." With that, his eyes rested upon Wallace and a smile crept onto his face. As he turned to leave, his eyes met Arsivus's and they remained there for a moment. The King gave a quick scowl toward him and then swept his cloak around himself and walked hastily out of the room.

Once he was gone, Raeolyn said, "Well, that was inspiring. I wonder who he has picked to win this year's tournament! I do hope I disappoint him." She smiled.

"You heard him. It is to be fair for all," Zenor yelled. "You had better watch yourself lady. I would hate to hurt such a pretty face!" Zenor's outburst only prompted another smile from Raeolyn.

Yura remained in the doorway and attempted to calm the mild storm that was forming. "There will be plenty of time to hash out your differences in the arena, but until then, let us cover the rules of the tournament. The first event will be archery, five shots from fives distances, and points will be awarded for marks that are hit. The next events will be dueling. First one-on-one, then two-on-one, and finally, three-on-one which will be the last event of the tournament. If for any reason at all a contender cannot finish, they will be expelled from the tournament. Be wary, even though the swords are dull, they all still have a pointy end. This is a battle competition, so injuries may happen. If you see yourself unfit to continue, you each will have a white flag that you can throw to give your surrender. Pairings for the dueling will be announced as we go. You each will have one sword from the armory, five arrows, one bow, one white flag, and a set of armor with shield is optional if you want it. We begin shortly. Are there any questions?" No one spoke. "None then? Well, best of luck to all of you!" Yura said as he turned and walked out of the room.

Janos turned to Arsivus and said, "I must be going now. Good luck, son. Remember, do your best!"

Arsivus nodded in agreement and said, "Thank you." With that Janos left the same way the King and Yura had. Arsivus went over and picked up the bow and quiver of five arrows he had held before. Behind him were Dricaryo and Raeolyn. Following them from a distance was Wallace, Huply, Zenor, and Ruvio. They made their way into the foyer and each grabbed a white flag from the table. Everyone passed by the armor set except Wallace, who chose to acquire a set for himself.

This made Zenor laugh out loud and he shouted out, "Are you afraid of getting hurt, boy? Maybe you shouldn't have even come today!" Ruvio laughed as Wallace shyly continued to put the armor on.

Raeolyn looked at Zenor and said, "By the time this tournament is over, you are going to wish you had made the same choice as him!" She walked past him humming a tune and went back to her bench with the guards.

"You best keep your distance and your mouth shut prisoner!" Zenor said shakily as Ruvio remained uncharacteristically quiet. All the while Arsivus noticed that Dricaryo hadn't said a word and had returned to his bed to await the final call to the tournament. Arsivus looked around the room. Everyone was keeping their distance from each other, except Zenor and Ruvio, who seemed thick as thieves sitting by the armory. Arsivus looked at his gear lying before him, and then took one more look around the room.

He let out a big sigh and said to himself quietly, "It is now or never. Let's give it our all, shall we?" With that he stood up and wrapped the bow over his shoulder and grabbed his arrows, then walked over to the corner to wait patiently for the call to come.

Back upstairs in the event room, Magnus was talking with Casily, Cardage, Doran, and Kadath. They were admiring the coliseum from the inside as the townsfolk began to quickly fill up the stadium. The sun was high and shining brightly on the sand floor of the arena. Assistants could be seen everywhere setting up the archery portion of the tournament. Bundles of hay were being placed behind the targets to catch any wayward arrows from ricocheting off and flying into the crowds.

There were mechanics in front of the targets, setting up obstacles for the contenders to shoot past. Some were moving and some were stationary. They were created to measure the ability of each shooter. The targets were set in a circle around the competitors, with five stations in all, each one increasing in difficulty. The first target was fairly close as it was intended to get the contestants comfortable with the pull back, the distance, and how the bow felt.

The second station was set up with a swinging pendulum that was gliding back and forth in front of the target, but the target was set back farther than the first. The third station had a rotating target set back farther than the previous, as well as a fire roaring in front of it, obscuring most of the target.

The fourth station had its target back farther yet, but a continuous waterfall flowed in front of it while the target bobbed up and down. The last station had the target all the way back at the wall. There was a swinging pendulum there, but it was very close to the competitors. There was a fire in front of the target, as well as a waterfall in front of the target. Although the last target remained stationary against the far wall, it was still the most challenging.

"Kadath, how is your boy at archery? Will he have problems with this setup?" Cardage asked loud enough so that everyone could hear and take interest.

"No, he practices every evening at home. These distances should not be a problem for him. Although, there aren't many waterfalls to shoot through at our cottage!" Kadath said as he smiled and the others in the room shared a laugh.

Doran pointed toward the gate as it was starting to open. "It appears that the tournament has begun. Here they come now!" Doran said as he let out a burp from the ale that he was drinking. As they watched the competitors come out of the tunnel, the door opened and Janos walked into the room.

"Well, your brother gave a rather inspiring speech before he left. There are to be three winners from this year's competition apparently," Janos said with a sly reply.

"Absurd!" Doran exclaimed. "Changing tradition to suit his own greedy desires. Such a shame." He shook his head.

"They are about to announce the introductions!" Magnus said as he walked toward the open balcony that overlooked the arena. Everyone fell in close behind until they were all out and watching.

From below, Yura was giving his speech. "Welcome, ladies and gentlemen, to this year's spectacular event. We have been waiting a long time for this day to come, and it is finally here. So please, grab your ale, hold your bread, take your seats, and be witness to one of the most memorable times of your life. Today we have seven individuals from around the kingdom and beyond, competing to earn the prestigious title of knight, but there is a catch. This year, there will be three that shall be crowned champion and join our ranks in defending this kingdom. Without further ado, here are your contestants.

We have Zenor, one of your very own. First-born of his name, competing for this coveted position. Alongside him, his brother and your prince, Ruvio, whose skill is of the utmost caliber. Huply, ladies and gentlemen. Strong as an ox and looks like one too. Wallace, a newly appointed squire and fully dressed for combat, I see. Next is our charity to you this year, a prisoner who has the chance at redemption. None other than Raeolyn, may her feats be great, as is her beauty. Next, hailing from the Western Kingdom, a champion in his own right, Dricaryo. Our last competitor for the tournament, producer of our herbs used in battle, a fine lad he is and strong he looks, Arsivus, ladies and gentlemen. Wish them luck, for they shall need it!

Our first event for today will be the archery contest you see before you; the bullseye's will count as two points, hitting the target will count as one, and no points will be awarded if a contestant hits outside of the circle or misses completely. Contestants, please take your positions." With the introductions done, the crowd cheered continuously as they had been filled with bread and ale and were in good spirits. Yura departed through the entryway as the large iron gate closed behind him. Zenor was set to go first through the trial, while the others waited in line behind him. Magnus watched from up above and took a sip of ale.

As Zenor nocked an arrow, the crowd grew silent. He held the arrow while he observed the target in front of him and let loose his arrow, bullseye!

Magnus nodded his head in agreement and said, "Most everyone should not have too much difficulty until the later targets, I think. It should be interesting indeed to see how everyone fares in this event." Zenor pressed on to the next couple of stations and hit the bullseye on the next two targets. On the fourth station, Zenor fired his arrow, but the water-fall quickly pushed the arrow down and hit the target for a score underneath the bullseye. On his last station, his arrow made it through, but it again was pushed down by the water-fall and landed just below the bullseye. Ruvio mimicked his older brother's marks with bullseyes on the first three targets and then clipping just inside the ring on his fourth which counted for a score. He finished by burying his arrow in the fire on the last station. As he finished, Zenor walked up to him and patted him on the back, and they shared a smile.

Huply was next, and he nocked his first arrow and let loose and hit just below the bullseye. "Ha, ha, ha, how could you miss that?" Zenor asked as Ruvio laughed with him. Huply simply walked to the next station and hit a bullseye. He continued to do that for the next two targets. On his last target, Huply missed it completely. Wallace was next and walked up in full armor and pulled back the bowstring with the arrow lodged into it.

He let loose and the arrow dug deep into the dirt right before the target. "Ooooh, ahhh!!" could be heard among the crowd, as well as a few stifled laughs.

Ruvio had his mouth open in disbelief, and Huply was the first to let out an audible sound. "Did you want to scoot closer and try again, kiddo?" he asked, which prompted laughter from Zenor and a few members of the crowd. Wallace looked down in embarrassment and was fumbling with his next arrow as he walked to station two. Arsivus saw that his confidence and courage were failing quickly, so he decided to take action.

He walked over and cut in front of Wallace and took his bow. "Wha-what are you doing?" Wallace asked politely but with some hesitation.

Arsivus held his bow and motioned to Wallace's armor. "Take off your armor. It is blocking your drawback. The string hit your chest and that killed your last shot. Without the armor, it would have hit its mark." Wallace nodded in agreement and tried to unclasp the hook in the back. Arsivus reached over and assisted in the task.

"Is this a dress rehearsal, or are we to be on with it?" Ruvio asked aloud, while Huply joined in and said, "Are you going to hold his bow for him, too?" which prompted more laughter from the crowd.

"That is enough!" echoed loudly through the coliseum. When everyone turned to see who said it, all eyes became fixated on Dricaryo. As he continued to lean on his bow waiting for his turn, he looked over at Arsivus and Wallace and simply said in a low but strong and reassuring voice, "Take your time, son." With that the crowd calmed down, and Ruvio crept back behind his brother to shield himself from the gaze of Dricaryo.

With Arsivus's help, Wallace's armor dropped off and hit the ground.

"There, stretch your arms quickly and you should be ready to go," Arsivus said and went back to his spot in line.

"Thank you!" Wallace said gratefully and picked his bow and arrow back up. He walked to the second station, pulled back the string, and let loose the arrow. It made a dull thud as it hit the pendulum on the way toward the target. "Bullseye!" the announcer yelled.

This filled Wallace with the confidence he needed, and he went to the next two targets and hit bullseyes without a second thought. Wallace walked to the last station, nocked an arrow, and let loose. It landed just inside the outer ring on the target so it counted for a score. But happy with his overall score, Wallace walked to the end of the line and waited as he attempted to hide a smile from his face.

Raeolyn stepped up to her first station and hit the mark. She hit just below the bullseye on her second shot, which prompted Zenor to chuckle. Upon hearing that and without changing stations, Raeolyn calmly grabbed and pulled an arrow back into her bow and turned toward the third target. She raised the bow and fired an arrow at the target from the second station. The arrow flew straight and true, right by Zenor's head and hit the bullseye on the target. Zenor was slow to react and jump out of the way, but he dove to the ground in response to her shot. After it had gone by his head, Zenor heard the crowd laughing at him. He jumped up to charge at her. By this time, Dricaryo had taken a step closer to Raeolyn, which stopped Zenor right in his tracks.

Arsivus couldn't help but smile, and Ruvio noticed it right away. "What seems to be so funny, farm boy? You won't be smiling for too much longer!" Ruvio shouted.

With that, King Thesias yelled from above so everyone could hear, "Enough, let us continue on with the tournament." With that Raeolyn grabbed her fourth arrow and walked over to the fourth station. She pulled the arrow back and let it go, hitting the bullseye easily. She walked to the last station, pulled the arrow back and let loose. It flew past the pendulum, through the fire, through the waterfall, and hit the target inside the ring. The crowd gave a loud and happy cheer as she was walked to the side.

"I guess it takes a woman to show you how it is done!" she said as she walked by Zenor. Zenor kept his mouth closed and said nothing, but his eyes were filled with anger and contempt. Dricaryo stepped up to the first station with his arrow in hand. The crowd was still applauding from Raeolyn's turn and they continued to clap and cheer for Dricaryo. He pulled back his arrow and let it loose. Bullseye! He stepped to the second target and fired. Bullseye! The crowd continued their applause. Dricaryo's third shot was pulled back and fired. Just as it entered the fire to pass through, a large ember flew up and hit the tip, which caused the arrow to fly to the right of the bullseye but still hit within the target. The crowd let out a sigh of displeasure as he stepped up to the fourth station.

His pace was steady but casual. He pulled back and let go another arrow that flew through the waterfall and hit the bullseye. The crowd cheered loudly. He walked to his last station and pulled back an arrow. He waited a moment to get the timing down for the moving pendulum. Once the pendulum had swung completely to the right, he let loose an arrow. It flew straight and true and hit the bullseye, which sent the crowd into an uproar.

Yura addressed the crowd wholeheartedly. "Ladies and gentlemen, we almost had a perfect mark, which has never been accomplished before. Dricaryo hit four of the five bullseyes!! Had it not been for that ember, he may have accomplished it." This excited the crowd even more as Dricaryo stepped aside and joined the others who had already completed the event.

"Our last competitor for this event, people of Affinity and everywhere else, please welcome, Arsivus!" Yura said. The crowd cheered as he walked to the first station. Arsivus gave a quick stretch and felt his back crack, which relieved some of the pressure he was feeling. He looked over at the other competitors. Zenor, Ruvio, and Huply were gathered around each other and appeared to not care what was happening outside of their little circle. Wallace was by his lonesome, and Raeolyn and Dricaryo were standing side by side saying nothing, but always watching.

Arsivus returned his attention to the task at hand. He looked at the target, nocked an arrow, and held steady. "Shtnk!" could be heard as the arrow struck with force into the center of the bullseye. The crowd applauded, and Arsivus moved to the next station. He took a deep breath and pulled back another arrow and steadied himself. He watched the pendulum coming and going, and as it swung way left, he released. "Shtnk!" again resounded through the arena as the arrow found its way to the center of the bullseye.

The crowd continued applauding and a couple of people yelled out their support. Arsivus moved to the third station and repeated his process. He breathed in a cool breeze that had infiltrated the stadium and he savored it in his lungs. He exhaled slowly as he pulled back an arrow and stared through the flames. His eyes went narrow and moments passed. He finally released his arrow with force. "Shtnk!" again echoed through the coliseum as his arrow penetrated the flame and struck into the center of the bullseye.

The crowd was on their feet cheering in hopes that Arsivus would be the first to hit all of the marks. Arsivus walked to the next station still feeling calm and confident. When he got there, he looked back at the other competitors. All of them were now watching him. Raeolyn was smiling at him in adoration, while Dricaryo had a faint smile on his face as he listened to the crowd cheer Arsivus on. Wallace was applauding as well, while Zenor, Ruvio, and Huply showed no expressions.

Arsivus turned back toward the target and saw it floating behind the waterfall. Arsivus tilted his head to the left as he bit his bottom lip in deep thought. "I'll have to shoot high to counter the water bringing the arrow down," he said, as he pulled the arrow back. "Unless I make the arrow go faster!" he said as he pulled the string back even more and let the arrow go. "Shtnk!" again blasted through the crowd as the arrow pierced the water with such great force that it barely moved on its way to the bullseye. The crowd erupted in applause and cheers. This even prompted a nod from Dricaryo and some excited clapping from Raeolyn. Wallace was beside himself as he was now running below the stands like a wild man trying to get the crowd more engaged in their cheering for Arsivus. Arsivus walked toward his last station while trying to hide his smile but failing to do so. From above, Magnus, Doran, Cardage, Janos, Casily, and Kadath were excited as well.

They were all celebrating and cheering loudly for Arsivus to hear as they drank their ales together. King Thesias from his viewpoint was less than impressed, as Arsivus had now bested both his sons in the archery contest. He was very unhappy with the contest so far. Captain Atalee, who was sitting behind Thesias's chair on his balcony perch, watched with uneasiness. He was happy that Arsivus was doing well because he did not want Zenor or Ruvio to win the competition, but he could not show the King his true desires.

Arsivus arrived at his last station. His nerves were in check and his confidence was high. He took a deep breath. It re-energized him as he let it out. He nocked an arrow and looked at the target. "Past the pendulum, through the fire and water, into the center," he said quietly to himself.

"Don't mess it up, farm boy. It is a long way back to your cottage!" yelled Zenor, who was jealous that Arsivus was doing so well.

"Ha, yeah, it seems as if your luck has run out, herb boy!" Ruvio joined in. Wallace was doing his part to get the crowd on their feet to cheer loudly in the hopes of drowning out the brothers.

Raeolyn shouted out as well, "You can do this!" which she followed up with a radiant smile.

Dricaryo even had words of encouragement for Arsivus. "By all means, don't stop now, lad!" he said.

With all of this going on around him, Arsivus smiled. He closed his eyes to concentrate and drown out all the noise around him. "Nothing but my best!" he said to himself as he opened his eyes and pulled back the arrow, his eyes steady on the target. The pendulum continued to swing, left, right, left. Arsivus let loose the arrow. It soared past the pendulum with ease. The arrow pushed through the heart of the roaring flames as though they weren't there. From the heat of the fire, the arrow continued into the cool, damp waterfall with no intent of stopping. "Shtnk!" again boomed throughout the stadium as his arrow found the center of the bullseye one last time. The crowd erupted with thunderous applause and all were on their feet cheering and yelling.

"Ladies and gentlemen, Arsivus has done it! He has a perfect score in all five stations. Congratulations, young man, on a job well done!" Yura commanded as the crowd continued to cheer, as did Kadath and the group of knights around him.

"He must have practiced quite a bit with that bow!" Doran said aloud to Kadath as they toasted to each other from up above.

"Like I said, every day he would practice with it, like he knew this would be his calling!" Kadath responded.

From down below Yura could be heard addressing the contestants and the crowd. "For our standings, we have Arsivus in the lead with ten points, and Dricaryo close behind with nine points. There is a two-person tie at eight points for Raeolyn and Zenor and a three-way tie between

Ruvio, Huply, and Wallace with seven. Contestants, please return to the armory and prepare for the dueling portion. We will take a little break to prepare the coliseum for the next events. Up next will be the one-on-one competition. We will see you in a little bit."

With that, Yura departed the arena foyer heading back to his resting area, and the contestants walked towards the large iron gate and waited to be summoned. As they walked, the crowd cheered them on. They could hear their names being chanted by the crowd as they walked through the coliseum and down the ramp into the corridors beneath the arena.

CHAPTER 20

The afternoon sun began to heat up the day. The stadium was full and everyone was now enjoying ale and a variety of foods. Magnus and his guests were afforded the luxury of having their ale and food brought to them so they could feast without missing any of the competition. The servants were busy filling the mugs of ale, as Magnus and his companions ate turkey legs and bread with honey. Doran looked over the edge and watched as the tournament helpers took down the archery components and began to make way for the dueling.

"What a great day!" Doran exclaimed as he took another bite of his turkey leg. "Arsivus is in the lead, it's a beautiful day, we have ale, and those brats are taking up the far end of the tournament. It is good to be a knight this day!"

Janos laughed and took a large drink of ale. Cardage quietly pondered how the rest of the day would go.

Magnus saw the look on his face and asked, "Cardage, what is on your mind?"

Cardage looked up and set his ale down. "I am wondering what will become of Midemos. How will he be used in the tournament? What will the people think of him?" Cardage said loud enough for everyone to hear.

Magnus walked over to the balcony and looked down on the coliseum grounds. Everyone went quiet. He pointed to the left side of the coliseum. "There, that is where I think he will come. If I remember correctly, there was an old shaft that was dug out years ago. My guess is that he will surface there. If what you say is correct, he would be too dangerous to bring up a stairwell in chains. The King would not want to suffer any losses of men. I think that is what he will do."

Kadath looked over at the area Magnus was pointing to and asked, "After the tournament, what will become of him? Will you set him free, or keep him imprisoned? I am sure the people who have never seen one will want it locked up for their amusement." Kadath's tone was solemn.

Magnus nodded his head in agreement as Kadath continued. "No one should be held against his or her will. If he has done nothing wrong, he should be set free. Freedom is priceless. After the tournament, you should give him his. So, he does not have to live a life of servitude, a life of chains."

Magnus continued to stare at the coliseum floor. "You speak truth, old friend. I shall see it done. I shall do it in front of everyone here and make it public so that none shall contest it."

"Freedom!" Cardage said. "It truly does have a lovely ring to it."

"I'll drink to that!" Casily said as she took a swig of ale. Magnus nodded his head, took a deep breath, and turned to the sky. Something caught his attention out of the corner of his eye and his gaze slowly sought it out among the clouds above them. He exhaled as he tried to speak. "Doran, I believe . . ." and with that, Magnus's voice trailed off and went quiet. Cardage looked over to him and saw his eyes fixated on the sky, his gaze unnerving. Cardage joined his gaze upward over the coliseum and saw something coming toward them. It was faint, yet its distinctive yellow wings and magnificent red body could be seen flowing toward them. Quickly, but as calm as a cool summer breeze, it soared through the sky.

Magnus was the first to speak. "Cardage, do you see it?"

Cardage nodded his head and said, "Yes, General. We must go at once." Doran and Kadath looked up and saw a miraculous bird coming toward them, the same bird from Goj that was given to Evra by Cardage for her to release if she was in trouble.

"General, how many of those birds do you have out there?" Kadath asked immediately.

Magnus, not taking his eyes off of it, responded, "Just one, and it was given to your wife. The rest are still residing here."

Kadath set down his ale and said, "I must go!" as he darted toward the door.

Magnus took his eyes off the bird and looked at Kadath. "Yes, you must." Magnus then turned to Doran and said, "I cannot leave at this moment. You are to go with him. Take some of the knights that are with Theros at the gate that are ready to ride but waste no time if they are not ready. Ride with those that you can immediately. I will follow with the rest as soon as I am able. Ride fast and hard, and know that a full company of knights are shortly behind you."

Doran gave a quick nod and was out the door with Kadath, on his way to go and prepare the knights.

Kadath looked back at Magnus, Cardage, Casily, and Janos and said, "Look after Arsivus in my stead. I will see you soon, my friends," and with that, Kadath and Doran bolted out of the door and were on their way to the front gate.

Janos turned quickly to Magnus. "Sir, let me join them. They may need more skill at their side!" he said impatiently.

Magnus shook his head. "No, I need you here. We are to follow soon enough, but if there is more treachery that has not been accounted for, we need protection here as well my friend." With that, Magnus picked up his ale and handed Janos his cup as well. Cardage walked over and grabbed his cup, as did Casily, and joined them in the middle of the room.

Magnus raised his cup and the others followed suit. "May they ride fast and hard, may the bird have just gotten out of its cage and returned home to see the tournament. May our friends arrive to find everything in harmonious order!" Magnus said with an encouraging tone, and with that, the four toasted and took a sip of the cold, dark ale.

Kadath was sprinting through the crowds trying to keep up with Doran. "Out of the way!" Doran yelled as he cleared a path for them to get to the gates as quickly as possible. Kadath had his hand on his sword to keep it from swaying from side to side as he was in full stride.

"Move!" Doran shouted again as the people who had been drinking ale all day and baking in the sun finally started to understand what was being said. Within minutes, both were free of the stadium and lines of people that were crammed inside.

"We must make haste. Let us be like the wind!" Doran said to Kadath as they continued to sprint toward the gate.

"There is a shorter path we can take. It brings us by Fallen Row and should be less busy and get us there quicker!" Doran shouted as he tried to maintain his breath.

"Let's take it!" Kadath responded as best he can. The two continued to run as fast as their legs could carry them down the stone-laden path.

"Ale was a bad idea," Doran shouted as they tried their mightiest to keep up the pace.

"Keep going Doran! We are almost there," Kadath said as they came upon the alleyway to Fallen Row. The two were in full stride now with a strong wind picking up the closer they got to entrance. Papers were flowing seamlessly across the street and dust was starting to rise up quickly in the most random of spots, although nothing else seemed to be moving. As they neared the entrance to Fallen Row, they saw a little girl sitting some ways down in the alley facing the entrance. She had blonde hair partially covered by a red hood and wore a black dress and white shoes. She did not move, but the wind seemed to be coming from her direction as they passed by.

Doran stopped at the entrance, prompting Kadath to do the same. They both spent a moment catching their breath as they looked down Fallen Row. A chill seemed to be forming in the air even though the sun was directly above them with no cloud cover. Kadath looked over at Doran and saw he was suspiciously eyeing the little girl in the alley. When Kadath followed his gaze, he saw the girl was now standing and facing them, although her head was down. Her hood was now off and her hair was flowing wildly, but there was no wind that could be felt. She took a step and then another toward the two men. With each step, the air seemed to get colder and colder, until she stopped at the alleyway entrance. Her pale face could now be fully seen, and her black eyes started at them ominously. She smiled.

Doran's hand remained on his sword, as he looked at Kadath and said, "Janos spoke the truth, this little girl must be the one he was talking about!" Kadath had recovered his breath and was ready to fight, ready to run, but most of all, ready to be on a horse heading home. With that thought running through his head, the little girl looked directly at Kadath and let out a laugh. A thick black smoke formed around her and then dissipated. When the smoke cleared, the girl was gone without a trace.

"Come, we don't have time for parlor tricks. We must be on our way!" Kadath said with urgency.

"Yes, I agree!" Doran responded and they both continued running toward the gate. Through the alleyways and streets, Doran navigated by shouting directions to Kadath, who was now in the lead.

"Left, turn right at the fountain, through that doorway!" After what seemed like a dozen twists and turns, Kadath and Doran arrived where Theros and Janos's detachment of knights were waiting with only Theros and four other knights still there.

"Doran, so good to see you, my friend. Why are you so winded? What were you two running from?" Theros asked curiously.

"The bird," Doran said and continued on as he took a drink of water from the horse's saddle and passed it to Kadath. "The bird has arrived. We must make haste immediately," Doran said loudly.

One of the knights that was waiting by his horse asked, "Is this the warning we were waiting for sir?" as he directed his question toward Theros.

Doran responded quickly, "We were told by General Magnus to take what we need and to ride immediately. And that the rest would follow with the General!"

"Very well, take what you need and be off. We have horses ready to ride, with provisions as well. Take these knights here with you, and we shall not be far behind, my friend," Theros said quickly. He turned around to face the knights and commanded, "You four mount up; you will escort Doran and his friend to his house and make no stops on the way there. The bird has arrived and we are already late." Doran quickly mounted the horse in front of him and Kadath did the same.

With that, the four knights mounted up and waited for Doran to spin his horse around. "See you in a bit, my friend. Good journey!" Theros said to Doran as he blew his horn to signal the gatekeeper to open the gates.

"Don't be too long, I fear the worst may come if you are," Doran said as he spun his steed around and kicked his stirrups to get the horse moving. Within seconds Doran was moving quickly and Kadath followed close behind with the four knights right behind him. The six made their way through Castle Affinity's gates with extreme haste. The gatekeeper closed the large doors and shut the steel gate behind them as they made their way toward the mountain pass. Theros climbed the tower next to the gatekeeper and watched as Kadath and company quickly made their way through the open fields heading toward the mountains.

"What happened?" Mulik asked.

Theros, not breaking eye contact with Kadath and Doran, responded, "We received word, the bird from Goj arrived this afternoon during the tournament. Evra must be in danger. The General sent six now, and the rest of us will follow when the General arrives."

Mulik looked over at the mountain pass and saw the six riding ferociously toward it and said, "They will make good time. The General mentioned that I was to be on the first detachment out. I received no orders, but I will ride when the General comes."

Theros replied, "Then you will ride with us. Hopefully we are not too late for whatever is coming." With that, Theros and Mulik continued to gaze out at the rugged mountains watching as Kadath and Doran became smaller and smaller in the distance riding toward his home with the knights in tow.

CHAPTER 21

"Competitors, grab your weapons. It is time to begin the dueling competition." Yura said as he entered the resting quarters attached to the armory.

"It's about time!" Zenor exclaimed as he got up from his seat. He began to stretch his arms as Huply and Ruvio followed suit behind him.

Ruvio asked, "Why did it take so long? Maybe we need to hire someone else to run this tournament after we win?"

Yura brushed the comments off and acted like he did not hear them. "Grab your swords, your shields, your armor, if you so desire, and make your way to the entrance. Line up alongside the wall and wait for further instructions." With that, Arsivus stood up and grabbed his sword and shield, as did Wallace and Raeolyn. Dricaryo grabbed just a sword and walked toward the entrance.

Wallace looked around nervously at everyone else and asked Arsivus, "Should I wear all of the armor?"

Arsivus, knowing that there was to be an attempt on Wallace's life, said, "Yes, wear it throughout the rest of the tournament. If it gets to be too much, throw your white flag. There is no dishonor in losing today. Understand?" Wallace nodded his head in agreement and put his armor on with the help of one of the assistants. Once everyone was armed, they all huddled together just shy of the iron gate.

Yura came around the corner and saw them all in disarray and in no particular order. "Ahh, simple instructions are a tough thing these days. Regardless, is everyone ready and prepared?" Everyone nodded their heads. "Ok then. Wait for my command to come out." With that Yura signaled the gatekeeper to open the iron gate and he walked out from underneath it. He walked into the center of the coliseum, which made the crowd get louder in anticipation of the upcoming duels.

"Ladies and gentlemen," Yura began as he waved his hands and spun around to address everyone. "We are about to begin the dueling contest. The rules are simple. It is one-on-one, and no-limitations. Fighters will defend for their lives and will strike their opponents for the win. The blades are dull but are dangerous with enough force. Who will survive, and who will forfeit? These questions will be answered in a few moments. There are three courts outlined here before you. Fighters are to stay within the boundary lines on the ground in white chalk. If a fighter for any reason at all departs the area, they will forfeit the match, resulting in a victory for their opponent. On their first court, we have Zenor fighting against Wallace!"

In the corridor, Ruvio laughed out loud and said, "Don't hurt him too bad, brother. It might be tough with all that armor on him to get a good hit in!" Zenor laughed as well, prompting Wallace to look down at the ground.

From outside, Yura said, "Gentlemen, please take your positions!" and with that both Zenor and Wallace exited the corridor and slowly made their way to the first court as the crowd continued to cheer them on.

Yura continued. "On our second court, we have Huply against Raeolyn. Fighters, take your positions."

Raeolyn walked by and said good luck to Arsivus as she left the tunnel and headed to the court. Yura continued on as he tried to be heard over the cheering crowd.

"Lastly, on our third court, we have Ruvio against Arsivus. Fighters, please take your positions." As Arsivus walked out of the corridor, he looked back and saw Dricaryo flash a quick smile.

Ruvio looked over at Arsivus and said, "Looks like this should be pretty easy for me. I have been waiting for this since we met in the alleyway when I took your little girl-friend. Let's see how you measure up in a fight, shall we?" With that Ruvio pushed Arsivus and ran out of the corridor toward the crowd. The cheers and voices lowered when they saw only Ruvio.

Dricaryo quickly walked up to Arsivus and said, "Don't let him get to you. Stay calm and methodical, and he shouldn't be a problem. Good luck." Arsivus nodded his head and ran out of the tunnel. As soon as he exited and the crowd saw him, the stadium erupted and the people were yelling as loud as they could. As Arsivus ran to his spot, he saw Ruvio looking forlorn that he didn't get a reception like that. As all of the fighters took their places, Yura had one final announcement.

"Fighters, this is a duel. That means that anything goes. If you are bleeding, you must continue. If you are hurt, you must continue. If you can no longer fight, throw the white flag or yield. We will start on court one, then court two, and finally court three. After the match, we will move on to the next event after a short rest period. Dricaryo has drawn a pass for this round and will not compete in this particular duel. Everyone that received a pass from the dueling round will be awarded half of a point. Winners will receive one point and the losers will receive nothing. Are there any questions?" No one spoke, so Yura motioned to the bell ringer high above. "Then let's begin!"

With that, the bell ringer banged the swinging bell and it echoed throughout the kingdom, announcing the start of the event. Zenor was the first to move. He darted toward Wallace, who was clad in armor from head to toe. Zenor raised his sword high and brought it down with a swift motion toward Wallace's left leg.

Wallace was slow to defend the strike and a loud "clang" rang throughout the arena as the edge of Zenor's sword struck true and glanced off. "Ugh!!" could be heard from inside the suit of armor. Zenor was quick to try to strike again as he spun around with his sword but Wallace saw Zenor spin and brought his shield up to block the blow.

"Clang" could again be heard resounding off Wallace's shield. The strike was so hard that it dented the shield and the metal bent in on Wallace's hand, squeezing it between the handle and the inner side of the shield.

"Oww, I can't get it off, I can't get the shield off!" Wallace yelled from inside his helmet as he tried to shake his shield off his hand. Everyone was watching in awe, hoping that the shield came off before Zenor struck again. Wallace wasn't accustomed to pain, and the throbbing was making his head dizzy and his eyes start to water. He opened his face guard with his sword hand so he could see better and tried to swing at Zenor from his hip. Zenor quickly brushed aside the strike and Wallace went in for another. This time it was a thrust straight into the chest of Zenor, but Zenor sidestepped and brought his sword down upon the hilt of Wallace's sword, loosening it from his grip and it fell on the coliseum floor.

Ruvio was laughing out loud as he was cheering on his brother, and Huply joined in the celebration of Zenor, both being as obnoxious as they could. Wallace, now stuck with one hand trapped within his own shield and the other without a sword, began to fight off strike after strike from Zenor who was trying to embarrass him in front of the crowd and knock him down. Wallace had no way of winning the fight; his only chance was to disarm Zenor. But he couldn't swing his shield around to do so in time. All he could do was continue to glance the blows off his shield and hope for a miracle.

After many strikes, Raeolyn finally couldn't take it anymore and yelled out, "Your white flag. Throw it out, Wallace, you need to throw it out!" Wallace had completely forgotten about the flag. As Zenor kept hitting Wallace and sneaking in blows against his shield and legs, Wallace fumbled to locate the flag. Once he grabbed hold of it, he threw it as high as he could to stop the fight. As the flag was coming down, Wallace lowered his shield and with that, Zenor stopped his attack mid-swing. The crowd cheered, not so much for Zenor winning, but because Wallace finally found his flag and threw it down, saving himself from any more punishment.

Yura came out, picked up the white flag, and handed it back to Wallace, and said, "Due to forfeiture, Zenor is declared the winner for this fight!" Zenor raised his hands as a champion would, but little applause followed his celebration. King Thesias was laughing from the bout.

Yura made the next announcement. "We have Huply against Raeolyn. Competitors, are you ready?" Both fighters gave a nod, and with that Yura signaled the bell ringer to begin the fight.

The bell rang out through the tournament halls. Huply ran forward in an attempt to mimic Zenor's attack, but it was met with much resistance. Huply's arm swung back as he tried to bring his sword down in similar fashion but failed as Raeolyn simply sidestepped his attack. Huply again brought his arm to the side to deliver a thrust toward her stomach, but again she left him thrusting through air as she leaned back and let the sword drift right by her.

"She appears very quick and nimble on her feet!" Janos exclaimed, to which Magnus agreed.

"I like her style!" Casily said aloud.

Cardage, still worried about Kadath and Doran, took a sip from his ale and then a bite of his bread and said, "She should do well, I think. She is far better with a sword than him!" Huply drew back and tried to swipe at her feet but she kicked the sword back, which infuriated Huply.

"Are you too afraid to engage me?" he asked her loudly, trying to embarrass her in front of the crowd.

"No, I am just waiting for a good enough strike to warrant my time!" she exclaimed even louder, which sent Huply into a rage. Sweat was now beading on his forehead as his face was turning red. His swings were getting sloppier as he progressed. Huply drew back again and thrust toward her neck and she used her sword to easily parry the blow. She moved in quickly, running her sword down the blade of his as she knocked his feet out from beneath him with a simple kick. Huply was on the ground breathing heavily and the tip of Raeolyn's sword was at his throat. Huply let his sword rest in the dirt as he slowly raised up his hand signaling his yielding to her.

The crowd erupted with laughter and cheered as she withdrew her blade and simply walked away toward where Dricaryo was standing. Wallace had finally gotten his shield off and was standing not far from them as Zenor came over and helped Huply off the ground.

Yura came out again and announced to the crowd, "Ladies and gentlemen, the winner by forfeiture is Raeolyn. Our next competitors will be Ruvio against Arsivus. Gentlemen, are you ready?" to which they nodded their heads. Yura motioned to the bell ringer and he chimed the bell loudly for all to hear. Arsivus swirled the sword in his hand as Ruvio took a few side steps around the court.

"Tell me if I hurt you, boy, because I will try!" Ruvio said as he tried to get into Arsivus's head. Arsivus continued to watch Ruvio's movements waiting for the right time to close the distance. Ruvio didn't give him a chance though, as he continued to side step to the very edge of the border. As Arsivus twirled his sword around again, Ruvio saw his chance and quickly darted in toward him. With a mighty thrust, Ruvio lunged forward in hopes of ending the match in one swing. His hopes were dashed when Arsivus moved to the side, and as Ruvio came closer to him, Arsivus punched Ruvio in the face with his sword hand. Ruvio dropped to the ground. He rose up and put his hand to his nose. He pulled it away and it was covered in blood.

"That was a cheap shot. That isn't dueling!" Ruvio exclaimed aloud, but everyone in the crowd drowned him out with their laughing and cheering. Ruvio immediately became angered and tightened his grip on his sword as he charged back toward Arsivus. This time, his sword was drawn back and he swung it toward Arsivus's head, which Arsivus blocked. Ruvio came again at him with a strong swipe to his side, which Arsivus blocked with his sword again. Ruvio tried to throw in a punch as quick as he could, but it was timed poorly and Arsivus simply dodged it while maintaining his stance. Ruvio backed up and grabbed his sword and came back at Arsivus with anger and impatience. Arsivus parried one blow and dodged another as the crowd cheered on.

"Kadath has taught him well!" Cardage said as Magnus looked on with joy.

Janos put his mug down and said, "He hasn't gone on the offensive aside from his punch, but he is winning the battle. Such fine patience for a man his age!"

Magnus nodded in agreement and said, "I agree, his mannerisms are much like his father's. He will prove to be a worthy asset if he wins!" Arsivus continued his game of cat and mouse with Ruvio, who continued to get more flustered with each missed swing. Arsivus lowered his guard and gave an opening for the top of his body. Ruvio started to close the distance between the two when Arsivus came forward with his sword low. Ruvio, in an attempt to gain an advantage, kicked dirt up into the air and into Arsivus's face, which drew immediate boos and contempt from the crowd. Zenor and Huply were now cheering wildly for Ruvio as Arsivus battled to cleanse his eyes and continued to block the incoming strikes from Ruvio.

"I suppose that wasn't a part of dueling either!" Ruvio said as he continued to rain down blows on Arsivus's sword. But Arsivus somehow managed to find the strength, fortitude, and skill to continue to find Ruvio's sword in his blind condition. Arsivus had a good feeling about his whereabouts in their court. He knew he was in the center, and Ruvio kept moving sideways as to not attack him in the front. Arsivus knew he only had to knock Ruvio out of the court boundaries to gain a win, so he now made an attempt to make that happen.

He parried the blows from Ruvio over and over again. Left, right, right, down, left, and right, each blow bringing Ruvio closer to Arsivus without him knowing it, due to him continuing to shuffle sideways with each strike. Finally, Arsivus had his partial eyesight back, enough to make out Ruvio's sword, his shape, and his motions.

Now was Arsivus's time to strike. "You have had your fun. Now it is time to end this!" Arsivus said in a strong voice. Ruvio brought his sword up and attempted to bring it down on Arsivus's head. Arsivus glided out of the way as Ruvio brought his sword back up and attempted to thrust it again.

Arsivus knocked the blow out of the way, which brought Ruvio closer to him. When Ruvio was within arm's reach, Arsivus dropped his shield and opened hand slapped him on the face, which brought an uproar of laugher from the stands and a shocked look from Ruvio. With Ruvio's hand to his face, Arsivus lifted his knee to his chest and kicked directly into Ruvio's chest, which sent him flying backward out of the court boundaries, where he landed squarely on his back as his sword flew out of his hand.

The crowd was cheering joyfully and singing praise for Arsivus as Yura came out and said, "Due to the boundary infraction, Arsivus is declared the winner, with interesting tactics I might add!" The crowd continued to cheer and Janos, Casily, Cardage, and Magnus toasted each other and cheered as well. Up above on King Thesias's level, Atalee gave a quick smile but retracted it as Thesias threw his goblet down into the arena and berated one of his assistants in his anger at his son's loss.

"We shall give the fighters a moment of reprieve to catch their breath and regain their composure and for the next round to be set up," Yura said. "Please refill your beverages, as well as your platters, and the festivities shall resume shortly. Fighters, please return to your resting chambers and await my return." And with that, Yura departed and the fighters returned to the tunnel while the crowds got up to replenish their beverages and food.

"Well done, Arsivus!" Magnus could barely be heard saying from above as Arsivus walked by.

"Well done, Arsivus, you sure showed him!" Wallace said as they walked down the corridor. Arsivus felt a little bit better now that his eyes were cleared, and he smiled as they walked.

"He got lucky. I would like to see him try that on me!" Zenor claimed.

"Be careful what you wish for, boy. You might just get it," Raeolyn responded to Zenor.

"No one was talking to you prisoner," Huply said.

One of the guards escorting them through the corridors spoke loudly for all to hear after Huply's remark. "Listen up, if any of you fight outside of the arena, you will be expelled from the tournament altogether. Is that understood? Keep it down until you are out there." That quieted the contestants down. They reached their resting chambers and all went to their respective places—Dricaryo to his bed, Raeolyn to her bench with her guards, Zenor, Ruvio, and Huply to the armory, and Wallace to his corner.

Arsivus went over to where there was water resting in a barrel, dipped his hand in and brought it to his eyes. Immediately he started to feel better and a cool sensation ran through his body. He looked at Wallace and saw he was still nursing his hand from when his shield had squeezed it. Arsivus grabbed one of the herbs from the water and brought it over to him.

"What is that?" Wallace asked as Arsivus knelt down and placed the herb on Wallace's wrist.

"These are called healing herbs; my family grows them. They aid knights with wounds sustained in battle. Since you were in battle, I see no reason for you not to have it," Arsivus said with a smile.

Both Raeolyn and Dricaryo were watching Arsivus and Wallace, but Zenor was the first to speak up. "Were you planning on tending all of his wounds? Maybe you would like to fight his battles for him as well. I know I would like that!" He said with a smug look on his face.

Arsivus, not looking away from what he was doing, simply replied, "I thought the pretty lady told you to be careful what you wish for, as it may just come true!" This brought a smile and a faint giggle from Raeolyn. Zenor let out a "hmph" and turned back to engage with his brother and Huply.

Arsivus continued to apply the herb. Wallace asked, "Why are you helping me?" Arsivus did not know how to answer without letting him know that Teslark had asked him to look out for him, which he knew may hurt his feelings or destroy his confidence.

Arsivus decided to keep it simple and said, "If honor was enough, you would already be a knight, but you need more skill if you are to win this day. I will assist you where I can, as much as I am able to see that it happens."

Wallace smiled and simply said, "Thank you!"

With that, Yura appeared in the room and said, "Contestants, the next round is about to start. Take your places in the corridor again and enter when called." With that, they all got up and made their way toward the door.

Arsivus stopped Wallace and removed his gauntlets for him. "Why did you do that?" Wallace asked. Arsivus threw them to the ground. "They are too heavy for you. They slow your response to a strike. Keep your armor on, but you don't need those."

Wallace again said thank you and they joined the others in the corridor.

Once they got there, Arsivus said, "Also, your hand won't get stuck again," and he offered Wallace a smile, which Wallace returned.

Yura made his way into the coliseum and saw that the stadium was packed full. Everyone was patiently awaiting the next round. "Ladies and gentlemen," Yura announced, "we start our next dueling competition and it should be very interesting. Our leader so far is Arsivus with eleven points. Next is Dricaryo with nine and a half points. Zenor and Raeolyn are close behind and tied with nine points. And Huply, Ruvio, and Wallace are tied with seven points. This next competition is a two-on-one where the single fighter may use two swords if he or she wishes, and the splits are as follows: court one will have Arsivus and Raeolyn against Dricaryo; court two will have Zenor and Huply against

Wallace, and Ruvio will receive half of a point as he receives a pass this round. Contestants, enter your courts." With that, the fighters entered the coliseum to enormous applause from the crowd and took their positions. The courts which were bigger now that there were only two drawn out in the arena.

"Court one, are you ready?" Yura asked and Arsivus, Raeolyn, and Dricaryo all nodded their heads as Dricaryo grabbed a second sword from the side.

Yura looked to the bell ringer and said, "Then let's begin!" Raeolyn was the first to make her move as she ran to the opposite side of Dricaryo. Dricaryo had Arsivus on his right side and Raeolyn on his left and was facing the second court and the stadium full of people. Raeolyn dashed in and came with a quick slice to the front, which Dricaryo parried with ease. This gave Arsivus a chance to move in as well, and he went with a swipe of the sword to try to disarm Dricaryo as fast as he could. Dricaryo rotated his arm and deflected the sword toward Raeolyn. The strength of Dricaryo's parry threw Arsivus off balance enough for Dricaryo to push him over to Raeolyn's side again. The crowd cheered on for all three competitors, as they had become the fan favorites.

Arsivus jumped in again with a high strike and Raeolyn followed suit with a low strike. Dricaryo parried both with ease and kept at Arsivus and Raeolyn, delivering his own high and low strikes.

"What do you think his strategy is?" Janos asked loudly.

Cardage took a sip from his ale and said, "The two-on-one is a tough match. You have to get your opponents alone, and quickly, or you will tire out and then you will be done. I believe he is going to try and throw as many strikes at them as possible to keep them busy while he keeps pushing them back and keeping them together so they are limited as to how they can attack him. That is what I would do anyway."

"That is a good tactic. I think Dricaryo might pull it off. You on the other hand," Janos said with a smile. "I don't think you could do it."

Magnus laughed from his position. He looked up and saw Atalee eyeing them. Thesias was nowhere to be seen on his balcony. Magnus gave Atalee a look asking where Thesias went, to which Atalee responded by shrugging his shoulders. Magnus, now annoyed that Thesias wasn't where he should be, turned his attention toward the fight. Dricaryo was still swinging his swords with ease from both hands as he continued to push Raeolyn and Arsivus back toward the edge.

Raeolyn was the first to notice what was going on and said to Arsivus, "We need to get behind him, and we need to do it soon." Arsivus continued to parry blow after blow and waited for the most opportune moment.

"I will call it," Arsivus said, as he was starting to memorize Dricaryo's pattern.

"Clink, clink, clink," was all that could be heard as Arsivus waited. Raeolyn finally said, "*Well?*"

Arsivus parried one last blow and yelled, "Now!" With that, they swooped to the sides, which caused Dricaryo to have his back to the edge of the border where they just were.

Raeolyn yelled out, "You go low and then high. I will do the same!"

Arsivus, not losing a step, yelled, "Let's go!" and the two started swinging their own strikes toward Dricaryo.

"Their teamwork is great!" Cardage said to the group.

"Excellent swordsmanship, one goes low, the other goes high, and then they rotate and switch," Janos commented aloud.

Dricaryo continued to fend off the attacks and gave a kick to Raeolyn, which sent her back but left Dricaryo's right flank open. Arsivus saw this and dodged a strike then rolled on the ground to avoid a downward attack but also to position himself in Dricaryo's unprotected flank. Dricaryo still had his sword on the ground because he was concentrated on fending off Raeolyn's attacks. With all his strength, Arsivus swung down and loosed the sword from Dricaryo's right hand, which startled everyone and made the crowd cheer loudly.

"Yes, great job!" Casily yelled from above to Arsivus. Dricaryo brought his left hand with his sword back to swipe at Arsivus and as he overreached to get to him, Raeolyn hit Dricaryo's sword from below and sent it flying into the air. The crowd erupted into applause. Now weaponless, Dricaryo had no other option but to forfeit the match. The crowd rose to their feet applauding all three of the competitors for a great match, which prompted Yura to emerge and attempt to speak over the crowd. "Ladies and gentlemen," Yura said, "due to a forfeiture of the well-fought match, the winners from court one are Arsivus and Raeolyn." Everyone was cheering loudly as the three stayed on the court and complimented one another on their style.

"Well fought!" Dricaryo said, as they were walking off the court and over to the side to watch the next match.

"You as well," Arsivus said as they put their swords down and stood next to Ruvio, who was looking anxious.

"I didn't think you would come at us like that. Your techniques were great," Raeolyn said.

"Not great enough. I wanted you together at first, but then when you both gave me the slip, I would have preferred you separate," Dricaryo said with a smile.

Yura could be heard talking over the cheers and the crowd, "Next up on court two, Zenor and Huply against Wallace. Fighters, any questions?" Zenor and Huply shook their heads no, while Wallace was debating whether to go with a sword or a shield for his second hand.

Arsivus looked at him and debated. He knew a shield would prove a better suit for Wallace, but two swords would give him an edge that they wouldn't expect.

Arsivus walked closer to Wallace and said, "Shield, take your shield." Wallace looked over at him and nodded his head. He could see the anxiety and fear in Wallace's face. As Arsivus was walking back toward Dricaryo and Raeolyn, he looked in the crowd and saw Korgal and Teslark in the lower levels. Arsivus looked to Teslark and gave an advice-seeking shrug, asking if his choice was correct. Teslark nodded his head in agreement.

"I have a feeling that this isn't going to be good for young Wallace," Dricaryo said.

Arsivus said, "These pairings are fixed; someone wants to make an example out of him."

From their side came a voice, "He just has bad luck, that is all," Ruvio said. "It isn't our fault that we are always paired against him." He grinned.

"There had better be some honor in these pairings or you —"

Raeolyn was cut off by Ruvio. "Or what, or you will what? You are a prisoner, and we are the King's sons. There is nothing that you or your friends can do to us. We are untouchable."

Then he moved toward the court to cheer on his brother. "Come on, Zenor. Let's go, Huply! Show this squire what being a knight is truly about," he shouted.

Yura signaled the bell ringer and the bell was chimed, starting the battle. Huply went in first swinging over his head to draw Wallace's attention. Wallace threw his shield up to block the blow, but while he was doing that, Zenor walked calmly to Wallace's right side and threw a quick jab to see if he was paying attention. Wallace saw him but was too slow to block it, and the jab hit him in the ribs. Wallace winced and started to favor his right side as Huply again delivered a heavy blow from up top that was demanding of Wallace's attention.

Zenor was taking his time now, for he was certain they would win. Zenor swung at Wallace's feet now, and every one of his strikes was filled with intent and landed squarely on Wallace's shins. A hot breeze filled the stadium, and Wallace felt it as he was having trouble breathing. Ruvio was having the time of his life watching this, and he could not stop cheering and laughing. Huply moved more to his right and feigned a strike from above, which prompted Wallace to raise his shield again.

When he did this, Huply kicked him in his unprotected ribs. "Come on, this isn't fair!" Arsivus said as he jumped forward with sword in hand and ran toward the court. One of the guards on the main coliseum floor was quick to step in and attempt to block Arsivus from joining in, but Arsivus dodged the guard with ease as another guard dove at his feet and tripped him up.

"Stay down, or you will be thrown from the tournament!" the guard exclaimed. The crowd got more and more quiet as the fight went on. The cheers for Wallace had dissipated and with each and every strike on him, more eyes turned away from the fight. All that could be heard was the clanging of metal as Zenor's and Huply's strikes landed upon Wallace, and Ruvio's laughter. Wallace was getting too tired to raise his shield to block any more strikes, and he slowly let it drop to the ground.

Upon seeing this, the crowd gasped and Arsivus yelled, "Throw your flag, throw your flag now." Wallace looked to Arsivus upon the ground and acknowledged his command. He took his eyes off the fight and searched with dazed eyes for his flag. He found it as the blows kept hitting him on his chest plate and his legs. Zenor saw that he went for his flag and heaved back his sword.

As Wallace threw his flag into the air, Yura called, "Ring the bell, the match is now over!" with haste in his voice. The flag was falling down toward the ground and the bell had been rung when Zenor moved forth with his last and final strike. He brought the broad side of his sword against the side of Wallace's helmet, which dropped Wallace right where he stood. The crowd erupted with anger and began booing.

"Nooo!" Arsivus yelled as he scrambled out from underneath the guard with his sword in hand. Huply and Ruvio were quick to join Zenor's side in a defensive stance as Arsivus made his way to Wallace's side.

"It's ok, farmer. He was just tired, that's all." Zenor said.

Huply jumped in, "He just wanted a quick nap. That could have ended much worse."

Ruvio, not to be left out, chimed in as well. "They went easy on him. They were merciful. Perhaps in the next round, we won't be." Arsivus checked Wallace and his eyes were open. There was a little blood coming down from his nose and some on his lips. His armor was dented and he looked completely scared.

"You fought well. Let me help you up and you can get some rest," Arsivus said and as he went to grab Wallace's hand, a rock hit Wallace in the arm.

Arsivus looked up and saw that Ruvio had heaved a small rock at him. "Maybe he would fight better with a rock. He would have a better chance at hitting at least one of us," Ruvio said and laughed. Fire burned like embers in Arsivus's eyes as he felt his blood boil on the inside. Arsivus stood up with sword in hand and started walking toward the three. Ruvio was the first to shut his mouth and he started to step back. Huply soon followed suit. Zenor was the only one to stand his ground. The crowd went wild seeing Arsivus walking toward them.

Yura tried to intervene and tried to calm the crowd but to no avail. His voice was easily drowned out by the cheers for Arsivus. Arsivus twirled the sword in his right hand as he bent down to pick up Wallace's sword as he walked by it. He stood up again with both swords and continued to walk toward them. Seeing this, the crowd got even louder and more excited. Arsivus looked out of the corner of his eye and saw that Dricaryo and Raeolyn were right behind him walking toward Zenor, Ruvio, and Huply. The stadium was ecstatic and filled with loud cheers calling for Arsivus to go after them. Ruvio and Huply fanned out, with Huply on the left, Ruvio on the right, and Zenor in the center. Arsivus stayed in the middle and Dricaryo went in front of Huply and Raeolyn in front of Ruvio. The crowd was now screaming for they all wanted the exact same thing, for Arsivus and his crew to pummel Zenor and his. Before the fight could begin, Yura called for the guards and within moments, twenty armed guards made their way onto the arena floor and stood in between the two groups, forcing them to walk away.

As soon as the guards were in place, Ruvio started in again with his mouth. "It is a good thing they showed up. I guess I won't get another chance to thrash you. It's a shame really, because I think the next round will be really entertaining. Your mother must be so proud of you, for whatever time she has left." With that, Zenor hit Ruvio with his sword and gave him a very stern look.

"What did you say?" Arsivus commanded, as anger flared up in him. Zenor quickly grabbed Ruvio and led him off the court.

"What did you say about my mother?" Arsivus yelled as Zenor left through the gate down below the arena. Arsivus looked up toward the crowd and saw Teslark and Korgal applauding for Arsivus, Dricaryo, and Raeolyn and their support of Wallace. Teslark pointed directly at Arsivus and then continued his applause. Arsivus saw this and acknowledged it with a nod.

All three of them helped Wallace to his feet, and Yura finally managed to get control of the crowd. "This has been an exciting day so far, hasn't it," Yura said. "Lots of emotions, lots of loyalty, lots of anger. Ladies and gentlemen, the winner from court two is Huply and Zenor due to forfeiture. We shall take another short break to prepare for the last round of the day. Due to circumstances, the fighters will be broken apart downstairs as we can barely keep them separated while they are up here. Arsivus, Dricaryo, Raeolyn, and Wallace, would you please return to your resting chambers? Zenor, Ruvio, and Huply have been moved to another side of the coliseum for obvious reasons. Wait for me to come and get you." With that the four walked proudly to the iron gate as the crowd cheered their names as loud as they could.

CHAPTER 22

"Wow, that went south very quickly. Wallace suffered some pretty serious attacks in that battle," Janos said.

"It wasn't supposed to be like this. Thesias has it all rigged," Magnus said as he was looking at the board.

"I don't know how much more Wallace can take. It would take a fighter of maximum caliber to survive a three-on-one," Cardage said. Magnus walked back over to the ledge and drank from his ale as he looked up toward Thesias's booth. All he saw was Atalee standing there with a mug of ale as well. Atalee shook his head sideways, as Magnus acknowledged Thesias's absence.

Magnus got an idea. "I will be back before the fight begins," he said to Cardage and Janos. And with that, he left the balcony and exited through the door down to the coliseum. "I wonder where he is going?" Janos said.

"I think down to the fighter's quarters to end this," Cardage said.

Very soon after, a large amount of cheering and commotion could be heard as the crowd applauded Magnus as he walked across the coliseum floor through the iron gates down below. "Ha, good idea, General! Very good idea," Janos said with a smirk.

Zenor, Ruvio, and Huply shuffled in to a side room and Yura closed the door behind them. "Ugh, I wanted one more swing at him!" Huply said with disappointment.

"You will get your chance; this next battle should be very fun indeed!" Ruvio said with pleasure. Zenor laughed it off as Ruvio joined in.

"I really got into Arsivus's head, didn't I?" Ruvio said, and he laughed some more.

"Yes, you did, you imbecile!" could be heard from the doorway as King Thesias entered the room.

"Father!!" Ruvio said as he scrambled to stand up.

"What were you thinking saying that, especially in front of the entire kingdom, you fool." Thesias demanded.

Ruvio searched for the right words, but they were all lost. "I, I, I thought—" was all he could get out before Thesias interrupted with a booming voice.

"That is the problem with you, you thought. But not about the kingdom, or my plans, but only about your petty ego. Hopefully nothing bad comes from you exposing our plan, for if it does, I shall have your head. Regardless if you are my son or not. Idiot!" And with that Thesias stormed out of the room.

Ruvio now looked downcast and had gone quiet as Zenor and Huply both tried not to laugh at him. "That was a stupid thing to say, but boy did it get him riled up!" Huply said, trying to encourage Ruvio.

"Ehh," was all that Ruvio muttered as he sat and stared at the fire before him.

"Just think," Zenor said. "Next round, we will fight again, and then soon be knights. No more chores or people looking at us with contempt. We will be respected as we should be." This drew no immediate response from Ruvio. They all looked into the fire imagining what life would be like after the tournament.

"When we get that pendant from his mother, we will be unstoppable!" Zenor exclaimed.

"I wonder if she will be hurt, or if she will just surrender it?" Ruvio asked.

"Well, enough of this clamoring, let's prepare for the next round," Huply said with encouragement as the three stood up and grabbed their swords and each of them a shield.

"How are you feeling?" Arsivus asked Wallace as he was taking off his armor.

"Bruised and beaten," Wallace said with a smile.

"Raeolyn, can you grab me some more herbs?" Arsivus asked as he helped Wallace with the clasps.

"Sure thing," Raeolyn said as she plucked five of them from the barrel and brought them over to Arsivus. Dricaryo was looking at more armor for Wallace for the next round and Arsivus was applying the herbs with Raeolyn's assistance.

"I should just quit now. There is no way I can win," Wallace said as he looked down toward the ground.

Arsivus looked at Raeolyn and then at Dricaryo, and said, "It is up to you. There is no dishonor in falling out. That was quite a fight you endured. No one would judge you harshly for your decision."

"He is right," Dricaryo added. "You have fought well so far. If you feel you cannot go further, do not push yourself."

Raeolyn jumped in. "There is always the next tournament. After some more practice you would be a fierce competitor."

As the herbs were being laid upon his body, Wallace said, "Thank you all. We did not know each other when we started, but I consider you to be my friends. I hope this tournament turns out well for all of you, but I cannot subside now. I must finish what I started." There was a moment of silence as everyone was thinking the same thing; that Wallace should drop out. But ultimately it was his decision and no one could make it for him unfortunately.

"Then you will need proper armor. Here, put this on!" Dricaryo said as he grabbed a new full set of armor that was lighter and more protective. He pulled it from a different rack not meant for the tournament, but he didn't care.

"You will need a lighter sword and shield as well," said Raeolyn. "Take these!" And she picked out a pair from the rack that were different from the normal swords given to competitors. Arsivus looked at Wallace and wanted to tell him to quit, but he could not.

Arsivus walked over to the barrel and picked up more herbs and brought them back to Wallace. "Stand up!" he said to him. Wallace stood and Arsivus started to place the herbs all over his body. He tied them down all around him so they stayed in place and provided healing wherever he was to get hit. "We will do our best to ensure you last until the end then. Dricaryo, let's get his armor on," Arsivus said. Dricaryo nodded and unhinged the armor and helped Wallace attach it to himself. Raeolyn brought over the sword and shield and gave it to Wallace. As Wallace stood there, Arsivus brought him some water and Wallace drank some of it.

"You look like a warrior!" a voice boomed. Everyone turned to see Magnus standing in the doorway.

"General!" Arsivus said. "What brings you down here?" Magnus walked into the room and looked around then motioned for all of them to gather around Wallace.

Wallace was now looking a bit uncomfortable. "What is it, sir?" Wallace clamored out somehow.

Magnus put his hand on Wallace's shoulder and said, "Son, you have fought valiantly so far. The next match is a three-on-one. You have been picked to be the one, and you can guess who the other three are. I want you to withdraw from the contest. King Thesias has declared that this fight can go to the death, and I am afraid you will meet yours at the hands of those men. This is no time to mince words. I want you to withdraw from the tournament."

Everyone was quiet, and Wallace was searching the ground for words and thoughts as Arsivus jumped in. "Wallace, please consider the General's words. You do not have to do this. You can back out."

"It would be wise," Dricaryo said.

Raeolyn agreed saying, "Yeah," with a solemn tone.

Wallace looked at each of them and shook his head. "No, I cannot. I told my mother that I would become a knight. I told my uncle that I would become a knight, and he would not run; therefore, I cannot run. Even in the face of certain loss, they fight because that is what they do. They fight for what they believe in. I will continue in this tournament, and I will fight for you. I will fight for them, and I will fight for me. Thank you for your kind words, but I reject your advice this time, friends."

Magnus nodded in acknowledgment. "Very well then, son. Best of luck to you," he said as he turned toward the door to leave.

Yura walked in shortly after and said, "Fighters, are you ready?" Everyone gave a quick nod except Wallace, which prompted Yura to ask, "Son, are you ready? Are you sure you want to continue?" he asked with a cautious tone.

"Just a moment. Can I write something down to give to you?" Wallace asked Yura.

"Yes, hurry though, the next round is supposed to start very quickly!" Yura responded.

"I will," Wallace said. He took a piece of parchment and scribbled down a few sentences. He wrapped it up and gave it to Yura. When he did this, he leaned in and whispered something to Yura as well.

Yura nodded as he listened, and then said, "I understand." Yura then asked again, "Is everyone ready?"

"Yes, let's go," Wallace responded with courage.

Yura took a moment and said, "Very well. This way, please." He led them out through the corridor to the iron gate.

"Same instructions as before. Wait here until I call you out, and best of luck to all of you." Yura departed to go address the crowd when some clamoring started behind them. They turned and saw Zenor, Ruvio, and Huply being led up the same corridor, although they were being set up on the other side of the walkway.

"Ahh look, he has a new set of armor. How cute," Ruvio said.

"It would be a shame if this one got all dented up as well," Huply added. This angered Dricaryo and he turned and started slowly walking toward the group. The guards immediately jumped in to stop any unnecessary bloodshed before the tournament continued.

"Save it for the fight!" they said as the guards set up a barrier between Dricaryo and the group.

Outside, Yura addressed the crowd once more. "Ladies and gentlemen, are you ready for our last fight of the day? This contest will feature a three-on-one fight. The same rules apply. One point will be awarded for victory. If someone doesn't finish, gets knocked out of the boundary, or cannot continue for any reason at all, they receive no points at all. King Thesias has also decreed that this fight may go to the death if the fighters so choose. That being said, they must defend for their life. I must remind the competitors that they still have use of the white flag in this competition. In court one, we have Zenor, Ruvio, and Huply against Wallace!" This prompted the crowd to boo at the drawings.

"See you out there, boy!" Zenor said to Wallace as the three of them ran to the court waving their hands in the air attempting to get some support from the crowd.

"Good luck to you guys!" Wallace said to Arsivus, Dricaryo, and Raeolyn as he walked by them.

"Wallace!" Arsivus said. Wallace turned to him. "Go for one of them at a time, and do not relent until he is taken out, then focus on another. Do this until they are all out of the fight, understand?" Arsivus said hopefully.

"I understand!" Wallace replied with a smile. "See you in the end," Wallace said as he exited the tunnel and entered the coliseum with a thunderous applause from the crowd as soon as they saw him. He took his position on one side of the enlarged court and his opponents were on the other.

"Ladies and gentlemen, we also have a surprise for you on court two," Yura announced. "For the three-on-one match, we have Dricaryo, Raeolyn, and Arsivus. Please welcome them with open arms." As they walked out of the tunnel, the crowd erupted again with applause and cheers for them. Their names could be heard echoing across the stadium, which brought smiles to their faces.

"Remember, the fighters must stay inside of the boundaries or they will forfeit the match. Any questions?" Everyone was quiet and awaited the call for the bell. Yura went on. "Then let's begin. Ring the bell!" and he motioned for the bell ringer to start the match. As the bell rang, Arsivus, Dricaryo, and Raeolyn were standing there confused, as their opponent was not yet present. The crowd shared in their confusion. Since they had no one to fight, they cheered on Wallace who, once the bell rang, charged forward to try to eliminate one of the fighters he was against. Wallace went right for Zenor, which caught all three of them off guard. With no hesitation, Wallace was bringing down strikes left and right, throwing in sweeping kicks, shield pushes, and body hits as fast as he could on Zenor.

The fast flurry of attacks was enough to push Zenor back to the edge of the border. "What a madman!" Huply exclaimed as Ruvio yelled out, "Let's get him." Both Huply and Ruvio attacked from the sides that Wallace was not protecting at this time. Ruvio's first strike caught Wallace on his right kneecap, but Wallace seemed to not notice. Just then, very large chains could be heard throughout the stadium being coiled up on a spool. Everyone went silent as the coliseum floor started to shake. It was in court two where the ground was reverberating the most, opposite of Arsivus, Dricaryo, and Raeolyn.

The ground shook as dust rose into the air. Two large metal plates in the floor were slowly being pulled apart, exposing a chamber underneath that had chains attached at the four corners. A loud roar was heard resonating from the depths of the chamber. Even Zenor and his crew had stopped fighting and were now watching with keen interest as to what was being brought up. Magnus came back into the viewing room through the door and immediately went to the edge. He looked up and saw Thesias smiling with pleasure from up above as Atalee peered down into the chasm as best he could.

Cardage was the first to say it, but they all knew who it was. "Midemos!" Cardage said as the horns could now be seen above the floor of the coliseum. The crowd was frenzied from the excitement mixed with fear. "*Roar!*" could be heard coming from down below as Arsivus, Raeolyn, and Dricaryo slowly stepped back and readied their weapons. Janos could see the beast was holding a large staff that was as tall as Midemos himself. It was made from thick black oak and had massive blades on both ends. The Eglician twirled the staff in the air for all to see.

"There is so much dust, you can barely see him from up here. But he looks just as regal as before, except they made him wear a helmet now, but such a strong creature nonetheless!" Cardage exclaimed excitedly. As the platform was nearly at the top, the crowd was going wild, for they had never seen a beast of that size. The guards on the coliseum floor were visibly shaken, and the mixture of fear and excitement was almost too much to handle.

Yura came back out of the gate and announced, "And their opponent," referring to Arsivus, Raeolyn, and Dricaryo. "He is a beast from out of our kingdom, an Eglician who has been held captive for some time once he landed upon our shores. His strength is mighty, his purpose is to survive. Ladies and gentlemen, I give you, Midemos!" But the crowd's cheers and auditory responses to the beast in front of them drowned out Yura as he pronounced his name to the crowd so that no one could hear it. With that, Midemos stared straight ahead as Yura walked up and unlocked the chains that were binding him.

Yura continued. "The King has decreed that if the beast wins this battle, he shall be granted his freedom. If not, he shall be given his final breath from these competitors. Let's begin!" he said as he left through the iron gate and it closed behind him. Midemos was squinting as he was adjusting to the brightness of the arena, as well as all of the dust that had risen from the ground, making it very tough to see anything at all. Raeolyn quickly swung behind him. Midemos saw her movement through the scattered dust remnants and altered his stance to defend against her. Arsivus joined her thought process and moved to his side while Dricaryo stayed to the right. Midemos moved again to counter their attack and everyone readied their weapons while Midemos's back was to the border of the court.

"We must attack him at once. He is too large for one-on-one combat. Everyone ready?" Raeolyn said with impatience.

Dricaryo lowered his guard for a second and looked at Midemos and said to himself, "That staff!" but was cut off as he was prompted by his teammate.

"Now!" Arsivus commanded as they all converged on him at the same time. Midemos, not having the freedom to move for quite some time, was quick to strike, but held back using lethal means. Raeolyn was the first to reach him and brought a hard swing down in front of his chest, which he swatted out of the way with his hunting staff and kicked her in the stomach, which sent her flying away. Arsivus was the next one to reach him as he ran toward Midemos. Midemos swung his staff sideways hoping to knock Arsivus out of the ring, but Arsivus slid underneath it and ended up on the other side of Midemos, drawing his attention away from Dricaryo. Raeolyn was up now and both her and Arsivus were striking from one side, giving Dricaryo a chance to strike from the other side. Dricaryo moved in through the thick dust to get a better look, but Midemos reached through and grabbed Arsivus and threw him to the side.

As Arsivus was being flung through the air, his right heel whipped around and kicked Dricaryo on the side of the head, which dropped him to the ground. Raeolyn was the only one left standing as she grabbed Dricaryo's sword and prepared to fight one-on-one while Arsivus reclaimed his footing.

"Clang, clang!" could be heard from the other court as Arsivus looked up and saw Zenor, Ruvio, and Huply all surrounding Wallace as Wallace was down to his knee. His shield was above him protecting his head from the strikes coming down like before. They got the jump on him while he was watching Midemos and them fight. All three were laughing as they hit him harder and harder with every blow. Ruvio spat on Wallace as Huply kicked him in the side of the head. Arsivus could see blood dripping from his helmet as Wallace stayed in his position.

"Ugh," could be heard from Raeolyn as she was thrown aside by Midemos, right next to Arsivus and Dricaryo, who were already on the ground.

"We need to figure out something!" Raeolyn said as she shook Dricaryo back to consciousness. Midemos took his time coming back to his competitors as he swung his large staff around. The three of them got up and Dricaryo took back his sword.

Arsivus said, "Wallace is in trouble." With that all three of them looked over and saw that Wallace hadn't moved, but he was still defending against his attackers.

"We are in trouble too!" Raeolyn said as Midemos drew closer.

Arsivus yelled to Wallace, "Focus on one, Wallace, just one!" With that, Wallace looked in Arsivus's direction and nodded his head. Midemos saw this and looked over at the young squire and then focused back on his opponents. Midemos saw that his opponents were more concerned with what was happening on the other court so he slowed his momentum down and glanced back at Wallace.

"These must be the ones that Sir Cardage told me about!" Midemos thought to himself as he looked at his competitors again.

The blows kept coming down upon Wallace and he was hurting now, but he was waiting for his chance. He had limited visibility, but he could see where Zenor was by the footwear he was wearing.

"Clang, clang, clang!" could be heard resonating through the stadium. Dricaryo was shaking his head after recovering from Arsivus's boot.

He looked up and over at Wallace. "This doesn't look good. He needs our help. Do we go to his aid?" Dricaryo asked aloud.

"That is no way to fight a battle. There is no honor in what those three are doing to him!" Arsivus said.

"It is simple, he is not battle worthy. He should not be in this competition. He appears lucky to have made it this far," Midemos said as he continued to look over toward the first court.

Dricaryo turned his full attention toward their opponent. "That voice!" he said. "It cannot be. Midemos?"

Midemos turned his attention back toward his opponents and responded, "Dricaryo?"

"Stop, stop this now!" Dricaryo yelled as he dropped his weapon.

"What are you doing?" Arsivus yelled out.

"I thought you were lost. I had all but given up hope," Dricaryo said. "My last attempt was to swear my loyalty to this King in return that he aids me in finding you."

Midemos lowered his weapon and said, "It was this King that took me prisoner in hopes of finding treasure."

Dricaryo, now more enraged than ever, said, "The King's entire family is corrupt. Those are his sons over there!" and he pointed to Ruvio and Zenor.

As Midemos looked over, King Thesias began yelling from above, "Lower the platform. Guards, kill the Eglician!" which brought utter confusion to the guards. Just then, when Zenor had halted his attack to see why his father was yelling, Wallace dug his foot deep into the coliseum sand. He dropped his shield and sword to the ground with intent. He ran with every ounce of strength he had left toward Zenor. He picked him up on his shoulder, much to Zenor's surprise. His legs burned from being beat on all day. His head was pounding from all of the strikes that he endured. But his rage was full. Full of being bullied, made fun of, and that was enough for him. He ran with Zenor on his shoulder to the edge of the court and threw Zenor up into the air before

Huply or Ruvio could do anything about it. As Zenor was coming down, Wallace hailed his arm back as fast as he could and lunged forward with everything left in his body and hit Zenor square in the nose.

Zenor went flying back as he screamed in pain, "Argghh!!!" and landed outside of the court.

Yura yelled, "Zenor has been eliminated from the fight. It is now two-on-one. Huply and Ruvio rushed toward Wallace and began hitting him as hard as they could. Zenor clutched his face in pain as he writhed on the coliseum floor. Wallace was now doubled over with no protection, no sword, taking hit after hit. Midemos roared loudly for everyone to hear. The sound was deafening and was enough to cease the strikes that Ruvio and Huply were delivering to Wallace.

Midemos said to Dricaryo, "Go help your friend!"

With that, Midemos stepped outside of the court, which prompted Yura to announce, "Midemos has forfeited the match. The winners are Arsivus, Dricaryo, and Raeolyn."

He barely finished his announcement when King Thesias yelled from his grandstand, "Kill the Eglician, kill the beast!" to his guards. The guards all rushed toward Midemos but were cautious because he was still armed with his hunting staff. He stood armed and waiting for the guards to come near. As they approached him with swords drawn, Midemos dispatched them as fast as they had arrived, single-handedly defeating the entire platoon of the arena guards.

"Arrows, lances, sleeping agents, throw everything you have at him!" Thesias begged his guards, as Midemos started to crawl up the stands toward where Thesias was sitting. This prompted Atalee to draw his weapon in anticipation.

Midemos made it to the lower deck and was soon surrounded by guards with lances on all sides. A lone archer stood next to Atalee and fired as fast as he could toward Midemos. Most of them missed, but four arrows lodged into his legs. One of the guards holding a pike lunged at Midemos and struck him in his other leg. He let out a roar that scared the rest of the guards away.

"Cowards!" Thesias yelled as he commanded others to throw the sleeping agents. One after another, the bottles of sleeping liquid were thrown at Midemos's head.

"Go, get your friend!" Midemos said as he slowly succumbed to the barrage of attacks.

"Midemos!" Dricaryo yelled. He turned back to see Wallace stumbling about.

Teslark yelled from the stands, his voice carrying above all the chaos, "Wallace!!" Arsivus looked to Teslark and then quickly to Wallace. Wallace stumbled but could hear Teslark yelling his name. Wallace looked at him briefly, and then turned around to see Zenor standing tall with blood streaming down his face. Wallace's helmet was twisted and halfway off his head. One of his eyes could see through an opening in the helmet while the other had been blocked off from view since the start of the round. Wallace stumbled and looked at Zenor. He tried reaching for his white flag. Ruvio and Huply had stopped their attacks while they stood in shock as they were able to see the damage they had caused upon the young squire, but Zenor still held his sword in his hand.

"Make a fool of me, will you?" Zenor said in a voice filled with hatred. Wallace attempted to say something, to do something, to fumble for his flag, but no actions befell him as he stood there in front of Zenor.

"Wallace!" Arsivus yelled as Dricaryo, Raeolyn, and he were in full sprint to get to his side of the court.

"Your friends are too late this time!" Zenor said as Wallace turned to see his three friends running in what appeared to be slow motion toward him, their mouths open, screaming his name. But he could not hear them, could not remember their names, or why he was even here in the first place. He feigned a smile and turned back around to face Zenor. But he saw darkness, emptiness, nothing. He could only hear the sound of steel piercing flesh. Zenor had lunged forward and placed his sword straight through Wallace's throat. Wallace couldn't breathe, couldn't think, and he couldn't move. He looked at Zenor and then slightly above him to the stands of the coliseum, and finally at the clouds in the sky. He felt the warm flow of his blood as it seeped down his neck and filled what was left of his armor. He lay there, unable to move, unable to breathe. The crowd fell eerily silent. Arsivus was the first to his side and knelt beside Wallace to attempt to comfort him. By the time that Arsivus bent down to hold him, Wallace was dead.

"Nooo!!" Arsivus yelled as he stood up and gripped his sword. Dricaryo had come to the left of Arsivus and Raeolyn to his right. There were no guards on the ground this time to break up the fight, as Midemos had taken care of all of them. Ruvio took his position next to Zenor, and Huply on his other side. Yura tried to stop the fight by using his words, but no one could hear what he was saying. The crowd was furious and scared and did not know what to do.

"Prince or not, you will die today!" Arsivus said to Zenor as he was about to lunge forward.

"Stop, or he will die!" could be heard from the stands. Dricaryo turned to look and saw Thesias standing above Midemos with an axe at his throat. "Cease your attack, and he will live. Do not, and he will surely die!" he said as Dricaryo gritted his teeth. Time seemed to stand still, and another command came upon them. "Cease now!" Thesias roared. Dricaryo spit in his direction and threw down his weapon. Raeolyn did the same as Arsivus held dearly onto his.

Arsivus looked back at Zenor and Ruvio and said, "It may not be today, but someday I will return this favor to you."

With that, Arsivus threw his sword down. Zenor smirked and said, "We will see about that, farm boy." The crowd was out of control. Spectators were running up and down the stands cramming for the exits, while others stayed put and screamed hostilities at the royal family. The noise was unbearable and constant. By this time Magnus, Cardage, and Janos had made their way down to the coliseum floor, leaving Casily above. They separated the fighters and walked them toward the iron gates to go underneath. The crowd cheered and applauded Arsivus and his group as they made their way below. Magnus and his group escorted them to their resting quarters. Zenor, Ruvio, and Huply were brought down separately by Yura, leaving the court to the sounds of boos and threats from the angry crowd.

CHAPTER 23

M agnus was the first to speak once they were all in the room. "You all fought well in the tournament, but that outbreak was not good. Dricaryo, I ordered some of my men to bring Midemos to the infirmary. He will be fine. The King has called all of his personal guards for fear of his life, which is understandable."

Arsivus shook his head in disbelief as Magnus continued. "He is afraid Dricaryo will make an attempt on his life. I have assured his majesty that you have other things to worry about."

Dricaryo put his sword down and said, "When can I see Midemos?" Magnus waited a moment and said, "Immediately after the ceremony. Until then, wait down here until Yura comes to retrieve you. The results will be given at the ceremony as well."

As Magnus neared the door he turned around one last time and said, "And by the way, congratulations!" And with that he left. Raeolyn looked confused and sat down, and

Dricaryo walked into the sleeping quarters, grabbed his large sword, and leaned against the wall with it in front of him.

Arsivus carried the swords back to the armory and grabbed an herb for Dricaryo. He handed it to him with a smile and said, "Sorry about the kick. It was your friend's fault!"

Dricaryo managed a smile, took the herb, and put it to his head. "No worries. I have felt worse."

Yura appeared in the doorway. "Please gather around," he said as he pulled out a piece of paper, the same piece that Wallace wrote on before the match.

Yura took a moment to reread the letter and then looked at each of the individuals standing in front of him. "I wanted you to know that Wallace was a thinker, an intelligent mind taken too soon. For his lack of strength, skill, or ability, his mind was sharp. He knew that if Zenor won the last fight, he would have the third highest score. Even if Dricaryo won every match he was in, Dricaryo would not be granted the title of knight. Wallace did not want to see that happen. That is why he fought so hard, and apparently why he went after Zenor first, to give everything he had in the fight to make sure Zenor did not win. He wanted Dricaryo to be granted the title. He knew that his physical ability would not gain him a win, or his skill with a blade. But he knew that others more deserving would be given the opportunity to do good if Zenor was taken out of the competition. This is what he wanted you to know, that he gave his all, for you three."

All three competitors dropped their heads in silence and thought about Wallace, and what he had done for them. "He will be sorely missed!" Dricaryo said.

"Aye, very much so!" Raeolyn commented.

"We will never forget what happened here today!" Arsivus replied. "So, let's be better for him."

"Agreed," came from the doorway as Teslark, Magnus, and Wallace's mother entered. "What Wallace did was knightly indeed. He gave his life so that others may prosper. There is no greater honor than that," Magnus said proudly.

Teslark came in and rested his hand on Arsivus's shoulder, and said, "You did everything you could. I will not forget this day either." That prompted Wallace's mother to come over and give Arsivus a hug and thank him for trying.

"He always wanted to be a knight, but he never really had any friends growing up," she told him. "I believe he thought of you that way. I am forever indebted to you for giving him that one last wish, of friendship!" she said as she fought back her tears. Arsivus thanked her for her kinds words, and Teslark escorted her to the door.

"General, it is almost time," Yura said to Magnus.

Magnus nodded in acknowledgment. "Yes, I do believe it is," he said. "Is everyone ready?"

They nodded in unison and Yura motioned for them to follow. "This way, please," Yura said as he led them out the door and toward the entrance to the coliseum floor one last time.

They walked up the coliseum corridor and toward the iron gate that slowly started to open up as they got nearer. Arsivus could hear the thunderous noise coming from the crowd.

"They are still cheering?" Arsivus asked.

"They have not left since the last fight!" Yura exclaimed. "They loved the tournament, the action, and they loved all of you." At the entrance, Arsivus, Dricaryo, and Raeolyn stood side by side looking at the stadium crowd. People were still wildly cheering for them to come out and celebrate, to be their victors, their champions from the fight. The crowd was on its feet, chanting and cheering, and those that could were whistling as loudly as they were able.

"Is this . . . for us?" Arsivus asked again, still caught largely off guard.

"It feels nice," Raeolyn said with a smile.

"You have earned it through your excellent efforts this day," Magnus said as he offered a wave to the people. Dricaryo was silent as he gazed about and Arsivus took notice.

"We will see him immediately after. Our herbs will heal him, I am sure of it," Arsivus said to him. This settled Dricaryo's mind for the moment and he turned his attention to the crowd and what they had achieved. "Very well," he said.

"They have taken Wallace to be buried, he will be placed with his kin. We will not forget him. Let's move to the center of the coliseum where the ceremony will take place," Magnus said, and he ushered them out with Yura. As the five of them came into view of the stadium and the crowd, the cheers were deafening. The three fighters felt a nice breeze come through the gates and flow gently over them.

"Ahh!" Arsivus said, as he took a deep breath of fresh air, held it as long as he could, and then released it. In the center of the coliseum, a royal blue carpet was rolled out over the dirt and a pearl-white platform had been erected for the competitors to stand on during the ceremony. As they drew closer to the stands, they saw King Thesias, Cardage, Janos, and Atalee coming from the other side of the coliseum to join them in the celebration. Behind them came Zenor, Ruvio, and Huply. Upon sight of them, the crowd immediately began booing loudly.

"Murderer!" could be heard from the stands as well as other hostilities from people that were not happy with Zenor being part of the ceremony. King Thesias tried to calm the people by waving his arms down, but it had no effect. The parties reached the center and Thesias sat in the middle of the stage on a makeshift throne. Magnus stood on one side and Atalee on the other with Cardage on Magnus's left and Janos on Atalee's right. Yura stood on the carpet below the platform directly in front of the King. The six fighters stood on the dirt facing the carpet. Arsivus, Dricaryo, and Raeolyn stood on Magnus's side facing Zenor, Ruvio, and Huply, who stood on Atalee's side. The crowd was incensed and Yura tried his best to keep it from becoming a mob by starting the ceremony.

"Ladies and gentlemen, we have reached the culmination of our events for the day. Today we have had reason to celebrate, as well as reason to mourn. There was adventure, surprises, and favorites, there was great combat, and there was great loss. We have experienced this together. General Magnus would like to say a few words before we deliver the results."

With that, the crowd erupted in cheers and applause as General Magnus stepped to the edge of the platform. "My friends, I pray that today's tournament was everything you had hoped for. It certainly was monumental, wasn't it? If I have learned one thing in my many years in combat, it is that trusted allies will never be forgotten. Today, we have witnessed what the best of the best may offer," Magnus paused as the crowd began to cheer loudly again, "as well as what the worst outcomes can potentially be."

The crowd immediately returned to booing Zenor. "I am not here to condemn, I am here only to judge. I believe the kingdom has lost a very important soul today. The young man named Wallace, who needlessly lost his life." Magnus said.

With that, Thesias in a calm but threatening tone said, "Careful General, about what you say next."

Magnus paused momentarily but continued his speech. "Wallace fought with true integrity, true spirit, and true strength. Although he did not succeed against his towering odds, he represented what knighthood means, to fight your enemies, no matter the cost, to fight for what is right, and to do it for those that you care about!" Magnus looked directly at Arsivus, Dricaryo, and Raeolyn.

"Wallace would have been an excellent knight. I would have welcomed him into our ranks if given the chance." This brought the crowd to their feet again with cheers and whistles from everywhere. "Also," Magnus said and the crowd quieted, "you saw what has been kept hidden from view for years without even my knowledge of his existence. An

Eglician whose name is Midemos. He was unfairly chained up below for a profiteer's desire."

Again, Thesias said, "General, this is your last warning. Do not do something you will regret."

Magnus paused for a moment and looked down at his hands. He looked over at Zenor, Ruvio, and Huply and they were all smirking at him. Magnus clenched his teeth and looked back at the crowd. "Midemos is resting now, with the help of our herbs. He is regaining his strength, and of that there is plenty. In my eyes, he has won his freedom and shall go free from the moment he is of full strength. You have my word!" Again, the crowd jumped to their feet and gave a thunderous applause that resonated deep into the city.

With that, Magnus motioned to Yura that he had finished, and Yura took center stage once more. "A great speech, from a great leader. Now, let us review the official results!" Yura said, and the crowd went silent in anticipation of hearing the results. "In the lead, with thirteen points and given the title of knighthood, Sir Arsivus!!" The crowd was ecstatic as Arsivus walked to the center of the blue carpet, all the while eyeing Zenor as he did. Yura continued. "Next, with eleven points total from the events, we have Lady Raeolyn!!" Again, the crowd lit up with praise. Raeolyn walked behind Arsivus and eyed Zenor as well until she reached Arsivus's left side. Yura waited patiently for it to quiet down a little and went on. "Finally, with ten and a half points, not only a champion in the Western Kingdom, but now a knight in the Eastern Kingdom as well, we have Sir Dricaryo!!"

Dricaryo walked toward Arsivus and stopped at his right side and they all faced Yura in the center. The entire coliseum erupted with cheers, clapping, and toasting of each other with ale. The cheering was so loud that it took Yura a couple of minutes to calm everyone down so the knighting could take place.

Yura again addressed the crowd. "Let the ceremony begin! King Thesias, your liege," Yura said as he bowed out of the way and Thesias walked down the platform to stand in front of the three winners.

Thesias raised his hands to quietly calm down the crowd. "You three have proven yourselves to be excellent fighters. Your teamwork was the best I have seen in a long time. You have scored the highest in the tournament and, therefore, will be granted the title of knighthood upon swearing your loyalty to me. Please . . ." Thesias said as he motioned toward the ground and the carpet beneath them. The three of them knelt on their right knees. "I will say your decrees, and once I am finished with all of them, you will all agree at once," Thesias said. Thesias walked up to Dricaryo and said, "Champion of the Western Kingdom, Dricaryo. Do you swear to uphold the truths and honor of this kingdom? To put all of its citizens and your majesties needs before your own. To withdraw from any and all previous misgivings of your personal nature from your past. To forgive wrongdoings upon yourself and those you know. To vigorously defend the crown, if be it, at the cost of your life?" Dricaryo paused for a moment and looked up at Thesias with anger in his eyes.

The King walked over to Raeolyn and said, "Raeolyn of the freelancers. Do you swear to uphold the truths and honor of the kingdom? To put all of its citizens and your majesties needs before your own. To put aside crime and the sell-sword life and be my personal handmaiden to be at my beckoning call. To vigorously defend the crown and all its desires, if be it at the cost of your life?" Raeolyn winced and looked up at Thesias as he moved on to the center.

Arsivus was looking at Magnus, and Magnus was gripping the hilt of his sword with anger. "Arsivus," Thesias said. "Do you swear to uphold the truths and honor of the kingdom? To put all of its citizens and your majesties needs before your own. To share with the kingdom the secret of your herbs, and to give the kingdom your skills and materials needed to produce such herbs. To vigorously defend the crown, if be it at the cost of your life?" Arsivus looked to Dricaryo to his right, and Dricaryo's stare was full of hatred. Arsivus looked left and Raeolyn was full of anger and she was breathing heavily. In front of them, Thesias was smirking at them and asked with a hint of sarcasm, "Well, champions of my tournament, what say you?"

Arsivus was the first to speak as he stood and looked at Magnus and then back at King Thesias. "I will not serve under those terms!"

The crowd cheered wildly, as Dricaryo stood as well and said, "Neither will I!"

Raeolyn immediately followed suit. "Count me out!" she said. Magnus offered a smile, as did Janos and Cardage.

Thesias, now fearing that he was losing control of the situation, brought Magnus to the forefront and said, "Make them understand, General!"

Magnus redelivered the oath of knighthood to the three. "Champions of the Seven Wizard's Battle, will you uphold the decree of the laws of Affinity, as long as they are just and fair? Protect its citizens with your lives, and never dishonor the people you serve?" After Magnus finished reading the decree, all three nodded and dropped to one knee again. "Let it be known that this day, Lady Raeolyn, Sir Dricaryo, and Sir Arsivus are now denizens of the kingdom, as well as its rightful protectors." With that Magnus withdrew his sword and tapped each of them on the shoulder. "Rise now, knights, and celebrate." The crowd cheered hastily as the three newly appointed knights rose and raised their hands to the sky to thank the crowd.

Thesias came to the front again and said, "What a joyous occasion. We have added these fine individuals to our kingdom." He clapped for them. "What's more is that there is one last addition to our kingdom. Zenor, Ruvio, and Huply, front and center, please. As the three came to the blue carpet, Thesias motioned for them to take a knee and said, "Do you swear to uphold the truths and honor of the kingdom? To put all of its citizens and your majesties needs before your own. To vigorously defend the crown, if be it, the cost of your life?"

The crowd was stunned into silence for a moment, after which, "What?" "This can't be!" "How is this fair?" and "This isn't right!" could be heard coming from the audience.

"What say you, gentlemen?" Thesias asked as they all looked to him.

"Yes, my liege!" they all replied in unison.

Thesias then withdrew his own sword and tapped each one on the shoulder and said, "Then rise, knights of my kingdom, protectors of my will, you shall be part of my most trusted agents." Thesias looked to the crowd and said, "Ladies and gentlemen, please welcome my newest addition to the White Guard!" The crowd gave a delayed and unenthusiastic applause. Magnus turned to Atalee and the fury was ripe on his face. Atalee's eyes were burning a hole right through the back of Thesias's head, and Magnus had never seen such anger in the young captain.

Magnus stepped to Atalee's side and shook his hand publicly to try to draw his attention away from what just happened. "Hold your ground, Captain. Do not do anything you will regret."

Atalee looked at Magnus and gritted his teeth. "What am I supposed to do? Your brother has singlehandedly ruined the White Guard by putting those wretches in with me," he said as he continued to hold Magnus's hand.

"Just flush them out in training. Certainly, they cannot complete what you have set in store for them?" Magnus asked with a curious tone.

With that thought, Atalee nodded. "Yes, that is what I will do. I thought losing the tournament would be enough. Apparently, I am not rid of these children as of yet. I shall ensure that they do not flourish any further to disrespect the White Guard. Thank you!" Atalee said as he loosened his grip. Magnus turned to look at the stadium with Atalee by his side. He saw Zenor, Ruvio, and Huply high-fiving each other and laughing with joy, while Arsivus, Dricaryo, and Raeolyn stood looking as shocked and angry as everyone else.

Cardage walked over to the General and said, "Sir, we must be going!"

"Yes, you are correct," Magnus replied. "Bring our champions with you to the front gate and meet me there!" With that Magnus turned and walked toward his chamber away from the crowd as it began to thin out. Arsivus was still standing with Raeolyn and Dricaryo when Cardage and Janos walked up to him.

"Congratulations are in order," Cardage said. "And we will celebrate. But first, you three must come with us immediately." With that, they walked out of the front entrance of the coliseum as the remaining crowd continued to cheer for them.

Casily was running through the corridors as fast as she could to get to the Fallen Row. She came upon it and entered the long stretch of knights locked in their cages. "Father!" she yelled out as she came up to his cage.

"Casily, what are you doing here?" Romez asked. "How was the tournament?"

Casily, a little out of breath, began to tell him of all the exploits, the archery, the dueling, the Eglician, Wallace, and every last piece she could remember.

"Wow, so he actually won! That is incredible news!" Romez said loudly with a smile on his face.

"Yes, that means everything is going according to our plan. You will suffer this not much longer!" Casily said as she reached in and held his hand.

"We must have patience now, for the timing must be perfect to have this work," Romez said. "Patience will be our key out of here once and for all, for all of us this time!"

Casily nodded her head in agreement. "I will be patient. I just hope that there is forgiveness at the end of all this, for me . . ." She paused for a second and let a sigh out before she finished her sentence, "from him."

"Darling," Romez said, "he will understand, he must understand. Believe in yourself, believe in me, and believe in the good in him. He will understand."

Casily let go of his hand and moved away. "I hope so," she said solemnly as she began running down the alley and out of Fallen Row. "I really hope so," she thought to herself as the walls whipped past her while she turned the corner heading toward the King's personal chambers.

"Why are we in such a hurry? Where are we going?" Arsivus asked as they moved quickly through the streets.

"Just a bit farther. We need to reach the gates quickly. We already have a mission from the General and we must be fast," Cardage said.

"I can see the guard tower. There, I see Theros and Mulik in the watch tower above the gate. We are almost there!" Janos exclaimed as he picked up speed.

"Let's go!" Cardage yelled encouragingly and they all began sprinting to make it to the gate. As Janos passed through the gate, he saw all of the knights were ready and standing by their horses.

"Theros, Mulik, it is time!" Janos yelled. Theros and Mulik turned around and they both gave a quick nod and headed for the stairwell. Cardage, Arsivus, Dricaryo, and Raeolyn caught up as Janos ran to the water pail and took a big drink. As soon as he was done quenching his thirst, he brought it to Arsivus and his crew. Arsivus took some and passed it on to Dricaryo and Raeolyn, who did the same.

"Will someone explain this mission? Everyone seems to have an idea of what we are doing except us," Raeolyn said.

Theros came down and pulled Cardage aside and asked, "What are they doing here?" Cardage took a drink from the water and said, "General wanted them with. Aside from that, they do not know anything of what has happened, but fetch them some horses and weapons." Theros nodded and directed one of his knights to do so.

Dricaryo grabbed his own horse from the stable and said to the knight about to give him a sword, "I brought my own."

Raeolyn looked at the knight and said, "You don't by chance have any short swords, do you?"

The knight went into the armory and came back with two of them and said, "One is silver and one is steel. Which one would you prefer, my lady?"

320

She grabbed both of them and said, "I'll let you know!" and she smiled as she walked to the stable to fetch her horse. Cardage grabbed a sword from the knight in the armory and brought it to Arsivus.

"Take this. I hope we do not need it, but we have to be prepared." Arsivus took it and grabbed the reins of the horse that was brought to him.

"Be prepared for what?" he asked loudly.

Dricaryo looked around. "Why are all these steeds and knights fit for light riding? Where are you intending to go?" he asked Cardage plainly.

"We are going to your home, Arsivus," Magnus answered from the entrance. Everyone turned to see Magnus on his horse, which also was lightly equipped. Magnus was dressed in his combat gear and had his sword and shield side mounted on his saddle.

"Freshen up. We leave immediately," Magnus said to his knights. With that, the knights took one last drink of water and mounted their horses. Arsivus, Raeolyn, and Dricaryo followed suit, as did Theros, Janos and Cardage.

"Mulik, I need you to stay here. You are to assume command in my stead. Here are orders confirming this in case you are challenged."

Mulik took the papers out of Magnus's hands. "I understand, sir. I shall see you when you return. Safe journey!" he said as he turned and headed to the palace courtyard. Arsivus steered his horse near Magnus and Dricaryo and Raeolyn followed.

"General Magnus, why are we going to my home?" Arsivus asked and then realized at the same time that he hadn't seen his father, "And where has my father been? I didn't see him at the end of the tournament at all. General, what has happened?" All of the knights were now turned toward Arsivus as he finished his last question. Their steely gaze penetrated the confidence that Arsivus had just possessed minutes prior.

Magnus looked at Arsivus and lowered his head before he spoke. "Son, we had word that your mother was in danger, so last night I sent a small detachment to your home to give aid if necessary. If nothing else, they would remain there to deter anything from happening. My men came across your mother a while back, and Cardage gave her a token, a bird, that if she were ever in trouble, she could release it and it would fly back here to us. During the tournament today, the bird returned."

Arsivus's horse fidgeted as it wanted to be on its way and Arsivus kept staring at Magnus. "Then what?" he asked impatiently.

"I had these knights waiting here for me for the end of the tournament, for I was to ride with your father and them to your home and ensure everything was all right. I spoke of this with your father and he decided it best not to tell you. When the bird arrived, we had no more time. He and Doran left with a handful of knights as soon as they could. They left after your archery event so they should be past the mountain pass by now. Maybe even at the edge of the Enegon Swamp, I do not know. But the threat against your mother has merit and she will receive every ounce of protection we can give her. That is why we ride now," Magnus said as he motioned for the gatekeeper to open the doors to the outside.

"You should have left sooner!" Dricaryo said as he made his way toward the open gate.

"Yes, you should have left much sooner. But we shall see this through together, General!" Arsivus said.

"Knights, form up and ride!" Magnus shouted as they stormed out of the castle walls on their way out of the city.

"The sun is still high in the sky. We should be able to make it there by dawn if we ride hard," Theros said to Janos when he caught up with him.

"I have quite the story to tell you when we have time!" Janos said to Theros.

"Oh really? Is it the same nonsense that Darius, Himus, Ioma, and Parcy were raving about?" Theros asked with a smile.

Janos mimicked the smile and said, "The very same!"

"You would believe us if you were there, sir!" Darius said, as he, Himus, Ioma and Parcy caught up to Theros and Janos.

"Well, when we get back, you can all revitalize the story once more. What do you think about that?" Theros asked.

"I think it is a grand idea. I shall buy the first round," Parcy said.

CHAPTER 24

The large band of knights had been traveling at full gallop for a while and were at the base of the mountain pass.

"Form up!" Magnus shouted as they closed ranks and lengthened out their line as they entered the pass. "I want three horses' wide, and a good visual distance between each group," he continued as the knights followed his command. Magnus took the center, with Raeolyn on his right and Arsivus on his left. In front of them were Janos, Cardage, and Theros, and behind them was Dricaryo. As the narrow stretches of the mountain pass surrounded them, the knights' formations grew tighter. Memories of the rugged terrain, sharp corners, and the creature that chased them through the pass in the pitch black just days before ran through Arsivus's head.

Magnus looked over and saw the frustration on Arsivus's face. "What is on your mind, son?"

Arsivus kept his focus on the path ahead and spoke. "A few days past, we came through this way and my whole life was different. I did not expect anything like this to happen, much less so quickly. My first and only time upon this path, we met a creature. It was in the dead of night, but the air was filled with chaos. This thing was clad all in black and chased us through the mountain. I stuck two arrows at least in it, but it kept riding. It finally gave way as we neared the castle. But it had these arrows that were unlike any I've ever seen." Magnus was silent as they continued to ride.

"What was it?" Raeolyn asked as they slowed down their pace due to the sharp corners ahead.

Arsivus looked over at her and then back at the path before them. "I don't know, and neither did Doran or my father. But from our counting, it killed at least several knights that we saw."

Magnus nodded his head and said, "This is true. We have been losing some knights as of late, with no reason as to their deaths or disappearance."

"What worries me is that the knights that were sent last night in the middle of the night could very well run into that creature," Arsivus said. "What worries me more is that my father and Doran and a handful of knights came this way this afternoon, and this was the place that we saw that thing last."

Dricaryo jumped into the conversation from behind them. "And they were only six men. At least we have an entire company with us. But for so few men, that was a bold move indeed," he said as Magnus appeared to take the criticism in stride.

"I have heard reports of an unidentified being in the region," Magnus said. "At first, I believed it to be folly, someone's nightmare. But as more reports came in of my men and women being attacked, we had to take the threat seriously. I sent a small detachment out several nights past, and they never returned. I was informed by Mulik that they were attacked on their return home. Doran also informed me that several knights were found on the other side of this mountain, dead, and one was impaled by strange glowing red arrows. I intended to send out a war party immediately, and then word came of your arrival, and the King's obsession with these pendants. I could not abandon you or your father in the castle while you were there. Kadath wanted you to finish the tournament, and I agreed. My intent was to investigate immediately after the tournament and study every piece of information about this creature before anyone else felt its wrath. And I intended to give you and your father an escort home with enough men to be safe. Naturally, every good intention is met with some criticism, but even I could not have foreseen your mother being threatened by the King. We have not received any more information about this creature engaging in attacks during the day, which is why I felt it beneficial to have your father and Doran leave during mid-sun. They should be well past this place and the dangers it holds."

Arsivus nodded and Raeolyn said, "It does make sense, Arsivus."

"I would do the same, if I were in your situation," Dricaryo agreed.

"I appreciate your words. I just hope I wasn't too late in issuing orders to leave," Magnus said. Arsivus remained quiet as they continued to make their way through the pass. As the sun continued to soar westward in the sky, the company reached the summit of the mountain where there was a large outcropping of space for everyone to congregate.

Cardage called out to the company, "Halt everyone, dismount and replenish. We leave again shortly!" Janos and Theros both dismounted and climbed to the highest peak they could find to get a good look at the other side of the mountain. Theros was the first to the top, and he gazed across the bright horizon.

"So much land!" he said as Janos joined him at the top.

Janos covered his eyes and looked toward the sun as it was beginning its slow descent into the earth. "There is the beginning of the swamp," Janos said as he pointed toward the far horizon in the west.

Theros brought his hand up to shield the sun so he could get a better look. "Ah, not much farther then, and we still have a half day worth of sun left. We should continue on," Theros said as a cool breeze came rushing up the mountain. The pair continued to look over the land as they felt a calm settle about them.

"A mug of ale?" Janos asked, as he picked up a nice smooth rock.

"Do you want for distance or target?" Theros said as he searched the ground for a rock about the same size as the one Janos had. He found a white one and picked it up.

"Let's go for distance this time," Janos said as he picked out the direction in which they would throw. "Toward the swamp, farthest one wins," Janos said as he took position. "Uggh!" he grunted as he heaved the rock as far as he could. It soared through the air and hit the face of a jagged outcropping of rocks and bounced back. "Ah blast!" Janos said as Theros stepped into his spot.

"All right, here we go," Theros said, and he grunted loudly as he released the rock. The rock soared well past Janos's spot and landed on the mountain path heading down the mountain. Once it made contact with the mountainside, movement could be seen down below.

"Did you see that?" Theros asked.

"Yeah, yeah, I owe you a drink when we get back. No need to send out pigeons to tell the world," Janos said.

Theros backhanded Janos on the shoulder. "No, look!" he said as they both peered down the mountain where Theros's rock landed. They saw a horse slowly coming up the mountain pass. Janos and Theros looked at each other, then down at the horse again. It had a light mount on it, much like their company had on theirs.

"The mount!" Janos said, as they looked at each other again. Without a moment to lose, Janos and Theros raced down the peak and came rushing into the resting area where the group was resting.

"General, we saw a horse coming up the path. It appears to be one of ours," Theros said as he tried to catch his breath.

Janos jumped in. "There was no rider, but that is definitely one of ours and it was outfitted for a light mount."

"Mount up!" Magnus shouted, and the knights dropped what they were doing and mounted their steeds.

"How far down the path was it?" Cardage asked.

"A good distance down," Theros replied, as he mounted his horse. Cardage looked toward Magnus and Magnus nodded back.

"On me!" Cardage said as he led the way down the mountain at a very fast pace. Half of the group took off behind Cardage.

"Fall in!" Magnus said as the remaining knights fell in behind him. The ride along the mountain pass took a little bit, but the entire company was galloping at the speed of an avalanche. Arsivus was next to Magnus, and the group that Cardage was leading had slowly gotten away from them. They took corner after corner with speed and precision, each hoping the horse's legs wouldn't give out or turn on themselves and send the rider flying down the side of the jagged rocks.

The pace slowed down as Cardage and his group reached the riderless horse. Cardage rode up alongside of it and grabbed the reins. The horse was spooked from the sudden oncoming of their party. Cardage looked the horse over and saw some dried blood on the saddle; otherwise, all of the gear was still there. Magnus and Arsivus caught up with the rest of the knights, and Magnus made his way to the front.

"And?" Magnus asked.

Cardage replied, "It is definitely one of ours, maybe the ones that were sent last night, though. This blood is hard dried on the saddle and on the mane. It wouldn't have dried that quickly if it happened this morning."

"Ok, everyone on their guard. We leave this pass as soon as we can. Cardage, bring this horse with us. We may need it for bodies . . . if we find any," Magnus said as he continued down the pass. Cardage nodded. He gave the reins to Parcy and he turned back around to follow Magnus down. The rest of the knights joined him, with hardly anyone saying a word. The ride was quiet but uneventful as they reached the base of the mountain. At the bottom of the pass, Arsivus was quick to look over to the base camp where he saw the knights before. But nothing was there, not even an indication that a battle had been fought. It was completely cleaned up. Even the fire pit was properly set up and had logs stacked for the next individuals to come through.

Arsivus kept his mouth shut. They did not have time to ponder the meaning of this, for they had some ways to go yet, and the sun was drawing deeper into the sky with each passing minute. As everyone reached the base of the mountain pass, Magnus called for everyone to gather around. They formed a circle around Magnus and drank water while their steeds rested a moment and chewed the grass beneath them.

Magnus turned around in the circle to make sure he had everyone's attention. "I will be brief. Doran, Kadath, and their knights should have reached their cottage by now. We shall be there soon enough. We will ride around Enegon Swamp as close as we can and head straight for their place. Be prepared to fight as soon as we get there. I want everyone in the mindset that we will fight first and save people after. Does everyone understand? If our friends are engaged in battle, we shall join them immediately upon arrival and fight until the threat has been extinguished. Any questions?" Magnus asked. Everyone was silent. "Good, I want full strides until we arrive. Knights, let's ride!" The knights gave a loud roar as they mentally prepared for battle and stuck their heels into the stirrups, driving their steeds into full gallop.

CHAPTER 25

They reached edge of the Enegon Swamp while the sun was still on the horizon. The group traced the edge of the swamp at full gallop while staying within close proximity to each other. A chill came through the air as they rounded the swamp and a brisk rain began to fall lightly from the clouds. Their path ahead was covered with freshly fallen leaves that were cold to the touch and crackled as the knights made their way over them.

"I didn't think the seasons were due for a change quite this early!" Cardage said as they continued to race against the sunset.

"Those are very beautiful!" Raeolyn said as she admired the golden-brown trees that overhung their path. "So old, so extravagant, it makes you really hate the word swamp. It completely distracts you from the beauty that it possesses," she said.

"You should see the Northern Forest when the seasons do change. It is marvelous," Arsivus responded. "We should be able to see it very soon."

Raeolyn smiled and said, "After this is all over, maybe you can take me there." This prompted laughter and some bubbly talk from the other knights.

As they made their way around the last bend of the swamp, they saw an outlying of trees that stretched from the east to the west. A bolt of lightning lit up the sky, illuminating the beginning of the forest far to the north.

"There it is!" Arsivus said to Raeolyn. "The Northern Forest, mighty and dangerous it may be, but magical at the same time."

Some of the knights shuddered as they remembered what happened last time they went to the Northern Forest. One of them said, "Magical, yes, dangerous . . . extremely!" The company continued on as the sky filled with thunderclouds. The raindrops were falling faster now and the lightning was closer.

Two hours had passed of hard riding when Magnus said aloud, "It shouldn't be much longer. Be prepared for anything!" More thunder echoed across the plains and through the trees as strikes of lighting were becoming more prevalent. The rain continued to fall the farther north the company went. In the distance, another large lightning bolt stuck and smoke could be seen rising high from the ground. As Arsivus peered through the rain and the brief unobstructed view that the lightning gave him, he could make out a small house on the distant horizon where the smoke was coming from.

"Arsivus!" Dricaryo said as he pointed to the smoke. "Is that your house?" he asked. Arsivus did not want to believe what he was seeing, but he recognized the layout.

Arsivus nodded his head and said, "It is. The smoke is coming from my house."

With that, Magnus shouted out loud enough to drown out the wind, the rain, and the thunder, "Knights!! Spread formation. I want a wall that no man would dare cross. Draw your swords, ride north, and ride fast. Prepare for battle."

With that, the entire company of knights dug deep into their reserves and their horses seemed to know what was about to happen. They formed into a long wall. They kept their heads down, partially to keep the wind and rain out of their eyes, but also to help shield themselves from flying arrows. They continued at full speed toward the cottage. Arsivus could see that it was indeed his home, or what was left of it. The home he knew only a few days ago was gone. What he saw was a pile of logs and ash. He could tell, even from a distance, that his home had been burned to the ground. The field where they had grown the crops was also burned. The smoke rose from the field as the raindrops fell. The storm had put out the fire, but flames of pain burned within Arsivus's soul.

As they approached the cottage, there was no movement. It looked deserted. There was nowhere for anyone to hide after the fire damage. The fields were flat and Arsivus's house was a pile of burnt logs. Magnus called for everyone to gather together.

"Darius, take ten knights and continue riding north. Return here when you reach a fork in the riverbed. Take note of all that you see," Magnus said. Darius nodded his head and pointed to ten men. "Come with me!" he said and with that, they were off at full speed. Arsivus and the others dismounted their horses.

"It looks like there was a battle," Janos said. "These tracks are fresh." He pointed to the ground by the entrance to the house.

"But where is everyone?" Dricaryo asked as he approached from behind.

"There's no trace of anything," Raeolyn said as she kneeled in the tall grass searching for footprints. Theros was the first to step into the rubble that was once the house. Cardage followed him.

"Here is the cage of the bird we gave her," Cardage said. He looked around and walked to the area where he remembered the storage room to be, where he last saw the pendant in the corner. "The pendant was right here . . . last I saw it," he said.

Arsivus was staring at the place where his house once stood. He was still in shock.

"This couldn't have happened more than a couple of hours ago. We must have just missed them," Theros said.

Ioma came forward and picked up one of the logs. "The fire would still be going if it wasn't raining," he said. "My guess is they left before the storm came."

Magnus nodded his head in agreement. He walked over to Arsivus and put his hand on his shoulder. "I am deeply sorry, my son. I had no idea this would happen."

Arsivus was still trying to keep his strength about him and accepted the kind words from Magnus. "Thank you. But if we aren't able to find any bodies of my family or your knights then they may still be alive."

Raeolyn stood up and walked over to him, as Magnus shook his head. "Son, we have to believe that your family —"

Raeolyn cut him off, saying, "No, Arsivus has a point. We don't see any bodies, not of his family, not of your knights, and none of those that attacked them. There was a battle here, but battles leave blood and bodies. I have found none." Her words filled everyone with a little hope.

"It makes sense, General," Janos said. Magnus looked around and started to consider the possibility that they could all still be alive.

"Very well, we shall not think of them as gone from this world." He turned to Arsivus and said, "I will have word out to every corner of the kingdom to search for them. My men shall leave no stone unturned. You have my word."

Arsivus nodded and said, "Thank you, General!"

Cardage looked to the sky and saw the last glimmer of sun as it began its final descent into the west as the storm has lessened. He looked along the horizon and saw a glimmer of something near the herb field.

"What is that over there?" he asked and everyone turned to look in the direction he was pointing. The sun was reflecting off something stuck in the ground. They all quickly ran to the field.

"It is my father's sword!" Arsivus said as he drew near it. "Well, his training sword anyway." It rested against a post that remained sturdy and unburned.

"It looks dull and well used," Magnus said. "It probably wasn't even an option for them to use in the fight."

Arsivus nodded and said, "It was a good teacher when it hit you, though."

Dricaryo was studying the sword as Raeolyn asked, "What was it that anyone would want with your family? Why would they burn your house and field? What were they looking for?" As she finished, Dricaryo pulled the sword from the ground and a bright blue aura filled the last remaining moments of daylight.

"They were looking for that," Cardage said as everyone stared at the stunning blue pendant attached to the end of the sword. No one spoke. They all just continued to stare in admiration.

"This was always kept in the house. Someone had to have known that they would be coming for it," Arsivus said, looking back at the house with a forlorn look. "So, they hid it in hopes it would land in safe hands," he said. Everyone was looking at Arsivus. He tried to process everything at once but could not focus.

Magnus broke the silence. "We must return to the castle. We need to strategize and think clearly. We will leave here tonight and get as far as we can. We will stop short of the mountain pass and cross early tomorrow. Gather your things. I have a bad feeling about this place."

As everyone agreed, Magnus said to Parcy, "Ride north and let Darius and his men know and then join us when you can." Parcy agreed and mounted up. Arsivus, still looking at the remains of his home, walked over to the General.

Magnus said, "Your mother's pendant will be in safe hands. It will ride with us back to the castle and it will stay out of my brother's hands, I swear it." Arsivus nodded, mounted his horse, and took one last look at his home. Magnus gave the call to start south and everyone fell in line, and they started moving.

"Let's go, friend," Dricaryo said as he came alongside Arsivus.

"We will come back. We will right this wrong," Raeolyn said. This gave Arsivus hope, for the future, and for his parents.

"You're right. Let's go," he said and they turned and rode away from the smoking ruins.

The group reached the base of the mountain well after nightfall. Darius and his men were still behind Arsivus and the main group but within sight as they could see the lit torches held by several of their bannermen. They stopped before the mountain pass and short of being within arrow-shot of the mountain.

"We will rest here tonight, and tomorrow by midday, we shall be back at the castle," Magnus said to everyone.

Cardage started to give orders. "Set a watch. Janos, make it happen. Get a fire going. The sun will be up in a few hours, and we leave again, so do not get too cozy." With that, Cardage dismounted his horse and stretched. The group gathered around the campfire and quietly chatted. After a short time, Darius, Parcy, and the other ten knights arrived.

Magnus looked up as they approached and asked, "Did you find anything?"

Darius shook his head. "There were no tracks, no signs of travel, nothing went north but the storm."

"I looked for tracks going east, but there were none," Raeolyn said.

Janos told the group he had checked for tracks going west and hadn't found any.

"We are in no position to make a move now anyway," Magnus said, as he contemplated the puzzling situation. "We will discuss this tomorrow back at the castle." With that everyone nestled in as best as they could in the chilly night and tried to rest up, knowing they would be departing in a couple hours. "We will sleep in shifts. Dricaryo, please take the first shift and make sure the fire doesn't go out. Everyone else, try and get some sleep. We have a big day tomorrow." With that, Magnus laid his back against a log and closed his eyes.

With the activity of the day, the knights found it easy to succumb to their weariness. But Arsivus couldn't sleep. He continued to mull over the events of the day. Dricaryo came and sat next to him.

"I never thought today would end. So much to take in. Some shut eye might do you some good," Dricaryo said as he took a sip of water from the pouch and passed it to Arsivus.

"Yeah, it's too much to focus on. I am kind of tired but tell me about Midemos. How did you guys meet?" Arsivus replied.

Dricaryo gave a short laugh as he thought of his friendship with Midemos. He smiled and said, "That is a long story."

But Arsivus was not to be deterred. "What is he like?" he asked.

Dricaryo paused for a moment, and then said, "He is a worthy opponent, and the fiercest of friends. There is no way he would have lost against us in that court in the tournament. There is no way he could not have gotten to the King if he truly wanted to. I have seen him fight twice as many guards than he did that were more experienced than those were. And he still walked away with nothing but a scratch. He spared the King and those guards for some reason. I would like to ask him next time I see him."

Arsivus was impressed. "So, he is a great warrior. How is it that he got captured?"

"We had just landed on the western shores. I was speaking with a local at the docks, and I saw Midemos heading to a forested area. I thought nothing of it, as he likes to explore his surroundings. On top of that, who in their right mind would mess with an Eglician. People were in awe of him, and all they wanted to do was ask questions. My guess is he got fed up with all of the talk and wanted some peace and quiet. By the time I turned back to the boatman, three men were now in front of me, and I had two spears pressed against my back from two more cowardly men. They said they wanted my friend as a prize. This was many years ago, but I remember their sigil, it was that of King Thesias, although these men were not knights or White Guard.

Soon after, they had me in chains and I could hear Midemos roaring in the woods. Shortly after, there was no sound. I remained in their prison for several months, until my captor made a mistake. I ended his life, as well as the rest of the slavers that resided there, and began my journey to find my friend. Once I heard of the tournament, that's when I made my way to the east. I spoke to everyone in every village I could about the King, the tournament, and much more. I learned that no one had seen an Eglician, so I presumed that the King had kept him chained up somewhere, hidden from view and still alive . . . or dead. But I needed to know the answer, and now I do."

Arsivus was full of more questions, but he could tell that Dricaryo was done talking for the night. Before Arsivus could say anything else, Dricaryo said, "Get some sleep!"

Arsivus lay down next to the fire and gazed up at the moon and stars shining down on the campground. His eyes slowly began to close.

The morning arrived earlier than many had hoped.

"Up! Get up and get ready. We leave shortly!" Cardage said for everyone to hear. Arsivus opened his eyes and saw that most everyone was busy packing up equipment and loading it on their horses. Arsivus rose and stretched out his body and felt soreness and pain throughout.

Magnus walked over and said, "How are you feeling today? After the tournament and a hard ride, are you up for one last journey?"

"Waiting on you, General," he said with a smile, as he quickly loaded his gear and mounted his horse. That prompted some laughter from the other knights.

Magnus smiled and said, "Good form, son." He turned and faced the mountain pass ahead. "Let's move out, same formation as when we came through. But let's move quickly. I would like to be through and home by the time the sun is at its peak," Magnus said. Everyone was in agreement as they set off toward the luminous path ahead of them. A brisk chill was in the air and the ground made crunching sounds when their horses tread upon it. They rode steadily through the base camp at the bottom of the mountain.

There was less hustle in the group today than there was yesterday. Arsivus could tell that the knights just wanted to get back to their homes. He kept thinking of the pendant they found at his house. "Who buried it?" he wondered to himself. "It must have been my father. He knew I would check around if I saw his sword standing there. But how would he know the sword would be standing? What if my mother planted it there before she released the bird?" So many questions ran through his head that before he knew it, they were halfway up the mountain. The air was uncomfortably chilly and most of the knights were cold to their bones, hungry, and sleep deprived. Arsivus admired their determination and will-power. He felt as if he would break any moment.

"We will make it to the top and take a small break before we head out," Magnus shouted to the group as they continued their ascent. The wind picked up the higher they climbed and air seemed to get colder. A screech in the distance cut through the silence and put everyone on alert, although it was not enough to warrant drawing arms.

"What was that?" Parcy asked.

"I don't know," Himus said. "But I think it's too far away for us to worry about." After a few moments a huge eagle swooped down on the path before them and picked up a small rodent. This put many of the knights at ease as they felt sure the screech had come from the eagle. The top of the mountain was almost in reach when the entire company came to a halt.

Magnus shouted, "What is the holdup?"

Someone from the front shouted back, "General, you need to see this."

With that, Magnus, Janos, Cardage, and Theros headed to the front of the line and looked at the jagged rock wall. Arsivus crept his way up between the knights who were sitting stationary.

When he arrived, he heard Janos saying quietly to the others, "That is what I told you about. This is what that little girl was saying to us. How many times do I have to say this? It has to mean something."

"We will investigate after we return and talk about it," Magnus replied. "We do not want to be spread too thin until we learn . . ." but his words faded when he spotted Arsivus reading what was written on the wall; "WE WERE THE ONES BEFORE, AND WE WILL BE THE ONES AFTER. OUR RETURN IS IMMINENT." Arsivus reached out and felt the coldness of the thick blood as it lay upon the wall.

"This wasn't here yesterday," Arsivus said quietly.

Magnus was quick to try to calm the situation by saying, "We don't know who wrote it, or when. Perhaps we just missed it since we were in a hurry. In either case, we need to hurry back to the castle." He looked at his commanding officers.

Cardage agreed and said to the troops, "We will not stop. We will continue to the castle immediately."

Magnus took one last look at the writing as Janos said, "They have to be linked, somehow. No one else was there to hear it."

"I understand, but we will discuss this when we get back," Magnus said. The serious look on his face let everyone know not to push him any further.

Theros decided to break the awkward silence. "Move out!" he yelled and they proceeded to race up the path again, with each knight getting a small glimpse of the message as they rode by. The company reached the peak and then started their descent when the clouds parted and the warm sun broke through, warming the knights and lifting everyone's spirit a little.

Arsivus noticed the persistence of the knights as they rode down the path. They had a mission, a purpose, and all of them had put their lives on the line for him, and for his father and mother for no other reason than being asked to. Arsivus truly felt blessed.

Before he knew it, Arsivus could hear Cardage yelling to the gate guard, "Open the gate! Open the gate!" They were back at Affinity. The gates slowly creaked open to make way for General Magnus and his knights. They flew into the corridor with the sun high in the sky and beating down upon them. As the gates closed behind them, a sudden feeling of doubt rose up in Arsivus. With everything that had happened so far, he hadn't thought about his future. "What was he to do, where was he to live, what was to become of him?" he silently wondered.

He looked around and saw the knights dismounting their horses and getting ready to head down the alley to get a round of drinks and some food before they rested. Dricaryo and Raeolyn were among them.

Arsivus spotted Casily standing in the corner and was overjoyed to see her again. "Finally!" he thought to himself. "Finally, someone I know I can rely on, who might have some insight as to what I should do." She was speaking with Magnus, and it looked very important. Arsivus looked at Magnus and could see he was carrying the pendant underneath his armor. He could see the bright blue aura shining out, but Magnus quickly grabbed a cloak and wrapped himself in it to conceal the pendant more.

Arsivus didn't want to interrupt her, so he started walking toward the other knights when he heard, "Were you going to just leave and not say hello?"

He recognized the voice immediately and turned to see Casily heading in his direction.

"You looked busy. I didn't want to interrupt you two," he said shyly as she got closer.

"You would never be interrupting," she replied with a smile, but it quickly faded as she said, "Magnus told me about what happened. I am so very sorry to hear that. I wish there was something I could do."

Arsivus shook his head and said, "No, there is nothing. I will look for them as soon as I am able. In the meantime, I will serve here under Magnus and his army as long as they will have me."

She giggled and said, "They are all the luckier to have you. You were magnificent in the tournament. I never thought you were that good. I think you definitely have what it takes to help me and —"

She cut herself off quickly as Raeolyn approached them and said, "Shall we have a drink, to put an end to a great but sad day?"

Casily jumped in and said, "I like that idea. Hi, I'm Casily, a good friend of Arsivus's."

Raeolyn looked at her and smiled. "Hi, I'm —"

Casily jumped in again and said, "Raeolyn. I know. I saw you in the tournament. You were wonderful as well. I think we should all get a drink and celebrate together." Arsivus nodded and Raeolyn led the way down the alley. The pub was overcrowded with knights from the trip, as well as their friends who stayed behind. Theros was happily drinking the free ale he won from Janos, and Cardage was slowly sipping his ale and looked to be in deep thought. Parcy had two mugs in his hands, and Ioma was chewing on some bread at their table. The noise inside from all the chatter was tremendous.

Raeolyn spotted Dricaryo sitting alone at a table and said to Arsivus, "I am going to go join him. Meet up with us when you can."

Casily stood closely by Arsivus's side. She leaned in and said, "It is too rowdy in here. Do you want to go somewhere else?"

Arsivus nodded. "Yes, let's go somewhere we can talk," he said.

Casily squeezed his arm and said, "I know just the place!" and she quickly pulled him outside. She led him through alleyways and streets to the great steps that led to the overlook sitting high above the sea. This time the heat was bearable and there was a nice, cool breeze flowing through.

"You can see the King's palace perched high above the rest of the city from here. It is basically within arm's reach if someone were to . . ." she hesitated and then changed her tone. "Let's go to the top again." With that, she took the steps in leaps and bounds to race to the top of the platform.

Arsivus was about to follow her up when he heard, "Well, look who it is. What is a lowly knight like you doing up here? This is where the White Guard resides, farm boy." Arsivus knew immediately that it was Ruvio. He turned and saw Ruvio and Zenor standing at the entrance to the higher portion of the kingdom, where the King, Magnus, and the White Guard resided.

"You have no reason to be this far up, boy. Leave now or we will make you." Zenor shouted loudly. Arsivus contemplated starting a fight, but he had no energy anymore, not after yesterday and today.

"I've more important things to attend to today, boys," he said as he followed Casily up the stairs, leaving both Zenor and Ruvio dumbfounded. By the time Arsivus got to the top, Casily was waiting for him, and there was no one else around. She came running over to him and wrapped her arms around him as tightly as she could. He looked at her, and her eyes pierced into his. He could feel his pulse racing like it had in the tournament when everyone was cheering his name. The wind picked up dramatically and she leaned in and kissed him passionately on the lips. His heart felt like it stopped. Every noise ceased to exist.

Her lips tasted like sweet cinnamon, and her sweet-smelling perfume invaded his nostrils. Her warmth kept him grounded while her arms pulled him in tighter to her body. Time as he knew it had frozen completely. After what seemed like hours, she released him. Arsivus was speechless.

"I was worried about you, and I missed you completely!" she said as she took a step back from him. "I just wanted to tell you that, before the day was done, in case I don't get another chance. I missed you," she said again.

Arsivus, still stunned, replied with the only thing that he could think of. "I missed you as well." Suddenly, the excitement of the past two days caught up with him. The culmination of events that had led up to this moment were taking their toll all at once.

"I missed you so much, but I am afraid I am exhausted. I feel like I need to lie down and rest," he said quietly.

"I understand," she replied. "Can I walk you back to your room?" she asked politely.

"Yes, I would like that," he replied.

She took his hand in hers as they descended the staircase. They traveled through the streets and alleys together talking about the fights and the tournament, and before Arsivus realized, he was standing next to the door to his room, the same room he and his father had stayed in when they first arrived at the castle. He looked down and saw they were still holding hands, which made him extremely happy.

Arsivus asked politely, "Can I see you tomorrow? I know it is only midday yet, but I feel as if I could sleep for a very long time."

Casily laughed and said, "I am sure you will sleep the entire day away after the events you just went through. Of course, I will see you tomorrow." She leaned in and kissed him on the lips one last time.

"Mmm, honey!" Arsivus said.

"What?" Casily asked.

"Your lips, they tasted like cinnamon the first time, and now they taste different," he said.

Casily smiled and said, "Sleep well, Arsivus. For tomorrow is a whole new adventure." With that, she took off down the street, out of Arsivus's sight in an instant. Arsivus walked into his lodging and looked around, half expecting his father and Doran waiting for him to congratulate him on a great tournament. But to his dismay, the room was empty, and the only noise came from the fire roaring in the fireplace. He bolted and barred his door. A feeling of sadness came over him, as he fell down on his bed.

"I am too tired to be sad right now, I just need to sle . . ." And before he could finish his thought, he was asleep fully clothed and fully exhausted from everything that had happened.

CHAPTER 26

"Wake up! By order of the King! Wake up!" Arsivus heard someone shouting. He felt a strong grip on his shoulder as his body was being shaken violently. He opened his eyes and tried to focus.

"What? How long have I slept?" Arsivus asked as he looked around in a daze. He saw some men digging through his personal things.

"Stand up!" yelled the man directly in front of him. Arsivus did not recognize him, but he knew he served the King just by the clothes he was wearing.

"Who are you?" Arsivus asked.

"I, good sir," the man said, "am the local magistrate. And you, sir, are hereby summoned to appear in front of the King immediately on very severe charges."

Arsivus was still half asleep and fully confused.

"What do you mean?" Arsivus asked as the magistrate's men picked him up and shackled his arms and legs together.

"Quiet now. There will be time for questions at your trial," the magistrate said.

"Trial? What trial?" Arsivus asked. He was completely awake now.

"Gag him!" the magistrate said to one of his guards. One guard placed a rag in Arsivus's mouth and put a rope around his head to secure it in place. "Place him in the wagon. King Thesias wants him there immediately," the magistrate said. The guard took Arsivus by the arms and drug him outside. The light was blinding, but the sun was just rising over the ocean.

Arsivus thought to himself, "I must have really slept the entire day through." He saw there were several guards standing by, ones he had never seen before, and they were all heavily armed. Arsivus didn't see anyone he knew, and fear was truly starting to grip him now. The guard pushed Arsivus into the cart and it took off immediately. Arsivus was lying down, so he did not know where he was going, until they passed the long steps leading to the ocean view where he and Casily were the night before.

"Are they taking me to the royal palace hall?" Arsivus thought to himself. "They must be. But why? What did I do? Is this about the pendant? Do they know that my mother had it the whole time? And now they want it from me. But I don't have it, General Magnus does. Where is he? He could clear this whole situation up." Rampant thoughts were now running through Arsivus's head, and he could not control them. Archway after archway passed above him as they took him deeper into the royal palace. Finally, the cart stopped and Arsivus could hear people scurrying about. He was stood up with the help from that same guard that gagged him before.

He was lowered onto the ground and the magistrate was barking orders to his guards. "March him up to the door and wait for me. You, turn the cart around. You, watch the entryway for any suspicious activity." Suddenly, Arsivus felt a sharp spear poking into his upper back. "Forward!" yelled a guard from behind him as he pushed Arsivus along. There were many steps leading up to the royal chamber and Arsivus took each one racking his brain for reasons why he was in this situation.

Once he got to the top, the guard said, "Stop just outside of the door, and do not move from the spot." Arsivus did as he was commanded. Inside the doors, Arsivus could hear all kinds of chatter, but none of it was audible.

The magistrate was close behind him and said, "Open the doors. Bring him before the King." The doors swung open and Arsivus saw that half of the kingdom filled the great hall. Large marble pillars of green, blue, and red and black ran the length of the royal chambers. The windows on each wall were open and an enormous chandelier hung from the ceiling. Arsivus looked up and saw vaulted ceilings above an entire second story that seated more guests. On the throne before him, Thesias sat with a stern look on his face. Magnus was to the right of the chair and Atalee was to the left.

Arsivus was pushed from behind and forced to descend the couple of stairs leading down to the main floor quickly. Nobles and townsfolk lined the chamber on both sides. As he walked toward the throne followed by a guard, the chattering ceased and the entire room became quiet. Arsivus heard the doors close behind him, which prompted him to look backward.

"That is close enough!" King Thesias shouted. Arsivus stopped in his tracks and turned his attention to the King. "You stand before me today accused of treason of the highest regard." Thesias stated. "How do you plead?"

Arsivus thought for a moment and then asked, "What treason do you speak of? I have done nothing in my time as a knight to bring discredit or shame to the crown."

Thesias shifted his position on his throne. "Do you deny your actions on Fallen Row? Would you deny those unto me here today?" Thesias asked with anger in his voice. Arsivus thought back and remembered when Casily took him there. He remembered meeting the knights and feeding them as well, and speaking with her father, Romez.

Arsivus now understood why he was there. "Sire, I was not a knight at that time. I did not know that feeding the knights of Fallen Row was a crime in the kingdom. I did so without knowledge of the repercussions."

Thesias's face twisted in anger and he blasted out, "WHAT are you talking about feeding the prisoners? You did way more than that. Last night you broke every one of them out of their cells and aided in their escape. Because of you, every previous resident of Fallen Row has now left the confines of this city and are scattered to the winds. No longer will they face my judgment or my rulings, but they are all set free on your account. What say you to these charges?" Thesias demanded. The crowd was now starting to get louder as

Arsivus was scrambling in his thoughts as to what Thesias is talking about.

"I do not know what you —"

Arsivus was cut off by someone shouting, "Lies! We saw him near the entrance leading up to the royal walkway yesterday afternoon. He was staring at the King's chambers until we called upon him, in which case he left immediately, scared that we had caught his planning." Arsivus looked down and shook his head, as he recognized Zenor's voice and saw him and Ruvio come walking out dressed in their White Guard armor.

"Yeah, he said he had more pressing things to take care of," Ruvio added

"Do you deny it?" Thesias asked.

Arsivus responded, "Seeing them, no, I saw them. But I was not there planning. I was there with my friend Casily. We were going to the overlook," Arsivus said.

"Ah, Casily, the one person who broke out of my prison, whose father was placed in Fallen Row for leading an insurrection against me. Who has shown public displays of disobedience to me and my laws, and who is also unable to be located right now. That same Casily?" Thesias asked slyly. The crowd now grew louder.

Arsivus tried to defend himself and said, "How could I break them out of their cells? I would need a key, or a lot of time to do it. After we returned yesterday, I met with Casily and then she escorted me home, afterwards I fell asleep. There would have been no time to do all of that."

"A key you say, like the one that was stolen from my personal chambers yesterday and is still unable to be found?" Thesias asked.

The magistrate jumped into the conversation. "Your majesty, in his defense, we searched his entire room, and we did not locate your key anywhere."

Thesias merely dismissed that statement and said, "Guards, search him." With that, four guards surrounded him and patted him down on all sides.

"What is this?" one of the guards said as he felt a hard piece of metal in Arsivus's belt on his back. The guard lifted the shirt to display a key wedged in between his belt and his bare back.

"Traitor!" could be heard ringing throughout the crowd.

The guard grabbed the key and brought it to Thesias. "Here you are, my liege," he said as Thesias swiped the key from him.

"Any more lies you would like to tell us before I sentence you?" Thesias demanded.

Arsivus did not know what to say. All he could do was think, "What happened? How did it come to this? Where are my friends? Where is Casily? She would be able to clear all of this up. Why doesn't someone speak up for me?" His thoughts were soon broken by General Magnus's voice.

"Your majesty, might I suggest his punishment not be the Fallen Row? Whatever his crimes were, certainly you can show forgiveness and leadership by something less severe." Magnus pleaded.

"He is your knight, General. He won your tournament. What would you do with someone who has grieved you this severely?" Thesias asked.

"Perhaps manual labor, or servitude. Something that is befitting for a knight with potential. The facts point to him being guilty, but there must be certain proof before penalties are imposed that cannot be taken back," Magnus replied.

"Hmm, you cherish this one, do you brother?" Thesias asked loudly. "So be it," he continued. "Your punishment from here until your death shall be excommunication. Never are you again to step into my castle, for if you do, death shall be the pleading whimper that comes from your lips after I am done with you. Be gone and from my sight and hope I never lay eyes on you again, Sir Arsivus." With that the guards came and took Arsivus away. As the guards led him back through the royal chambers, he spied Zenor and Ruvio laughing near their father as Magnus looked on with worry.

"Into the cart, prisoner," the guard said as he poked the spear into Arsivus's waist. Arsivus descended the stairs and saw the cart below, waiting to take him to the gates of the city, where he would leave them forever.

"In you go," the guard said as he pushed Arsivus into the wagon. The horses neighed as the driver gave them a little whip to start moving.

Arsivus was deep in troubled thought. "What just happened? How did I get the key? Did someone break in and plant it on me while I was sleeping? Who freed all of the prisoners? How could they if I had the key? Who knew that I would be asleep? Why couldn't Casily be found? Where was she now that I need her?" All of these questions were spooling in his brain, and before he knew it, he was back at the city gate. He saw General Magnus, Cardage, Theros, Janos, Mulik, Dricaryo, and Raeolyn standing there before him.

The magistrates' guards hauled him from the cart onto the ground and released his bindings. The guards stepped back into the cart and sped off.

"I didn't do it!" Arsivus stated immediately.

Magnus was slow to say anything, so Raeolyn spoke up for him. "We know you didn't. You wouldn't do that without at least inviting us to join you," she said with a smile.

"What will happen?" Arsivus asked openly.

"You have been steered in a certain direction for reasons beyond our control," Cardage said sadly. "You still retain your title, but it will not be recognized here, I am afraid."

"So, I am to venture alone then. I understand and I accept," Arsivus replied with a heavy heart.

"Who said you are to be alone?" Dricaryo asked.

"We have already received our first mission, courtesy of General Magnus, of course," Raeolyn said. "And that is to escort Sir Arsivus to his home. The way I see it, you don't have a home. So, until you find a new one, we are your shadows," she said with a smile.

"As long as you would like us to be there," Dricaryo said.

Arsivus smiled and said, "I would like that a lot. Thank you all!" As they gathered their weapons, armor, horses, and gear, they took turns saying their goodbyes. Theros was first and then he was off to join Mulik in some policing business in the market section.

Janos walked up to Arsivus and shook his hand. "Good journey, and fortune. Come back with news!" he said with a wink as he put both of his hands on Arsivus's hand, and then moved them to his shoulders. He then moved on to Dricaryo.

Cardage came up and said, "I know it wasn't you. While you are gone I will see to this case myself. You have my word. If you ever need anything, let me know and I will be there."

With that Cardage moved on to Raeolyn and said his goodbyes and then on to Dricaryo. "Good luck in your journey, my friend. I have a parting gift for you if you will have it?" Cardage said to him.

Dricaryo looked suspicious. "What is it?" he asked. Cardage motioned toward a cart being drawn down the alleyway. As it pulled up, Cardage hailed for it to stop and the driver left. Cardage opened the back door, and Midemos stepped out as the cart shook back and forth under his weight.

"Was that really necessary?" Midemos asked, as Cardage grabbed the hunting staff from the side storage unit.

"I just thought that I would play my part in having every prisoner that King Thesias wanted locked up, escaping within a day of each other." Cardage said, as it gave way to some laughs from everyone.

Magnus was the last to say goodbye. He visited everyone and then came up to Arsivus. "Son, there is a path ahead of you, and only you can walk it. Someday, I hope, every-thing will make sense. But until that day comes, I believe your mother would want you to have this." And with that, Magnus handed him the beautiful blue pendant that his mother always displayed in their home.

Magnus took hold of Arsivus's hands as he said, "Keep it safe. There are many powerful people in the world who are looking for these. And that includes my brother. It is best if it stays as far away from him as possible. What better place for it to be than with an excommunicated knight!" he said as he let go of Arsivus's hands.

Arsivus tucked it away immediately and said, "General, thank you for everything. You shall not be forgotten. I will remember what you have taught me. I hope our paths cross again soon!"

Magnus looked him in the eyes and said, "I am sure they will, son. I am sure they will!" With that, Arsivus, Dricaryo, and Raeolyn mounted their horses as Midemos joined beside them on the ground. Magnus called out one last time for Arsivus and his crew, "Open the gates for our knights!" as the four made their way out of Castle Affinity. Once they were clear, the gatekeeper kicked the switch, and the gates closed again as the workers below strung up the large wooden block to secure it in place. Magnus walked to the gate tower and climbed to the top to watch his friends make their way westward, to find journeys untold.

Arsivus rode slowly on his horse as the others were by his side.

"So, Arsivus, where will our adventure take us?" Raeolyn asked cheerily.

Dricaryo said, "We could go north, into the Northern Forest. Or we could go south to the Old Kingdom and explore the witches and their lairs. Or we could go west, as far west as possible and back again."

Arsivus didn't respond but was looking down in his hand.

"What is it?" Raeolyn asked.

"As we were leaving, Janos slipped something into my hand. It is a map," Arsivus said.

"Where does it lead?" Dricaryo asked.

Arsivus looked more closely at the map and then handed it to Midemos as he said, "This was the parchment that was left when Janos and his men were visited by those things that appeared in Fallen Row. The same ones that Janos said wrote the phrases inscribed on the rocks on the mountain pass."

Midemos looked at the piece of parchment and said, "I know this place. We as a clan always avoided it. This is the Great Hall that resides within the Western Kingdom. Strange things happened when we ventured too close. Is this where you would like to go?" Midemos asked.

Arsivus nodded his head and said, "It is the only clue we have as to what may have happened to my parents, Doran, and the other knights. Also, the fact that they showed up and no one saw them except the knights during the tournament is strange indeed. That information may be something we can bring back to Janos and Magnus if we find something. If nothing else, it is worth a shot," Arsivus said as his spirits started to rise again.

"Looks like we are headed west then!" Dricaryo said as Raeolyn cheered happily.

"As long as there are no sleeping agents along the way, count me in!" Midemos said. With that, the four started to make their way toward the mountain pass to take their journey westward.